EMIT

A novel by: Barbara Cross

Library of Congress TXu 1-832-801

EMIT: a novel/ by Barbara Cross. First Book edition: Feb 2013

Summary: After Paige Devon meets Daniel Haydin, her normal life is thrown into utter chaos when she discovers that he works for a secret U.S. agency. Her home is bugged and she is under constant surveillance by a team of agents. Besides keeping Paige alive, Daniel has a big secret he is hiding from her.

ISBN-10: 0988478315
ISBN-13: 978-0-9884783-1-2

West Cove Press New Jersey United States of America

Printed in the United States of America

This book is dedicated to my beautiful daughter, Alix, for inspiring Paige.

To my wonderful niece, Jane McKee, for helping mold Lily.

To my mother, Gabriela Srednicka, for her love and being the best "Gabby."

To my sister, Maria McKee, for all her support in everything and telling me to never give up. Thanks for believing in me.

I love you all.

CONTENTS:

LOVE'S PHILOSOPHY

The fountains mingle with the river,
And the rivers with the ocean,
The winds of heaven mix forever
With a sweet emotion;
Nothing in the world is single;
All things by law divine
In one another's being mingle;--
Why not I with thine?
See the mountains kiss high heaven
And the waves clasp one another
No sister flower would be forgiven
If it disdained its brother;
And sunlight clasps the earth,
And the moonbeams kiss the sea;
What are all these kissings worth
If thou kiss not me?

- Percy Bysshe Shelley

PREFACE

As I stared at his unmoving form, my eyes filled with tears. After all, this was my fault. When I was asked to keep this secret, I never imagined anything like this was even possible. Everything I was involved in was dangerous, yet somehow I felt safe and believed that my family would be unharmed.

My parents always said if someone told me to keep a secret from them not to listen. So what did I do? I ignored their advice. All the red flags and all the warnings screaming in my head didn't dissuade me either.

Because of that decision, I was standing in a hospital staring at my dad who was in a catatonic state. Why didn't I tell my parents? I thought I was protecting them, but was I just being selfish?

Entrenched in this bizarre world where everything seemed so impossible, but was actually real, I succumbed to the adventure. All my perceived notions about what I would and wouldn't do went right out the window.

1. CENTRAL PARK

"Joy in looking and comprehending is nature's most beautiful gift."
Einstein

It was the end of June and more than the climate of Manhattan was changing. Residents were leaving the city to go to camps, vacations or their summer places. Throngs of tourists had invaded the city and the hustle and bustle was much more chaotic now.

I loved spending summers in the city, but this year, I had plans to be in London with my grandparents. However, that all changed when five days before I was coming, Nana broke her leg. It was a rainy day and she tumbled down the slippery outside steps. A next-door neighbor called an ambulance and she was taken to a nearby hospital.

Dad, an international law attorney, was working on a case at his firm's London office and rushed to the hospital after Aunt Lucy, his sister, called him.

A couple of days later, Dad called and said that I'd be staying at Aunt Lucy's house.

"Why?" I whined. "I don't want to go there!"

"Your visit will be too much for Nana right now."

"I could help her and Granddad," I argued.

"Sorry Paige, but there's no discussion here. Nana feels horrible, but she has to rest. You can stay at Aunt Lucy's house or you can stay home."

"Fine. I'll stay home," I said angrily and hung up the phone.

I'd already nixed staying at Aunt Lucy's when we were in London during my spring break. Aunt Lucy overheard that I might spend the summer in London and asked if I wanted to be her mother's helper since she needed to hire someone. Watching my two crazy cousins, Liam and David, ages eight and ten, respectively, wasn't at all appealing. I told her that I wanted to visit Nana, but maybe next year. If I went now, I'd be stuck with the boys and the babysitter in the suburbs an hour from London.

As I played on the computer, I had an idea, so I ran downstairs.

"Mom, can I stay at Emma's? I'll be really close to help Nana if she needs me." Emma moved to Nana's street when we were both four and whenever I visited, we were inseparable.

"Absolutely not. It's rude to invite yourself," she answered.

"What are you talking about? Her parents have asked me to stay with them for years."

"You're not staying there," Mom repeated.

"But why? It makes no sense," I badgered.

"I'm uncomfortable about those boys."

Emma's older brothers, Lane and Damian, were nineteen year-old identical twins.

"What? Why?" I asked totally confused.

"Nana says they're wild and they got arrested last month," Mom said uncomfortably.

"Come on. It was for jumping into the Chelsea Gardens. It wasn't anything terrible."

She glared at me. "They were drunk and were writing graffiti on the walls. You're not staying there, so just forget about it."

"This isn't fair," I moaned.

"You can go to London, but you must stay with Aunt Lucy."

"I'll be bored to death. I want to stay in Chelsea!"

"You can take the Tube anywhere."

"If I can't stay in Chelsea, I'm not going," I wailed.

"That's your choice, so stop complaining."

I skulked to my room frustrated with the outcome and Skyped Emma.

"I'm not coming," I blurted out angrily and sighed.

"Why?" Emma asked sadly.

"Nana doesn't want me to stay with her and my only choice is Aunt Lucy's house."

"Stay at my house," Emma begged.

"I already asked and my mom said no." I couldn't tell her that Mom thought her brothers were complete derelicts. "I'm bummed too. At least, I'll see you the end of August. I have to go," I said and rushed off the phone.

Ever since I was eight months old, we always went abroad the last two weeks in August. While Mom and I visited with my grandparents the first week, Dad worked in the London office and then the second week, we went on a family vacation.

Last year, it was Paris and the year before it was Rome. My parents never told me where we were going, so it was always a surprise.

When I went back into the kitchen, the house phone rang and it was Nana.

"I'm so sorry for being clumsy and ruining your summer."

"It was an accident. You just rest and take care of yourself. I'll see you very soon."

***

When I came downstairs Friday morning, Mom was heading out the door.

"Morning sleepyhead. I need to do some research at the MET. Want to come along?"

"Yeah, I do, " I said excitedly. "Let me grab a yogurt and throw some clothes on."

Visiting museums was something we enjoyed doing and the Metropolitan Museum of Art was my favorite. I loved to draw and paint and my so-called masterpieces were scattered all around the apartment.

Mom waited in the living room and got on her computer. "Your father's sleeping, please be quiet when you go upstairs."

"What time did he get in?" I asked.

"It was after you went to sleep. There was a delay at Heathrow. Then he was in his office till almost four this morning. He's going to work from home today."

When we walked outside, the air was warm and stifling. We

lived on West 69th Street and Mom wanted to walk through the park.

Seeing no empty cabs, I had to agree.

Central Park, as usual, was swarming with people. Joggers, bicyclists, and dog walkers were everywhere.

I asked Mom about working at Harper's Bazaar. She was an art director there.

"I asked yesterday and they hired too many interns this summer. They can't use you."

"Too bad," I said sadly. "It would've been fun."

"If anything changes, they'll let me know."

"Okay. I'll ask Dad about his firm."

By the time we reached the museum, I was so hot and sticky.

Mom said, "I have to go to the American Wing. Do you want to meet up later?"

"I'll come with you."

The sun was shining as we entered the Engelhard Court and as we rode the glass elevator, it felt like we were still outside. We roamed the period rooms and Mom took pictures on her cell.

While I was playing with a touch screen, I lost her. I glanced at my phone and we had been there almost two hours. I really had enough. I went downstairs, sat on the edge of the Frog Fountain and texted Mom that I was hungry.

She answered that she'd be down in ten minutes and we'd go for lunch.

I noticed a really cute guy walk by reading a museum guide. He was tall, very tan with light hair and looked like a model. I felt like

I'd seen him before, but had no idea where. He went into the American Wing Café and disappeared from view.

When Mom appeared, I asked, "Can we eat over there?"

I hadn't seen the boy exit and I wanted to get a better look at him. If he was a model, maybe Mom knew who he was since she worked for a fashion magazine.

Noticing the long lines, she said, "Let's go and see how long the wait is at the Petrie Café."

As we walked away, I turned and saw him exit the café and head in the opposite direction.

Inside the restaurant, as I ate my pasta, Mom talked about a photo shoot in Central Park.

"We're doing it at Belvedere Castle and at the obelisk next week."

My gaze drifted out the window to Cleopatra's Needle, the obelisk directly behind the museum. The tall four-sided stone pillar with the pyramid-like shape on top always made me think of an arrow pointing to heaven. Whenever I had plans with friends to go to the museum, the obelisk was our meeting place. No one could miss it!

"I have to go to Madison Avenue and pick up your dad's birthday present. I found a pair of fun cufflinks, but had to order them since they only had the display pair left."

Cufflinks were Dad's obsession and Mom always tried to find something unique. At the store, I saw that there was an elephant on one side and a mouse on the other.

"What are you going to get him?" Mom asked, as we exited the store.

"I still have time, but probably a book." Dad loved history books.

We began our trek back through the park.

The humidity had subsided and there was an intermittent breeze wafting through the air, which made it much more bearable.

As we approached the Conservatory Water Pond, Mom ran into her friend, Bianca.

While Mom updated her on Nana's accident, I sat on a bench and pulled out my sketchpad and book. Looking around, I found myself engrossed with the adults and children casting their model boats. Tiny sails billowed in the breeze as the radio-powered boats zipped around the water. The adults were enjoying themselves as much as the youngsters.

I heard a scream behind me and turned to see a woman picking up a crying child off the ground. The little girl had a bloody gash on her knee and the woman was comforting her. Directly behind them, I noticed a blonde-haired boy wandering under the trees and realized that it was the same guy from the museum.

As I watched him, his actions really sparked my curiosity. What was he doing?

It looked like he was picking up chestnuts, but some looked green, so I wasn't positive. Whatever they were, he scrutinized each one by holding it up. Those he deemed acceptable were put in a shopping bag that lay on the ground nearby and those that didn't pass muster, he tossed away. The vision of this gorgeous guy scouring for nuts made me laugh.

Suddenly, he turned and looked right at me.

Flustered, I looked away and pretended to watch a little boy chasing bubbles. Did he hear me? That was impossible! I was so far away.

After a few minutes passed, I nonchalantly turned around to see what he was doing. At that moment, he looked my way and our eyes locked. He looked familiar. Who was he?

Nervously, I grabbed my bag to get my book. I saw my street-vendor bought sunglasses at the bottom and put them on. I instantly felt somehow hidden. Emboldened, I peeked over my shoulder. He had resumed his foraging.

When he started walking north, I looked over at Mom and she was still absorbed in her conversation, so I got up to follow him. Rationalizing that it was just keeping me entertained while I waited somehow made me feel better.

As he walked on the grass, I stayed on the parallel pathway. I trailed at a safe distance and felt like a pathetic stalker.

He looked about my age. He was wearing tan chinos, a white polo shirt, and brown loafers. On his left wrist, he wore a silver watch. His clothes were professionally pressed because of the meticulous seams on his pants. It was obvious that he cared about his appearance and that made me feel extremely sloppy. I had thrown on a pink tank top and a white cotton skirt. Both garments could've used the swipe of an iron. My hair was in a high ponytail, but I could only imagine how it looked by now.

He began picking flowers off a bush and he put them in a small plastic bag. How weird! If I had the courage, I'd walk over and ask what he was doing. What if he didn't speak English? I'd be standing there like an idiot pointing at a plastic bag.

Abruptly he stopped, looked at his watch and glanced around like he was expecting someone.

He plopped on the grass and reached for his cell. I walked a little further then nonchalantly turned around and returned to a bench facing him. That way, I wouldn't have to turn around to look. He was lying sideways on the grass, leaning on his elbow, staring at his cell.

Oblivious to everything around me, I realized that Mom was next to me talking. "Sorry. What did you say?" I asked, glancing up at her.

"I'm running over to Bianca's to see their new pug. Do you want to come?" As I thought of an excuse, she interjected, "Or I can meet you at home."

"Uh. I'll stay here and wait for you. I'm ...really tired," I stammered.

"Okay. I'll be back soon."

I continued watching him behind my sunglasses. He was lying on his back and hadn't moved in a while. He might've fallen asleep. Feeling pretty pathetic, I removed my glasses and buried my head in my book. After ten pages, I couldn't remember what I read, so I slammed the book shut in frustration. Looking up, I was shocked to find him standing in front of me.

"Oh!" I gasped loudly and dropped the book.

"I'm so sorry. Did I scare you?" he said. His eyes were an amazing color blue.

I shook my head and stuttered, "No... no. Not at all."

He bent down, picked it up and handed it to me. "Here you go." I heard an English accent.

"Thanks."

While reaching for it, our hands touched and I felt a spark.

"I've been gone for a few months and was wondering if there were any good films out?"

That's what Dad called movies too. What was the last movie I saw? Nothing was coming to mind. "I'm sorry. I can't think of anything."

"Don't worry about it." He smiled and ran his fingers through his hair.

I saw a man walk with a newspaper and quickly added, "You can check today's paper."

"Thanks, I'll do that. Enjoy the book," he said as he left.

I'd definitely seen him before. Maybe he was an actor.

He sat down on the grass much further away than before.

I texted my cousin, Lily, and realized how dumb I was. Why hadn't I used my iPhone to search for movies? He had a phone too, so he could've done the same thing. Maybe he just wanted a recommendation instead of picking something blindly. Why didn't I ask him about his plant collecting? Instead, I just stared at him like a fool.

I saw Mom hurrying towards me.

"Let's get going. I hope Amber hasn't woken your dad."

Amber was our six year-old, liver-colored, field spaniel. The moment I laid eyes on her at two months old and saw her beautiful chocolate coat, the color amber came to mind. Ergo, that's how she got her name.

As we headed home, I turned to look at him and he was sitting up looking in our direction. It seemed like he was looking right at me.

I noticed the trees behind him. "Mom, are those chestnut trees over there?" I asked pointing.

"Yes. Why?" she asked.

"I think somebody was picking chestnuts, but some were green, so I wasn't sure."

"The green ones are called burrs and the nuts are inside. The red horse chestnuts are toxic."

I wondered if I should tell him, but it looked like he knew what he was doing. I missed Mom's comment and asked, "What did you say?"

"Don't you remember that game called conkers?"

"Yeah, I do." I remembered kids striking chestnuts until one broke and the strongest chestnut won. "It was a silly game."

As we passed the Bethesda Fountain, Mom stopped to watch a juggler. Not at all interested, I looked around and saw him approaching. Oh my God! He must have been right behind us. Mom started walking and I had to follow. I began panicking. What did I look like from the back?

Mom was talking about the puppy, but I was having trouble paying attention. "Her name's Desirée. She's six months old, all black and weighs ten pounds. Amber will love her."

"That's nice," I said tersely, hoping she'd cease yapping. Her incessant talking wasn't allowing me to think straight.

I wanted to stop and let him pass, but I didn't know how.

Maybe he wasn't there anymore and I was frantic for nothing. I tried in vain to look sideways. How could I find out?

As we passed Cherry Hill, it came to me. I rummaged through my bag and pulled out my lip-gloss. After applying it, I purposely dropped it when I put it back in my bag. The round container rolled down the path. Mom stopped when she heard my gasp of "uh-oh." I retrieved it from the edge of a bush and at that point he passed us.

When he exited the park at 69th Street, he went right on Central Park West. I watched him disappear into the crowd and thought about the boy with the blue eyes all the way home.

I needed to talk to my cousin Lily. We told each other everything and had no secrets. Lily was spending the weekend with me and I wanted to tell her about the boy in the park.

At home, Amber greeted us at the door.

Dad called down, "Hi you two. I just walked her."

I went upstairs to see him and asked about Nana.

"It's going to be a really tough time for her," he said.

"Mom said you hired a nurse."

Dad nodded and said, "Nana will need a lot of help."

"I wish I could be there to help her."

"Well since you refused to stay with Aunt Lucy, what are you going to do this summer?"

"Look for a job. Is your firm hiring?"

"All the summer help has been hired, but I'll check tomorrow."

I went to my room and grabbed my laptop to check Facebook.

There was a private message from Daphne and Grace. They

were my two closest friends in school, probably best friends, but nothing like Lily. They wanted to do something tonight and said to call Daphne's cell.

I grabbed the house phone and called Daphne. "Hi, I got your message and that sounds great. Lily will be here this weekend." Everyone knew Lily.

"Oh, good. Where have you been? I've been trying to reach you all day."

"I went to the MET with my mom. Did you call my cell?"

"Yeah. I texted you three times and never got an answer, so I called but it said your voicemail was full. I sent the Facebook message and was about to call your house phone."

"What? That's so weird!" I grabbed my cell from my bag and there were no texts. I called my voicemail and there were no messages. "Daphne, there are no texts or messages on my cell."

"That's really strange. Whatever. What do you want to do tonight?" asked Daphne.

The boy in the park had mentioned movies. "How about a movie?"

We agreed on a new romantic comedy and made plans to meet in the theater lobby. I knew that Grace and Lily would be fine with the movie choice.

I sat on my bed and stared at my photo wall. One entire wall was covered with photos. My walls used to be lavender, but last year, I painted three walls a sky blue color.

My photo wall was left alone because I was too lazy to remove all the photos. The purple was barely visible except around the edges and it sort of looked like a frame. The bedding was a lavender, pale green and pale blue flowered fabric and the curtains were a pale green and pale blue stripe.

I went downstairs and sat in the living room to wait for Lily after she texted that she was nearby. Amber was snoring on the couch totally oblivious that I was sitting there with her. She was the biggest couch potato and only moved if she heard her leash or her food bowl.

Lily lived in Westchester. Our moms were sisters, so we saw a lot of each other and we spoke or texted daily. In the fall, we'd both be seniors in high school.

In looks and personality, we were complete opposites. Lily had blue eyes and blonde hair like both our mothers, who are Swedish. I, on the other hand, had very long, straight, dark brown hair and brown eyes. My dimples were the one feature that no one missed. Even with our differences, we called ourselves "Identical Cousins" and had a silly song we made up to go with the name.

Lily was very practical and rational in her outlook and opinions. When it came to any high school drama, she always chose the path of least resistance. Her approach to life was to step back and discern the situation before reacting. As for me, I was much more emotional and tended to react immediately without thinking. However, when we were together, we melded our strengths and we balanced each other nicely.

When she walked in, I hugged her hello and said, "Come on, let's go upstairs."

I dragged her by the arm and accidentally tripped her.

Lily looked at me like I was deranged and said, "Please, let go of my arm."

"I'm sorry. Are you okay?"

"I'm going to have a huge black and blue, but I'll survive."

I slammed my bedroom door shut and excitedly said, "I have to tell you something."

Lily asked, "Okay, what? You're acting really weird."

"Well, today I saw this guy at the MET and then I saw him later in the park...." I began, and then paused when I realized how stupid it was going to sound.

"Yeah? Who was it?"

I stared at Lily not sure how to continue. "Well, nobody I know," I admitted. The second the words came out of my mouth, I regretted it and felt so dumb.

"What are you talking about?" Lily wanted me to get to the point.

After I told her the whole story, Lily just stared at me incredulously. She was about to laugh out loud, but when she saw my hurt look, she covered her mouth and suppressed it.

"Okay, so what? You'll never see him again, so forget it."

"I know you're right," I reluctantly agreed.

Always rational and calm, that was Lily in a nutshell. "By the end of this weekend, you won't remember him."

Lily began telling me about her first week working at her dad's finance firm. She said the work was dull, but after receiving her first paycheck today, she promised to stop complaining.

I told Lily about the movie plans and she went to take a shower.

Amber started barking and Mom told me to take her out. Still daydreaming about him, I couldn't believe it, but I thought I saw him. Halfway up the block, he was crossing the street and then he disappeared from view. Great! Now, I'm seeing him. For a second, I had considered sprinting after him.

I returned glum from the walk and didn't bother telling Lily that I was now having visions of him. She'd probably really start laughing, and I'd die.

At the theater, I glanced around the lobby hoping for a miracle. Did I really think he'd be here? Those kinds of things only happened in the movies.

Daphne and Grace appeared right after us and we rushed inside to find seats. We weren't able to find four together so we had to split up.

Before calling it a night, we took a walk on Columbus Ave and even though I knew it was irrational, I found myself looking around for him.

"Paige, earth to Paige. What do you think?" asked Daphne.

I shrugged my shoulders and said, "I don't know." I had missed a large part of the conversation and had no idea what they were talking about.

"What's wrong with you tonight?" Daphne asked.

"Nothing, I was just thinking about someo... something," I corrected myself. I looked over at Lily who was grinning and I glared at her to stop. I couldn't handle all three of them laughing at me.

"I'm thinking of getting a tattoo on my ankle. Do you like a heart or a star? I'm taking a poll."

"I like them both." I'd personally never get a tattoo because I hated pain. After having my ears pierced in fifth grade, I was scarred for life.

"Come on, pick one."

"I guess star. What did you say?" I asked Lily and Grace.

"They also said star," Daphne answered.

"Don't you have to be eighteen?" Lily asked.

"There's a guy on St. Mark's Place that doesn't check ID's," Daphne explained.

"Like I keep saying, I think you should wait and do it at a good place," said Grace. Lily and I agreed.

"I'm not waiting," Daphne said, sounding annoyed.

Grace looked exasperated and asked me, "What are you two doing tomorrow?"

"Lily begged me to go shopping," I moaned.

"You'll survive." She knew how much I hated it. "By the way, Stars is having a huge sale tomorrow," Grace told Lily.

"Yay! We'll be there," Lily answered excitedly.

When we got home, Carl, the doorman, handed me a package for Dad. I left it on the table in the foyer and took Amber for her last walk.

My queen-size bed was perfect for sleepovers, but tonight I just couldn't get comfortable. Lily was exhausted from her full week of work and getting up early to catch the train, so she quickly fell asleep. I turned off the TV and hoped I'd get sleepy in the dark.

***

When I opened my eyes, it was seven o'clock and Lily was still sleeping, so I quietly slipped out of bed. Why was I up this early? Maybe since I hadn't done anything all week, I wasn't that tired, but I didn't feel refreshed, either. This was crazy! I couldn't stop thinking about a stranger I met in the park. If it weren't so pathetic, it'd be humorous. Lily was right. If one of my friends told me this story, I'd laugh hysterically too.

It was hot and humid outside, but shopping was the only thing on Lily's agenda. The weather wouldn't deter her. When she had asked to shop all day, I had agreed without mentioning that I hoped to find him strolling around the Upper West Side.

Our first stop was Stars. As always, the store was packed and I saw Daphne and Grace helping customers in the back. Besides being best friends, they lived on the same block and both worked here together. The store was managed by Daphne's mom and owned by Jordan Walker, a well-known model. She opened the shop two years ago and it quickly became 'the' store on the Upper West Side. Besides the unique décor, it carried the newest trends and fairly priced merchandise. There was a section with T-shirts of famous and up-and-coming music bands and T-shirts with quotes from songs, books and movies. There was an entire wall of funky flip-flops and a large jewelry wall.

When Daphne saw us, she came over and whispered, "Lily, I pulled some things for you from the sale rack."

While Daphne went in the back room for the merchandise, Lily looked through the sale racks and then had to wait in a long line for one of the coveted fitting rooms.

I went in the office to talk to Grace because she was on break.

Many stores later, I felt nauseous and when we reached the Time Warner Center, I finally had enough.

I sat on a bench and said, "Lily, go ahead, I'll wait here for you."

When she finally came out, we headed home to get ready for the New York Philharmonic concert in Central Park. My parents loved classical music.

Lily was taking forever in the bathroom trying on her new clothes and Mom was tired of waiting. "Paige, we're leaving. We'll see you over there."

When we arrived, I found my parents talking to another couple and waved to them. I spotted some kids from school, so we went over there.

As the music wafted through the air, Central Park was magical. The full moon, the lights and stars bathed the area in a spectacular glow. When fireworks filled the sky at the end of the performance, it was amazing.

***

Sunday morning after breakfast, Lily asked, "Can we go to Soho today?"

I was sick of shopping, but I wanted to get out of my neighborhood to stop looking for him.

As we turned onto West Broadway from Spring Street, I got a feeling that I was being watched. I glanced all around but saw no one looking at me.

After two hours, I couldn't shop anymore.

"Lily, can we please do something else?"

Lily reluctantly said, "Fine. What?"

"How about we go to the High Line?"

"No, we were just there two weeks ago," she complained.

We finally agreed on the Museum of Natural History and jumped on an uptown train. We got a slice of pizza near the museum and then ran in acting like kids.

This had been our favorite museum when we were young and we especially loved the Butterfly exhibit. Our moms would literally have to drag us out of the vivarium.

We went to our favorite spot, the Hall of Ocean Life. It was home of the ninety-four-foot-long blue whale, and every time I walked into that room, I still felt such excitement. When I was twelve, a friend had a birthday slumber party there and I'll never forget waking up beneath the whale.

After roaming around, we headed to the Rose Center for Earth and Space.

On our way out, I stopped at the information desk and asked about volunteering. As the lady behind the desk was giving me the information, my cell rang.

"Paige, Martin, Marina and Anna are here. Where are you?" Martin, my older half-brother, was there for dinner and I had completely lost track of time.

"I'm sorry. We're on our way."

"What's the matter?" asked Lily.

"Martin's there and we're late."

After Mom married Dad, she moved from the city to Dad's house in Westchester. He'd been married before and had joint custody of Martin, my half-brother. He was fifteen years older, was married to Marina and had a one year-old daughter named Anna, which made me an aunt.

When Martin was heading to college, Mom convinced Dad to move back to the city. Everyone told my parents that the city was no place to raise a child, but they didn't listen and I'm glad. I had the best of all worlds, the city, Lily's place for suburbia and Grammy's house at the beach. After selling the house, my parents bought a three-bedroom duplex on West 69th Street.

Back home, we tried playing with Anna, but she was completely mesmerized by Amber. Anna was making funny noises and it really seemed like she was trying to talk to Amber. It was hysterical. Amber escaped into the den and Anna had no idea where she went.

I overheard Martin telling Dad that they went to the Central Park Zoo and how much Anna loved the carousel.

"You should've called me! We would've met you there. I love the snow leopards."

"We did. Marina called and left a message. You never called back," Martin said.

"I never heard my phone ring."

I looked at my cell. "And I don't have any messages." There was no indication of a missed call or a voice mail and my missed calls log was empty.

Marina looked at my phone and said, "That's weird. I know I called." She showed me her phone log.

My cell phone was doing odd things. There was clearly something wrong with it.

Lily tried texting me a few times and that worked. Mom said the cell was only four months old and if it kept happening, we'd go to the phone store.

Marina asked if I could babysit in a few weeks and I was thrilled to have something to do.

When Anna started getting cranky, Martin said that it was their cue to make a quick exit.

Lily and I helped them to the garage and then took Amber to the park. She was telling me a story about Noelle, her best friend in Chappaqua when I saw him. He was walking into the park and I nearly screamed.

"Lily! That's him! Over there," my voice cracked from excitement as I pointed. This was so unbelievable! After obsessing about him all weekend, there he was in the flesh.

"Where? Oh, the blond guy?" she said, once she spotted him. He was walking really fast. I caught a glimpse of him near the 7th Regiment Memorial statue and then I lost sight of him. At least, he was still around. That was good and bad because if I hadn't seen him maybe I would've forgotten about him. We walked around, but couldn't find him.

"If he lives around here, maybe you'll run into him again," Lily said.

***

Lily left for work Monday morning and I missed her immediately, even though, I'd see her Friday on Long Island for the Fourth of July weekend and Grammy's birthday.

My cell was ringing and I saw that it was my friend, Eden.

"Hey stranger, long time no speak."

"I know. How are you?" I asked.

"I'm good. Are you free today? I want to talk to you." She sounded sad.

"I am. Is everything okay?"

"Yeah. I just want to see you."

"I'm home. Do you want to come over?"

"Okay. I have something to do first. How about in an hour?" Eden asked.

"Sounds good to me."

Eden, Daphne, Grace and I had been inseparable since fifth grade. In the beginning of our junior year, Eden started dating Paul, a boy from another school, and we hardly ever saw her anymore. They were together every possible minute and the four of us had drifted apart.

When we complained, she said, "True friends wouldn't make me feel bad for being in love."

We just wanted to see her occasionally, but we gave up trying.

As I waited, I got a text saying that she was sorry that she couldn't come over after all.

I wasn't surprised because she canceled all the time, but I was still disappointed.

When Mom got home, we decided to order Japanese food.

"What would you like?" she asked while looking at the menu.

"Just a spicy tuna roll and firecracker shrimp."

I went to my bedroom to wait and got on the computer. There

was an invitation on Facebook from Reed, a boy from school. Reed had asked me to the last school dance in May. I only liked him as a friend, so I lucked out that we had theatre tickets for the same night.

His message was that he was going to hockey camp for the summer and was having a get-together tonight before he left. It would be nice to see some kids from school.

When I heard the doorbell, I ran downstairs for dinner. I was starving.

Mom was paying the delivery guy and I took the bag. As I entered the kitchen, the house line rang and it was Daphne.

"Paige, I've been texting you all day. Are you still having issues with your phone?"

"I guess. One day it's fine and the next it's crazy. I have to go to the phone store. Are you going to Reed's tonight?"

"Yeah, that's why I've been trying to reach you. Grace and I are going. Can you go?"

"I'm not sure I should. What if he asks me out again?"

"Tell him you like somebody else or that you just want to be friends. Problem is, once a guy asks you out and you say that, they never want to be friends. Remember Colton?"

"I know. That's exactly why I'm worried. Colton hates you now. I'll call you back after dinner. I'm really not sure if I'm in the mood for a party."

Mom walked in and overheard the ending. "Sweetie, go have fun. You were just complaining how bored you were."

She was right. I couldn't hide from every boy that liked me.

I called Daphne and made plans to meet them in front of Reed's building. Reed lived on West 79th Street and Daphne and Grace lived on West 82nd Street.

When I got to Reed's, they were waiting for me. As I approached, Grace was animatedly telling Daphne something. What did they have left to talk about? I suppose, that same question could apply to Lily and me, but we didn't go to school together, work together and live on the same block.

It was impossible not to notice Grace's striking appearance. Her mom was African-American and her dad was Irish so Grace had beautiful blended features. With long curly brown hair, big brown eyes, light brown skin and full lips, she really was stunning. Daphne was Italian with shoulder length black hair and hazel eyes. Jokingly, we called ourselves the 3D's for 'the dark three.' When Eden was part of our group we had called ourselves the Four Musketeers. After Eden ditched us for Paul, Daphne came up with our new name. Eden had red hair so the 4D's name wouldn't have worked for the four of us anyways.

"Hey, you two look great. Perks of working in a clothing store, huh?" I joked.

"Yep, but we also have to deal with crazy shoppers, so it's a trade off," Daphne said.

"Yeah. There's this insane woman who keeps returning everything she buys," said Grace.

Walking into the building, Daphne asked, "You ready?"

"I guess," I answered hesitantly.

"Maybe he likes somebody else by now," Grace added, reassuringly.

As we rode the elevator up, I hoped I wasn't making a mistake.

Chad, Reed's older brother, answered the door. He was really cute and had long brown wavy hair that almost reached his shoulder. He had graduated this year and I had no idea what he was doing in the fall. When I was a freshman, he was a sophomore and we had an art class together, but since then, I had barely seen him.

"Hi, girls."

"Hi. How's your band?" I asked, noticing his guitar.

"Great. We have a gig tonight."

"What are you doing next year?" I asked.

"I'm going to Julliard."

"Wow," we all said almost simultaneously.

"Reed…you have some more friends here," he yelled. "Gotta go, have fun." Although Chad and Reed were only a year apart, they had their own circle of friends. Reed was a muscular jock and sports consumed his life and Chad's passion was music.

Reed materialized and I could tell from his expression that he was happy I came.

"Hi, come on in. We're playing video games and just hanging out."

There were five guys and three girls from school standing in the living room and a pretty blonde girl I didn't know sitting on the floor talking to Evan, Reed's best friend. Reed's mom told us to help ourselves with the drinks and snacks on the counter in the kitchen. After grabbing a water bottle, I returned into the living room and sat on the couch. I thought Daphne and Grace were right behind me, but Reed sat down next to me instead.

"I heard your London trip got canceled."

"Yeah, my grandmother broke her leg."

"So what are you going to do this summer?"

"I don't know yet. Hopefully find a job. When are you leaving for Canada?"

"In two weeks. Are you around for Fourth of July?" he asked.

Oh no! Please don't ask me out. "No, we're going to my grandmother's on Long Island. It's her birthday," I said.

Evan came over complaining about the remote and dragged Reed away. Grace quickly sat down and squeezed my arm. I opened my eyes wide at her and breathed a sigh of relief.

Daphne was talking to Deidre, a girl from school, and the blonde girl. Wherever Reed went, she watched him like a hawk.

When Daphne came over, I asked, "Who's that blonde girl you were talking to?"

"Her name's Josie. She moved into Reed's building from Paris about two weeks ago. She's really nice," Daphne added as an afterthought.

"Does she speak English?" I asked.

"Yeah, she's from California. She lived in Paris for two years because of her dad's job."

I looked over and Josie was watching us.

In a short time, there were about twenty people there. Daphne spent most of the night flirting with Evan, which was strange because she always said that he was a jerk.

I was talking to Grace and Deidre when I saw Vanessa walk in and I was surprised and annoyed at the same time. Vanessa's best friend was Carla, Reed's ex-girlfriend. When Reed broke up with Carla in the spring, she was heartbroken and she still wanted him back. The rumors were that she wouldn't leave Reed alone and was almost stalking him.

As soon as Vanessa spotted me, it was like daggers were being thrown at me. Carla and Vanessa heard that Reed had asked me to the dance and because of that they hated me. Every time they passed me in the halls, they'd laugh and make snarky comments. Luckily, I had no classes with them, but sometimes their comments really got to me.

All night long, Reed was nearby and always jumped into my conversations. I glanced around and saw Vanessa talking to Josie. When they both started giving me dirty looks, it was obvious that Vanessa was talking about me. It was funny watching them together. Josie was a blond Barbie doll and Vanessa was Chinese with long black hair. They were complete opposites.

"It looks like Vanessa is talking about me," I whispered to Grace.

Grace looked over and lifted her water bottle and mouthed, "Do you want a picture."

Vanessa turned away and laughed with Josie.

"Don't. It's not really worth it," I said.

"Why not? She's an idiot. You should go over there," Grace insisted.

"What's so crazy is that I never even went out with Reed. What would they be like if I did?"

"I think you should tell them off or tell Reed. He'd get really pissed at both of them."

"I'll think about it." When I glanced back at Vanessa, she gave me the finger. I didn't want to stay any longer and deal with this nonsense. "Grace, I'm going home."

"Don't let her get to you." Grace hadn't seen what she did and I wasn't telling her.

"I'm just tired. I'll talk to you tomorrow."

I wasn't in the mood for Vanessa or Josie. Perhaps with me gone, Josie and Reed would find each other. Carla and Vanessa could move on and hate Josie.

When I went over to say goodbye, Reed insisted on walking me to the door.

"I'll call you before I leave for camp."

I managed to say, "Sure."

I gave him a hug goodbye, but by the time I got to the elevator, I worried that he might have gotten the wrong idea and regretted it.

***

My books were strewn all over the place. While most of my friends bought clothes, I bought books and could get lost for hours in a bookstore. Lily thought I was crazy.

As I put my books away, I saw a folder protruding from under my bed. Inside, I found my school's required summer reading lists and assignments for my classes that needed to be completed before school started. I'd signed up for a poetry class called English Poets.

I'd taken a Shakespeare class last year and loved it so much that this year I decided to tackle poetry. Nana loved poetry and on every visit, I'd find a poetry book in my room. Her favorite poets were

Elizabeth Barrett Browning, John Keats, Percy Bysshe Shelley and Lord Byron. Luckily, those four poets along with William Blake, Lord Tennyson and William Butler Yeats were part of the curriculum. I had to check if we had any of the poetry books and if not, I'd have to go to the library.

When Amber started barking, it gave me an excuse to stop cleaning to go for a walk.

Back in my room, I noticed my electric and acoustic guitars and my keyboard in the corner of my room and decided to write a song. I got so involved that I lost track of time and didn't realize how late it was.

Mom called up that she was home, so I went downstairs and found her in the kitchen. She reminded me that they were having a dinner party.

I really didn't feel like being home anymore, so I called Daphne. "What are you doing tonight?" I asked.

"Nothing special. Why?"

"I'm bored. Can I sleep over?"

"Sure. That concert we tried to get tickets for is tonight at Rumsey Field. Want to go, sit on a bench and listen?"

"Okay. We can close our eyes and pretend we're inside," I joked.

We had a great time. I normally had trouble falling asleep at friends' houses, but not tonight.

***

In the morning, I walked with Daphne and Grace to Stars and went inside to find a present for Grammy's birthday. I eventually settled on a beautiful knit peach summer scarf. While Grace gift-wrapped the gift, I asked Daphne if there were any job openings at the store. She didn't think so, but would check with her mom later.

Before I left, Grace asked if I wanted to meet at Café Lalo that evening. She had family visiting and had to stay for dinner, but wanted to get out of the house afterwards. I said sure.

When I got home, I called the Museum of Natural History and a lady told me that I needed to apply with the Department of Volunteer Services. First, there was an application to complete and with that you had to send a resume. Then, there would be a preliminary interview. Since I was under eighteen, I needed a permission letter from my parents. If I passed all these steps, I would be interviewed a second time and finally placed.

By the end of this long process, I fully understood, it would be fall and I would be back in school. I checked some other museums and the process was the same. Even volunteering was difficult.

Nonetheless, I decided to fill out the applications online anyway. I could volunteer on the weekends during the school year if I got accepted or at least be ready for next summer if need be.

I called Mom and she was at the obelisk for the photo shoot so I jogged over. For a research paper on Egypt in seventh grade, I wrote about obelisks and since then I'd been fascinated by them. This one was the only ancient Egyptian obelisk in America. Napoleon had admired this one, but thought it was too deteriorated, so he chose a different one for Paris. Cleopatra's Needle is the name given to all three Ancient Egyptian obelisks removed from Egypt. They were re-erected in London, Paris and New York City. Amazingly, the twin of the Manhattan obelisk was in London and I'd seen it many times. It made me feel like New York and London would forever be linked and intertwined. The obelisk in Paris came from a different site and its twin still stood in Egypt. Obelisks were placed in pairs at entrances of temples. Now most stand alone apart from their mates. It's sad in a bizarre way because they were constructed as mates and then they were torn apart.

After about an hour, I got bored and left. My cell rang and it was Grace. "Hey, let's meet at the café at eight o'clock. If I'm running late, I'll call you."

When Dad got home from work, he said his office did need me, but only on a part-time basis. I jumped up from the couch and screamed, "YAY!" Mom rushed out of the kitchen.

"I'm working at Dad's office!" I shrieked at her.

"That's great, but please quiet down," Mom said, shaking her head.

Surprised by my outburst, Dad patted my shoulder and said that Maria, the office manager, would call to tell me when to come in.

How could they be this blasé? I had something to do and it actually paid!

After dinner, I went to meet Grace at Café Lalo. I took a table by the window, ordered a cappuccino and stared at all the people passing by. Grace was almost twenty minutes late and just when I was going to call her, she rushed in.

"I'm so sorry. My mom wouldn't let me leave. I tried calling you. Did you forget your cell?" Grace asked breathlessly.

"No, it's right here. It never rang." I checked my phone, but there were no calls.

The door opened and in walked Carla and Vanessa. They spotted us and began laughing.

"Oh, no," I said and covered my face with my hands. "This will be torture."

Carla was sporting a pixie hair cut and it actually looked really nice on her, which I wasn't happy to admit.

Grace said, "Don't let them get to you. They're idiots."

They sat two tables down from us and kept whispering and staring. Grace began imitating them and they looked really annoyed. When Grace waved to them, Carla gave her the finger.

"Wait till the next time, she comes to Stars," Grace said threateningly. "I'm so rude to them already, but Daphne and I are very careful that her mom doesn't get mad at us."

"I'm surprised they still shop there."

"They like those T-shirts from London that only our store carries."

"Why don't they order them online?"

"The shipping cost from the UK is really expensive."

Suddenly, Carla said loudly, "I hate shirts with zippers. Only sluts wear them to make it easy for the guys."

She was talking about me, so I looked at Grace and pulled my zipper up and down exposing my pink polka-dotted bra. Grace and I started laughing so hard that we had tears in our eyes.

Carla yelled out, "Can you quiet down over there?"

"Mind your own business," Grace shot back, which caused us to laugh even more.

We left before them and as we passed their table, Grace said,

"No wonder Reed broke up with her. She's such a bitch and what a stupid haircut."

She looked so mad that I almost expected her to leap across the table and attack Grace.

***

Thursday morning, we headed for Grammy's house on the North Fork of Long Island.

Mom had taken Thursday and Friday off so we were getting an early start to the long weekend. Dad would take the Jitney out on Friday night.

Headphones on, pillow on the window and book in lap, I was ready for the ride. While Mom listened to the radio, I listened to my IPod.

Suddenly, Mom slammed on the brakes and I woke up.

"What happened?"

"Sorry. That black car cut me off and I almost hit him."

I was unsettled by the jarring way I was awakened and thought about the strange dream that was interrupted. I was walking in Central Park on a sunny day and suddenly everything went dark and cold. As I tried to leave the park, the path home kept disappearing. I asked people for help, but no one understood what I was saying and a feeling of despair enveloped me. Suddenly, a horse carriage materialized and the boy with the blue eyes motioned to me to get in. When I approached, he reached for my hand and pulled me up.

I stared out the window feeling very sad from the memory of it.

2. HAVEN

"If you want your children to be intelligent, read them fairy tales. If you want them to be more intelligent, read them more fairy tales."
Einstein

There's a road sign in Cutchogue saying it's the sunniest place in New York State.

Grapevines are planted for miles and miles an there are over forty vineyards. Farms and nurseries are everywhere. Life is simple and that's why I loved it. It was also the special place where my family always came together.

We called it the "Unhamptons" because it's very different from the South Fork. We enjoyed the Hamptons and visited Cooper's Beach for the ocean. When we returned, we always appreciated the peacefulness of the North Fork all the more.

On the way, we stopped at Briermere Farm to pick up a blueberry cream pie.

As we pulled into the gravel driveway, the front door of the cedar-shingled house opened and Grammy rushed out to greet us.

"I'm so happy to see you," Grammy said as she approached.

As I carried in the groceries, the aroma of baking hit me as I entered the foyer. The house always smelled of pies and cakes. I went up to my room and threw on my bathing suit. I pounded down the stairs two at a time, charged out to the pool and dove into the crystal clear water.

Floating on my back, I glanced at the house and saw Grammy watching me from the kitchen window. Ever since Lily and I were little, Grammy felt very uncomfortable unless there was a grown-up outside while we swam. One of Grammy's friends died in a tragic pool accident and Grammy had been scared ever since. Even as we got older, she still lurked nearby pretending to garden whenever we were in the pool. I smiled and waved. When she disappeared from the window, I presumed that Mom had coaxed her away. A few moments later, Grammy came outside with a towel, magazines and a bottle of water.

"I brought you some things."

"Thanks so much, Grammy." She put everything on the table and went back inside. For a second, I'd thought she was going to stay and lifeguard.

Tired, I got out and sat on the chaise daydreaming.

Mom walked out of the house. "We're going to Southold to visit one of Grammy's friend."

"Okay, have fun."

"I'm not sure about that. You remember Eileen?" I nodded. "She hit a deer yesterday."

"Is she okay?"

"She's fine, just pretty banged up. Her car is totaled, though."

"Wow."

"We should be back in an hour."

As I zoned out, I looked around the property and wondered why I'd never drawn or painted it.

On the ground floor were Grammy's bedroom, a guestroom, two bathrooms, kitchen, living room, den and dining room.

Upstairs, there were three bedrooms and two bathrooms. Lily and I shared a bedroom upstairs and our parents had the other two rooms.

Grammy's Christmas present from Mom and Aunt Cecile, an interior decorator, was a makeover of the ground floor and the three of them had fun decorating together. The walls in the living room were painted sandy beige. There were pale blue couches with white and yellow pillows. Hurricane vases were scattered around the room filled with sand, shells and candles in case of a power outage during a storm.

The kitchen was painted a pale yellow with sea green cabinets. All the fabrics used on the ground floor were yellow, blue, green and/or white. On a yard sale run, Mom found big green and amber glass bottles and had them converted into lamps. The bedrooms upstairs were all painted linen white and the splashes of color came from the bedding and the curtains.

My favorite place was the outside stone patio, which was covered by a long sand-colored retractable awning. There was a large square aluminum table and chairs that seated twelve. On the side there was a long wicker couch and large wicker chairs for relaxing. Even in the rain, we were able to enjoy the outdoors.

Around the pool, there were ten lounge chairs and six huge tan market umbrellas. In one corner, there was a large round teak table.

Lavender bordered all the gardens and sitting on the patio, the scent was unbelievable. Lilacs, roses, Montauk daisies, blue hydrangeas, lilies, peonies were just some of the flowers that grew in her garden.

The neighbors were amazed because their plants didn't grow half as well.

Grammy's house was on Horseshoe Cove Beach facing Little Peconic Bay. The area was called Nassau Point and Albert Einstein had rented a cottage here in the summers of 1938 and 1939. He said that it was "the most beautiful sailing ground I ever experienced."

I loved being at Grammy's, but it wasn't perfect unless Lily was there too. We were more like sisters than cousins and like sisters; we've had some crazy fights over the years. One dispute over a yellow crayon will live on in infamy. Now, we reminisce about all the silliness and realize every memory good or bad made up our history together.

I glanced up at my bedroom window and saw a dark shape swoosh behind the curtains. It really looked like someone was up there. Amber was inside and if a stranger was there, she would've been barking like crazy. Looking through the patio glass doors, I saw Amber enter the kitchen from the front foyer and flop on her dog pillow with not a care in the world. I glanced through the side gate and Mom's car wasn't in the driveway. The apparition must have been the light or my imagination.

I jumped back in the pool to do some laps.

As I turned to head the other way, I saw Mom and Grammy standing by the edge.

Grammy looked angry. "You know that you're not allowed to swim if you're home alone."

"I'm so sorry. I forgot."

Grammy was visibly upset and without saying anything, she turned and walked away. Years ago, a friend of Grammy's had a horrible pool accident in her home and since then Grammy has been vigilante that no one swims alone.

Mom shook her head and said, "Come on. You're not two. You know that's her one rule."

"I'm really sorry," I repeated. No longer in the mood to swim, I got out and watched as Mom caught up to Grammy.

Frustrated, I grabbed Amber's leash and walked down the beach to get away from them.

Amber had webbed paws and she loved the water. As I walked, she swam alongside. Eventually tiring, she'd walk on the sand in front of me. After each brief respite, she'd jump back in. All of a sudden, she charged out of the water. I looked down the beach and spotted a yellow lab approaching. For a good ten minutes, they chased each other around making sand storms. They were panting loudly so I took my water bottle and filled my cupped hand. They slobbered all over me and just as I began to wonder where the owner was; a man whistled and the dog took off. Amber tried to follow. I grabbed her collar, put her leash on and headed home. I toweled her off, changed my clothes and went for a jog.

Later, we watched a movie and when it was done, Mom asked me to take Amber out. The beach was desolate and up ahead, I saw a person near the trees and I nervously turned around.

***

The next morning, we had breakfast at the Cutchogue Diner. When we got back, Mom and Grammy started looking through cookbooks for menus and recipes for the weekend barbeques. I was so happy to be here. If I went to London, my parents would've been here without me.

"Sweetie, we're going food shopping. Call the farm and see about riding. If you can ride today, schedule it for later."

"Okay," I said and called Meadow Hill Farms. I was able to get a hack for today, which was riding without an instructor and was only allowed for experienced riders.

My obsession with horses started when I was six years old on the drive to Grammy's house. As we passed several horse farms, I saw kids riding and saw a sign that said 'Pony Camp.' I pestered my parents until they signed me up and I've been riding ever since.

After that summer camp, I took lessons in the city at the Claremont Riding Academy. When the facility closed, I was heartbroken. Luckily, my horse trainer moved to Westchester and I continued riding there.

I texted Mom the time of my ride and then found my riding clothes in a laundry basket in the closet. As I sat on the window seat, I glanced out and saw the boats from the New Suffolk sailing club heading towards Robins Island. I grabbed my camera and took some photos.

When I was done, I put the camera in the case and threw it on my bed. As I put on my sports bra, I noticed a guy jogging barefoot on the beach heading towards our house.

In a few moments, he was right in front of the house and it looked like the guy in the park. How was that possible? I ran to my bed, grabbed the camera and tried to zoom him into view, but only his back was visible.

I threw my shorts back on and raced to the beach. I looked all around and spotted him walking on Fleets Neck Beach. He must have swum across the channel since there was no other way to get over there.

When I turned to go home, I stepped on a shell and felt pain on my heel. Looking down, I saw my pink and black colored zebra-striped knee-high riding socks and realized how ridiculous I must look. Besides the socks, I was wearing a yellow sports bra and red shorts. Shaking my head, at the wacko I'd become, I quickly ran inside before anyone saw me.

When Mom and Grammy got back from shopping, I got my saddle out of the garage.

"Mom, can I drive over? I have to practice."

She handed me the keys and crossed herself.

"Mom, please stop!"

"I was just fooling around." I wasn't sure if I believed her.

We made it to the barn with Mom screaming less than usual, so I thought it was a good drive. Mom got into the driver seat. "Have fun. I'll be back in an hour."

I ran in with carrots, excited to see Milton, a gray, part quarter horse and thoroughbred. After leasing him for a couple of summers, we had a special bond.

"Milton," I called out and he stuck his head out of the stall.

"Hi. I've missed you." I rubbed his nose and he nudged my arm for the carrots.

I brushed him down and since Carlos and Julio, the grooms, were busy with a hay delivery, I got Milton ready myself.

We walked outside and Sara, the riding instructor, was giving a group lesson in the school ring, so I headed for the far riding ring, which was empty.

"Hey stranger," Sara called out as I passed. "Nice to see you."

"You too. I've missed this place and Milton," I added.

"I'm sure he missed you as well."

I had a great time trotting, cantering and galloping. Flying through the air was exhilarating.

Afterwards, I washed Milton in the outside shower stall and got soaked in the process, but it felt good. Suddenly, two black sedans sped by and I was really surprised. There were signs all along the driveway warning drivers to slow down because the horses could get spooked and buck off the riders. The cars disappeared, but I knew they'd be back since there was no exit over there. Sure enough, they raced by faster than before.

I put Milton in one of the pastures and went to watch Sara teach.

As I sat on the fence, Sara called out, "Can you help me with the poles?"

"Sure," I said and jumped down.

"Did you see those cars before?" Sara asked, as we each grabbed an end.

"Yeah, I did. I couldn't believe how fast they were driving."

"I know. I screamed slowdown, but they didn't," Sara said angrily. "I yelled for the kids to get off their horses. When they went behind the property, I called the police and waited in the road. They came out and drove on the grass around me."

"It was probably a car service and they thought this was a winery." Some people hired cars when they went winetasting.

I saw Mom driving up the driveway and ran inside to grab my bag and saddle.

As we exited the farm, the two black cars were parked across the street and a police officer was talking to one of the drivers. Why were those cars still around almost thirty minutes later?

I felt so gross and sticky that I ran up to shower. There was horsehair all over my arms and face. As I walked out of the bathroom, someone screamed, "Boo."

I jumped for dear life and there stood Lily laughing. "Wow, you were really scared!"

"You almost gave me a heart attack. Don't do that."

"Why did you shower?" Lily asked, as she put on her bathing suit. "I want to go swimming."

"I went riding. Why are you here? Weren't you catching the bus with our dads tonight?"

"The office didn't need me today, so I came out with Mom."

"Why didn't you tell me?"

"I wanted to surprise you."

I wanted to tell Lily about my possible sighting of him, but decided to wait till later.

After we got out of the pool and Lily was wrapping herself up in a towel, I said, "Lily, I saw that blond guy from the park jogging on our beach this morning."

Lily sighed and sat down on a chaise. "Give me a break. That's impossible."

"It looked just like him. I swear. I know it sounds crazy, but I'm pretty sure it was him."

"There's no way. You're hallucinating."

"But it's possible it was him," I insisted.

"I'm 99.999% sure it wasn't him. Want to bet ten dollars?"

I didn't, but said, "Sure." It wasn't like we would ever know anyway.

Lily put on her ear buds and closed her eyes. She was done talking about imaginary people.

I checked Facebook and texted some friends. When that got dull, I decided to start my school reading since I found one of the books. The first poem on the list was written by John Keats called 'To A Lady Seen for a Few Moments at Vauxhall.'

> Time's sea hath been five years at its slow ebb,
> Long hours have to and fro let creep the sand,
> Since I was tangled in thy beauty's web,
> And snared by the ungloving of thine hand.
>
> And yet I never look on midnight sky,
> But I behold thine eyes' well memory'd light;
> I cannot look upon the rose's dye,
> But to thy cheek my soul doth take its flight.

—

I cannot look on any budding flower,
But my fond ear, in fancy at thy lips
And hearkening for a love-sound, doth devour
Its sweets in the wrong sense: - Thou dost eclipse
Every delight with sweet remembering,
And grief unto my darling joys dost bring.

Time normally makes memories fade, however, that wasn't the case here and I felt a little less foolish fantasizing about a stranger. The words "sweet remembering' explained that perfectly since my reaction to the boy in the park was comparable.

"How come you look so miserable? Stop reading that stuff and let's do something."

"Sure, what do you want to do?" I asked, snapping out of my doldrums.

"I don't know, but I need some exercise. How about tennis?" Lily rose from the chaise.

We went inside to ask one of our moms for a ride and they wanted to join us.

"If the courts are full, we'll play doubles," Mom suggested.

"Otherwise, we'll play singles," Lily countered.

When we arrived, there was one court available so we had to play with our moms.

As we were leaving the park, I noticed two cars idling in the parking lot with dark tinted windows. It looked like those same two cars from the morning.

Back home, we were doing laps when our dads appeared.

That night, there was a new moon and it was eerily dark on the beach when we took Amber for a walk. Apart from the intermittent house lights, the only illumination came from the boats in the bay.

"It's really eerie out here when it's this dark," Lily said.

"I know. The other night I got scared being out here alone and turned around."

There was a boat that had its lights on and as we passed, it went completely dark. From the light of a nearby boat, I saw that someone was standing on the deck.

***

Lily and I woke up and smelled baked goods all the way upstairs. In the kitchen, we found everyone preparing a birthday breakfast for Grammy.

"Happy Birthday, Grammy!" we yelled out together and kissed her.

Mom was scooping scrambled eggs into a bowl and Aunt Cecile was making a fruit salad. Uncle Ian, who hated to cook, was preparing the coffee and tea. Dad was flipping pancakes and making a terrible mess. Grammy looked upset and sat down at the table.

As Mom put the eggs on the table, she whispered, "Don't worry, I'll clean it up."

"Paige, are you riding today?" asked Lily while reaching for a blueberry muffin.

"Yeah, I have a lesson. Want to come?" I asked, knowing what she'd say.

"No way. Never again."

I laughed. One summer, Lily was bored waiting for me to come home every day, so Aunt Cecile signed her up for a two-week session.

The first day she had a lot of fun, but that wasn't the case on her second. Lily was told to clean a horse stall and she adamantly refused to do it. When a girl began mucking my stall, I got upset and Lily thought I was insane. "Why do you care if someone picks up the horse poop?"

"I want to do it myself," I whined.

"Are you crazy?" Lily stared at me in utter disbelief.

After camp, Lily ran to her Mom and shrieked, "Did you know that you paid for me to clean stalls?" Lily was convinced that the pony camp was just a ruse and that parents were paying for their kids to do child labor. That was the end of Lily's equestrian life and she never went back.

After breakfast, I drove to my riding lesson.

Sara set up the gates and I was thrilled to jump the rails. Towards the end of my lesson, something spooked Milton and I saw a man in a suit walking behind the bushes.

Sara saw him too and called out, "You can't be over there. This is private property."

Without saying a word, the man walked down the hill towards the street.

As Mom and I left the farm, a dark car was blocking the driveway. This was so weird.

"What are they doing? Beep the horn."

Before I did, the car pulled away.

The rest of the day we hung out by the pool. When Lily started playing her guitar, I read some more poetry.

A poem called 'When I Have Fears That I May Cease To Be' was really depressing.

> When I have fears that I may cease to be
> Before my pen has glean'd my teeming brain,
> Before high-piled books, in charactery,
> Hold like rich garners the full ripen'd grain;
> When I behold, upon the night's starr'd face,
> Huge cloudy symbols of a high romance,
> And think that I may never live to trace
> Their shadows, with the magic hand of chance;
> And when I feel, fair creature of an hour,
> That I shall never look upon thee more,
> Never have relish in the faery power
> Of unreflecting love;--then on the shore
> Of the wide world I stand alone, and think
> Till love and fame to nothingness do sink.

Since his parents, grandmother and brother died, Keats was cognizant of his own mortality or he wrote this poem when he was ill. Keats died when he was twenty-five. Time was the theme of the poem and it alluded to fulfilling dreams of fame and love. In the end, Keats knew that he would "stand alone" since dying was a solitary journey.

That evening we had reservations to celebrate Grammy's birthday at her favorite restaurant, The Bayview Inn in Jamesport. We sat on the outside deck and as I looked down the street, I saw two dark cars idling nearby.

"Dad, I keep seeing dark cars with tinted windows everywhere."

"So have I. The North Fork is getting very popular and there are a lot of wine tours so there are a lot of car services out here now. I read that it's a booming business."

"It's better than people driving drunk," Mom added approvingly.

"Even with that, I keep reading about many alcohol-related accidents," Grammy said.

***

Sunday morning, Lily and I joined our dads on the driving range. Lily liked golf, but I only went if she asked me to come.

"Thanks for coming," Lily said smiling, knowing exactly how I felt.

"This is so boring. You owe me."

"Fine, how about later we go to the beach and look for your fantasy man."

"Sounds like a plan," I shot back, ignoring her sarcastic tone.

Mom, as pre-arranged, picked me up at the golf course and drove me to Meadow Hill Farms for my hack. There was no one there, so I was alone. When I was almost done, I noticed a black car pull in the driveway. It slowly inched up the path at a snail's pace, made a K-turn halfway up the long driveway and stopped in the middle facing the riding ring. I really felt uncomfortable being watched and shortened my ride.

As I brought Milton back to the barn, Carlos, one of the grooms was bringing a horse out to the pasture so I asked, "Carlos, do you know whose car that is over there in the driveway?"

"No, I don't know."

By the time Mom picked me up, the car was gone. As we exited the farm, I saw that it was now parked outside. I had no idea what was going on with all these cars.

Back home, I found everyone in the kitchen prepping for the

barbeque. By two o'clock, the house was full of company. Grammy had invited some neighbors and it was lively outside.

I was in the kitchen cutting watermelon when Martin, Marina and Anna walked in.

I was so shocked. "What are you guys doing here?" I said so loudly that Anna started crying.

"I'm so sorry Anna. Look here's Amber," I said and that made her stop. Marina put Anna on the floor and she immediately crawled after the dog.

"I see that Dad didn't tell you we were coming," Martin said and I shook my head no.

"Grammy invited us," said Marina.

"I'm so happy you made it," said Grammy as she walked inside from the patio.

"Happy Birthday." Martin gave her a big hug. "Thanks for inviting us."

"You are welcome anytime."

Marina handed Grammy a big gift-wrapped box.

Grammy carefully opened it and it was a beautiful turquoise ceramic bowl. She loved it and after wiping it down, put the green salad in it.

While Marina and Martin took their bags to the guest room, Lily and I took Anna outside to play on the beach. She scooped the sand in her hands, but began to cry when the sand got wet and stuck on her hands. I carried her into the kitchen and cleaned her up.

***

Monday morning, Lily and I found everybody outside. Anna was in the pool with Martin, so I walked in and put her on a raft. As I pushed her around, Amber jumped in to retrieve a ball. Anna was so surprised that Amber was swimming that she almost toppled in.

Later that afternoon, Uncle Ian drove us to Greenport for the yearly carnival. The adults would meet us in the evening to watch the fireworks. While waiting for one of the rides to start, I looked around at the people and thought I saw him, walking towards the parking lot.

"Lily, look over there, that's him," I said excitedly and pointed.

Lily looked at me and said, "I was just kidding before about searching for him."

"Just look," I said. She looked reluctantly, but by that point he had disappeared.

"Forget it, he's gone now," I said angrily.

"I'm sure that it wasn't him. Seriously, what would he be doing here?" Lily asked.

"I don't know." I shrugged. "He must have a doppelganger out here because it really looked like him."

Lily shook her head and moved up in line and the subject was dropped.

Around ten o'clock, Aunt Cecile called Lily's phone and after our parents and Grammy found us, we watched the fireworks together. Martin and Marina stayed home with Anna.

When we got home, everybody sat outside by the pool. Exhausted, I headed upstairs, turned off the lights and stared out the window. Suddenly, I noticed alternating flashes of light coming from

Fleets Neck Beach and a boat docked by our beach. It really seemed like some sort of code. It had to be kids fooling around since grownups would use cell phones to communicate, not flashlights.

***

The next morning, I went for my hack. Thank goodness, I saw no strange cars.

When I got back, I found everyone snoozing by the pool. Anna was inside taking a nap, so apparently everyone did the same outside.

After lunch, everybody started packing up to leave. The weekend was ending.

"Paige, I have to give Anna a bath to get the chlorine off. Come and watch, so you know what to do when you babysit," said Marina.

The last time I helped, Anna was just a little blob. Now, there were rubber ducks, a floating frog and a toy whale thrown in the tub. Anna was having a ball.

"So I hear you'll be working part-time at your dad's," Marina said.

"Thank goodness. I was getting so bored," I admitted.

"You can visit us any time and even stay over. Anna would love to spend time with her aunt."

"Yeah, that sounds like fun. I'll call you. I can take the bus or maybe Mom could drive me."

After everybody left, I took Amber for a fast walk on the beach. As I approached a boat, a figure retreated below deck. On my way back, the person was back on deck, but as I got nearer, they went below again.

When I got back, the car was packed and Grammy looked really sad as we said goodbye. I knew she was lonely out here since Grandpa died four years ago. That's why in the fall and winter, Grammy visited and stayed with us in the city and also Lily's in Chappaqua.

Mom drove and stopped at the Krupski and Wickham farm stands for produce. I listened to music and texted people the whole way back.

3. MEETING

"Few are those who see with their own eyes and feel with their own hearts." Einstein

Monday morning, it was raining cats and dogs. Daphne called and said it was her day off, so she came over and we hung out all day together.

When Dad got home from work, he said that his office needed me the next day and I had to report to Maria at nine. I was thrilled to finally have something to do and it actually paid!

Daphne stayed for dinner and afterwards helped me pull together some outfits for work.

I had trouble falling asleep that night and knew that it was because I was nervous about work.

***

I woke up way too early and put on my TV. Dad came in to tell me that he had an early meeting and would see me at the office. I found Mom in the kitchen talking on her cell and she waved to me. I still had over an hour, so when Amber barked, I decided to take her for a quick walk. When I got to the corner, I saw him. He entered the park and I lost sight of him. Damn! As soon as the light changed, I charged across the street and saw him walking on a path. As I caught up, Amber started barking at a passing dog. He turned around and his blue eyes looked right at me. I was face to face with my fixation.

"Hi. Are you following me?" he asked and grinned. If I weren't so taken aback by the comment, I would have blushed. How arrogant and presumptuous. I was, but he didn't have to ask me.

"The last time I checked this was a public park," I answered testily.

"I'm sorry. I was just kidding. Have we met before?" His bright blue eyes glistened in the sunlight and pierced my soul.

I nodded. "You asked me about movies near the Conservatory Pond," I managed to say. It bothered me that he didn't remember me since I hadn't stopped thinking about him.

"Oh, that's right."

I stared at his dark skin and had to ask, "Why are you so tan? Tanning salons?" It was the beginning of summer and no one was tan yet.

He seemed amused by my comment and said, "No. I was in Australia for six months. By the way my name's Daniel." I knew his name! That silenced me and I just stared at him.

"And you are?" he asked smiling. His white teeth were blinding me.

"Oh. I'm Paige," I answered nervously and smiled. What was wrong with me?

—

"Well, I definitely didn't see you smile the last time because I wouldn't have forgotten your dimples."

"Oh, those, I can't do anything about it... sort of born with them," I remarked dismissively, embarrassed by his comment.

"You don't like them?"

"Not really," I confessed. It sounded silly, but it was true. Everybody always commented on them and it was annoying. When friends stuck their fingers in them, I was mortified.

"Well, I think they're great. Who's your four-legged friend here?" he asked.

"This is Amber."

Amber, who usually hid behind my leg whenever I talked to people she didn't know, was actually wagging her tail and sniffing Daniel's leg. He bent down and started petting her. Amber, who always shied away from strangers, sat there and let him. This was so out of the norm that it was weird.

"She's a field spaniel right?"

I was impressed. "Wow. Nobody ever knows what kind of dog she is! Most people say cocker spaniel."

"I've spent a lot of time in England, so I know the breed."

"What a nice dog," Daniel said, as Amber kept nuzzling him.

"Yes, she is," I agreed. "This is really bizarre because she never lets strangers pet her."

"She must know I love dogs."

"Do you have one? Maybe she smells yours."

"No, I travel too much, maybe one day," he answered.

I didn't know what else to say, so I just stared at him.

"Do you live around here?" he asked. "I live on West 72nd Street." He lived only three blocks from me!

"Really, I live on West 69th Street."

"We're neighbors," he said, smiling.

As he scratched Amber under her chin, I noticed three black dots on the palm of his left hand. The way they were spaced it could've been a triangle if lines were drawn to attach them. "What's that? A triangle?" I asked motioning to his palm.

He laughed it off and said, "No, it's just a silly tattoo."

I didn't want to leave, but knew that dad would be angry if I was late. "I have to go. Today's my first day at work," I said.

"No problem, I have to run too. I'm meeting a friend at the Bowling Greens. It was nice meeting you."

"Okay, bye," I remarked. Okay bye… what was wrong with me? Well, what else could I say? I was still reeling from the fact that he lived only three blocks away. Maybe, that's why he looked so familiar.

Now that I had actually seen him, talked to him and knew his name, Lily might be more interested. I called and it went to voicemail. I left a message for her to call me.

Arriving at my building was actually quite surreal because I couldn't remember the walk back. I rushed Amber into the apartment and went to tell Mom that I was leaving. She was at the kitchen table and still on the phone.

"Mom, I'm leaving."

She mouthed, "one second."

I sat down on the counter stool to wait and since Mom's laptop was on, I quickly checked Facebook. There were over ten notifications, so I checked my wall to find postings from friends congratulating me. What were they talking about?

Comments like 'It's about time', 'Finally' and 'How cute! Paige has a boyfriend!' What was going on? The last comment was written by Eden and it said, 'Reed's so nice.' Why would she write that?

I checked Reed's status and saw that he posted that he was in a relationship with me.

WHAT? Didn't he think we should be actually dating before he posted that? In spite of my anger, I had to deal with this later since I had to get to work.

I logged off and pushed the laptop away. "Mom, I have to go," I yelled in an annoyed tone just as she was ending her call.

"Good luck today," she said. She walked over and kissed me on the cheek, not realizing how mad I was.

"Yeah, great luck," I muttered, angrily.

"What's the matter?"

Ignoring her question, I said, "I have to go to work. I do want to kill someone, though."

Mom said, "Paige, don't be so melodramatic."

I reached for my bag and ended up knocking it off the counter. Everything fell on the floor. I was so annoyed. The joy I had felt over seeing Daniel was now clouded with the Reed problem.

I arrived right on time and was ushered to Maria's office. She was an older lady at least sixty years old, with blonde highlighted hair and she was extremely professional. She had me fill out employment forms and told me that I'd be helping Todd Madison with clerical duties today. She picked up the phone and asked him to come to her office. Todd appeared quite quickly. He had brown hair, was wearing a bowtie and had on wire-rimmed glasses. I noticed that his fingernails were painted black, which seemed extremely strange at a law firm. Maria introduced us and when Todd heard my last name, his eyes opened wide.

"Well, well, welcome," he said enthusiastically and took me to a machine at the back of the office. There were files placed in two sections on a long table.

"These all need to be photocopied. This group has to be done today and when you're finished bring them to me. I'm in the room to the left of Maria's. If you have any time left, you can start this second pile."

All morning I copied and thought mostly about Daniel, but the Reed mess always brought me back to reality.

Dad came downstairs around lunchtime and asked me to join him in his office. Sonia, his secretary, ordered us sandwiches. While we ate, he talked about a big case he was working on. I wasn't really listening, but did hear that he was going to Paris on Monday.

After lunch, I went back to photocopying and felt like I was being watched. When I heard a noise behind me, I turned around. There was a tall guy with glasses and curly brown hair leaning against the wall.

"Hi, can I help you?" I asked.

"Do you have a lot to do?" he asked.

"Yeah, I'll be here for awhile, sorry," I apologized. "I still have all of that." I motioned to the piles on the table.

"Wow, no problem. You'll be here for weeks," he said chuckling. "I'm Jared by the way. Are you new?"

"Yeah. Today's my first day. I'm Paige." I didn't volunteer my last name because of the nepotism factor, but Jared hadn't shared his last name either.

"Oh… you're a real newbie. You poor thing," he chuckled. "This is my third summer interning. It's not all bad, just be careful, there are some crazy people that work here." I wasn't sure if he was serious or just kidding. I wondered if he was one of them.

Jared had a large bandage wrapped around his left hand.

"What happened to you?" I asked motioning to his hand.

"Oh…I had a fight with a copy machine. Be careful they're quite temperamental and they fight back," he joked.

Everything that came out of his mouth was really funny. He must keep his co-workers very entertained when he wasn't annoying them.

"If you need any insight on anything, come find me." Jared whistled as he walked away. Dad said I was the only high school intern, so Jared had to be in college or law school.

I went to find Dad, so we could walk home together.

"Are you leaving soon?" I asked.

"I have a few things to finish up. I'll see you at home."

As I turned to leave, Maria said she'd call when the office needed me again.

The entire walk home, I worried about the Reed not knowing what to do.

Mom was in the kitchen, busy cooking dinner and it smelled

great. Whenever Mom had time, she loved to experiment and Dad and I were her guinea pigs. Usually, she wasn't happy with a cookbook recipe so she'd find another one online and then combine the two. Mom loved spices and she'd double or triple the amounts with mixed results.

The kitchen walls were painted pale green and the cabinets were white. In the back of the kitchen, there was an oak cabinet filled with colorful pottery.

"Hi honey. How was your day?" she asked when she saw me standing in the doorway.

"It was okay."

"What did you do?"

"I just photocopied." I plopped in a chair at the round table that my parents found at a garage sale in Long Island years ago. It had been painted white, so they stripped it in Grammy's garage and refinished it.

"That's good. Sweetie, get me some cilantro, please."

I jumped up and went to the herb garden container on the windowsill.

"Are you okay?" Mom asked. "You're very quiet."

"I'm fine just tired. I'm going upstairs to change."

In my room, I struggled with calling Reed. I didn't want to call his cell. At his party, he said his cell was broken, but what if he got it fixed and he was with his friends? I also didn't want to text anything since Dad always said to be careful what you email or text people. I guess it was the lawyer in him.

I found the student registry and called his house. Chad answered.

"Hi, Chad. It's Paige. Is Reed home?" I asked nervously.

"He's out. Did you try his cell?"

"He said it was broken."

"Oh, I don't know about that. I'll leave him a note that you called."

"Thanks, Bye," I said and hurried off the phone.

Glancing on my wall, I saw a post from Daphne. It said, "I'm happy for you two" written half-an-hour ago. I'm going to kill her.

Dad got in an hour after me and said he knew we were having Indian food from the aroma in the hallway. During dinner, the house phone rang and it was Daphne, but I didn't answer. I wanted to talk to her privately not in front of my parents. When I called her back, she suggested a walk and I agreed. I'd wait to tell her how mad I was in person.

When I saw her approaching, I must have looked annoyed because the first thing she said was, "Are you okay?"

"No. Why did you post that comment about Reed?" I asked coldly.

"Oh, you aren't together?" she asked.

"Don't you think I'd tell you if I was dating him? Why didn't you check with me first?"

Looking at me incredulously, she said, "I did. I tried all day. I saw the post this morning then called you like six times. I texted, emailed and left voice messages, but I didn't hear back from you. When I saw Eden's post, I thought it was true. I called your house phone tonight hoping you'd tell me about it."

"I was at work all day and there's no messages from you on my phone." This was crazy.

Daphne checked her phone and said, "Look. The six calls and here are the texts. Let me find the email."

"This is ridiculous! I have to go to the phone store."

Frustrated, I threw my phone in my bag. "So what do I do about Reed? I just want to be friends."

Daphne was looking at me and shaking her head. "Girls in school would die to date him. Just go out with him. He really likes you and we could double date if Evan ever asks me out," she added smiling. I was right she did like Evan.

Daphne started talking about Evan forgetting about my problem entirely. "Evan was flirting with me, but he might like Josie."

"I don't know about that. I think Josie likes Reed.

Daphne cheered up hearing that. "Really?"

"I'm pretty sure. She couldn't keep her eyes off him."

"That would be good for you. Deidre said that she's coming to our school in the fall."

"Maybe Reed will fall for her and leave me alone. I shouldn't have hugged him goodbye."

"You hugged him?" She looked at me awkwardly.

"Give me a break. It meant nothing. So what should I do, so he doesn't hate me?" Looking for some, any kind of advice.

"Oh, just go out with him," Daphne said, sounding annoyed.

"You go out with him," I said angrily.

"I used to like Reed," Daphne admitted. "Now, I like Evan."

"What? You never told me that you liked Reed," I said, surprised at the news.

Daphne stared at me uncomfortably and finally spoke. "I didn't tell you because I felt stupid. He was dating Carla and then he was after you. I really didn't want to be sloppy thirds."

"That doesn't make sense. I never went out with him."

We were best friends yet she never told me about her feelings for Reed. I should talk since I said nothing at all about Daniel.

Daphne shrugged her shoulders. "Whatever. I don't know what you can do. Reed posted it on Facebook and now he's going to look like a fool when you dump him. Forget about being friends. That's never going to happen."

Feeling absolutely miserable, I knew that Daphne was right. This wouldn't end well. "It's like he's trying to force me to date him," I rambled.

Why didn't I like Reed? He was nice, popular, and cute. I wondered if it was because he had dated Carla, the antithesis of me, for over a year. Carla was Spanish and very loud and gregarious. She was the girl version of Reed as far as athletics were concerned. The difference was that Reed was nice and she was a horror. She played sports year round and was adept at a lot of them. She was a gifted athlete, but was a miserable human being. Playing on some varsity teams her freshman year, then all varsity teams since then, the coaches treated her like the second coming. Her head was so swollen from all the accolades that she treated everybody in school who wasn't a teammate with contempt. In school, she only conversed with her teammates, girls on other Varsity teams or her absolute favorite, the boys. No one else mattered. Since I was only on the JV tennis team, I didn't exist to Carla.

Daphne was on Carla's softball team and said that the coaches continually stroked her ego and kowtowed to her.

One day, Daphne overheard Carla telling the coach that she was too tired to go to practice. She didn't come that whole week and when she returned, she left early every day. She came and went as she pleased and her teammates were sick of the preferential treatment. All that mattered to the athletic department was that the team won.

In gym class, if someone couldn't do something up to her standards, she rolled her eyes, smirked and laughed out loud. She was never reprimanded because she made sure the teachers weren't nearby to hear her. Carla knew how to play the game. In the presence of teachers and grown-ups she was the politest, sweetest girl and had the entire faculty fooled. No one in school complained about her because the teachers never believed that she was a bully.

In the halls, whenever Reed said hi to me, she gave me venomous glares. When they broke up last year and she found out that he asked me out, she became even more unbearable. How could Reed have ever dated her?

After discussing Reed ad-nauseam, I couldn't talk about him anymore. "He caused this mess so if we can't be friends it's all his fault," I said angrily. "I have to go. I'll talk to you later."

I called Lily as I walked home and it went to voicemail. Where was she?

As I entered the apartment, Lily called so I ran to my bedroom.

"Where have you been? I've been trying to reach you all day."

"Sorry, my phone died and I forgot to bring my charger to work today. What's up?"

I told her about Reed and she wasn't sure what to do either.

"I don't get it. Why would anybody do that? He's going to look ridiculous when it gets around that you aren't dating."

"I know. Why hasn't he called me back? He's supposedly my boyfriend," I joked.

Maybe he tried, but with my phone acting crazy his calls didn't go through. If he couldn't reach me, maybe he'd leave me alone.

"Just call him again and get it over with. Try his cell this time. You'll drive yourself crazy worrying about it."

All of a sudden, I realized I forgot to tell Lily the most important news of all. "Oh my God Lily, I have to tell you something. I met that blond guy today. His name is Daniel."

She was actually speechless for a moment. "Are you kidding? That's amazing!"

"I know. I got so tongue-tied that I couldn't think straight," I admitted. "At least, I know he lives in my neighborhood, so maybe I'll see him again."

Lily laughed and said, "If you don't, you can always stalk 72nd Street."

"Thanks, maybe I will."

***

When I opened my eyes, it was ten o'clock. I couldn't believe I slept so long.

After I ate some yogurt and strawberries, Amber and I headed out to the park. I knew Mom or Dad had already taken her out, but I hoped to bump into Daniel. I looked all around and even strolled by the Bowling Greens. With no success and feeling pathetic, I went home.

As I entered my building, my cell rang and it was Reed. I didn't want to have the conversation in the lobby or the elevator, so I ignored the call. When I had called him, I was angry and brave, but now I didn't know what to say.

After Daphne's, not to mention Lily's, dire predictions, I needed some more time. Maybe I could just hide out until he went to Canada and it would all blow over.

Tired of thinking about Reed, I went for a jog and as I entered the park on 79th Street, to go to the reservoir, I passed Daniel jogging out of the park. I stopped, but he didn't notice me.

After my run, I showered and went to the library. Then, I hid in my bedroom for the rest of the day, read poems and tried not to think about Reed. I refused to look at Facebook, afraid of what people were saying.

Lord George Byron's biography described a troubled and tortured soul, which I found very disturbing. Although he was a handsome man from a wealthy family, he had a clubfoot and an alcoholic mother. Due to sexual abuse by his nanny, he grew up to be a wanton adult and his contemporaries condemned him on moral grounds. He supposedly had an affair with his married half-sister and there were rumors of an incestuous relationship with his daughter. Because of the accusations, he left England to escape the scandal. By his own account, he had slept with about two hundred women in his time in Venice alone. Supposedly, women were always throwing themselves at him.

How pathetic! Was I just as crazy for obsessing over someone I didn't know because he was good-looking?

Reviewing the required list, I read the next poem.

SHE WALKS IN BEAUTY

She walks in beauty, like the night
Of cloudless climes and starry skies;
And all that's best of dark and bright
Meet in her aspect and her eyes:
Thus mellowed to that tender light
Which heaven to gaudy day denies.

One shade the more, one ray the less,
Had half impaired the nameless grace
Which waves in every raven tress,
Or softly lightens o'er her face;
Where thoughts serenely sweet express
How pure, how dear their dwelling place.

And on that cheek, and o'er that brow,
So soft, so calm, yet eloquent,
The smiles that win, the tints that glow,
But tell of days in goodness spent,
A mind at peace with all below,
A heart whose love is innocent!

Unrequited love seemed to be Byron's inspiration for this poem and it made me think of my unexplainable and unexpected feelings for Daniel.

My bedroom door opened and Mom startled me.

"Hi, Honey. Sorry, I didn't get a chance to call today." She kissed my head.

"It's fine," I said, but it came out sounding pathetic.

Looking at me suspiciously, she sat down on the bed and asked, "Something wrong?"

I didn't want to talk about it. There really was no point.

"No," I said sullenly.

As she got to the door, she stopped, "If you'd like to talk, I'll be in the kitchen."

Awhile later, I realized that I did want to talk to her, so I went downstairs and told her.

"You have talk to him, because the longer you wait, the worse it might be."

"Yeah, I know. I just don't want him to hate me," I moaned.

"If that happens, it wasn't your fault."

I walked into the living room, sat on the couch and texted Reed. After a few exchanges back and forth, we agreed on meeting at the IMAGINE mosaic. How appropriate! Maybe it would inspire this talk to remain peaceful. I took Amber for moral support and also as an excuse for a getaway.

We walked over to Strawberry Field and I started thinking about John Lennon's life and death. This part of the park was named after the Beatles song "Strawberry Fields" and for an orphanage in Liverpool, England. The black and white mosaic, inscribed with "IMAGINE" in the center was the focal point of the Garden of Peace. Whenever I saw the word, I sang the Imagine song in my head.

I got there before Reed. I took the Lord Byron poetry book out of my bag and tried to read, but it was impossible to concentrate.

I saw him approaching and he looked just as nervous as I felt.

This was going to be bad; I knew it. Putting my book down on the bench, I braced myself.

We exchanged pleasantries and Reed sat down.

I had to get this going before I chickened out. "We really need to talk." He stopped smiling. "I saw your status and I don't understand," I blurted out and waited for his explanation.

"I'm sorry. I didn't do it. Evan did and I really had it out with him. If you go on my wall, it's gone and I posted that Evan's a moron."

"Oh." I was stunned. It wasn't a real posting!

"I wanted to get it off before you saw it, but people had already started commenting on it. When you didn't call back, I thought you saw I deleted it."

"No, I haven't been on Facebook." I breathed a sigh of relief.

When I looked over at Reed, he seemed uneasy and asked, "Are you dating anybody?"

I paused and answered truthfully, "No, I'm not." Please don't ask me out!

He sort of nodded his head and said, "Okay."

Before he could say anything else, I quickly asked, "When will you be back from camp?"

"The last week in August. I'll call you when I get home. I won't have a computer there, so I can't stay in touch and the camp doesn't allow cell phones."

"Wow, you're going to be really roughing it," I kidded.

"Yeah, they want us to focus only on hockey."

He wasn't happy, but I was. I wouldn't have to deal with him all summer. Perhaps there'd be girl hockey players at the camp and he'd fall in love with one of them.

"I'll be in London till Labor Day, either way, I'll see you in school," I added.

"How about a rain check for a dance this year?" he asked.

I jokingly said, "Maybe."

"Maybe?"

"I'm just kidding," I answered and didn't definitively say yes or no.

"That's good." Reed looked at his watch and said, "I have to go and meet my parents. Chad has some gig and I'm being forced to go." He rolled his eyes. I guess he wasn't a fan of Chad's music.

"Okay, have fun in Canada."

As he walked away, I closed my eyes and was thankful that this nightmare was over.

When I opened my eyes, Daniel was standing right in front of me. How did he always sneak up on me?

"Hey, you okay?" he asked and sat down. Amber scampered right over to him and Daniel scratched her head. She had totally ignored Reed, even though; she had met him numerous times.

"Hi! I'm fine, just a little tired." I was so excited to see him.

"You seemed upset talking to that guy." He had stopped petting Amber and she nudged his hand with her nose until he resumed.

He'd been watching us? "Oh, no, I wasn't upset," I said.

"Was that your boyfriend?" he asked.

"No, he's a friend." This couldn't be happening. My fantasy man was here and he was talking about Reed.

"What are you reading?" Daniel picked up the poetry book.

"Wow. Lord Byron. That's really amazing." There was a pause. "Lord Byron went to my school. I know his poetry really well."

"You're kidding, right?"

Daniel shook his head no.

"You like poetry?" I asked.

"I do. I know that's strange," he added.

"Not strange, different," I remarked. "Who's your favorite poet and poem?"

"Lord Byron and his poem 'Darkness.'"

"Sounds ominous," I said jokingly. There was no response to my comment, so I wasn't sure if he had heard me. What happened to him? He seemed a hundred miles away.

Amber started tugging on the leash trying to reach a passing dog. I jumped up so that she could say hello. Daniel stood up and after the other dog left, asked, "Want to take a walk?"

"Sure! That'd be great." Since Reed had made a speedy getaway after our conversation, there was still time before dinner.

For some reason, Daniel escorted me out of the park and we headed towards Columbus Ave.

Hoping he was my age, I asked, "Are you in high school?"

"No, I graduated last June, a year go," he answered very slowly.

"So you'll be a sophomore this fall? What college do you go to?" I wondered.

"I'm not at school. I've been working and traveling around."

"Did you apply somewhere and get deferred?" I never heard of people taking two years off before. One year for a gap year was the norm.

He stopped talking and looked at me with a curious look. "No, I'll decide when I'm ready. What about you?" he asked.

"I'm a senior in high school," I answered, watching his reaction.

"Really! I thought you were older."

"I hear that a lot. I'm seventeen. I'll be eighteen in December. How old are you?"

"Nineteen."

"Did you go to high school in Manhattan?"

"No, I went to Harrow, a boarding school in London. It was my Dad's alma mater," he answered. That explained his good manners. "My parents were from London."

"So is my dad. Wouldn't it be funny if he knew one of them?"

Daniel looked at me awkwardly and said, "You never know, but my parents passed away."

"Oh...I'm so sorry. What happened?" I asked, incredulous to hear that they were dead.

"They were in a car accident my freshman year," he answered quietly. Daniel quickly regained his composure and managed a cute smile. "I'm sorry for getting gloomy."

"Please, don't apologize." I felt bad and sad for him simultaneously. "Do you live alone?" I asked, trying to steer the conversation in a different direction.

"No, I live with my Uncle James, my Dad's brother. I'm working for him part-time."

Daniel didn't like to talk about himself, but I persisted in asking questions.

He eventually told me his uncle was married, had two kids and normally lived in DC. He was here this summer for business. When I brought up college again, he explained that he had a trust fund and had decided to take some time off before heading back to school.

"Enough about me. Where do you work?" he asked.

"At my dad's law firm. I just go in when they need me."

"Does he specialize in any law?"

"Yeah, international law."

It got totally quiet and I started feeling uncomfortable. The silence was killing me, so when Lily popped into my head, I told him all about her. After exhausting that topic and he still wasn't talking, I remembered that he was in Australia, so I asked him about it.

As we walked, he told me all about the Great Barrier Reef.

"So for six months, all you did was play in the sun and tan?" I asked and put my pale arm next to his. I was white as a ghost!

"Mostly, I did read some books though."

"Anything good?" He was definitely too good to be true.

"I don't think you'd like my taste in books. I read a lot of non-fiction stuff."

"Non-fiction and poetry? You're right; you are a strange nineteen year-old."

Daniel shrugged his shoulders and said, "I told you so."

"I'm kidding. Are you reading anything now?" I wondered.

"Not yet. I just finished reading a book on Einstein."

"Einstein vacationed out on the North Fork of Long Island near my Grandma's house!" I said trying to impress him.

"I recall reading something about that," Daniel said grinning. "So do you like Byron's poetry?"

"Some I like, some I hate, and some I don't understand at all.

"If you ever need help, just ask."

"I might take you up on that." Even if I had to pretend I needed help, I thought. "Did Lord Byron really go to your school or were you joking?"

"He did a long time ago, not with me," he said and winked. "As a matter of fact, Lord Byron wrote a poem about the school."

He looked at his vibrating cell and said, "Wow. I have to run. I have an appointment. Do you want to have breakfast or coffee tomorrow morning before work?"

Anything, anytime, but I couldn't really say that, so I casually said, "Sure."

"How's eight o'clock at that cafe." He pointed to a little place right on Columbus Avenue.

"Okay," I blushed. I couldn't believe this; I had a breakfast date with Daniel. Daniel bent down, petted Amber goodbye and as he walked away, he winked and my heart jumped. His looks weren't the only great thing about him.

Mom was on the phone when I came in. She covered the receiver and whispered that Dad had gotten stuck on a long-distance call and dinner would be later. If I was hungry, I should help myself. I said I'd wait and went to call Lily.

She was on the train and the clamor was ear shattering. She couldn't hear me at all and said she'd call me back.

I was daydreaming about Daniel when Lily's call forced me

back to earth. As I told her the whole saga about Reed and Daniel, she was silent and didn't interrupt once. She was obviously riveted or incredulous; I wasn't sure which.

"Unbelievable."

"I know, but why is he talking to me?"

"You're pretty, smart and fun. Anyone who dates you would be lucky," she added.

"I just don't get it." I was being such a baby. Now that he was talking to me, I was getting insecure and scared. Talking to Lily did quiet some of my concerns.

When I heard Mom calling me, I got off the phone. As I reached for the plates to set the table, I started humming.

"You seem better. How was your talk with Reed?" Mom asked.

"Oh Mom, it was a misunderstanding. A friend of his posted it as a joke. Do you believe it? We're still friends," I beamed happily. "Everything's fine!"

My phone vibrated, alerting me to an incoming email, which reminded me of all the problems I'd been having with my phone. "Mom, I'm still having issues with my phone."

"Can you make calls?"

"Yeah, it works outgoing."

"You're going to Lily's tomorrow so, we'll take care of it next week."

"Okay, but it's a mess. I'm not getting all my calls, email or notifications from Facebook and my call log is not working at all," I added.

I called Lily and we finalized our plans to meet at Uncle Ian's office on Park Avenue.

I kept talking about Daniel and Lily interrupted me mid-sentence and said, "Enough. I'm going swimming. I'll see you tomorrow."

I grabbed my poetry book and looked for the two poems that Daniel had mentioned. I found the "Darkness" poem. There was such an overwhelming feeling of hopelessness. Words of destruction, depicting the end of the world and the end of humanity, made the poem nightmarish with all the horrible images and connotations. Shocked, I couldn't fathom how this poem could be his favorite. Perhaps Daniel discovered this poem after he lost his parents and could relate.

Quickly, I started looking for the other poem, to rid my mind of this one. Only one poem had the word Harrow it was called "On a Distant View of the Village and School of Harrow On The Hill." The poem was full of memories and recollections.

Tired of reading poetry, I put the book away and started writing a song. Inspired by my crazy emotions, I called it 'Longing.'

Still long to feel the touch of your hand once again
To feel the warmth of your skin.
Even after you left,
Your voice still lingers in the air.
I can't stand when the sound of your voice enters
my heart and my head and all I can think of is you.

Trying to pretend your standing right beside me
and there's the times I picture your face.
And believe you still care.
But how could you ever care about me?
All my longings are just illusions of the heart.
That can never come true.

To long now that you're gone
I can see that without you by me
It's like a part of me has simply gone away.
You left me my heart shattered and cracked
and it will not be whole again.
The footprints you left on my heart
will never be washed away.

Trying to pretend your standing right beside me.
And there's the times I picture your face
And believe you still care.
But how could you ever care about me?
All my longings are just illusions of the heart.
That can never come true.

4. STORM

"What does a fish know about the water in which it swims all its life?" Einstein

I woke up out of a fitful sleep. Since I first noticed Daniel, I hadn't slept well. I was having really weird scary dreams. Snippets came to me and I remembered being terrified. It was probably caused from reading that horrible 'Darkness' poem. I showered and dressed.

Mom, still in her bathrobe, was pouring water into the coffee pot as I entered the kitchen.

"Good morning. Why are you up so early?"

"I couldn't sleep. I got up to finish packing for Lily's," I explained.

"Can you take Amber out since you're all dressed?" she asked.

"Sure." I walked towards the foyer with Amber close behind.

Mom called out, "Paige, do you want anything for breakfast? I could make you eggs."

"Oh no, thanks. I'm meeting a friend for breakfast," I said matter-of-factly and left.

When I brought Amber back, Mom was upstairs and Dad was in the den on a phone call. I waved and quickly ran out the door.

As I approached the cafe, I worried about being stood up. Thankfully, I saw Daniel walking from the opposite direction and I waved.

"Hi. I wasn't sure if you'd be here."

"What do you mean?" I asked since I was just thinking the same thing.

"I'll tell you inside," he said and opened the door.

We sat at a table near the window and I stared at his beautiful almond-shaped eyes. He had on chinos and a pale blue polo shirt, which made his eyes look even bluer. He had a chiseled jaw and there were a few tiny freckles on the top of his nose that I hadn't noticed before.

"Why did you think I wasn't coming?"

"What I meant was, if something came up, we wouldn't have been able to reach each other. I wasn't positive you'd make it." He handed me a business card. "That's my phone number for the future."

"Thanks," was all I could say. I had his phone number and his name was Daniel Haydin. "Haydin? If there was an e, you could say you were the Hayden from the Hayden Planetarium."

Daniel asked, "Oh, really? Do you still want to have breakfast with me even though I have the wrong name?"

"Hmmm....Let me think about it," I joked. Daniel gave me a hurt look. "I'm kidding."

When the waitress came over, I ordered Earl Grey tea and over-easy eggs and Daniel ordered coffee and a mushroom omelet.

"You're a coffee drinker. That's not very English of you," I teased when the waitress left.

"I have coffee in the morning to wake up. The rest of the day, it's tea. No coffee for you?"

"No, don't like the taste. I do like cappuccinos though."

He kept asking me questions about school, teachers and my friends. I answered them because I didn't want to be rude, but I wanted to hear more about him.

When I asked if he was on Facebook, he said, "No. It doesn't interest me." Too bad, that meant I couldn't lurk him.

"Daniel, the day we met in the park, what were you doing?" He looked at me like he didn't understand. "You were picking nuts and flowers then putting them in a plastic bag."

"Oh, a friend in DC asked for those samples. I mailed them to him."

"What was he doing with them?"

"I really don't know." He shrugged and changed the subject. "Any plans this weekend?"

"I'm going to Lily's in Westchester."

"Really? I'll be up there too."

"Where are you going?" I asked curiously.

"Visiting an aunt in Chappaqua," he answered.

I stared at him with my mouth open. "I'm going there too!" It had to be fate. Daniel in Chappaqua! I got excited thinking about it.

"You're kidding? I'm driving up tonight. Would you like a ride?" he asked.

"Thanks... I'm catching the train with Lily and my uncle." Going with Daniel would've been great, but my parents would never allow me to drive up there with a total stranger.

"No problem. If something happens and you need a ride, call me," Daniel said.

He said he'd like to meet Lily and asked about having breakfast in Chappaqua. We made plans to meet at Susan's Café at ten o'clock the next day.

His cell beeped all through breakfast and he'd look at it, but wouldn't answer it.

"Maybe you should answer it. It might be important."

"It isn't. Should I swing by and pick you two up in the morning?"

"Uh, I think it's best if we meet you there," I stumbled over my words awkwardly.

Daniel realized what I meant and said, "Oh, a stranger taking you both away in a car."

"It's just that my aunt doesn't know you and she'd want to meet you," I said.

"And you're embarrassed to introduce me?" he asked, sounding amused.

"Oh...no...no...I'm not," I stammered, mortified that he thought that.

"Don't worry. I understand," he said smiling and insisted that he wasn't insulted.

Daniel's cell phone went off again and this time he excused himself and went outside.

When he returned, his mood was gloomy. He angrily thrust his cell phone down and it slid across the table. Before it fell off, I grabbed it and handed it to him.

"Are you okay?" I asked.

He nodded, but he seemed upset.

"Tell me about Lily. Does she have any pets?" Daniel was adept at switching conversations mid-stream.

"No. Her Dad's allergic to animals and has to stay away from Amber. On second thought, she does have a fish named Bubbles."

"Interesting name."

"Yes, Lily's very creative. She's had Bubbles for six years now. Isn't that awfully long?" I asked. Daniel didn't respond. "I was positive her parents were replacing Bubbles whenever he died, but Lily said it wasn't possible because Bubbles had special markings."

Daniel just stared at me and I felt so self-conscious.

"How long do fish live?" I asked and waited for him to answer. It felt like eternity.

"I really don't know." Daniel looked down at his phone. "I'm sorry, but I have to get going."

Outside on the sidewalk, Daniel said, "I'll see you tomorrow at Susan's Café." He rushed off and grabbed a cab at the corner.

My cell rang and I fumbled around in my bag to find it. I answered without checking. "Lily?"

"No, it's Daphne. Who were you with in the coffee shop?" she asked excitedly.

"Oh, hi. That was Daniel. Where are you?" I asked, looking around to see if she was nearby.

"At work. I had to come in early for a delivery. Reed and I walked by and Reed almost had a heart attack." Reed seeing us was actually a good thing. "So who is he?"

"A guy I recently met." No point in telling her that he was a total stranger that I met in Central Park. "What were you doing with Reed?"

"We bumped into each other and he walked me to work. He talked about you, of course, and then when we saw you, he got very quiet. I felt bad for him."

"Oh...I wish you two would date." That would be the best solution. If things didn't work out with Evan, I would try to get Daphne and Reed together. They would make a great couple.

"Daphne, I have another call. I'll call you later." I hung up with her to take Lily's call. I told Lily about our new plans for breakfast and she said she couldn't wait to meet him.

Now, because of Daniel, I was thrilled to be in Manhattan for the summer. Honestly, I didn't know how long he'd be around. I expected him to disappear the same way he had materialized.

When I got back it was eight thirty and Dad was still home, so we walked to work together.

At the end of the day, I was really excited knowing that I'd see Daniel tomorrow. When I arrived at Uncle Ian's office building, they were waiting outside.

"Hi Duncle," I said and hugged Uncle Ian and then Lily. Duncle is what I've called Uncle Ian since I was young. One day, Lily combined the words dad and uncle together, so we could call Uncle Ian the same name. Uncle Ian's been like a second dad to me, always there in his quiet, reserved manner. Lily eventually reverted back to dad, but every once in a while I still call him duncle.

In ninth grade a teacher started calling me Buttercup and it stuck with the kids at school in ninth grade. At first, I was annoyed, but I eventually got used to it. On one of my school sweatshirts instead of monogramming it with Paige or Devon, I put Buttercup. In tenth grade, the kids stopped and that's when the nickname moved to my house.

After Dad heard Daphne call me Buttercup, he started calling me that. When he said it in front of Nana, she said that the name really suited me and from that day on, also called me Buttercup. Thankfully, Mom and Grammy never jumped on the 'Buttercup' ship.

We rushed to Grand Central and on the train; Uncle Ian sat elsewhere to read the paper, knowing that we wouldn't stop talking.

"Noelle's meeting us tomorrow at Susan's Cafe," Lily said. Oh, no!

"Why?" I moaned.

"I changed the sleepover for tomorrow night. She asked why and I told her about breakfast."

"I only wanted you to meet him. He'll think I'm such a baby bringing my friends along."

"He wanted to meet me, just tell him that I already had plans with Noelle." When I continued to look miserable, she said, "We don't have to come."

"No, never mind. Maybe it'll be better with you guys there," I conceded.

My cell was buzzed and there was a text from Reed. 'Have a great summer. Call you when I get back.' Reed was a problem to deal with in the future and I wasn't wasting any more time on him. As for Daniel, now that was another story.

When we got to Lily's house, Aunt Cecile was busy cooking dinner. I loved being at Lily's. After spending weeks there during summer vacations, the moment I'd passed the threshold, I always felt at home. The house was a split-level, so walking through the door; the front entry was halfway between the upper and lower floors. There were two short sets of stairs, one running upward to the living room, kitchen, dining room and bedrooms, and one going downward toward a finished basement area with Uncle Ian's office, the family room and the guestroom where I slept whenever I visited.

After I dropped my bags in my room and changed, I found Lily in the kitchen eating chips, salsa and guacamole. While Aunt Cecile put the fruit crisp in the oven, we munched on the food and talked.

Aunt Cecile made her famous shrimp corn chowder. After we ate, Lily and I were stuffed and couldn't move from the table.

"I guess we'll have the quesadillas for lunch tomorrow," Aunt Cecile said.

Lily moaned, "There was more food?" I was unable to say anything.

"It's not my fault you guys ate too many chips," she scolded us. "What about the fruit crisp?"

This time, I groaned, "No more food." We plopped on the couch in the living room.

"Do you like working at your dad's office, Paige?" Aunt Cecile asked.

"It's alright. I'm just filing and photo copying."

"Do you get to see your dad? I know how big that firm is."

"I'm on another floor, but I sneak by and see him."

Lily told Aunt Cecile about meeting Noelle for breakfast.

"Sure, I need to run errands in town anyway," Aunt Cecile said.

We didn't mention Daniel. Since I hadn't told Mom yet, it was better not to bring him up.

***

In the morning, I felt like I slept better, but it was probably due to sheer exhaustion.

I jumped in the shower before heading upstairs. Lily was in her room making a scrapbook of our Paris trip from the summer before. It had been Lily's sixteenth birthday and her parents surprised her, and me for that matter, with a trip to Paris. My parents didn't tell me in case I blabbed to Lily.

On Lily's birthday, we spent the day exploring Paris. We had dinner on the island of Île Saint-Louis and afterwards, took a taxi to the Eiffel Tower. The views were amazing and Lily and I took tons of pictures.

Looking at Lily's scrapbook, I was impressed. "You're almost done."

"Yeah, almost. Can you get me copies of your photos?" Lily asked.

"Yeah. I made copies, but I don't know where I put them. I'll look when I get home."

"Have you started yours yet? I know how you procrastinate."

"Very funny, but I did, and then got sidetracked." Lily laughed at that. "Stop. I better finish it before this summer. I really wish I knew where we were going. Have your parents said anything? Mine won't tell me anything, as usual."

Lily shook her head no. "All she said was that Dad didn't know when he could take off. If we go anywhere, it'll be last minute or we'll just go to Grammy's."

My parents only told me where we were vacationing when we were on the plane going. The reason for this was because when I was young, I got super excited about a vacation to Italy. I started looking through the guidebooks and picked sites to see. At the end of the trip, when we hadn't visited any of my choices, I had a complete meltdown in the middle of the hotel lobby as Dad checked out. I sat on the floor and refused to leave. Humiliated, Dad picked me up and carried me to the taxi. All the way to the airport, I cried. They decided to surprise me from then on, but I think they just liked torturing me.

In early June, I protested, "Mom, I'll be eighteen in December."

She answered, "Next summer, we'll plan the vacation spot together, okay? This year, you'll find out in August." Thankfully, this would be the last summer that they would do this to me.

I sat there looking at Lily's photos. My reminiscing was interrupted by Noelle's call to make sure that we were still going for breakfast.

Aunt Cecile drove us into town and we met Noelle at Starbuck's.

At ten o'clock, we walked over to Susan's Café and grabbed a table outside.

I was on edge waiting for Daniel to come that I wasn't listening to the conversation.

Noelle stopped talking, stared at me and said, "Hey, calm down. It's only breakfast."

"I know," I answered testily and hoped that Noelle wouldn't be her nonstop talking self.

"How's lifeguarding?" Lily asked Noelle.

She started talking and wouldn't stop. Sitting there listening and waiting was torture and as the minutes passed, I became more irrational. "Noelle, please do me a favor and don't babble like that when Daniel comes. Also, don't ask tons of questions, he'll think we're imbeciles."

Noelle looked visibly hurt and then she got angry. She rose and stormed into the shop.

Lily glared at me and said, "Why are you being so crazy? If you continue like this, I'm not staying."

She was right. What was wrong with me? I apologized and begged her to stay.

Noelle came out with two coffees and visibly upset. "I couldn't carry out your tea. If you want it, it's on the counter." She gave Lily her coffee. "I'm sitting at another table. Then I won't embarrass anyone."

"No, Noelle, please don't. I'm really sorry."

Noelle was apprehensive of my mood change. "You're being so ridiculous," she said, but went inside and got my tea. She was

---

probably worried that I'd spill it on somebody.

When my cell said 10:20, I knew that I'd been stood up. My greatest fear was being realized. Noelle and Lily were exchanging knowing glances, but I had no energy to yell at them. It was almost 10:30 and he was nowhere in sight. Lily had tried getting me to call him at 10:15.

Lily was getting frustrated and repeated her earlier argument. "Call him. Maybe something happened. He doesn't have your number for crying out loud."

When I refused again, Lily stood up to leave.

"Fine," I snapped and hoped there was a plausible explanation.

Daniel answered. "Hello?"

"It's Paige. Where are you?" I asked with an edge of anger.

"I've been hoping you'd call. I got stuck in the city. I was about to call the café." He seemed relieved to hear from me. "I was borrowing my uncle's car and he needed it." Maybe that's why his phone had buzzed constantly at breakfast. "I'm leaving the city in an hour. Can we meet there tomorrow?" he asked.

After I hung up, I told them what happened and asked if they'd come back with me.

"Of course. I need to see why you've become so crazy," said Lily, rolling her eyes at Noelle. Noelle groaned, but agreed to come too.

After breakfast, we went to Lily's pool club.

It was almost a hundred degrees and it was great being wet. We played Marco Polo with almost fifteen kids and it was insane.

After eating turkey wraps for lunch, we lazed by the pool, read magazines and talked. Out of the blue, it suddenly started thundering. Promptly the lifeguards closed the pool and everyone began packing up. The sky was dark and ominous and then the rain poured down. As we raced up the hill to Lily's house, it was relentless in its intensity. It felt like someone was throwing buckets of water on us, and the wind was incredible. The thunder sounded so close and the flashes of lightning were scary.

By the time we got in, we looked like muddy drowned rats.

"Mom, we're home. Was it supposed to rain today?" Lily called out.

Aunt Cecile walked into the kitchen surprised to see us. "I was just about to drive down and get you. Why didn't you stay put? You shouldn't run around in the woods when there's lightning."

"Sorry," we all said, but smiled at each other because we had fun.

Looking at the floor, she saw the mud. "Stay in the kitchen. Do not move," she commanded.

"We need towels," said Lily.

"I'll get them." Aunt Cecile walked out saying, "It should stop soon. It's just a passing storm."

After showering, we decided to stay at Lily's for the sleepover and not go to Noelle's. Aunt Cecile said it was fine, but they were going out. As I looked out the window, the dark storm clouds were slowly dissipating.

"Girls, have the quesadillas and the soup from last night," Aunt Cecile said before leaving.

Noelle called her parents and they were going to the movies.

We grabbed food to bring downstairs and planned on watching a movie. I made my favorite popcorn with melted butter, garlic powder, red pepper flakes and lots of Parmesan cheese. It was one of Mom's creations and I loved it.

As we watched the movie, we heard the storm still raging outside. Around ten, we paused the movie so that Lily could go get some water bottles. She was on her way back downstairs and the power went out. The house went completely black.

"Oh, no!" Lily shrieked.

I didn't know what to do, so I reached for Noelle and held her arm tightly. Only between bursts of intermittent lightening were things visible. Lily went into the laundry room and brought out flashlights. We found hurricane candles in the hall closet and lit them.

"We have a generator in the garage, but we have to wait till my parents gets home. Don't worry. Our house alarm goes to a battery backup if the power goes or the phone lines go out," Lily said, acting brave, while calling her parents cells. Getting no answer, she hung up without leaving a message. Noelle called her parents and they also didn't answer. All four parents disappeared just when you needed them most.

I called Mom and was relieved that at least she answered, even if she wasn't nearby. "Mom, it's me," I whispered, feeling that if I spoke loudly the monsters would find me.

My vivid imagination was working overtime in this darkness.

She knew from the sound of my voice that I was upset. "Why are you whispering? What's the matter?"

After I told her what happened, she assured me that Aunt Cecile would be home soon. I'd been through blackouts before, but it was very different out here. When it happened in the city, everyone would rush outside, talking and complaining and you never felt alone. Out here in the suburbs, it was quite alarming since it was so desolate. Lily's house was on two acres and the neighbors' houses weren't visible, or even nearby, so you felt totally alone. Behind Lily's property, there was only the swim club, which was immense and deserted. I looked out the window and saw a car in the parking lot with its lights on.

The three of us sat on the couch with the candles lit and talked about the situation. When my cell rang a few minutes later, I presumed it was Mom and didn't check the screen. Lily and Mom were the only people that called me, all my friends texted. I answered trying to sound upbeat, "Hi, Mom. I'm better now."

"Paige, everything okay?" It was Daniel.

For a minute, I couldn't speak. "Hi. Yeah, I'm fine. Are you in this blackout too?"

"Yes, I am. Are you all right?" he asked again.

"Oh, I'm fine… I'm at Lily's with her friend, Noelle." After I told him that her parents were out for the evening, Daniel offered to come over and keep us company. He seemed overly concerned, but it was just a blackout.

"Let me check with Lily."

I looked over at her but it was too dark, so I couldn't see her face. I shone the flashlight at her and she had a confused expression. "What?" she asked.

"Daniel wants to know if we want him to come over. He'll wait with us till your parents get home." I tried to sound normal but I mouthed, "please" to Lily repeatedly, so that he didn't hear.

She shrugged and said, "Sure, I guess … if he wants to." I knew she said yes for me, but she also sounded relieved. In this darkness, even the flashlights made menacing shadows. I gave him the address, hung up and started jumping up and down.

Lily reminded me that we really didn't know Daniel and that concerned her. Noelle looked apprehensively at me and asked how we met. I told her the whole story. Noelle rationalized that all three of us had phones to call the police and besides that, Lily's parents would be home soon.

Lily called her mom's cell and left a message that Daniel was coming over. Knowing that someone knew, they settled down.

We ran upstairs with all the candles to illuminate the living room. Lily and Noelle ate cheese sticks and sat on the couch waiting for him. I ran into the bathroom to brush my teeth. I had added so much garlic powder on my popcorn that I was afraid I'd kill him with my breath.

When I returned, Noelle asked Lily if her parents would be okay with Daniel being there.

"With you guys here, it's fine, but if I was alone, I'm not sure they'd handle it very well."

Ten minutes later, we saw lights on the wall and jumped up to see a car pull into the driveway. Lily turned off the house alarm and I ran to the door with a flashlight to help guide him inside. He had a light on his keychain that he was using to maneuver around the walkway.

"Hello," he said as he grinned at me while I shone the flashlight at his beautiful face. "So I am getting to see you today after all."

"If you call this seeing me," I joked and was happy it was dark now because I felt like I was blushing.

Daniel chuckled and said, "How are you guys holding up? It's really amazing how dark it is when there's a blackout in the country."

"I know! I thought the same thing."

He followed me into the living room. The room looked cozy with all the candles and didn't seem sinister anymore.

I introduced him to the girls. At first, it was awkward, but Daniel started asking them questions about school. He was adept at getting people to talk, but said very little himself.

However, when Lily asked about Australia, Daniel got quite talkative.

"Did you go there alone?" asked Noelle.

"I did. I met a friend for a little while, but then I went to the Great Barrier Reef alone."

The talk turned back to school. Since all of us would be seniors in the fall, college was always on our minds.

"Paige said you're taking time off and not going to college yet. Why?" Lily asked.

I didn't need to ask Daniel anything since Lily and Noelle were asking all the questions for me.

"I want to travel around for awhile."

"Are you working?" asked Lily.

"Yeah, part-time."

"But how can you do that?" nosy Noelle asked.

Daniel asked, "You mean financially?"

Noelle nodded and said, "Yeah. How can you afford it and only work part-time?"

"My parents died and when I turned eighteen, I was able to access the trust fund they set up."

Noelle's face crumpled and I could tell that she felt terrible. I had forgotten to tell her about his parents. "I'm so sorry. What happened?" asked Noelle.

"They were in a car accident in Utah. It was January of my freshman year. I had gone back to school after the winter holiday." Lily and I looked at each other because we went skiing in Utah last February on break. "They hit a patch of ice and their car went down a mountain cliff."

The mood was somber for a while. Daniel got very quiet and I felt so bad for him. It must be horrible to constantly tell everyone his parents died.

Lily glanced over at me and raised her eyebrows. She asked Daniel if he grew up in Manhattan in an obvious attempt to change the subject.

"No, I was raised in Washington DC, went to school there till eighth grade. Then, for high school, I went to a boarding school in London."

"There are tons of boarding schools here. Why so far way?" asked Noelle.

"My dad went there and I wanted to go."

"Well, I guess if you hadn't gone, you might've been with your parents on that ski trip," Noelle said, insinuating the unthinkable.

I was so floored by what she said and asked, "Noelle, are you for real?"

"What? It's true. Don't tell me you hadn't thought that," Noelle accused.

I shook my head at her like she was insane. Before I could comment, Lily jumped in while Noelle remained oblivious to her inappropriate comment. "If you live in DC, why are you in Manhattan?"

"I was going to work in DC this summer, but my uncle got called to New York last minute." That was quite a coincidence since my plans had also abruptly changed. We could've been in different parts of the world and never met.

When the lights came on, the brightness was jarring. Lily and Noelle finally saw Daniel in his full glory. He really was striking.

Noelle kept asking Daniel about his trust fund and I prayed that she didn't ask him how much money he had. I'd die. Before Noelle had a chance, we heard the front door open.

Lily jumped up and nervously called out, "Hey, we're in the living room."

Aunt Cecile walked in, saw Daniel and said, "Hello, I'm Cecile Hamilton, Lily's mom."

"Daniel Haydin, nice to meet you." He stood up and shook hands with Aunt Cecile as Uncle Ian walked in.

"We were wondering whose car was in the driveway. Ian Hamilton." They shook hands.

"There was a blackout tonight and the lights just came on," Lily explained. "Daniel's a friend of Paige's. He's in Chappaqua visiting his aunt and came over to keep us company."

"I hope you don't mind," said Daniel.

"No, of course not. I'm so glad that Lily wasn't home alone tonight," said Aunt Cecile.

"I tried calling, but your phones were off," Lily said.

"Sorry, my phone died. Your dad left his at home."

"I better get going. I'm sure my aunt is wondering what happened to me. It was nice meeting all of you. Good night," Daniel said.

It had stopped raining so I walked him out to his car, which was a black BMW.

"Do you still want to meet for breakfast?" I asked not sure if he still wanted to get together.

Daniel looked at me and said, "Of course, unless you don't want to?"

"I do. I thought maybe since I saw you tonight...." I stopped talking.

"Paige, what does the blackout have to do with breakfast?" He looked confused. "I'll see you at ten. Pleasant dreams."

I walked back into the house on cloud nine.

Noelle was grinning. "You're right. He's sooo cute and sooo nice!! So... what happened?"

"What do you mean? I walked him to his car." I was totally confused. I glanced at Lily with a look like what was she talking about. Lily widened her eyes and shrugged.

"Did you kiss for heavens sakes?" Noelle asked sounding frustrated.

"Give me a break, Noelle. We just met. I don't even know if he likes me."

It was almost one o'clock. Noelle stayed with me in the guest room and kept talking about Daniel, so I pretended to fall asleep.

***

The next morning, while Noelle slept, I snuck out and went upstairs. I couldn't believe that Daniel had been in Lily's house. I wanted to pinch myself in case I was dreaming.

Walking into the kitchen, I found Aunt Cecile reading the paper. "Morning, Paige. Lily told me that you are all meeting Daniel at Susan's."

I nodded. "We were supposed to yesterday, but he got stuck in the city," I answered, trying to sound very casual.

"He seems very nice, but how old is he?" she asked.

I told her he was nineteen and hoped that the questioning wouldn't last too long.

"Does your mom know him?" she asked.

"No, she doesn't. Aunt Cecile, we're just friends. I'll tell her when I get home," I said trying not to seem upset even though I was.

"Is Lily in her room?" I was trying to get away as quickly as possible and started walking down the hallway.

Aunt Cecile said, "She's outside on the deck, talking on the phone."

When I got outside, I overheard Lily making plans to go swimming. She waved at me and finished her call. "Want to ask

Daniel to come to the pool? It'll be fun."

"I'm not ready for that besides he might think it's juvenile to play Marco Polo."

Lily said I was being ridiculous, but she gave up trying to change my mind.

Aunt Cecile dropped us off and we got the last available table outside at Susan's. It was very hot, but all the tables inside were taken. The girls wanted to go swimming and I felt guilty dragging them out again.

Daniel's car pulled up in front of the cafe just as a car pulled out of a spot. I saw that he wasn't alone. When he stepped out of the car, he looked like a male model from a Ralph Lauren ad. He was wearing a white linen shirt and beige linen shorts. He seemed oblivious to the way he looked. His friend looked older and was dressed in tennis whites.

"Good morning. You all survived the night," he said in a mischievous tone.

"You make it sound like you had doubts," I joked back.

"Of course not," he said and winked. "This is my friend, Pierce. I didn't think you'd mind if he joined us. I didn't want to be outnumbered."

"Are you afraid of us?" joked Noelle.

"You never know," Daniel kidded back.

We ordered food and everybody talked except Pierce. He looked like he wished he were somewhere else. Lily and Noelle tried talking to him, but he seemed very disinterested in anything they had to say. Maybe he didn't want to bother with high school girls.

"How do you two know each other?" Noelle asked. Her nosiness was usually annoying, but today I didn't mind.

Pierce looked over at Daniel to answer.

Daniel said, "Pierce lives near my aunt. We met years ago."

"Where does she live?" Noelle asked.

"Near the Wampus Lake Reservoir."

"Is that nearby?" I wondered out loud.

"No," Noelle said. "It's on the opposite side of town."

Daniel excused himself and went inside and Pierce seemed nervous being left alone with us. Noelle asked him questions but Pierce only gave curt responses. We learned that he was in his last year at NYU and lived in the Village. He was home this weekend for his mom's birthday.

Daniel returned and said, "Paige, we have to get going. I paid the bill so take your time."

"Okay," I said, flabbergasted by their quick exit. "Nice meeting you, Pierce." He looked at me and nodded uncomfortably. What a strange guy!

Daniel turned around and jovially added, "Be careful in the pool, ladies. Make sure to put on sun block."

"Okay, Dad," answered Noelle. They got in the car and drove off. I hoped that he wasn't spending a long time in Chappaqua. The city would seem so empty without him.

5. BLOCK PARTY

"Reality is merely an illusion, albeit a very persistent one." Einstein

We got up early Monday morning and caught the train back to the city. As Uncle Ian and Lily walked to work, I spotted a cab dropping someone off at Grand Central and I jumped inside. Feeling hot and tired, I wanted to get home as quickly as possible.

Exiting the cab, I saw Mom across the street taking Amber for a walk. I waved to her. When I entered the lobby, Carl handed me a package for Dad. I put it on the table in the entry foyer and admired the hydrangea arrangement.

Mom loved flowers and most of the paintings and photographs hanging in the house were of flowers. She weekly bought various bouquets and made beautiful arrangements. There was always a vase filled with flowers in the kitchen, dining room and foyer. Once when I suggested dried flowers, Mom said that in feng shui teachings, it wasn't good to have dead flowers, something about bad energy. Whatever that meant.

After I got out of the shower, Mom came in to my room and said she was working from home. She needed to pick things up for a photo shoot and asked if I wanted to come. I said sure. She reminded me that Dad was leaving for Paris after work and to call him.

As I brushed my hair, I heard my cell beeping. It was a text from Daniel. "Can you have lunch today? Am going out of town tonight." That put me in panic mode. Where was he going?

Instead of texting back, I called him and said, "Hi, lunch is great."

"Want to meet at Rosa's near Lincoln Center at noon? Do you know where that is?"

I told him I did. We even liked the same types of food. Before I could ask him anything, he said he had to run and would meet me there. I'd have to wait to find out.

Mom appeared in my doorway and I had to fill her in on Daniel because if I didn't, Aunt Cecile would. How could I tell her I met him in Central Park and that he was a complete stranger? She wouldn't care that he was nice; she'd be thinking "serial killer." I knew her.

I started by saying that I had just made a lunch date and was going to pass on going with her.

After she asked who I was having lunch with, I filled her in on the whole story. Her demeanor quickly changed. When she heard his age, Mom began pacing around my room straightening up, a sure sign that she was upset. She folded some clothes that were on a chair, and stated, "If you go out with him, I must meet him."

"Mom, please, it's just lunch," I pleaded.

She pretended not to hear me and asked, "Where does his uncle live?"

"On West 72nd Street, but I'm not going to his apartment. We're going to Rosa's."

Ignoring my comment, she added, "We don't know anything about him."

"You're really not being fair. If it was a boy from school, it would be okay even if we knew nothing about him."

"At least I'd be able to find things out from another parent."

"If I was in college, you couldn't," I countered.

"You're not in college, so don't bother using that as an excuse." She became silent and then said, "Give me his cell number." This couldn't be happening.

"You're kidding, right?

She shook her head no.

"Mom, please, don't be ridiculous," I begged.

"I'll only call if absolutely necessary."

"Describe necessary." I tried to remain calm, but if she called him, I'd die.

"If you don't come home, is it okay if I call him then?"

I felt absolutely safe with him, but nodded my head yes and said, "I understand."

"It's about time. I want to meet him."

"I promise next time, if there is a next time." If Mom knew that Aunt Cecile had met him, she'd be upset.

She relented. "Fine. Next time, he picks you up at the house, or no date. Do you understand?"

"Yes," I said, trying to mollify her.

Mom sighed and exited without another word or his cell number. I went to my closet and started looking at clothes. I had to get out of this apartment. I put on a beige gauze skirt, a pale green tank top and beige sandals. Hurriedly, I brushed my hair and applied some pink lip-gloss.

I ran downstairs and at the front door yelled bye. I didn't wait for a response, not wanting to have another conversation.

It was a bit early, so I window-shopped to waste time.

Grace was walking up the street and I knew she'd ask about Daniel since Daphne must have told her about him. I hadn't spoken to either of them all weekend though we had exchanged some texts.

"Hi Grace, sorry I didn't call you back. I just got home this morning."

"It's okay. You look nice," Grace said, looking me up and down.

"Thanks," I responded. I could tell by the way she was looking at me that she was waiting for me to say more.

"Where are you going?" I asked, hoping she didn't ask me the same question.

"Back to the store, I had to run an errand. Where are you going?"

"I'm having lunch at Rosa's."

"With who?" she sing-songed.

"A friend."

"That guy Daphne saw you with?" she continued.

"Yes, his name's Daniel," I said and began slowly moving away. Please let me get out of here.

"Oh... Daphne said he was hot." Yes, he was hot and I felt a twinge of jealousy. Grace seemed unaware that I wasn't engaging in this conversation and was actually trying to escape.

"So are you dating him?" she continued with the questioning.

"If I was, I'd tell you. We're just having lunch," I coldly replied.

"You're acting like you're going to a funeral. What's wrong with you?"

Why was I being so crazy?

Grace was right. Ever since Daniel had come into my life I had been a horror to my friends. First, I had it out with Noelle and now, I was doing the same thing to Grace. "I'm sorry, Grace. I'm just not ready to talk about him yet. I'm afraid I'll jinx it."

Part of that was true, but more precisely, I was afraid he'd leave and I'd be crushed. Hearing about him from friends I'd confided in would be torture, so I decided to speak of Daniel only to Lily till I knew where, if anywhere, this was going. Normally, I was quite private with my emotions anyway and now with the strong feelings I had for Daniel, I was even more gun-shy.

Grace kindly let me off the hook. "You really have to lighten up. I have to get back to work. Call me later and tell me how it went. Want to go for a walk or something later?" she asked and made me feel guilty all over again.

"I'll call you later. Dad's out of town and I'm not sure if Mom has something planned," I fibbed not wanting to hurt her feelings again. I wanted to stay home since I had been away all weekend. My bed and TV were calling me.

Daniel was waiting outside talking on his cell. My heart jumped and all my doubts vanished.

He was wearing faded blue jeans, a plain white T-shirt and black sunglasses. His hair was slicked back like he had just jumped out of a shower and he looked amazing.

"Hi, you look lovely." Lovely, who says that? It sounded like my father.

"Let's go in. Our table's ready."

He led me inside and I followed him as he veered around all the people. The hostess took us upstairs to a corner table by the window. After ordering our lunch, I couldn't wait anymore and had to ask where he was going.

"To London, but the trip was canceled."

I was so happy to hear that. "I thought you might be leaving for good."

"You can't get rid of me that easily," Daniel said smiling.

"Why was your trip canceled?"

"Squatters moved in to my house and I wanted to see if I could do something about it." He had a home in London! "My lawyer said that I didn't have to come. He's starting the eviction process and will get them out."

"Evict the squatters? Don't they just arrest them?" I asked confused.

"No, I have to formally evict them. Squatting isn't illegal if entry isn't forced."

"You're kidding?"

"No. I'm not. I know that it's crazy. I had a problem with squatters a few years ago and my uncle took care of it through his contacts in London. After that, I hired a couple to live at the house full-time. They went on vacation for a month to visit family in Poland, so I asked a friend to check on the house and she called yesterday and said she saw people inside. I've instructed the lawyer to offer them money, so possibly that will expedite things. Squatting's been a problem in Britain since at least the fourteenth century."

Daniel didn't seem that concerned with his illegal visitors, so I dropped the subject. We talked about his family and he told me about his uncle. His name was James Haydin, worked for the US government and lived primarily in DC. Daniel said he was going to DC soon to visit his family because he came directly to New York from Australia. Every time he mentioned travel plans, it felt like my heart stopped beating.

"Are you close to your cousins in DC?" Daniel looked uncomfortable, but I had no idea why.

"Not really, I see them mostly on holidays. We really have very little in common. They're both married." Daniel had no parents, no siblings and much older cousins; it explained why he acted so mature.

When I asked what his parents did, Daniel proudly said, "They both went to Oxford and were physicists." He raised his eyebrows as if I should understand something from that answer.

It hit me. "Oh, that's why you read Einstein."

Daniel smiled and said, "Yes, that was the reason, but I've always been fascinated by Einstein's genius. One of my favorite quotes by him is 'A happy man is too satisfied with the present to dwell too much on the future.'"

"That makes sense. People should live in the present instead of always thinking about the future." Daniel stared at me strangely. "What's the matter?" I asked.

"Simple as that quote seems, it's quite complex." I didn't know what he meant, so I changed the subject.

"Where on 72nd Street does your uncle live?"

We both reached for some chips and our hands brushed. I felt a tingle. It was so weird like static electricity.

"The Dakota. I'm sure you know the building."

"Are you kidding? That's my favorite building." John Lennon lived there and got shot in front of that building. Every time I walked by that secretive and imposing building, I wondered what it looked like inside.

When Daniel said I was invited over anytime, the thought of going to his uncle's apartment actually made me very nervous.

After lunch, he walked me to my building and I noticed Mom sitting in the lobby reading a magazine. Oh no! When she saw us, she walked outside. This was so humiliating.

"Oh... hi... Mom," I said, glaring at her. She ignored me and scrutinized Daniel. "Mom this is Daniel Haydin. Daniel, this is my mother, Lena Devon."

"Nice to meet you, Mrs. Devon."

Mom started asking him questions. Poor Daniel, he couldn't get away from being interrogated. First by me, then Lily and Noelle, and now my mother.

When Mom asked him about college, Daniel glanced over at me and said, "I might start college soon and stop putting it off, Ma'am."

Ma'am? It must be the English boarding school influence. Even Mom's eyebrows arched as she turned to me. Daniel said he had to run and I hoped that Mom didn't scare him away.

"Well, he's cute and charming. Different somehow," she commented.

Different? I wasn't even going to ask. "Why were you waiting for me?" I asked, ignoring her comments. "It's embarrassing that you're spying on me."

"I figured since he lived on 72nd that he might drop you off. Why didn't you tell me he was in Chappaqua? I spoke to Aunt Cecile and she said she met him."

"He called after I had talked to you and offered to stay with us till Aunt Cecile and Uncle Ian came home. That was it."

"Well, you still should've told me. I don't appreciate hearing things from Aunt Cecile."

"I'm sorry," I said but didn't really mean it.

Mom knew I wasn't being sincere because she glared at me and said, "It bothers me that we know nothing about him."

She was being crazy. "His uncle lives in the Dakota. One of your friends might know him. Well, maybe not. His uncle lives in DC mostly and only comes to New York for work."

Mom left to run her work errands. I had enough of her hysteria and went upstairs. Maria called and said I was needed at work on Tuesday and possibly Thursday.

After dinner, Mom and I took Amber for a walk in the park. Thankfully, all the way to and from the reservoir, Daniel was not brought up. Enough had been said for one day.

Lily called when I got home and I told her that he had a house in London.

She said, "You know I like him, but try not to get too attached. With a home in London, he can leave anytime he wants."

"I know, but it's too late because I really like him. Please don't mention that he has a London place to anybody. They'll constantly ask if he's leaving and it'll drive me insane."

"Sure, but maybe he'll surprise us and stay around for a while."

After we hung up, Mom and I started watching a movie, but I left before it ended.

I remembered that I had gotten a journal, but had never used it. I searched my closet and found it in a box. I didn't want to forget anything. On the first page, I wrote Daniel & Paige. I wrote about my feelings for Daniel and wrote everything that had happened since the first day I saw him. When I finished, it was three o'clock. I hid the journal under some clothes in the drawer of my nightstand and went to sleep.

***

Before I left for work, I saw an invitation on Facebook that Chad's band, Sunspots, was playing at a block party on Wednesday night. A lot of my friends had RSVP'd that they were going. It sounded like fun so I texted Lily and asked if she wanted to go. Lily texted me right back and said "Sure." Anything that involved music, Lily was in.

The day at work dragged, probably due to my lack of sleep. The filing duties were so tedious that I couldn't focus and my mind kept wandering to Daniel.

As I left, Sonia, Dad's secretary, stopped me by the elevator and asked if I could bring a file home, saying Dad would need it when he got back from his trip. Luckily when I walked out of the building, a cab was dropping someone off so I jumped in.

As I walked in, my cell rang and it was Daniel. I threw the file on the couch and the papers spilled on the floor. I raced upstairs for privacy since Mom was in the kitchen.

When I asked about his day, he answered, "Just had some appointments and handled personal stuff." For a nineteen year-old, he sure had a lot of appointments.

"Oh, what happened with your squatters?"

"It's really strange. The lawyer went over and no one was there."

"Were they hiding?" I asked.

"No. The lawyer had the alarm company come out and investigate and they said the house wasn't tampered with."

"That's so weird!"

"I know. A friend is staying there until my housekeepers get back next week."

"That's good."

"Yeah, I'll feel better about it. Do you have any plans tomorrow night?"

"Lily's coming over and we're going to a block party. Would you like to come with us?"

"If I'm not intruding." Was he kidding?

"You're definitely not, please come."

After the call, I ran downstairs, ecstatic that we had a date. Upon entering the living room, I noticed the scattered papers on the floor, so I gathered them up and placed the file in the foyer.

I took Amber for a walk and when we got back, I stood in the foyer admiring it while taking off her leash.

The walls were painted a soft golden yellow. On the left wall, there was a demilune console table and beyond that the stairs leading to the second floor. On the right side, the bathroom had a topiary-printed wallpaper in a sunny antique wash. Straight ahead, the French doors opened onto the living room that was painted a darker shade than the foyer. In the living room, there was a door on the left that led to the kitchen and on the right was the den/library that also functioned as the guest room. At the end of the living room was the dining room that also had an entrance into the kitchen. Upstairs there were three bedrooms and two bathrooms. The third bedroom was changed to Dad's office after Martin got his own place.

Mom had dinner plans with a friend in the Village, so I was on my own. When Grace and Daphne called, I invited them over. I didn't want them to think I'd turned into Eden and had ditched them for a guy. About five minutes after Mom left, the house phone started ringing, but since all my friends called on my cell, I ignored it. Then I thought it might be Dad, so I checked the caller ID, and saw it was a private number. When the answering machine picked up, the caller hung up, so it had to be a telemarketer. It must be hard being one these days since everyone screened their calls and didn't pick up for strange or unknown numbers.

After getting my laptop from upstairs, I put music on in the living room and chatted with friends on Facebook while I waited for the girls to arrive.

Mom decorated our apartment in a French-style. Honeymooning in the South of France, she fell in love with Provence. She blended what she saw with some of her own ideas, so our apartment was both eclectic and very European. Aunt Cecile helped Mom pull her vision together. The look was rustic, old-world with a warm and casual feel. The living room couches were covered in pale yellow toile fabrics and the chairs and pillows were covered in red and green plaids, checks, and stripes. It was warm, cozy and casual.

When Lily called, I told her that Daniel was coming with us to the block party.

"I'll stay home, so you can go with him alone," she offered.

"No way. You're coming too."

Grace and Daphne finally arrived and although I wanted to watch a movie, they only wanted to talk about Daniel.

"Do you like him?" Grace wouldn't let up.

"Yes, I told you I did," I moaned, wishing I hadn't invited them since I was now getting tired of the conversation. "The problem is I think he'll be leaving soon, so I doubt anything will come of it." I already felt insecure about Daniel and all their questions started making me feel worse. I asked them to watch the movie and to stop talking about Daniel.

The house phone rang at least five times but no one ever left a message.

***

Wednesday morning, I started reading a poetry book, but I needed some fresh air, so I went for a jog in Riverside Park.

When I got out of the shower, the house phone started ringing.

Caller ID showed it was an unknown number, but when the answering machine picked up, they hung up. It rang again and the same thing happened. When it rang again, I silenced the ringer and went up to my bedroom.

I picked up the poetry book again and found a poem by Lord Byron.

THEY SAY THAT HOPE IS HAPPINESS
Félix qui potuit rerum cognoscere causas. –Virgil

> They say that Hope is happiness—
> But genuine Love must prize the past;
> And Mem'ry wakes the thoughts that bless:
> They rose the first – they set the last.
> And all that mem'ry loves the most
> Was once our only hope to be:
> And all that hope adored and lost
> Hath melted into memory.
> Alas! It is delusion all—
> The future cheats us from afar:
> Nor can we be what we recall,
> Nor dare we think on what we are.

First I needed to find out what the line by Virgil meant and who Virgil was. After Googling him, I found out that Virgil was a classical Roman poet and the sentence, translated from Latin, meant: 'Happy is he who has been able to learn the causes of things.'

There are things that happen in life that have no explanations. The last paragraph made me think of the future.

As you get older, your opinions and beliefs change and the person you were in your youth becomes just a memory just like the poem alleges.

After some nonstop reading, I felt I'd accomplished something.

Just as Mom got home, Amber began whimpering at the door. Needing some fresh air myself, I took her out. It had been cloudy all day, but now the skies were clearing up. Hopefully, the block party would be a success. Daniel called and said he was stuck in a meeting on Wall Street. He asked for the address and said he'd meet me there.

As I reached my building, I noticed a strange man across the street waving and motioning for me to come over. Having no idea who he was, I quickly went inside.

When Lily and I got to the elevator to leave, I realized I forgot my cell so I ran back to get it. Mom was standing in front of the answering machine and looked confused.

"The phone didn't ring, but the machine answered and a message.

"Sorry, I turned the ringer off. The phone kept ringing and I was trying to read."

"Who was it?"

"No one ever left a message and caller ID said it was an unknown caller. It was probably some telemarketer. Bye Mom, love you."

We got to 85th Street and there were people everywhere. After wandering, we eventually spotted Daphne and Grace near the stage talking to Eden and Paul. The band was so loud that I could barely hear anybody.

Eden yelled, "There are three bands. This is the first one. Chad's band is next."

I noticed Billy, Eden's older brother, standing nearby. He

attended Boston University and would be a sophomore in the fall. In high school, he was known as a player. He was rarely home when I visited her and if he was, he ignored us. In school, whenever I said hello, he'd look at me like he had no idea who I was. It was so embarrassing that I stopped acknowledging him.

I saw Billy approach and figured he'd dismiss me as usual. "Hi, Paige, how are you? Long time no see," he said and gave me a hug.

"Oh, hi," I stammered, while glancing over at Lily with a confused expression. Daphne and Grace, emboldened by the fact that Billy was friendly for once, pounced on him. No wonder he had a lot of girlfriends, they were completely mesmerized by him. I turned my attention to watching the first band and wondered when Daniel would get there.

Chad walked over to Billy smiling. "Hey, Billy thanks for coming." Chad noticed Lily, so I introduced them and they started talking. I couldn't hear what they were saying. When they turned to look at the band, their hair was almost the same length, falling just to their shoulders. They really had a lot in common since they both loved music and played guitar,

When Chad left, Lily nudged me smiling.

Daphne, Grace and Lily moved closer to the stage, but I wanted to stay where Daniel could find me. As I watched the first band, I saw Evan and Josie walking together near the stage. Daphne saw them too because she started whispering to Grace and nodded in their direction. I was still hoping that Reed would like Josie.

Billy started telling me about school and his summer job and it seemed like he was flirting with me, which was strange because I thought he had a girlfriend.

"So what's going on with you?" he asked. Before I could answer, a hand touched my back and I twirled around to find Daniel smiling at me. My back tingled and looking into his eyes, I wondered if he knew the effect he had on me. As I moved to make room for Daniel, I stumbled and he grabbed my arm.

"Are you okay?" Daniel whispered in my ear. I could only manage a nod.

At that moment, Evan and Josie walked by and they glared at me. Evan I understood, but what was Josie's problem? She should've been happy that I was with somebody else. She must have seen the Facebook post that Reed and I were dating and now she hated me.

I introduced Billy and Daniel, but Billy quickly left.

Daniel joked, "I think you have an admirer." When I said no way, Daniel just shook his head and smiled. The idea of Billy liking me seemed absurd.

Chad's band began playing and they were quite good. I recognized Nick Logan, but had no idea who the other three guys were.

When they finished, Daphne and Grace came back and were excited to meet Daniel.

Daphne whispered that she was upset that Evan came with Josie. I told her not to worry because they probably were just friends. Personally, I thought that he was too immature especially after his stupid stunt with Reed's Facebook page.

Chad returned to where we were and resumed talking to Lily. He glanced over at Daniel and I wondered if he knew that his brother liked me.

As soon as the third band, a screamo band, started all conversations stopped because the noise was deafening. I expected the police to come and shut them down. We were standing too close to the speakers and when my ears started to ring, I asked Daniel to move further away. I leaned on a fire hydrant and I noticed a man staring at me from the other side of the street. He looked like the man who had motioned to me near my building. Instead of watching the band, he was watching me and he looked really angry.

I got freaked out so I shuffled behind Daniel. When I looked again, I saw the man walking away. He must have confused me with someone else.

Daniel glanced over and mouthed, "You okay?" I smiled and nodded. When the band stopped playing, I waved to Lily and pointed that we should leave. Chad took out his cell and it looked like Lily was giving him her number.

As the three of us squeezed through the crowd, I saw Daphne talking to Evan and Josie.

Daniel wanted to walk us all the way to 69th Street, but I wouldn't let him. He'd have to walk back up to 72nd Street and that made no sense. When we got to his street, Daniel left us and insisted that I called when we got home.

Lily immediately started talking about Chad and I got a weird feeling that we were being followed. I kept turning around, but had no idea where to look. There were people everywhere.

When we got inside, I called Daniel. "Okay, we made it home

alive."

"Great. I'll call you tomorrow."

I walked in the kitchen to get a glass of water and Mom said she was taking Amber for a walk. As soon as she left the house phone rang. I reached to get the phone, but it was missing from the base. I heard the answering machine pick up and it was another hang up.

6. PHOTOGRAPH

"Coincidence is God's way of remaining anonymous." Einstein

Lily and I walked to work and hoped it wouldn't rain since we both forgot our umbrellas.

I spend most of the day filing, which was a little better than marathon photocopying.

At the end of the day, I walked home through the park. It had only been three weeks since I first saw Daniel, but now it seemed like he'd always been a part of my life.

Suddenly, I felt somebody grab me. "Oh my God!" I screamed and turned sideways.

Daphne was standing there laughing, thrilled by her ambush. "You were in a trance."

"You scared me to death."

"Thinking about anybody I know?" she asked.

"Daphne, please stop," I begged. "So what happened with Evan last night?"

Daphne got excited and said, "You were right. Nothing's going on between them. Josie called Evan and asked him to go with her."

"I figured as much."

"As we stood there talking, Nick Logan walked over, and Josie started flirting like crazy. They ended up leaving together and Evan walked me home."

"Good, I'm glad. They were really weird last night. When they passed me, they both gave me the dirtiest looks."

"Evan I get, but why would Josie?"

"I have no idea. She obviously has an issue with me."

When we reached my street, we said goodbye and made plans to talk later.

I entered the apartment and put the file on the table. Dad was talking on the phone in the den and waved at me as I passed.

I sat on the couch and waited for him. My head started spinning, so I closed my eyes.

"Hi Buttercup."

His voice woke me up and I said groggily, "Hi Dad. I can't believe I fell asleep. How was your trip?"

"Good, but I might have to go back next week." Dad began explaining something about some corporations, but I had no idea what he was talking about.

"Are we still going to Grammy's this weekend?" I asked when he was done.

"Yes, I'm taking tomorrow off, so we'll leave late morning and miss the traffic."

"Sounds great to me," I said happily. "I left a file that Sonia said you needed in the foyer."

I went in the kitchen and asked Mom if she needed any help.

"Just set the table," she said and handed me the plates.

Mom had made a caprese salad and some shrimp kabobs over rice. It all looked delicious, but I started feeling queasy and just played with my food.

"Are you okay?" Mom asked when I put my hands to my temples.

"I have a headache." I started feeling dizzy. "Maybe, it's the heat."

"Go lie down. I'll bring you some medicine."

The medication worked and feeling better, I wrote a song called 'I Want to Tell You.'

I want to tell you all my feelings
I want to tell you everything
But I'm worried that my honesty might make you run away.
What if you can't handle what I'm saying
And you can't stand to be around me
If it creeps you out will you stay around or will you leave me

Be great if you felt the same way but what if you don't
Will I just end up with more pain
I'm scared that I love you
I'm scared of wrecking our friendship
I'm scared of sabotaging everything we have
I'm scared that I love you and that I'm afraid to tell you
I'm scared you'll disappear once again.

I'm sure you're the one I'm meant to be with
I can't stop how I feel for you
Are you capable of loving me or is this just crazy?
I'm sure you love me as a friend.
Is it something more to you too?

I'm hoping you love me too and that you're not afraid.

Be great if you felt the same way but what if you don't
Will I just end up with more pain?
I'm scared that I love you
I'm scared of wrecking our friendship
I'm scared of sabotaging everything we have
I'm scared that I love you and that I'm afraid to tell you
I'm scared you'll disappear once again.

After I finished the song, I stared at the ceiling wondering how Daniel felt about me. I heard a buzzing noise and realized it was my cell. I forgot to turn it on when I left work.

"Are you sitting down?" Lily asked excitedly.

"Yeah, what's up?" I said and got back on the bed.

"You won't believe this, but Daniel was in Paris last summer. I have a picture of all three of us on the Eiffel Tower," she shrieked.

For a minute, it didn't register. "What are you talking about?" I said stunned.

"I was working on my scrapbook and found a photo of him standing behind us. I emailed it to you."

I went to my computer and sure enough it was him. He was standing sideways talking to a girl. I could only see her back. She had long brown hair and had on wooden bangle bracelets.

"I can't believe it."

"All this time, I thought you were stalking him, but he's been stalking you." She laughed and said, "I'm obviously kidding."

"I know. I'm going to look through my photos. I'll call you back."

I grabbed my photo box under my bed and started searching.

Sadly, my pictures had no Daniel in them. At least, we had one. Daniel and I had another thing in common, Paris. I couldn't wait to tell him.

When Mom came in to say goodnight, I showed her the photo. "What a small world," she muttered, as she walked out.

I wanted to call Daniel, but felt funny.

All of a sudden, as if on cue, my cell rang and it was him. "I was just thinking of calling you," I confessed.

"You can call me anytime."

"You were in Paris last August, right?" I began.

"Yes, how did you know?" he asked.

"We were there for Lily's birthday and she found a photo of you standing behind us on the Eiffel Tower. We were destined to meet," I said and quickly got embarrassed by my comment.

"Yes, I guess we were. I was vacationing with some friends," he said. "I'd love to see the picture. Can you email it to me at DanielHaydin@mail.com?"

"Sure. I'll do it right now." I had his email!

He opened it and said, "It's definitely me."

We talked about France for a bit and then Daniel asked, "Are you around this weekend?"

"No, we're going to my grandmother's on Long Island." I loved going to Long Island, but now with Daniel in the city I wanted to be in both places at once.

"Have fun. I'll call you next week. Maybe we can do something."

"I'd like that," I admitted. I printed the photo and put it in my bag. That way, I would have him with me at all times. I took out my journal and wrote about the block party and the photo.

***

A crazy dream woke me at six o'clock. I couldn't remember it, except that I was scared. My headache was back, so I grabbed the medicine and reached for my water bottle, but it was empty.

I went downstairs and found my parents talking at the kitchen table.

A call from France woke them around five o'clock and they weren't able to fall back asleep.

Thank goodness, I had put my house phone in my bedroom on silent mode.

A new secretary had called, having forgotten about the time difference. Dad called her a flibbertigibbet, his favorite word for incompetent people. The secretary told Dad that she found some files he left behind. Dad asked her to overnight the files to the New York office and said he wasn't missing anything. He had no idea what she was talking about.

Since we were all awake, we got an early start for Long Island. Halfway there, Dad realized he forgot to bring the file that I had brought home. He left a voice message for Sonia to send a different file by Federal Express.

When we arrived, Grammy was outside puttering in the garden. Mom went to help, Dad rushed off to make calls and I took Amber for a walk. The beach was totally deserted.

When I got back to the house, Aunt Cecile was pulling into the driveway.

Lily and Uncle Ian were catching the bus after work and were expected around eight. I changed into my bathing suit and jumped in the pool.

Around two o'clock, bored with swimming, I took Amber for a walk to the Causeway Beach for a change.

As we were heading down the beach, I noticed a black car with tinted windows pull into the parking lot. No one got out and I couldn't really see anyone from my angle. When I came by again on the way home, the car was gone.

I found a note on the table that Grammy, Mom and Aunt Cecile had gone food shopping. I heard Dad talking on the phone in the den, so I got my books and camped out on a lounge chair by the pool to read poetry. All the poetry now reminded me of Daniel.

When Lily and Uncle Ian finally arrived, Dad took orders for grilled fish and salmon burgers. As I ate, I saw a motorboat anchored off the beach right in front of Grammy's house. The boat was on a private buoy, so it most likely was a neighbor enjoying the night.

I wasn't that hungry, so I jumped in the pool and waited for Lily to finish eating. When she was done, Lily ran towards the pool and dove in.

As Lily surfaced, I yelled to her, "Hey, you have to wait two hours before swimming."

"Sure, I'll jump right out," Lily laughed and started doing laps.

One summer, Mom, Dad and I had visited friends in Piscara, Italy and we went along with their relatives to the beach. After eating lunch, I jumped up and ran right into the water while the other kids just sat on the edge of the water and watched me enviously. I kept asking them to come in, but they said they weren't allowed.

Our friends told us that all the locals waited two hours after eating fearful of cramps.

The adults gave my parents dirty looks, appalled that I was allowed to swim. This wasn't the only strange thing. If they ate watermelon, they had to wait three hours to swim and some people wouldn't even bathe.

When I first told Lily the story, she wisecracked, "So if you eat pizza and watermelon do you have to wait five hours?"

Later that night as I looked out my window admiring the full moon, I noticed that the boat was still there and the lights were on. The evening was cool so we opened the windows and enjoyed the night sounds.

***

The following morning, Lily wanted to kayak after breakfast. The motorboat was still there and with nothing better to do, we paddled towards it to investigate.

As we reached the boat, we saw a person disappear below. As we pulled away, the person reappeared. Lily thought that was strange and we paddled back towards the boat. Again, the occupant went below.

"I'm not leaving until I see who is on that boat," Lily stated. We paddled back and forth hoping the person would appear eventually.

My arms started to ache and I moaned, "Let's forget it. Who cares?"

"Fine," Lily agreed.

We were about to turn the kayak towards home when the person came out. Standing on deck was Daniel's friend. It took a minute to remember his name.

"Pierce?" I called out to get his attention and wondered if he'd remember us.

He was visibly startled. "Hey? What are you two doing here?"

"Our grandmother lives right there," I answered and pointed towards the house.

"That's amazing. I'm sorry, but I forgot your names."

"I'm Paige and that's Lily. Why have you been here all night?"

"My friends were coming last night from Connecticut, but something happened and they couldn't come till today. Since I was already anchored here, I waited."

"Do you live around here?" asked Lily.

"My family has a place on Robins Island."

That island was privately owned, so Pierce's family had to own it. We tried to talk to him, but it was just as painful as the first time.

"I've always wanted to go there," I mentioned. Pierce didn't respond and walked around the boat tying some buoys to the railing.

We got the hint and left. "Bye," we called out. Pierce waved. I had to go and ride Milton anyway.

I looked out the window before we left and the boat was gone.

It was a stressful ride over. Mom kept yelling, "You're too close to the car in front of you. Slow down. Turn now." By the time we got there, I wanted to kill her.

When I saw Milton, I calmed down. I trotted around the ring and noticed a black car parked at the entrance to the farm. What's with all these cars? What was going on? My imagination went wild. Was

I being watched? I realized how stupid that was. Why would anyone be watching me?

I laughed at the absurdity of what I was thinking and when I was done, I gave Milton a bath. I called Mom that I was done and was told Uncle Ian would get me on his way home from golf. Mom wasn't letting me drive anymore today.

By the time we left, the mystery car was gone.

When I got back, I found Lily by the pool and told her what I thought.

She laughed. "Yeah, sure. Our lives are too boring for anyone to bother watching us."

She had me there, but since Daniel came into my life, I wasn't bored, just very intrigued.

* * *

On Sunday, we went for a long bike ride and then spent the day by the pool. I grabbed a stack of magazines and began reading while Lily Skyped people on her laptop.

I was hoping we'd leave right after dinner, but nobody seemed in any hurry. Lily was engrossed with working on a new song and I was the only one anxious to go.

Grammy said, "I think you all better head out. I worry about you driving late at night." On that note, everyone headed upstairs to pack.

Before leaving, Mom and Aunt Cecile told Grammy not to get carried away in the gardens and to take it easy while we were gone. Aunt Cecile and Mom had offered to get her a gardener last year, but Grammy said no. Fall and spring cleanups and weekly mowing of the lawn were fine, but no stranger was allowed to touch her gardens.

Lately, she had allowed us to help with a few things, but the majority of the time, we just meandered around and she would tell us about all the different plants she loved.

We got home around ten o'clock and I crawled into bed. My cell rang and it was Daniel.

"Hi. Where are you?" he asked.

"69th Street. Where are you?"

"72nd Street. I heard you ran into Pierce."

"Yeah, it was so weird," I admitted.

"It's really a small world."

"My mom said the exact same thing after I told her about the Eiffel Tower."

"Great minds think alike," joked Daniel.

"Since I met you, strange things keep happening."

"What do you mean by strange?" he asked sounding confused.

"I mean Chappaqua, Paris, now Pierce in Cutchogue. It seems we're somehow ...connected." I couldn't express what I meant correctly. "Does Pierce's family own Robins Island? What's his last name?"

"His last name is Tallmadge, but his family doesn't own the island anymore. Years ago when the island was sold, his family made a deal and were able to keep their house."

"Every time the island gets sold, they get to stay?" I asked.

"I'm not sure. I think so," Daniel answered.

"That's amazing."

"I guess it is. I was wondering are you free for dinner tomorrow night?"

"Yes," I answered quickly, smiling ear to ear. "I am."

"Well, I know you wanted to see the Dakota. How about we eat here?"

"Ah…yeah …okay," I answered a bit apprehensively.

"Are you sure?"

"Yes, I'm positive," I answered and agreed to meet him at seven in front of his building.

After we hung up, I called Lily and told her about the plans.

"Are you telling your mom?" Lily quizzed.

"No."

"I don't think that's smart."

"I'm not telling my her, so forget it."

"You better text me all night and let me know that you're okay," Lily insisted.

I couldn't sleep so I got on the computer and did some research on Robins Island. As I scrolled down to the history section, I found that Caleb Brewster and Benjamin Tallmadge, two espionage agents of General George Washington, purchased it in 1784. Pierce's family had a spy in its past! It turned out that a Wall Street financier owned Robins Island.

***

After Mom and Dad left for work, I went for a jog and found myself at the Delacorte Theatre. I stopped to look at the Romeo and Juliet statue. This was my favorite of Shakespeare's works. My thoughts went to Daniel and I hoped that our relationship would fare much better.

After I got out of the shower, Daphne texted that she had the day off, so we made plans to meet up for manicures at a place on Broadway. When I told her about my dinner plans, Daphne insisted that I get something new and after our nails dried, dragged me to Stars. Daphne put together at least ten outfits that I didn't like.

"I just want to wear something I feel comfortable in," I explained.

"I give up. That you don't like to shop is so weird to me."

Mom called and said she was meeting Dad at the office for some business dinner, so I would be on my own. It was perfect. I wouldn't be asked where I was going. She told me to feed and walk Amber.

Daphne came back to the apartment and helped me pick an outfit. We settled on white jean shorts and a yellow gauzy top.

"That's perfect," Daphne said.

Leaving the apartment, I got super nervous. Mom had a point. I really didn't know Daniel and I was going to his apartment. At least, Lily and Daphne knew where I'd be.

"Is he ordering food or is he cooking?" Daphne wondered.

"I doubt he cooks," I answered. I was so glad that Daphne walked with me and kept me calm.

On the corner of 72nd Street, I saw Daniel standing outside the fortress-like building talking to the doorman. Seeing his gorgeous face made all my worries disappear.

As we approached, he saw me and did a double take when he spotted Daphne. "Hello, ladies."

"Hey Daniel, just dropping Paige off. I have to go home and

babysit my sister." She gave me a hug goodbye.

Daniel nodded to the guard and we walked through the arched entryway. We passed the first gate then the second. There was a fountain in the middle of the courtyard and I felt like I had stepped into a different era.

On the sixth floor, Daniel opened the door to reveal a huge foyer with a wood-burning fireplace. It was so beautiful and I was speechless.

The ceilings were so high that I felt I had walked into a mansion and not a New York City apartment. We walked down the hallway on the left and passed several doorways. At the end on the left side, Daniel stopped at open French doors. As I walked up and looked in, it was the living room and it was massive. There were floor-to-ceiling windows and because of that tons of light shone threw the windows. Two large couches, two settees, four chairs, a grand piano and a fireplace were in that room and it was still spacious.

"Wow," was all I could say afraid to enter. I felt like I was looking at a magazine page. "This is so beautiful."

Before we walked in, I heard a noise coming from a room behind us. Daniel called out, "Hello?"

"I'm in the library. I'll be right out."

"That's my uncle." Suddenly, I wasn't sure if I felt better or worse. He didn't want to be alone with me, I thought.

The pocket doors slid open and a gentleman came out. He looked like an older version of Daniel, but with darker hair. He walked over and introduced himself, "Hi. I'm James Haydin." Without allowing me to respond, he continued brusquely, "Paige, right?" Daniel had told his uncle about me? That did make me feel good.

"Yes," I answered meekly. "You have a beautiful apartment."

"Thank you," he said without any emotion or social pleasantries. He turned to Daniel and sounding very businesslike said, "I have a meeting at the Knickerbocker. It shouldn't take too long." As he walked down the hallway, he turned around and said, "Nice to meet you." He seemed to be in an unpleasant mood unless that was his normal demeanor.

Daniel ushered me into the living room. There were beautiful landscape paintings on the wall and nothing was out of place. When I looked out a window, I saw two balconies and the apartment had amazing views of Central Park.

Daniel asked if I wanted a tour and when I said yes, he led me into the room that his uncle had been. It was the library and it was filled to the rafters with books. My mouth opened wide at the sheer size of it.

"This is unbelievable," I gasped. Leather armchairs and couches were placed all around the room and there was another large fireplace. "I would live in here."

I picked up a book lying on the desk called These United States filled with photographs of American landmarks.

"These are so beautiful," I said and Daniel looked at them over my shoulder.

"Yeah, I love that book."

Daniel got a call and left the room. While I waited, I sat down at the desk and noticed a sparkly object sitting in an open box. Peering inside, it looked like a crystal cylinder with a blue line in the middle, which seemed to be glowing and pulsating.

Daniel walked back in. Holding it up I asked, "What's this?"

"Oh…I don't know. It's my uncle's." Daniel took the crystal and put it in a desk drawer. He seemed to be in a hurry to exit the library. His uncle probably didn't like people nosing around in there. I realized that there weren't any personal photos anywhere.

"Did your aunt decorate this apartment herself?" I wondered looking at the sconces in the hallway. Aunt Cecile would love this apartment.

"I don't know."

Daniel pointed to the two doors on the left and said they were bedrooms, but didn't show me inside. At the foyer, we went to the right wing of the apartment. Daniel stopped at a doorway to the massive dining room with yet another fireplace. In the middle of the room was a large rectangular wooden table. I counted the chairs and it seated sixteen people. The sterling silver and crystal shone in the hutch. The walls were covered in pale grey fleur-de-lis wallpaper and the windows had soft blue silk curtains.

The next room on the left, he called the family room/media room. When we entered, it was really dark and Daniel reached for a remote control. The blackout shades automatically lifted revealing dark green walls and large tan suede couches and chairs. The biggest flat screen TV that I'd ever seen was hanging on one wall.

As we exited that room, Daniel pointed down the hallway and said, "There are two bedrooms down there." It was obvious he had no intention of showing me any personal rooms and for a moment, I felt like I was on an official museum tour.

We crossed the hall from the family room and Daniel opened a closed door and said, "This is the billiard room." Of course, it was. Didn't everyone have one of those?

Coming back down the hall, we entered the huge kitchen. It had stainless steel appliances, two huge islands and a banquette was nestled by the large windows. I reached for my cell to take a picture and realized how obnoxious that would be, so I put my phone back in my bag. Daniel noticed so I quickly said, "I thought my phone buzzed."

"For a minute, I thought you were going to take a photo."

I laughed and made a silly face at him. Not admitting that I had almost done just that.

Daniel opened a drawer and pulled out some menus.

"What would you like to eat?"

"I really don't care."

After going back and forth for some time, we decided on a pizza and a Caesar salad. We sat in the living room to wait for the food to arrive. Daniel put on some classical music, which was soothing and helped calm my nerves. He walked across the room and opened a large, built-in wooden armoire with glass doors and inside was a wine rack and refrigerator on the left side and on the right a sink and lots of glasses. He brought over a bottle of sparkling water and glasses.

In the corner of the room, there was a guitar and I remembered that Daniel said he played. I asked him to play something, but he said, "Maybe later, I don't want you to lose your appetite."

"I'm sure I wont. Later, there are no excuses," I warned jokingly.

I walked over to the piano and started playing a Sara Bareilles song.

"Why don't you sing? I'm sure you have a nice voice."

Feeling self-conscious, I refused. I only sang in my bedroom or with Lily.

When I finished, I looked around the room. "I can't believe your uncle doesn't live here fulltime. This is amazing."

"Well, his job and family is in DC."

"Then why does he keep such a large apartment in New York?"

Before he could answer, the doorbell rang and he went to get the pizza.

Daniel came back holding the box and said, "Let's go in the kitchen."

I sat at the table and Daniel brought over plates and glasses.

"Do you have red pepper flakes?" I asked.

Daniel nodded and grabbed the bottle from the spice rack in the cabinet.

As I sprinkled the pepper on my pizza, Daniel was amazed at the amount.

"Wow! You'll be breathing fire soon," he joked.

"Very funny," I said and kept shaking.

"My uncle likes red pepper too, but you win the prize."

"Where does your uncle work?" I asked.

"I told you. He works for the government."

"But where in the government?"

"The NSA."

"What does that stand for?" I asked, knowing that I should know.

"The National Security Agency."

"Oh...right," I said feeling stupid. "What does he do there?"

"He's an intelligence analyst."

"So what does the NSA actually do?"

"It's responsible for foreign communications and foreign signals intelligence." When Daniel saw my confused expression, he continued. "Basically, they protect US security systems. They prevent adversaries from accessing classified national security information. They also collect foreign intelligence to support military operations that fight terrorists' actions, here and abroad."

"Do you mean like the CIA?"

"Yes and no. The NSA is concerned with communication intelligence. They collect information from foreign communications and protect our government's communications from being accessed by other countries."

"Do you mean computer intelligence?"

Daniel nodded, stood up and went to the refrigerator for more bottled water. When he sat down, he changed the subject by asking me a question. The conversation about the NSA was over.

We were talking about France when Daniel's uncle walked into the kitchen. "How was your pizza?" he asked, noticing the box on the counter.

"Good," We answered simultaneously and laughed.

His uncle looked at us, but didn't seem amused. "I need to make some phone calls," he said brusquely and walked out of the room.

Daniel asked, "Do you want to get out of here? Go for a walk and get some dessert? I'll give you a rain check on the guitar solo."

Outside, we headed towards Columbus Avenue. Daniel was in a great mood and we stopped at a café a block from my house. We sat outside and shared a lemon tart and a cup of chocolate peanut butter ice cream. We were having fun teasing each other, but it was short-lived once Daniel answered his cell.

"What! ...I'll be right there," he said, visibly upset. He stared at me and looked dazed.

"Are you okay? What happened?"

He said, "I'm sorry. I need to go. I'll walk you home."

"Don't worry. I can walk home by myself."

"I insist. I'll feel better knowing where you are." That remark concerned me. Why did he have to know where I was? He never told me what happened and before I could ask again, we were at my building.

Daniel quickly ushered me into my lobby and said, "Good night. I'll call you soon." As he exited the building, a grey SUV pulled up and he jumped inside. I didn't even say goodbye or thank him for the evening. My parents still weren't home so I took Amber outside and tried to make sense of the evening.

When I got back, I glanced down at my cell and saw that it was dead. Now my battery wasn't keeping a charge. I had forgotten to text Lily. I called her from the landline and she was so happy to hear from me. She'd been freaking out.

After I told her the strange way the night ended, she said, "I'm sure everything's fine, but I have to tell you something really weird. The photo of Daniel is gone. It's not in my book where I put it or on my computer. It totally vanished."

"Maybe you misplaced it and hit delete after you sent it to me. Don't worry, I'll email it to you." I went to the computer. Nothing happened. The screen stayed black. "My computer's not turning on. Wait here it goes." I opened the photo file and couldn't believe it. "Lily, my photo's gone, too." I don't know why, but I didn't mention the copy that I had in my bag.

"This is freaking me out. How could it disappear from my scrapbook and on both of our computers?" Lily asked. I had no idea. We made plans for her to come over the next day.

After my phone charged, I read all of Lily's texts and saw that Martin had texted. I called him back and found out that all three were home sick. Martin reminded me that I was babysitting next Tuesday and that they'd be over Sunday for Dad's birthday.

I was lying on my bed when I heard my parents come in. They stopped in my room and then Dad went to his office to finish some briefs, while Mom stayed behind.

"How was your night? What did you do?"

"It was fine. I had pizza with Daniel." I prayed she wouldn't ask where.

"I told your father about him and he'd like to meet him."

"Fine," I said, gritting my teeth. I knew there was no point in arguing about this anymore. "Just so you know, I met his uncle tonight and he works for the NSA. They're not psychos."

"I never said they were. That's a serious agency," Mom said, raising her eyebrows.

"Is it a spy agency?" I asked.

"No." She stopped, thought for a bit and added, "I do remember that there was some sort of scandal. About computers, I think. Ask your dad, I'm sure he knows."

I started getting a funny feeling. Computers? She left the room and I went to see Dad in his office. He was on his computer and looked up as I entered.

"Hey Buttercup."

"Dad, do you know anything about a scandal involving the NSA?"

"The National Security Agency?" Dad asked.

I nodded.

He looked back down and answered while he typed, "Well, some time back the NSA was charged with illegally bugging telephones of the general public and installing hardware to monitor computer communications. Why?"

Telephones and computers? "Just curious. Mom mentioned a scandal. Daniel's uncle works there," I said.

"Really! Speaking of Daniel, I'd like to meet him."

"Yes, Mom told me. I'll invite him over soon, so you can grill him," I said angrily.

"I'm not interrogating him. I just want to meet him," Dad objected.

In a huff, I stormed off to my room and sat at the computer. I researched the NSA and saw that the information for the NSA was listed as classified. Phone tapping and computer hacking? My intuition was saying that something was going on and I wanted to talk this out with Lily. Even though, I knew she'd say I was crazy.

Before bed, I wrote in my journal and filled the pages with the

Pierce sighting, the Dakota dinner and all my new worries. I felt better after having written it down, but it all seemed so ridiculously impossible! I fell asleep highly amused at myself for thinking that Daniel was a spy and that people were watching me.

In the middle of the night, I woke up dreaming about masked men chasing me. Was my subconscious trying to tell me something or was my imagination working in overdrive? I lay in bed staring at the ceiling hoping to quiet all the noises in my head.

7. AMBUSH

"Whoever is careless with the truth in small matters cannot be trusted with important matters." Einstein

In the morning, Lily called to say she was sick with a fever and not going to work. I was upset because I really needed to talk to her. Even after explaining away things before I went to sleep, I knew something strange was going on and that things weren't what they seemed.

As I headed for the door to leave for work, Mom called out that she'd walk with me. She had a meeting near Dad's office. At 55th Street, Mom left and I got a sick feeling that I was being watched. I rushed into the building.

Jared stepped in the elevator after me and distracted me from my paranoid thoughts.

"Morning. Not walking with your Dad today?" he asked. He must have found out who my father was.

"Not today. He had an early meeting. I actually found my way to work all by myself."

Jared laughed like he didn't believe me.

"On second thought, my mom did walk with me," I admitted guiltily. Someone I didn't know in the elevator chuckled.

"Thought so," he wisecracked. "I knew you couldn't find it yourself."

I made a face at him as we exited. Jared chuckled and went in the opposite direction.

Work did distract me. After I finished photocopying, Todd Madison showed me how to scan files into the computer. At the end of the day, I went to see Dad in his office and found him talking to Maria. He seemed aggravated so I waited outside. Maria left looking harried and Dad motioned me in.

"Sonia's out sick. I'm so busy with this case and I can't find some files," he muttered and said he had to cancel his Paris trip. Distracted and upset, he said he'd be working late and he'd see me at home.

When one of the paralegals came in, Dad gave me a hug goodbye and told me to head home. I offered to stay and help, but he said there really wasn't anything I could do. As I left, three more people entered Dad's office looking very somber. I wondered what was going on.

When I walked outside, Jared was talking on the phone near the revolving door and called out, "Hey Paige, can I ask you a question?"

I nodded. He handed me a note.

"Do you know this restaurant on Columbus?"

"Yeah, you'll like it. It's really good," I offered.

"Is it on 69th Street?" he asked.

"No, its on 71st Street. I live on 69th."

"Thanks. You want company walking home?"

"Now you don't think I can walk home alone?" I joked.

"We're both going in the same direction and you never know, you might need a bodyguard."

Mom called and said she was at the Lincoln Center library doing some research for work and wanted to go out for dinner once she was done. Since I wanted to do more research about the NSA, but felt funny using the home computer, I told her I'd meet her there.

On the way, Jared told me all about law school and how intense it was. Passing a bookstore, I told Jared I had to get a present for my Dad's birthday and he said he'd come in too. I found a new history book that I thought Dad would like.

As I was paying, Jared was looking at a magazine and he still had a bandage on his left hand.

Hoping to hear something other than the copy machine attacked him, I asked, "So what happened to your hand?"

"A crazy co-worker stabbed me. I'm thinking of filing a lawsuit. Do you think your dad will represent me?"

"I doubt it." I gave up. He was never going to tell me. He was such a joker.

He ended up walking me all the way to the library, saying he was meeting his friend in an hour and had time to kill. Arriving at Lincoln Center, I tried saying goodbye to Jared on the street, but he insisted on walking me to the door.

"I have to escort you to the door. My bodyguard certificate will be taken away otherwise."

"Okay, you preformed your duties admirably. Thank you," I said, once I got to the door.

"If you ever need my services, please call. My hourly rate is very fair," he said handing me his business card. It just had his name and phone number.

"Thanks Jared. If I ever need a bodyguard you will be the first person I call."

Jared smiled and headed down the street. What a nut job!

I ran in and decided to check out James Haydin. The NSA website didn't have any information on him. Nor was there anything anywhere else, no images, no data, nothing. There was nothing on a Daniel Haydin anywhere on the Internet either. I read more about the NSA scandals and learned that the NSA's work was limited to communications intelligence not spying on people.

I found Mom on the second floor and we went to a sushi place near home. After dinner, I offered to take Amber for a quick walk, but Mom said she needed some exercise and wanted to take a long walk. I wasn't in the mood, so I stayed behind. As soon as she left, the house phone started ringing and wouldn't stop. Every time I looked at caller ID, it said unknown caller and they never left a message.

When Mom returned, I thought about talking to her about my crazy concerns, but decided against it. She was already worried about Daniel and I'd just make things worse if I were wrong.

I curled up under a big chenille blanket on the couch in the den to watch a movie. The walls were painted a dark maroon and the couch was covered in a cream and red paisley tapestry. There were two dark cream-colored leather armchairs near the gas fireplace. Photos of me at horse shows covered one wall.

I started out in the Hunter and Equitation division, but switched to the Jumpers division because of the speed and the objective form of judging.

It was all based on how fast you covered the course without errors. In the other disciplines, it was all about what the judges thought of you, and your horse.

After the movie ended, I went upstairs and found Mom reading a book in bed. She had the news on so I sat in a chair and watched.

"A man was found in Central Park today with amnesia and the police are asking the public for help in identifying him. If anyone knows this man please call the number below or your local police station." I stared at the man's face and he seemed so familiar.

"Mom, do you know him?"

Mom looked up and said, "No, I've never seen him before."

"That's weird. I've seen him somewhere."

When I told Mom I had the next day off, she asked if I'd come to her office and help her.

That night, I woke up from a nightmare covered in sweat. In my dream, the man with amnesia was chasing me and he shot me in the back. It felt so real that I actually felt the pain. I rolled over and tried to go back to sleep.

***

I regretted going to Mom's office. It was a total disaster. Photos, magazines and beauty products were everywhere. She was a neat freak, so this made no sense.

"What happened in here?"

"Oh, this has to be all thrown out. I went through it yesterday, but didn't have time to finish."

For lunch, we grabbed a sandwich at a nearby Au Bon Pain.

We finished around four and Mom had nothing else for me to do, so I played on the computer until it was time to leave.

Dad called and said that he'd be working late again.

After dinner, Mom and I took Amber for a walk in the park. It was a dreary grey evening.

"So, what's going on with Daniel?" she pried.

"Nothing. I haven't heard from him."

"Oh really," she said and it sounded like she was pleased.

That really infuriated me. "Please, stop talking about Daniel," I demanded.

Mom stared at me and said, "Calm down. Why are you acting like this?"

"Because I can tell that you're really glad that I haven't heard from him."

"I'm sorry. I'm just concerned."

"There's nothing to be concerned about. Absolutely nothing is going on, so stop." We walked in complete silence all the way home.

Daniel called that evening, but his tone was so casual and weird.

"How's it going?" he asked.

"Fine. What happened the other night? You seemed upset."

"It was about work. I forgot to do something. My uncle was

really annoyed with me."

"Oh. What have you been doing?" I asked.

"Just working. Are you going to Long Island this weekend?"

"No, we're staying here. My parents have a wedding on Saturday and my dad's birthday is on Sunday. We're having dinner with my brother."

"You have a brother?"

"Yeah, his name's Martin. He's actually my half-brother, same dad different moms. He's fifteen years older and is married to Marina." What's wrong with me? I had been so pre-occupied with Daniel that I forgot to mention my own brother. "Martin has a daughter, her name's Anna and she turned one in June, so that makes me an aunt," I added.

As we talked, Daniel started sounding more normal and actually laughed a few times.

"I wanted to ask you to a film this weekend, but I see you're busy," Daniel admitted.

"No, I'm not. My parents are going to the wedding, not me," I explained. "I'd love to see a movie." No matter what was going on I really liked Daniel and I'd talk to him in person.

"Great. I'll call you Saturday afternoon."

My heart skipped a beat. What was I worried about? Nothing had happened. How could Daniel be a spy? A photo disappeared so what was the big deal? The only thing that kept nagging at me was how did it vanish from both our computers? How was that possible? I really was at a loss to explain that one.

Since Lily wasn't going to Grammy's either, we made plans to spend the weekend together. On Saturday, we'd spend the day together and as always, Lily suggested shopping. Later when I saw Daniel, Lily could hang out with Daphne and Grace or wait for me at home.

After we hung up, I decided to read some poetry and grabbed the John Keats book.

I picked "Bright Star…" because it sounded upbeat.

BRIGHT STAR, WOULD I WERE STEDFAST AS THOU ART

Bright star, would I were stedfast as thou art--
Not in lone splendour hung aloft the night
And watching, with eternal lids apart,
Like nature's patient, sleepless Eremite,
The moving waters at their priestlike task
Of pure ablution round earth's human shores,
Or gazing on the new soft-fallen mask
Of snow upon the mountains and the moors--
No--yet still stedfast, still unchangeable,
Pillow'd upon my fair love's ripening breast,
To feel for ever its soft fall and swell,
Awake for ever in a sweet unrest,
Still, still to hear her tender-taken breath,
And so live ever--or else swoon to death

This love poem was eerily poignant. A man was watching his love while she slept. Since death was inevitable, he wished to be a star. In that way their love would last forever since a star had, or so he thought, a limitless life. The poem was a paradox of immortality and love. Knowing that Keats died at twenty-five from tuberculosis made me understand why he wished for immortality.

***

Dad went to court and was out of the office all day. He called when I was standing at the elevator to leave and asked me to bring some files home. I waited for Sonia and she handed me a large shopping bag.

I walked up Fifth Ave and entered the park at 59th Street. As I strolled on a path listening to my iPod, I saw two men walking towards me.

They were still quite a bit away from me, but I moved onto the grass for them to be able to pass. When I did that, they stopped and glared at me. One of them looked like the man from the block party. I got scared and froze in place. There were a lot of people around, so what could they actually do? They exchanged words, moved onto the grass directly in my path and resumed walking towards me. The man I didn't recognize was reaching for something in his jacket pocket. I didn't know if I was hallucinating or not, but it looked like a gun.

I was about to turn and run in the other direction, but the dream that I got shot in the back popped into mind. Was that nightmare a warning? I heard someone approaching from behind and was terrified. Suddenly, Daniel was standing in front of me. I stared into his eyes and knew that I was involved in something really dangerous.

"Hi!" he said. He bent down and hugged me. I didn't know what he was doing. He suddenly lifted me up and turned me so that my back was facing the men.

I knew the hug wasn't real, but I was so happy to be in his arms. I felt safe.

As Daniel released me, I managed to ask, "What's going on?"

I glanced behind me and saw that they had stopped moving. One was on his cell.

Without answering my question, Daniel put an arm around my shoulder and pushed me back to where I entered the park.

We walked in silence. Something bad would've happened if Daniel hadn't shown up, I knew that.

"What's going on?" I repeated. "Who were those men?"

"What men?" Daniel asked flippantly, attempting to pretend nothing happened.

I said angrily, "What did they want? And don't tell me you don't know."

"Not here. Let's go to my apartment."

When we got to the street, he raised his arm and a black car with tinted windows materialized. This was the type of car I'd been seeing all over Long Island and now all the pieces were falling into place. I hadn't been imagining anything; I was being watched. Terrified, I began shaking. Daniel put his arm around me and I suddenly realized that his interest in me wasn't romantic at all. That's why he hadn't kissed me or even tried.

The driver nodded at Daniel, but they said nothing to each other. I refused to look at Daniel and stared out the window feeling so deceived.

Once we were safely inside the Dakota, I collapsed on the sofa. He was watching me and I waited for him to speak.

The silence was killing me. I demanded, "Are you going to tell me what's going on?"

Daniel kept looking at his cell as if he was reading something.

He finally put down his phone and faced me. "I'm sorry, but I can't tell you what's going on. Please trust me, you're safe. I won't let anything happen to you."

"What do you mean you can't tell me?" I said loudly, wondering if his uncle was around.

"I can't talk about it. It's classified," he answered, as if that should end my questions.

I wanted to scream at him, but decided that before I antagonized him I had to get some information. "You work for the NSA and you're spying on my family?" I asked acting composed, but inside I was enraged.

After a long pause, he admitted, "Yes. I'm protecting you."

"What do I need protecting from?"

"It's classified," he repeated and kept staring at his cell.

"From our first meeting in Central Park, you've been watching me?"

"Yes," he admitted reluctantly.

I couldn't believe it. I never needed to search for Daniel. He'd been following me all along. I felt like such a fool! "Did you delete your photo from our computers?"

"Yes, there can't be pictures of me."

What did that mean? Suddenly, I thought of Pierce being in Cutchogue. "Has Pierce been watching me too?" I asked. Daniel nodded. I suddenly remembered my sightings of Daniel out there. "Have you been on Long Island?" Again, he nodded.

"Oh, my God, I wasn't crazy," I exclaimed, but I felt crushed. "You've been using me." It was one thing to think it, but completely different to have it confirmed. I wasn't able to hold my emotions in check any longer. "You've been pretending to like me. How dare you?"

"It hasn't been all work. I do like you and that's been a problem."

Temporarily, I was on cloud nine because he admitted that he liked me, but none of this made sense. The NSA has nineteen-year-old spies. "How old are you?" I demanded angrily.

"I told you. I'm nineteen," Daniel said.

All of this must have something to do with my dad. "Is this about my Dad or his firm? Does my dad have something they want and they want to use me to get it? Were they planning to kidnap me?"

"No, that's not what's going on here. We've already investigated your dad and he has nothing to do with this. We've narrowed down the threat to you."

"ME? What threat? What are you talking about?" This had to be some joke. "You're kidding right?"

"No, I'm quite serious. Something catastrophic will happen in the US and you're involved. Our job is to stop it." My head was spinning and I felt dizzy. People were after me and I was in danger.

"That was why you were in Chappaqua the night of the black out. Was that a real black out?"

Daniel nodded and said, "It was. We were concerned that it wasn't. That's why I stayed with you until Lily's parents came home." Again, he reminded me that I was his job.

"Where were you?"

"The parking lot of the swim club, behind Lily's house," he

admitted.

"I saw a car out there during the storm. What do these people want from me?"

"We're not sure yet, but they think you have whatever they need."

"I don't have anything!"

Daniel said nothing.

"Who are they?" I asked.

"We'll know soon."

Daniel's cell rang and he went out of the room to take the call. I texted Mom and told her I was running an errand. I stared at my cell and realized that my parents could be in danger. Daniel walked back in just as I started to panic. "I need to go home and warn my parents."

He knelt in front of me and took my hands. "You can't tell them. I won't let anything happen to any of you. Please don't say anything to anyone, not even Lily. It would change things."

"What do you mean? Change what?" I asked confused. "You're not making any sense."

Daniel got flustered and stood up. "That's all I can say. Just know that you're all safe."

Even though I didn't want to, I did trust him. "I won't say anything, but if anyone gets hurt, the deal is off. As far as Lily's concerned, I'm not promising anything."

"If you tell her, just tell me, so that we're not surprised and can protect her if need be."

"Are you telling me that she could be in danger too?" I shrieked.

"Yes, it's actually best that you don't say anything. We're..." Daniel said and his cell beeped. "Excuse me, let me check this. We need to know who those men in the park were."

"One of those men, I've seen a few times now."

Daniel put his cell down and was surprised. "Where?"

"Once across the street from my building, at the block party and today in the park."

"The agents said they've never seen them before."

"How is that possible? You're following me. Wouldn't you see somebody else that was following me? You were even with me at the block party."

"I was a little preoccupied with all your friends and we presumed you were safe since I was with you. We'll check satellite footage and the camera surveillance."

As Daniel talked to his uncle, I closed my eyes and rubbed them, trying to give myself time to think.

Daniel finished his call and I asked, "Were the things you told me about yourself true?"

"Mostly."

"Mostly?" I was annoyed at that statement. "Is this your uncle's apartment or did you rent it for your job?" I asked looking around the room.

"This is my apartment. My uncle is staying with me." Daniel watched my reaction.

"You have a home in London and an apartment in New York!"

"Yes, both properties were left to me."

"You can stay in New York? You don't have to leave?"

He shrugged. I was hurt, but did I have a right to be? He worked for the government and this was his job. I'd fallen for a spy and he'd be leaving when the job was done. My hard, angry exterior totally crumbled and I began to cry. I didn't care that he saw a blubbering idiot since it didn't matter in the scheme of things.

Daniel looked uneasy, but put his arms around me. I leaned my head on his chest and sobbed.

"Nothing or no one will hurt you," he said softly, trying to comfort me. His voice was so soothing that I was afraid to move and lose the closeness with him. His phone rang and he released one arm, but kept holding me with the other. After hanging up, he said that the agency was tailing the men and that they were ex-French Secret Service agents.

"My dad's working on a French case right now. Maybe this does involve him."

"Yes, in part it does, but the crucial part will not …I mean doesn't," he stated.

"Why do you keep saying will?"

"Just trust me. I've already said too much. Just know that the NSA is protecting you."

"When I googled the agency, it said the NSA doesn't follow people around."

"We're a division of the NSA and our rules are different."

"What division?" I stared at him, surprised that he actually admitted anything.

Daniel quickly closed up and answered dismissively, "It's classified."

"Even the name? Give me a break?" I snickered and turned away from him. I was sick of this.

Seeing my frustration, he relented. "The division is called EMIT. There is no record of it and it doesn't exist. Understand?"

I nodded my head and I thought of my phone. "My cell phone has been acting weird. Are you guys responsible for that?"

Daniel nodded and said, "Yes, I'm sorry but you'll continue having problems with it."

"Even if I get another one, I'll have the same problems?"

Daniel nodded.

"But why? I don't understand!"

"We put a tracking device in it and it causes some problems with older cell phones. They're working on correcting it."

"It's not old. I just got it four months ago. It's the latest iPhone," I whined. "Besides, my cell has a GPS so why do I need a tracker?"

Daniel ignored my comment and went back to staring at his cell.

"Damn, our team lost those men!"

I had enough and told Daniel that I wanted to go home, where I felt safe.

The walk home was totally silent. Daniel kept looking at me, but said nothing.

At my building, I saw Dad getting out of a cab and when he spotted us, he waited. I had to introduce Daniel.

"Dad, this is Daniel Haydin. Daniel, this is my dad, Oliver Devon."

They exchanged pleasantries and Dad invited Daniel to come inside. He accepted. What was he doing? At the same time, his job was to watch me. No point in skulking around corners.

When we walked into the foyer, Mom was surprised to see Daniel and her look said it all, 'So this was your errand?'

She invited Daniel to stay for dinner and we actually had a great time. The only awkward moment came when she asked him where his parents lived. After hearing that they were no longer alive, she looked at me like she was going to kill me for not telling her.

Daniel and Dad talked about England and Daniel's boarding school. History and world affairs were Dad's favorite subjects and it seemed like Daniel knew everything about everything. They talked about all the anti-American sentiment in the Mideast.

I said, "Since 9/11, things keep getting worse, especially since that crazy movie came out."

Daniel agreed, "It's definitely a big problem."

"American culture is viewed as immoral in those parts of the world," Mom added.

"Our views are diametrically opposite of theirs. Islamic fanatics believe that all the wrongs in the world are an American depravity issue. As long as they continue to teach that to the youth, they'll continue breeding terrorists," said Daniel.

"Well, honestly, it must be hard for the people there to believe in America's good motives when they are always being bombed," I said.

"Mahatma Gandhi says, 'I object to violence because when it appears to do good, the good is only temporary; the evil it does is permanent.' The problem is that sometimes there is no other option," Daniel insisted.

They discussed the turmoil in the Middle East, the Taliban, the oil situation, the Israeli-Palestinian conflict, North Korea and the economic meltdown.

Dad was impressed by Daniel's knowledge and said, "Daniel, you're so knowledgeable about the Mid-East." I realized how uninformed I was.

"I studied the Middle East at school, the history, religion and all the conflicts in that region. I found it fascinating."

When they started talking about English football, I realized that Dad and Daniel had a lot in common. They were engrossed talking about the Chelsea, Fulham and Arsenal teams.

Daniel's cell rang and he walked into the living room. I overheard him say that he was at our house for dinner and would be home soon. Why didn't his uncle know where he was, if I was being followed? Or did his uncle call to tell him to leave?

Daniel told us that he had to go. Well, that answered my question. I walked him to the door and he whispered, "Stay strong."

When I went back to the kitchen, I waited for the comments to begin.

"I liked him. He's very bright," Dad said.

"He's mature for his age, which is surprising," Mom said.

"What do you mean by that?" I asked suspiciously.

"That someone that smart would be taking so much time off from school. He seems to need guidance. If his parents were around, he'd be in college." If Mom knew what Daniel really did, she'd be crazed.

"It's tough for a child to lose his parents. I'm sure he'll get his act together," Dad said.

"His parents left him a trust fund and he can do whatever he wants," I said and left the room. I couldn't take it anymore.

I sat on my bed and called Lily. I didn't say anything about what happened in the park. We never kept secrets from each other, but now I was trying to keep us both safe. I wondered why Daniel felt so confident that all would be well. How could he know for sure?

I wrote everything down in my journal in great detail so I wouldn't forget what happened in the park. Someday, I might actually need to tell the authorities if something horrible ever happens. I made a copy of the Eiffel Tower photo and placed it in the journal just in case something happened to the one in my purse.

Again, I woke up from another nightmare. The dream must have been a byproduct of the day's events. Two faceless men chased me and cornered me in an alley. Hoping it was a robbery; I threw my handbag and begged them to take it. They laughed and I felt hands covering my mouth making it impossible to scream. Panic seized my body and I woke up.

I was unable to go back to sleep. I could've been killed today. I knew that I should tell my parents about Daniel, but I was afraid to. Every cell in my body was telling me not to endanger them. My parents always told me never to listen if someone told me to keep a secret from them. Yet, here I was doing just that.

Suddenly, I remembered that I never gave Dad the file from the office. Is that what those guys were after? I tiptoed downstairs and found the shopping bag in the den.

I took the file upstairs and found a sealed envelope lying inside. I was afraid to open it so I placed the envelope inside a book on my nightstand. I hoped that Dad didn't need it. If he didn't ask for it then it wasn't for him.

I really needed to find out what was going on. Maybe Sonia was involved in this? She gave me the file and she was out sick on Tuesday. This had to involve Dad's office. I didn't care what Daniel thought. He had to be wrong. I went downstairs for water and left the file on the table in the foyer.

I tossed and turned all night and started thinking crazy thoughts about Daniel. Was he the bad guy? The darkness was making me delusional because I trusted Daniel. The next time I saw him, I would give him the envelope. He'd know what to do with it.

8. SURVEILLANCE

"The important thing is not to stop questioning. Curiosity has its
own reason for existing." Einstein

When I woke up, I began freaking out about those men in the
park. I didn't want to leave the apartment. Were they after that
envelope in the file? Or me?

Dad and I we walked to work together and I was on pins and
needles the whole way there. At work, everything seemed normal,
but Sonia was out sick again. She looked perfectly healthy the day
before and I wondered if she was involved in this horror.

After work, Lily met me in the lobby and we walked home. I
couldn't concentrate on what Lily was saying because I was
nervously looking around. At least, I knew that the agents were
following us and was relieved about that. Please keep us safe, I
prayed to God. Lily sensed that something was wrong because I
wasn't responding to her questions.

Lily asked, "Are you all right? You're acting weird."

"I'm fine," I lied.

"I know something's wrong," Lily said angrily. I had to tell her something.

"I'm just worried about Daniel. I like him, but I have a feeling that he's leaving soon."

Then a crazy thought occurred to me. If they were all looking for that envelope in the file and I never gave it to Daniel then he'd have to stay and protect me.

What a great idea!

On second thought, that was a stupid idea. I wanted him to stay for me, not to just protect me.

"What makes you think he's leaving?" she asked.

"I just get this feeling," I confided truthfully. Daniel would leave when this case was finished. I knew that. "He does have a home in London."

"If he goes there, you'll still get to see him since you're always visiting your grandparents in London," she added, trying to lift my spirits.

"I guess but..." I stopped talking when I remembered I was being followed. I didn't want them to hear me. "I just don't want to talk about this anymore. It's too depressing."

Lily was getting tired of my sulking. "Cheer up, please. He's not gone yet, so be happy while he's here. Have you heard from him about tomorrow night?" Lily asked.

"No, I'm not even sure if that's still on." Things had changed drastically since he asked me.

"Well, if you're not, we'll go to the movies ourselves," Lily said and that comment made me feel worse. Lily started telling me about some boy named Zach that had asked her out. Lily's story kept my mind off Daniel.

"I guess you forgot all about Chad?"

"I like Chad, but it's difficult. He's a GUD, geographically undesirable?"

"I thought you said an hour wasn't that bad."

"It's far," Lily said sadly.

Back at the apartment, we went to my bedroom. We jumped on the bed and my cell rang. It was Daniel.

"Hi, just checking on you. Are you feeling better?"

"Yes, I feel great! And you, what are you doing?" I asked sarcastically.

"Not much. The usual," he answered, sounding frustrated by my tone.

"Are we still doing something tomorrow?" I asked, tired of Daniel calling all the shots.

"If you still want to," he answered.

"Yes, I do, but I just want to talk. I don't want to go to the movies."

"There's not much more I can tell you. If you don't want to see a movie, we can do something else. How about Shakespeare in the Park?"

"It's really hard to get tickets. You have to wait on line for hours," I said testily.

"I'll see what I can do. Is Lily coming?"

"No, Lily's not coming," I said impatiently and ended the call. It annoyed me that he knew she was over. I wish they'd stop spying on me.

Lily was staring at me like I had two heads. "What was that all about? You sounded so annoyed. Why don't you want to do anything?" Lily asked pointedly.

"I really don't know him well and if he's leaving soon why waste time watching a movie?"

"How did he know I was here?"

"Oh, I told him yesterday," I lied and dragged Lily downstairs to get some food.

We stayed in and watched movies all night. It was so nice having Lily over even if I wasn't being honest with her.

***

After breakfast, we went for a long walk in Central Park with Amber. Talking all the way, we discovered that we were right by the Swedish Cottage Marionette Theatre. We looked at each other and started laughing thinking.

One summer, Nana gave me a marionette and I became obsessed with being a puppeteer, so on my ninth birthday, Mom had my party at the theatre, which included a marionette show. Mom made me invite the whole class saying it wasn't nice to leave anybody out. Vanessa, who was so mean to me in school, actually showed up. After cluing Lily in about Vanessa, we stayed clear of her. The show started and we heard a commotion. Vanessa was hysterically crying. Her mom hadn't left yet and she took Vanessa out. In school the next day, I found out that she was terrified of the marionettes and now whenever Lily and I see the Cottage we think of her.

Maybe that was another reason Carla hated me. Once on Facebook, someone put up a question asking everyone to post things we were afraid of and someone mentioned Vanessa's fear of marionettes. She wasn't afraid anymore, but the joking still hadn't stopped.

Later that week, someone left a marionette in front of her locker and Carla told everybody that I did it. Even after Evan said he knew who did it and it wasn't me, Carla and Vanessa didn't believe him.

I gave up defending myself. My friends knew it wasn't true.

Walking back, Lily's cell rang and after finishing the call, she told me that there was a change in plans for the evening. Noelle and her mom were coming into the city to see a Broadway show. Noelle's dad was sick, so they had an extra ticket and since I was busy anyway, Lily said yes to their invitation. They were picking her up for dinner and then Lily would go with home them to Chappaqua since she had a birthday party on Sunday.

Daniel called and said he got the Shakespeare tickets. What was I thinking? Of course, he was able to get tickets, if anyone could, it would be him. I didn't want to see the play, but he sounded so pleased with himself that I didn't say anything. Maybe the play wasn't such a bad idea - after all, it was a beautiful night.

"Can we grab a bite to eat after the play? I have something to do before."

"Okay." He'd have to talk then.

After Mom and Dad left for the wedding, we took Amber for a quick walk. When we got back, Noelle's mom was parked at a fire hydrant waiting, so Lily ran in and got her bags.

I grabbed an apple and had some time before I had to get dressed, so I went to my room and jumped on my bed. While listening to music, I stared at my photo wall and noticed the photo of the statue of Benvenuto Cellini on the Ponte Vecchio Bridge in Florence. Along the railing surrounding the statue, couples would lock a padlock and then throw the key into the river to profess their undying love for each other. Back then I thought it was silly, but I was also eight years old. Now, it seemed very romantic.

I noticed the photo of me scowling in front of the Statue of David to the right of the Ponte Vecchio photo. Thinking about that trip made me laugh. Visiting museums started at an early age for me but the first visits weren't pleasant ones. After some meltdowns in a couple of London museums when I was young, my parents decided to spare the general public from my outbursts by leaving me with my grandparents on all their museum outings. However, that all changed on Dad's business trip to Florence. They decided that I was old enough to behave properly, but I think it had more to do that they had no babysitter. The first day, Dad had meetings, so Mom and I wandered around the city. I loved the Piazza della Signoria, a large plaza with a lot of animal statues. The Fountain of Neptune and an equestrian statue were my favorites.

That evening for dinner, we returned to the plaza and afterwards strolled around eating gelato. Dad stopped in front of a statue and said it was called "David" but that this one was a reproduction. The real statue had been moved indoors to protect it from the elements. When he said we had plans to see the original "David" by Michelangelo at the Academy Gallery the next day, I said I wasn't going. I didn't need to see another David, that this one was enough. Besides, it was just a statue of a naked man, nothing interesting. Glancing at each other, my parents ignored my outburst and I thought that since the conversation was over, I had won.

In the morning, as I was being roused, I realized I was very wrong. I buried my face into my pillow to escape the light as my mother drew the curtains open.

"I don't want to see any more old stuff," I cried.

Dad tried reasoning with me and explained that I could sleep anytime, but when would I visit Florence again. Honestly, I didn't care, but I got up when I saw how angry he was getting. At the gallery, I moped and sulked the entire time. Mom took some great pictures of me scowling by the David statue.

Now as I looked at the photo, something in the background caught my eye, so I rose from the bed to get a better look. I had to be imagining things, I thought as I approached. I leaned in closer and couldn't believe what I was seeing. I yanked the photo off the wall and knocked over the porcelain lamp. It crashed on the floor.

"Oh my God!" I screamed. This was impossible. Shock, disbelief, anger swirled in my head and tears welled up in my eyes.

Almost instantly my cell rang. I stared at the photo again thinking my eyes must be playing tricks on me. Nothing had changed. It was still the same image. Glancing at my cell, I saw that it was Daniel.

I answered and said, "Yes?"

"Are you okay?" he sounded alarmed. "What happened?"

It then hit me; he'd **HEARD** the crash. "Do you have my room bugged?" I shrieked.

There was a long pause and he answered, "Yes."

"My whole house is bugged? Every room?" I yelled. My mind was reeling from the knowledge that he'd been hearing **EVERYTHING**. I was so embarrassed about all the things I'd said about him.

"Yes, but not the bathrooms."

"How nice of you," I seethed through clenched teeth.

"Let me explain," Daniel said beseechingly.

"You've heard all my conversations with people on the phone and in person. What's to explain? That pretty much sums it up."

"Yes, but..." he tried to say something.

I didn't want to hear it. I interrupted him. "Are my computers bugged?"

"Yes."

"Have you bugged my cell too? It's not a tracking device, is it?"

"It's both," Daniel admitted. "Please ..."

"How dare you? Is this some sick joke?" I yelled. "Are you having fun tormenting me?"

"Of course not, it's not like that. I'm trying to keep you safe. We all are. That's the only reason for all of this."

"Well, I'm sure you've had some good laughs at my expense," I yelled.

"I didn't laugh at anything you said."

"I can't believe that I trusted you. I'm such an idiot."

"Please don't say that."

Was he kidding? I wanted answers and that's all that mattered right now. "Please come over." What was I saying? I didn't want him in my apartment. "No, wait. I'll meet you in the lobby." I felt angry and betrayed.

"I'm presuming that you don't want to go to the play?" Was he kidding? He just told me that he'd been bugging me and he thought I would sit and watch a play with him.

"No, I don't want to see a play," I screamed into the phone.

"I'll be outside in ten minutes," Daniel said.

I didn't know what to make of the photo and I wanted an explanation or I had to tell somebody. Who should I tell? All of this seemed so crazy! First, I was almost attacked by goons in the park; now, I learned that besides being under constant surveillance, my home computers and cell were bugged. Dad said that the NSA had gotten into trouble for doing something like this before. Even if I told somebody, nobody knew about EMIT. Who would believe me? One thing I knew, my parents and Lily would.

When I reached the lobby, thinking that I'd have to wait, Daniel was already standing there. He must've been outside in a car spying on me and that's why he couldn't have dinner before. Carl was helping a tenant outside with their luggage, so Daniel and I had a few moments to talk.

"What's wrong?" he asked and seemed upset, but that no longer mattered.

"Are you kidding? I just found out you're bugging my apartment. How dare you ask me what's wrong?" My voice got noticeably shriller by the time I finished.

"It's for you safety, while we figure out how to keep these guys from getting to you again," Daniel said presciently.

"Did you say again? They're coming after me again?"

"Yes."

"How do you know that?"

"We know."

"How? Oh, it's classified!" I said snidely. I stood there feeling trapped in some sick prank.

"Please tell me, what's going on!" I begged.

"I can't say anything more than what I've already told you. I won't let anything happen to you." Then he looked at me and asked, "Why did you scream?"

"Why did I scream?" I was still trying to comprehend what Daniel had said about those goons coming after me again. His question jogged my memory and I motioned for him to follow me outside since Carl was returning.

As we walked towards the park, I turned and handed him the photo and asked, "Explain this to me. You must be at least twenty-seven years old now if you were nineteen when this picture was taken. You look exactly the same as you do today. I was eight in this picture."

He stared at the photo, his face went white and he looked visibly stunned. After a few moments, he said, "Can we go to my apartment, so I can talk to you? I can't have this conversation in the street."

"I'm not going anywhere with you? How old are you?" I grabbed the photo from him and stuck it in my jeans in case he tried to destroy it like Lily's photo.

Daniel answered slowly, "I'm nineteen."

"How old are you in this photo?"

"I'm sorry, but that's classified." Daniel glanced sideways and I noticed one of those cars parked across the street.

"I'm sorry. I can't do this," I said loudly, but lowered my voice when people passing stared. "You are clearly lying to me."

Daniel tried to speak, but I turned and walked quickly away from him.

He called out, "I'm not lying to you."

I stopped and waited for him to catch up. "Then how old were you in this picture?"

Daniel looked away. "I can't say."

I wanted to scream. "Well, don't call me until you can." Daniel grabbed my arm as I turned, but I shook free. "Please, just leave me alone."

He followed me to my building. I went upstairs and didn't know what to do. Should I tell my parents? I really did trust Daniel, in theory, but I knew something strange was going on. How could he look exactly the same as he had nine years ago? I stared at the picture. If he was nineteen now, he would have been ten years old then.

My head was spinning and I didn't know what to do. This was impossible, yet somehow I believed Daniel or wanted to. Did he have an older brother he never told me about? I never asked if he was an only child. My phone rang. It was Lily but I didn't want to talk, so I ignored her call. Then Daniel called, but I didn't answer his call either.

I took Amber for a fast walk in front of the building, knowing that the doorman would see if anything happened and then ran quickly inside to get away from all the craziness. My heart was breaking and I began to sob. Suddenly, I realized my room was bugged and I had no privacy. I needed some noise, so I turned up the volume on my radio and filled my pillow with tears.

***

I found a note in the kitchen from my parents saying that they'd gone for a walk with Amber.

There were fresh bagels on the counter so I took a cinnamon raisin one out of the bag. On my way to the refrigerator, the house phone rang. Who keeps calling?

I answered and heard a French sounding male voice, but there was static on the line.

"I'm sorry. What did you say?" I asked, hoping this was a call for dad.

"Meet me in the lobby in five minutes. Bring the envelope and no one will get hurt, girlie."

I slammed the phone down. I reached for my cell to call Daniel. It didn't matter that he lied; I still thought he was inherently good. As I fumbled for my cell inside my jean pocket, it started ringing and it was Daniel.

"We heard everything. Do you know what envelope he's asking for?"

Hearing his voice made me question my decision to tell him anything. He'd been lying to me and I really didn't know what to do anymore. "No," I lied.

"Listen, I'll be in the lobby. Go find out what he wants," he instructed.

They wanted me, a seventeen year-old girl, to meet some goon. Were they crazy? Who were the good guys and who were the bad guys? Maybe I should call the FBI or the CIA. I was in such turmoil and my head was spinning.

"I'm not going anywhere," I answered, slowly recovering from the frightening call. "You go and meet him and arrest him. Then, you can find out everything you need."

"We can't. We need you to do it."

"Are you crazy?" I screeched.

"I won't let anything happen to you. I promise. You're safe, and you're going to be safe," Daniel said, trying to reassure me.

"How do you know that? Are you God? No one can say that. You never know what can go wrong. I don't want to be involved in this. Please stop bothering me," I snapped.

"These people are looking for something and you're the key."

"I'm not doing anything until you tell me the truth because I don't trust you." I hung up. Ten minutes later my house phone rang and when the machine answered it was a hang up. That continued until my parents got home and then it stopped. All those previous hang-ups were for me I realized. These people were watching me and knew when I was home alone since the landline only rang when I was by myself.

Daniel didn't call back and I was miserable. I had hoped that he would keep trying, but the faster I accepted that I was just a job, the faster my broken heart would heal.

I overheard Mom talking about dinner and had totally forgotten it was Dad's birthday.

"Dad, I'm so sorry… Happy Birthday." Giving him a hug, I ran upstairs to get his gift.

After he opened it, he seemed really impressed and said he had planned on buying the book this week.

While I sat on the couch, I started feeling really queasy. I put my head on a pillow and closed my eyes. Mom asked if I was okay.

"I'm just tired." I really wanted to say I was feeling sick, but I didn't want Martin to cancel dinner. Anna had just gotten better from some bug.

I went to my room and wondered what to do. Nothing made any sense. When I heard the doorbell, I ran downstairs and saw Anna burst out in laughter as Mom tickled her. She handed her to me when the oven timer went off.

We sat in the dining room, my favorite room in the apartment. There was a beautiful mural painted on wallpaper affixed to the walls. Mom said she wanted to take the mural with us if we ever moved. Flowering trees adorned the corners and the limbs reached out with leaves and flowers, which extended across the four walls. Painted in pale hues, the effect was very romantic and dreamy. The curtains were a pale grey dupioni silk. Mom found the antique crystal chandelier in a Parisian antique store and had it shipped home.

Right after cake, they left. Martin carried a sleeping Anna in his arms.

Dad looked at his watch and said there was time to catch a foreign film that he wanted to see. I didn't want to go and shortly after they left, the phone started ringing. I silenced the ringer and crawled into bed. I just wanted to hide.

Lily called and I knew I had to talk to her so I answered the cell.

"You're not returning my calls. What's going on?" she asked.

"I'm sorry. I'm just frustrated about Daniel and..." I suddenly remembered they were listening. My God, I kept forgetting the whole house was bugged.

"And what?" Lily asked. "How was your date? Did you go to Shakespeare in the Park?"

"No we didn't go."

"Why? What happened?"

"Nothing happened. He's been playing games and I don't like him."

"What are you talking about?" Lily asked totally confused.

"He's been lying to me and I don't trust him," I ranted so that all the listeners heard.

Lily was so confused. "I'm coming over tomorrow night and I want the whole story."

Part of me was hoping that Daniel would call and tell me I was wrong, but there was no phone call. I just didn't know what to do or think anymore. Nothing was the same. Everything had changed; my life was now not my own. Everything that I held absolute was slowly being undermined: my privacy, my decisions, my views and most importantly my word. I wasn't being truthful with anyone now, not my parents, not Lily and not even with Daniel.

I glanced around my room and decided to search for the bug. An hour passed and I had no idea where it could be. As I eyed the computer suspiciously, I realized the NSA's expertise was in computers so perhaps it was hidden in there. Since I had no idea how to find and remove it, destroying the computer was the only solution. I couldn't believe that I was standing there actually contemplating ruining my computer. I'm going insane. When I glanced at my laptop, I realized that it was probably bugged, too.

Feeling defeated, I gave up and decided to go online and see what I'd been missing with my friends. I couldn't deal with any more of this garbage. Everyone was having a great summer except me.

Looking at my emails, there was one from Eden. She was throwing a party and since I hadn't RSVP'd to the first invitation, she sent me a second invite.

I got my cell and called her. "Eden, it's Paige. I'm sorry. I never got the invitation."

"That's weird. I also left you two voice mails and you never called me back. I thought you were mad at me. I was going to call Daphne and Grace and ask them what was up."

How many messages or emails had I missed because of their surveillance equipment? Didn't it defeat the whole purpose? Or were they listening to my messages and because of that they got deleted?

"Can I bring Lily?"

"Sure, that'll be fine."

I needed to get out and be with people. If Daniel didn't care about me, what was the point of moping? He never told me he cared; only that he was keeping me safe.

I still needed to figure out what to do with the envelope though.

It obviously wasn't for Dad since he hadn't mentioned that something was missing. Then again why would he tell me? He'd tell Sonia. I sat on the floor and used a letter opener. If it was something important, I'd didn't want to destroy it. Inside, I found a folded piece of paper and on it there were a bunch of handwritten numbers. I hid the envelope under my mattress.

Reaching for my journal, I wrote what happened the last few days. I made a copy of the Statue of David photo and placed it inside the journal. Now I had two photos of Daniel from my past. I hid the journal in the bottom of my closet.

***

I opened my eyes and it was morning, the thought of leaving the apartment scared me to death. When I got downstairs and Mom told me that Dad had already left, I told her I felt really sick. There was no way I was going to work alone. I called Maria and left her a message.

Mom wasn't sure it was a good idea for Lily to stay over, but I said that I was just under the weather and didn't have a fever. Mom looked at me like she knew I was up to something.

"Lily can come over, but if you're still sick tomorrow, I'll babysit Anna," she offered.

"I'm fine," I kept repeating.

Mom looked at me suspiciously. "I just walked Amber, so you don't have to go out. I have to go. I'll come for lunch and check up on you."

Shortly after she left, the house phone began ringing. I was relieved that they didn't have my cell number. Daniel said I was safe, but how did he know that? Was I just making the situation worse by not giving Daniel the envelope? If I did, he might leave and I didn't want that either.

Mom came home and I saw from her expression that she was worried about me. She took Amber out for a walk. When she got back, she made me a turkey sandwich.

As I ate, she asked, "What's going on? You seem off somehow and I don't mean ill. Is this about Daniel? You haven't mentioned him recently."

"Daniel and I aren't seeing each other anymore, so you should be happy."

"I'm sorry. My only concern about him was that we didn't know anything about him."

"Give me a break. He's nineteen. What else is there to know about him? I think we know enough. He went to boarding school, his parents are dead, he has a trust fund, and his uncle has an apartment in the Dakota. You make it seem like he's a criminal. It's so crazy!"

"You have a point. What happened with you and Daniel?"

I had to tell her something so that she'd stop talking about him.

"He doesn't like me and I don't like him either." Humiliated enough over everything that the agents and Daniel had heard, I wasn't going to let them think that I was home pining away for him. Why give those agents anything else to laugh about?

I talked Mom into letting us go to Eden's party, saying that I felt fine and really needed to get out. She said yes without arguing and probably thought Daniel was the cause of my sudden illness.

Lily came over after work and as I dressed, she peppered me

with questions. Thinking about my predicament was one thing, trying to explain it was quite another.

"I'll tell you everything when we get back from the party. I really want to go have fun and not think about Daniel right now."

"Fine, but I want the whole story later."

I had every intention of telling her, but now I was waffling again. What was wrong with me?

The party was at Eden's apartment on 78th Street and Riverside Drive.

"Call us when it's over. We'll walk over with Amber and get you," she offered because at night it's pretty desolate around there.

"Don't worry. I'll get someone to walk us or I'll get a cab." If she only knew that I was totally safe since I had protection from the NSA 24/7.

On our way over, Lily told me that she'd been talking to Chad a lot and wondered if he'd be at the party. I said I only knew that Daphne and Grace would be there and she was disappointed.

When we arrived, we found that the party was on the roof of Eden's building. It was a Hawaiian-themed luau and Deidre placed leis around our necks as we walked through the door. I looked at the Hudson River and saw boats bobbing up and down at the Boat Basin. The music blared from an iPod and there were about thirty kids there already.

I spotted Eden and we walked over.

"Hi, cool party."

"Thanks. It's really a going away party," she said. When she saw my confused expression, she added, "I'm moving. My dad got transferred to California."

"I'd love to move to California," said Lily. "Where in California?

"Pacific Palisades," she answered and made a face.

I was so surprised. "I'll miss you. Why didn't you tell me?"

"I was going to that time I was coming to your house, but I got upset and canceled. Every time I talk about it, I cry. I don't want to move, but I have no choice. Soooooo." She raised her hands in the air. "I figured I'd throw a party."

"When are you leaving? Can we get together before you go?"

"Sure, I'll be here until the end of August. My mom's going out next week to go house hunting, but I'm not leaving until I'm forced to," she said and I saw her eyes glisten.

I hugged her and said, "I'm so sorry. Would your parents let you stay and finish the senior year? Maybe at my house if my parents said yes."

"I already asked them that and they said absolutely not."

"Sorry, Eden," said Lily.

Paul sidled over and asked Eden to dance. What was Paul going to do without her? They had been inseparable. Eden's parents had always complained about the amount of time that Paul and Eden spent together, so the move was probably a blessing for them.

I spotted Daphne and Grace dancing with some boys that I didn't know. They must've been Paul's friends from his school. Eden's parents and two couples were sitting at a table talking.

Lily brightened up when she saw Chad in the distance.

"Chad's here, I'm so happy,"

As we walked over, I noticed he was talking to Billy, Carla and Vanessa. Ugh! I forgot that Eden and Carla were friends.

Once when I asked Eden, "Why?" She said that Carla wasn't that bad and I dropped the discussion.

Our friendship was strained already at that point and I wasn't going to allow Carla to cause more friction.

I grabbed Lily's arm to stop her and said, "I'm not going over there."

Lily stopped dead in her tracks when she saw them. Deidre was walking by, so I asked how her summer was going.

"It's been great. I'm interning at a theatre company. It's so much fun," Deidre said. She was really involved in the drama department at school.

I saw Chad looking around and when he spotted us, he left the group and bee-lined right for Lily. I whispered, "Chad's coming."

"Hi! What a surprise! I thought Paige might be here, but I never expected to see you."

While they were deep in conversation, Billy suddenly appeared and joined my conversation with Deidre. When she saw four new people walk in, she left to give them leis.

Alone now, Billy whispered in my ear, "So, I heard you broke Reed's heart."

I must have turned purple from embarrassment. I nervously glanced around to see if Carla was nearby or if anyone heard him. Someone told him something, but Reed and I never dated, so it was ridiculous.

"No, I didn't," I quickly countered.

"Yes, you did," Billy said knowingly, amused by my discomfort.

"We're just friends," I said.

"Reed likes you, but he thinks you might be dating somebody." Billy watched for my reaction. Reed told Billy! How crazy?

Sighing, I said, "No, I'm not dating anyone." I felt depressed saying that, but it was true. Since Daniel didn't like me, I was definitely single. Billy seemed pleased by my answer and I really hoped that Daniel was wrong about Billy being an admirer. I wasn't in the mood for him, besides they were moving to California.

As we continued talking, Carla and Vanessa walked by and totally pretended that I didn't exist. They asked Billy where the restroom was and walked away cackling. I thought I heard them say "Bustedcup." That was only one of the derogatory versions of Buttercup that they had made up and they'd whisper them whenever they passed me.

Lily was talking to Chad all night and it seemed that whenever I turned around, Billy was always nearby. He was a great distraction and I forgot about the spy drama for a while.

Chad and Billy offered to walk us home at the end of the party, so I called Mom to tell her we were on our way home and had escorts.

When we exited the building, Carla and Vanessa were getting into a cab and seeing us called out, "Bye Billy, bye Chad."

Lily and I were invisible, which was actually a good thing.

Lily yelled out, "Bye girls!" Carla and Vanessa glared at her.

Chad looked at me and smiled like he knew why his brother's ex-girlfriend hated me. He copied Lily and said, "Bye girls." Lily laughed.

We started walking home and I wondered where the NSA agents were hiding. Had they eavesdropped on the party? What was the point in that? The goons weren't going to be there.

It started drizzling and Billy put his arm around me to keep me dry. It actually felt nice to have someone be that attentive. Billy said he was excited about the California move, but wouldn't get out there until Thanksgiving. He had job at a Wall Street firm this summer and then would go right to Boston University from here.

When we got to my building, Billy turned and looked at me, "You want to catch a movie one night?"

Why not? We could be friends. "Sure."

Billy smiled, "I'll call you tomorrow." He leaned forward and gave me a kiss right on my lips. It was a fast kiss and I was really taken by surprise.

In the elevator, Lily stared at me and said, "I saw Billy kiss you. What's going on?"

I shrugged. "I don't know. That kiss was weird. I just want to be friends."

In my bedroom, Lily sat on the bed and demanded that I finally tell her what was wrong. Now that it was time to talk, I worried about Lily's safety and changed my mind about divulging Daniel's spying activities. I told Lily to come in the bathroom while I washed my face. I didn't want them listening to my conversation and Daniel said the bathrooms weren't bugged.

Once inside, I told Lily that Daniel said he only wanted to be friends. After a litany of questions, Lily believed me and stopped nagging.

"You only want to be friends with Reed and Billy, so you should understand. I liked Daniel, but he seemed so old for his age," she said as an afterthought.

"He did," I agreed. Maybe that's because he probably isn't, I thought.

"Maybe it's because he lost his parents or having gone to boarding school," Lily suggested.

I shrugged and said in a British accent, "I don't know, but the British are very proper."

Lily laughed and then tried mimicking me but failed horribly. We jumped on my bed. I got on my computer to peek on Facebook and there was a friend request from Billy. I accepted and we lurked his wall and photos.

Lily said that she really liked Chad, but they lived so far apart. "I don't believe that saying, 'absence makes the heart grow fonder.' I think the 'out of sight, out of mind' statement makes more sense."

"I don't believe that. If it's meant to be, distance or time won't change true feelings. There are stories of people that fell in love at a young age, broke up, got back together later in life. They said that they hadn't stopped thinking of each other. I believe in true love."

"You're such a romantic. You've watched too many Disney shows," Lily said smirking.

9. ASSAULT

"Memory is deceptive because it is colored by today's events."
Einstein

Since I was babysitting for Martin tonight, I wasn't able to work, so Lily left alone.

Around lunchtime, Billy called and asked if I wanted to catch a movie the next night. Billy would be going back to college soon anyway, so what would be the harm? Even though his kiss worried me, I said, "Sure. Is Eden coming too?" Really hoping that she was joining us.

"She's busy. It's just you and me." It might have been a mistake to say yes.

Mom was working from home and I hid in my room to do some English homework. I read my last required John Keats poem called "This Living Hand."

> This living hand, now warm and capable
> Of earnest grasping, would, if it were cold

And in the icy silence of the tomb,
So haunt thy days and chill thy dreaming nights
That thou wouldst wish thine own heart dry of blood
So in my veins red life might stream again,
And thou be conscience-calmed--see here it is--
I hold it towards you.

I thought it was about Keats living on through his written word. It was very apropos that time was a dominant theme. To see death all around and be ill at a young age, Keats focused on life and immortality.

When it was time to head out to Martin's in New Jersey, I was relieved that the garage was in the basement of the building and that the elevator went straight there so that no one would see us leave. Getting out of the city and away from everything was exactly what I needed.

I looked around and didn't see any dark cars, but they heard where I was going, so I wasn't fooling anybody. If they followed me to Long Island, two hours away, they'd follow me over the George Washington Bridge to Martin's.

I was looking forward to playing with Anna. Many Saturday nights, I babysat Luke, a five year old, who lived down the hall. Lucia Vardin and John Costra were his parents. Luke had a full-time nanny during the week, but on weekends, I was one of the babysitters who filled in.

Lucia and Luke were spending the summer at their weekend place in Woodstock. I really missed them. Our floor had been quiet without Luke's lively outbursts and mad dashes to the elevator. He was absolutely adorable!

Lucia was a Panamanian-born singer/actress, with dark, long, curly hair and was very exotic looking. She dressed like a rock and roller most of the time. I loved her music and listened to her CD's almost daily.

Her band preformed all around the city and I saw many of her shows at Joe's Pub. She was vivacious and fun to be around. Many days, I would visit her and pour out my silly insecurities. She politely listened and encouraged me to look inward for the answers. Very spiritual, Lucia was into yoga and Buddhism. Incense burned in her apartment and once she dragged me to one of her yoga classes. I wondered if she would have liked Daniel.

I had bumped into John a few times in the lobby and he told me that Luke was having a great summer. John worked in the city during the week and went upstate on the weekends.

On the drive, I started to relax. Mom would drop me off and then drive Marina to the mid-town restaurant.

After a list of instructions, they left. Anna was cranky at the beginning, so I distracted her with a new toy that Mom had brought for her.

While I fed Anna dinner, she grabbed the spoon and tried to feed herself. The high chair got smeared and baby food was everywhere, even in her hair. The more I laughed, the bigger the mess she made. I reached for my cell and took photos as Anna scowled at the camera.

She desperately needed a bath, so I carried her at arms length out of the kitchen. She had so much fun splashing around with the toys, but when I noticed her wrinkled fingers, I pulled her out.

I put on her jammies and read her some books including my

favorite, "Goodnight Moon." I noticed that the pink dream catcher, a Native American object used to ward off bad dreams, I bought Anna was hanging on the doorknob.

When I was young, I had a lot of nightmares and when someone told Mom about dream catchers, she got me one.

Mom had made up a song and sang it to me every night while rubbing my back. Tonight, I sang the same song to Anna at least six times.

Bad dreams go away
Anna doesn't want any bad dreams today
Only happy happy dreams
Happy dreams today
Think of happy things, think of happy thoughts
Think of playing games, taking a bubble bath, reading books,
(Mom put in whatever I did that day)
And now it's time for bed
Now it's time for bed
My little munchkin head,
Mommy and Daddy and Aunt Paige love you so
and now it's time for bed

By eight-thirty, Anna was sound asleep. After cleaning the kitchen floor and the high chair, I called Lily and we talked about nothing. I glanced out the dining room window to discover that there was a dark car parked across the street. I set the house alarm, closed the blinds and sat on the couch watching TV. Around midnight, I heard Marina and Martin come in, I waved hello and without talking went to the guestroom to sleep.

***

In the morning, Marina offered to drive me home later if I

wanted to spend the day with them. Of course I did, anything to postpone going back and dealing with psychos.

We took Anna to the mall and wandered around the stores.

I saw Pierce casually strolling behind us. What a dull assignment it was watching me. I'm sure it was exactly what he thought he'd be doing when he signed up to be a spy. Follow a teenage girl around. *Ridiculous!*

After lunch, Marina drove me back and all the anxiety returned. I really wanted to go for a jog but I was too terrified. I spent the rest of the day playing games on the computer while watching a One Tree Hill marathon on the TV. I heard Mom come in and ran downstairs.

"Hi Sweetie, did you have fun with Anna?" she asked.

"Yeah, she was great. I have pictures on my cell that you have to see." I grabbed my phone.

Mom laughed. "She's quite the character."

"Oh, Mom, I'm going to the movies tonight with Billy, Eden's brother."

"Isn't Billy in college?" she asked sounding confused.

"Yes, he goes to Boston University."

"Okay, have fun." She knew the family, so she didn't overreact this time.

Dad was on the phone in the living room. When he hung up, he came into the kitchen and said, "Marina just told me a strange story. Her next-door neighbor said there was a suspicious car parked across the street all last night. When she called the police, they told her that a security team was guarding somebody." Turning to me, he asked, "Did you see anything?"

"I saw a car with dark windows," I answered truthfully.

My parents left for a charity auction and told me to walk Amber if I got home before them.

Billy wanted to see some action movie and I really didn't care. It actually was very exciting with all the explosions and speeding cars. I glanced around and spotted Pierce. Was he the only agent they had? At the same time, he was the only one I knew.

After the movie, Billy put his arm around me. I really didn't want him to, but I didn't know how to take it off. He talked about college all the way back to my building.

To get away from him, I used Amber as an excuse, but it backfired. He offered to walk her with me. If my parents were home, I wouldn't have to deal with Billy. I called and when there was no answer, Billy quickly added, "It's late. I'll go with you." I didn't know how to say no politely, so I said fine. When we got into the apartment, I needed to use the bathroom. Billy went and sat on the couch to wait and he tried to pet Amber, but she ran away.

When I returned, Billy was leaning on the couch with his eyes closed. It looked like he had fallen asleep, so I went over and shook him.

"Billy, wake up," I said totally annoyed. All I wanted to do was go to sleep. Billy's eyes opened and he grabbed me in a bear hug. He held me tightly and started kissing me.

"Please stop!" I said. Struggling from his grasp, I was getting really angry. "Billy, stop." Pushing him off wasn't working; he was too strong and I was getting nowhere.

"Paige, I really like you." He forced me down on the couch. His hands began roaming over my body and he groped me with one hand while he held me tightly with the other.

"What are you doing?" I screamed.

He kept trying to force his tongue in my mouth. Repulsed, I thrashed my head from side to side and held my lips firmly closed. "Billy, stop!" I screamed whenever I was able.

Momentarily, he stopped, but continued holding me down firmly and pleaded, "Come on, don't tease me. You're driving me crazy."

"Please stop," I begged.

His hand was sliding under my T-shirt and he unsnapped my bra. His hands were grabbing my breasts. Panic was setting in and I tried pushing his hand away. He reached for my jeans and was trying to pull the zipper down. I screamed and he covered my mouth with his hand.

Suddenly, there was loud banging on the door.

A voice called out, "Open up in there or I'm calling the police." It sounded like Daniel.

Billy got startled and he dropped his hold on me. I escaped and ran to the door.

Daniel was standing there looking furious. "Are you okay?" he asked, looking at my disheveled clothes. Embarrassed and ashamed, I couldn't speak and Daniel rushed in.

"Get out!" He stared at Billy. Billy didn't move. Daniel screamed, "Now."

"Hey, Buddy, calm down, everything's fine. We were just fooling around, that's all," he said smirking.

Fury flashed on Daniel's face and he stepped towards Billy with his fists clenched. It looked like he was going to punch him. "It's time you left, Buddy," Daniel hissed.

"No, it's time you left, Buddy," retorted Billy.

Daniel looked at me and asked angrily. "Would you like me to escort your date out or do you want him to stay?"

"Get him out of here," I pleaded and looked at Billy with disgust.

"Paige, I thought we were having fun." He actually looked confused.

"How dare you? You pig, I said no! If you don't leave right now, I will call the police," I screamed. I really wanted to hit him; I was so enraged and felt so violated. His hands had been all over my body and I was sickened at the thought.

"I thought you were playing hard to get."

"You're an idiot!" I screamed. "No means no, you jerk." He walked out the door without apologizing. I sat on the couch trembling.

Daniel stood there seething. "What are you trying to do? Are you trying to hurt yourself on purpose or is this just a maturity thing because I'm about to lose it!" he snapped.

"What are you talking about?" I couldn't breathe and my legs were shaking.

"Why did you invite him to your apartment?" Daniel implied lividly.

"Are you saying that I asked for this?" I was so mad that my voice cracked. Daniel just stared at me and didn't answer. Amber came out of the den and smelling Daniel she got all excited. I still had to walk her. Following me outside, we walked in silence. I couldn't wait to get back inside the apartment and forget this ever happened.

"How did you get by the doorman and get to me so fast?"

"We have an apartment in the building," he said, ignoring my gaze.

"You what...?" I screamed.

"We need to be close. Tonight, you were lucky that we were. A thank you would be nice," he answered angrily.

He was right. If he hadn't been here, I don't know what would've happened.

"Thank you, but please leave me alone. I can't take this anymore," I yelled and headed for the door that Max, the doorman, was holding open. He looked at me with concern, but said nothing. If Daniel lived in the building, what did the doormen think was going on? All six doormen were probably as confused as I was.

The elevator opened and when I didn't exit, Daniel put his arm around me and escorted me out. Taking my house keys out of my hand, he opened the door and led me to the couch.

Daniel put his arms around me and said, "I'm sorry I yelled at you. I know all of this has been a lot for you to deal with, but you have to be careful." It felt so good being in his arms. "I was so angry that I really wanted to hurt him." He looked at me with such concern that it was hard to believe that he didn't care.

"I can't do this anymore." I got up and faced him. "I know what they're looking for."

"You do? What is it?" Daniel asked looking really confused.

"I'll be right back." I went to my room and got the envelope.

This would all end tonight. I wanted my life back, even though I'd never see Daniel again. I thrust the envelope into his hand. "Here, I don't know what this is. It's just a bunch of numbers."

Daniel opened the envelope and looked at the sheet of paper. "I have to tell you something."

"I don't want to hear it. Do whatever you need with it. Just please, leave me alone." I ran upstairs and slammed my bedroom door. Tears streamed down my face and I was miserable knowing that I no longer had a hold on him. I washed my face, put on my pajamas and went downstairs to get some water. I jumped to find Daniel still in the living room petting Amber.

"Why are you still here?"

Daniel stood up and said, "We have to talk."

"I told you I'm done, so I don't want to know anything. I want my house debugged immediately or I'm telling my parents." No more nonsense. I tried moving around him to go in the kitchen, but he stood in front of the door. I had no choice, but to listen.

"Only you can take care of this issue with the envelope. It has to be you."

"What are you talking about? Only me what?" I asked puzzled by his words.

"You have to give it to them," he said.

"I'm getting out of here." I started walking back upstairs. *He was crazy!!*

Daniel rushed over. "Please! You have to listen."

I stopped, looked at him and said, "I don't know what you're talking about. I'm not doing anything. Take the info and give it to them yourselves."

Enough with this insanity; he had to leave. My parents couldn't find him here. I walked over and opened the front door, hoping he'd get the hint. I found his uncle glaring at me.

"Can I come in? Is everything all right?"

Why did he look so perplexed? Hadn't they been listening to my every word? "Sure. Maybe you can get Daniel out of here," I said, as Daniel defiantly sat back down.

James shut the door and walked over to Daniel. "What's going on? Is this about the fellow that you threw out?"

"No. Paige found the info we need."

"That's great news," said James.

"Paige refuses to be involved anymore. I've been trying to reason with her."

I stood in the foyer wishing they'd both leave.

"I see." James sat down and Daniel handed him the envelope. He took a photo with his cell and handed the envelope back to Daniel. Looking at me reproachfully, he started talking to me like I was an annoying nuisance. "Paige, what Daniel said is true. Only you can take care of this, otherwise the outcome isn't assured."

"Assured? You're not making any sense," I shrieked, frustrated beyond belief. I sat down in the armchair across from them.

"We are trying to stop something that will happen in the future."

"The future? Is this some joke?"

"That's all I can say, but only you can handle this. Please just go about doing what you normally would and we'll be there if and when you need us. We are entrusting you with this information for the safety and security of the United States."

His cell rang and after hanging up he said, "We need to go. Paige's parents just entered the building."

They got up and started to leave. "I'll call you later. Please don't worry. I won't let anything happen to you, I promise," Daniel said and handed me the envelope. I don't know why I took it. I should've flung it out the door behind them, but I was too emotionally drained by that point and just stood there like a zombie.

After turning off the lights, I locked the door and raced upstairs. I didn't want my parents to see my red eyes. My cell rang and it was Daniel. I picked up, "Yes. What else do I need to do? Arrest them for you, too?" I asked sarcastically.

Daniel ignored my comment and said, "I'm sorry that I've caused you so many problems. I'm not supposed to get personally involved, but I figured that if I got to know you I could help you figure this out. I'm sorry if you got the wrong impression."

"What do you mean wrong impression?" I asked suspiciously.

"I'm sorry Paige, but I have a girlfriend. I should have told you about Juliet before."

I almost died. "Wrong impression? Are you serious? You've been eavesdropping on me, so you heard I liked you. Why didn't you tell me you had a girlfriend when we first met? Then I would've known you just wanted to be friends and you still could've protected me."

"I'm sorry."

I was livid, but I had to keep my voice low. "Does she live in New York?"

"No, she lives and works in Europe. We have a long distance relationship at the moment."

"Wait, were you in Paris and Australia with her? Is that the friend you were talking about?"

"Yes."

"Problem is that you left out the word girl before friend. You know the maturity thing you were talking about, maybe you should look in the mirror. I guess you've learned how to lie well for your job, like your age and your girlfriend. Your uncle should be so proud."

"I'm sorry..."

"I have to go." I hung up and sobbed in my pillow, so that they couldn't hear me. If he lied about a girlfriend, he lied about his age because he had to be at least twenty-seven.

I had to get out of New York. I'd ask my parents in the morning if I could go to London. As long as I stayed with Aunt Lucy, they'd let me. Anything was better than this nightmare.

Juliet? She even had a beautiful name.

Now every time I would think of, read or watch Romeo and Juliet, Daniel and Juliet would come to mind. *Thanks for ruining my favorite play!* I guess Daniel was her Romeo. *Yuck!* That thought made me feel even worse.

Thinking about their long distance relationship inspired me to write a mean song. I thought of both Billy and Daniel and put all my anger in the song. After the night I had, the song made me feel better in a strange cathartic way. I named it 'Long Distance Relationship.'

He says you're the only one. How do you know that's true?
You've only known this guy for a week or two.
There could be tons of other girls lining up at his door
Cuz when it comes to action you know he always wants more.

I know that you cried when you two had to part,
But did it really have the same effect on his heart?
Or were you just another girl like the one's before?

I know you think that you know him well and that he wouldn't
lie,
But just sit back and see how things look from my eyes.

You're in a long distance relationship.
You're blind to what's on the inside.
Only seeing what's on the outside.
When you're in a long distance relationship
You never know what's going on when you're not around.
You might just have your heart broken down.

You say you've found Mr. Right,
but how come he's always try'na pick a fight
with you and everyone else around him?
Is that really what you're looking for?

Even you have to admit that his comments are perverse
And his sweet talk lines couldn't get much worse.
He's sick. Not my pick. Why can't you see?
This whole damn thing just disgusts me.

I know you think that you know him well and that he wouldn't
lie,
But just sit back and see how things look from my eyes.

You're in a long distance relationship.
You're blind to what's on the inside.
Only seeing what's on the outside.
When you're in a long distance relationship
You never know what's going on when you're not around.
You might just have your heart broken down.

10. HIT & RUN

"A man should look for what is, and not for what he thinks should be." Einstein

My cell phone woke me and staring at the screen, I saw it was Lily.

"Hi. What time is it?" I asked trying to sound awake.

"You're still sleeping? Get up, it's almost nine, I'm about to walk into work. How was your date with Billy?"

"It was horrible. He attacked me, kissing and groping me. I swear I should've had him arrested. He wouldn't take no for an answer. It was so scary." I explained how he came upstairs to walk Amber and then assaulted me. When I got to the end, I stopped.

"And? How did you get him to leave?" asked Paige.

I couldn't say Daniel saved me because that would start more questions. "The doorman brought up a package and I made him leave. Should I tell Eden?"

"I have to get in the elevator now. Want to have lunch, so we can talk about it?"

"I'm not sure if I can," I fibbed. "I'll call you later." I was too scared to go outside.

Mom was in the kitchen and asked how the movie was. "It was fine. Mom, can I go to London and stay with Aunt Lucy?"

"What brought this about? When we suggested it, you vehemently opposed it."

"I just want to go. I'm so bored here. Dad's office doesn't really need me."

"I don't see why not. When do you want to go?"

"Tomorrow?" I asked and smiled. "Please!"

"In a rush are you? I'll call the airlines and check. You better start packing."

I jumped up and hugged her. "Thanks Mom."

I went in the basement and got the luggage out of the storage room. I packed, but it didn't take that long. With nothing else to do, I read some poetry. I hadn't read any books lately, which was so unlike me. Daniel and spy garbage was all that I'd been concentrating on.

At the same time, I didn't want to forget any of these memories, so I retrieved my journal and filled in the latest details of my Daniel saga.

I stared at the two photos of him. Daniel looked exactly the same. But there was an eight-year difference between the photos. How was this possible? I didn't want to carry his photo around anymore, so I placed all the copied photos and the originals inside

EMIT

the journal and put it in my keepsake box at the bottom of the closet.

I went on Facebook and unfriended Billy. I also blocked him because I never wanted to see anything pop up about him.

While checking my emails, I read one from Emma, asking when in August I was arriving at Nana's. She wanted to plan a summer bash and wanted to make sure that I'd be there. I emailed her back and told her my new plan.

Staring out the window, I texted Lily that I'd meet her for lunch. Knowing that the NSA was following me, made me feel better. Besides, I had to get rid of the envelope if I wanted any peace from all this.

I wanted to leave for London without constantly looking over my shoulder for goons. I grabbed a wristlet and slipped the folded envelope inside. It would be a lot easier to whip the letter out if I was approached. I didn't want to rummage through my big handbag or walk around with it in my hand. Daniel and James told me to do what I thought was best.

During lunch, I told Lily about my London plan and she got upset. "Is this because of Daniel or Billy?" she asked.

"I just have to get out of here, Lily. I think I'm going crazy." I started getting emotional and blurted out, "I can't handle that Daniel has a girlfriend."

"What?" Lily looked dumfounded and I realized that I never told her. I was keeping so much from her, it was hard to keep track. I couldn't keep this charade up. I wasn't a liar like Daniel. I hoped that my eavesdroppers didn't hear my outburst. I didn't want Daniel to know how much I cared and how much pain I was in.

Staring at me, she said, "You never told me that."

"I didn't?" I said playing stupid and regained my composure. "Well, he does and her name's Juliet. Isn't that really nice?"

"Is this why you've been so upset?" Lily asked. "When did he tell you this?"

I shrugged my shoulders and shut my eyes. "Does it matter? He has a girlfriend. Bottom line is he's been leading me on. I don't want to talk about him anymore. Please," I begged.

"Okay, I'm sorry." Lily looked so confused, but I couldn't tell her the real story. I had to keep her safe. "Daniel and Billy are both losers," Lily said, trying to make me feel better.

I nodded in agreement. "So what should I do about Billy?"

"You have to tell Eden. She's his sister. Maybe she'll talk to him."

"What if she gets angry or doesn't believe me?"

"So? What if he rapes someone?"

"You're right. I'll call her tonight and I'll leave with a clear conscience." Suddenly, I had a brainstorm and shrieked, "Why don't you come with me? My aunt won't mind. They have plenty of room and we'd have so much fun together."

"I can't. I made a commitment at my Dad's office. They would have hired somebody else for the summer."

After lunch, I began walking home praying that someone would ask me for the envelope. I was so dumb for not going to the lobby when Daniel told me to. I walked up Sixth Avenue and decided not to go through the park. My last walk there still haunted me, so I walked up Central Park South.

I hoped that I wouldn't see Daniel. It'd be easier to forget him. Who was I kidding? Like that was even possible. I'd never forget him. At least, I'd always have my photos and my memories. No one could take that away from me.

As I daydreamed, I started to cross Central Park West in the middle of the street. To my left, the light was red so I started walking. When I was in the middle of the street, I suddenly saw a dark blue car run the red light. Everything moved in slow motion. The car was speeding and I watched it racing towards me. Oh, my God! The car was about to hit me straight on but suddenly veered and clipped me on my left side. I was struck and went flying in the air. There was a loud crash as my body hit the ground. At first, I felt nothing, but then pain started shooting down my arm and leg and my head was pounding. I think I blacked out because when I opened my eyes, there were people all around me. Scanning the crowd for Daniel, I spotted Pierce trying to get through the people hovering around me. A woman was talking to me but I didn't know what she was saying. She had a thick Spanish accent. Where was Daniel? Didn't he tell me that nothing was going to happen to me?

"Are you okay?" Pierce asked as he knelt down.

"No. My left arm really hurts," I managed to say. The pain was excruciating.

A group of men in suits appeared and ushered the crowd away from me. I'm not sure how much time passed, but I heard sirens blaring and hoped it was an ambulance for me.

I picked up my right arm and was surprised to see the wristlet bag still on my wrist. It hadn't fallen off. I overheard someone say to call my mom. Pierce asked if I had my cell and I said it was in my wristlet. I heard him tell her that it was a hit-and-run. On top of everything else I've been dealing with, this had to happen. At least I was alive, I should be thankful for that.

I was taken to St. Luke's Hospital and Pierce was right there keeping an eye on me. With the pain that I felt, I knew my arm was broken. As I waited in the emergency room, I saw Mom rush in frantically. She looked so worried and seeing her so upset made me cry. I waved so that she could see I was alive.

"Paige, baby, I'm so sorry," she said and wiped my tears with her hand. "What hurts?"

Through sobs, I answered, "My whole left side and my head. I think my arm is broken." I felt everything swelling.

"You could've been killed." The doctor came in. X-rays and CT scans were ordered and I was wheeled to Radiology.

When I returned, Dad was waiting with Mom. He rushed over. "How are you feeling?"

"Not so great."

The doctor appeared and said I was very lucky that the car wasn't going faster. "The radius bone in your lower arm is broken. What's truly amazing is that your legs weren't broken." Then why did they feel like they were? I wondered. "We'll put on a temporary plaster cast to immobilize the arm and wait for the swelling to subside before the permanent cast is put on."

Mom asked, "What were the results of the scan? Is there a concussion?"

"No concussion just bruising from where the head hit," the

doctor said.

I spotted Pierce standing near the door. I guess Daniel was done worrying about me.

Dad was asking a ton of questions, but I couldn't concentrate because I was getting groggy from the painkillers. I did hear, "It takes about six weeks for an arm break to heal." There goes my London trip again. My parents would never let me go now and that meant I would be stuck in this nightmare.

"Buttercup, the doctor said you could go home, but advises you stay overnight just in case."

"No, please, I want to go home," I pleaded, looking at Mom for help. I wanted my own bed and house. Knowing that between the doormen, the EMIT agents in the building, and everyone listening to everything in my house, I'd be safe there.

Mom came to my rescue. "Oliver, she'll rest better at home. You know how hospitals are. She'll never get any sleep. I'll take care of her and if anything happens we'll bring her right back." Reluctantly, Dad agreed.

We took a taxi home and everything hurt from the bouncing. Bursts of pain shot through my arm and I flinched. I clenched my teeth and suffered silently, fearing that if I complained, my parents would return me to the hospital. At least, it was my left arm; I was a righty anyway. The cab dropped us off at the building and I was so glad to be home. Dad had to go to a meeting and said he'd be home as soon as possible.

Mom made me lie down on the couch in the living room, and said, "Stay here till I get back. I'm going to run down to the pharmacy and drop off these prescriptions. When I get back, I'll help you upstairs to your bedroom."

The phone rang as soon as I was alone, but I knew I had to answer it. "Hello?"

"Girlie... the next time it'll be much worse. We want that envelope. We'll call again to make arrangements." His voice made my skin crawl.

What was I doing? These people could've killed me.

My cell rang and while answering it, I dropped it to the floor.

"Sorry, I dropped it," I yelled. Every move hurt from the jostling. "Hello."

"Paige, it's Pierce."

"Where's Daniel?" I had to know.

"He's out-of-town on assignment."

Just great! On to his next case, leaving me to fend for myself, so much for the 'I won't let anything happen to you' nonsense.

"Next time they call, please follow their instructions and we'll take it from there."

"Fine, I will. Bye." I didn't want to talk to any of them. I called Lily to tell her what happened, but it went to voice mail.

Mom helped me upstairs when she returned and helped me change my clothes. Dad walked in and before he could say anything, my cell began ringing.

"Answer your call, Buttercup, I want to talk to your mother." He leaned over and kissed the top of my head.

As I answered, I heard Lily say, "I just heard what happened. How are you?"

"To be honest, I feel like death on a cracker," I joked, trying to make light of the situation.

"Be serious, please."

"I want to go to sleep, wake up and find out it was just a bad dream," I admitted.

"I'm so sorry. At least it wasn't your leg," Lily said trying to find something positive to say.

"Yeah, but I'm stuck here. My parents won't let me go to London now. Aunt Lucy doesn't need to deal with two patients."

I was getting sleepy, so I ended the call, but between the pain and the horrible nightmares, I hardly slept.

***

When I woke up, I felt like I'd been hit by a train. Everything hurt. Glancing at my legs, I saw they were covered in huge black, blue and yellow bruises. I called for Mom and when she saw them she gasped.

She found the sweatpants I asked for and helped me put them on. I didn't want to see my legs. This was going to be horrible since I couldn't dress myself. I guess it was better that I broke my arm in the summer. Trying to put on winter clothes as opposed to summer clothes would've been horrific.

When I complained that I didn't want to be stuck in my bedroom all day, Mom agreed and thought it was best that I stayed in the living room, so I didn't go up and down the stairs all day. She set up the couch with pillows, blankets and put my laptop on the coffee table. I lay there and tried to ignore the pain coursing through my body. Amber kept me company and stared at me like she knew something was terribly wrong.

Whenever the painkillers kicked in, I was able to fall asleep.

Mom finally left me alone to run an errand and the phone rang. It was Nana joking that I broke my arm because I was jealous of her broken leg.

That evening, Martin, Marina and Anna came over. Mom ordered Chinese food and they left after Anna fell asleep in her stroller.

Afterwards, my parents asked if I could handle the drive to Long Island for the weekend. I quickly said yes. I'd rather sit in a chaise and look at the water, than sit on a couch and stare at the walls. Painkillers and rest was all that I needed for now. Cutchogue wasn't London, but it would do. The envelope would wait because I needed to get out of here.

***

I found Dad in the kitchen drinking coffee.

"Morning, Sweetie. How are you feeling?"

"The same," I said shrugging. What else could I say?

"I'm sorry. It's going to take time to heal."

"I know. I can't wait to go see Grammy."

"Oh, Aunt Cecile, Uncle Ian and Lily wanted to come in today and see you, but when I told them we were heading out to Grammy's, they're going to meet us out there," Mom said.

"That's great!" I was excited to see Lily.

"You'll be able to rest out there and recover from this accident," said Dad.

If Dad knew that it wasn't an accident, but was intentional, he'd be furious.

When those goons had first called, Daniel told me to go and see what they wanted, but I said no and refused. As a result, I had a broken arm and Daniel was gone anyway.

When we arrived in Cutchogue, Grammy ran out of the house. "I've been so worried about you," she said, as she hugged me gingerly.

Grammy wouldn't stop hovering and Mom seeing that I wanted to rest, dragged her away to do some gardening. I sat on a chaise by the pool thinking about Daniel. I hoped that wherever he was, he was happy. He really was a great guy and his girlfriend was lucky while I, unfortunately, would remain jealous forever. Enough! I had to stop thinking about him.

Lily arrived about an hour later.

"I can't believe this happened to you," Lily said.

"Me either."

I read and hung out with Lily all day. It was so relaxing.

"Mom, can I stay with Grammy till we have to leave for London?"

"I'll check with Grammy, but I'm sure she'd love it. You need to see the orthopedist next week, so I'll bring you back after you see him."

As long as I knew I could come back here, I could wait.

I knew I was being watched because I spotted a boat anchored close to Fleets Neck Beach.

At least, it wasn't anchored smack in front of the house. There also was a car parked by the entrance to Grammy's road. Our road was a dead end so if you parked at the entrance you'd see anyone entering or leaving. Weren't the neighbors wondering about the parked car?

Since reading was about the extent of what I could do, I continued with my poetry. I grabbed the Elizabeth Barrett Browning book. In no mood to read her biography, I looked for a required poem on the list.

THE SOUL'S EXPRESSION

With stammering lips and insufficient sound
I strive and struggle to deliver right
That music of my nature, day and night
With dream and thought and feeling interwound
And only answering all the senses round
With octaves of a mystic depth and height
Which step out grandly to the infinite
From the dark edges of the sensual ground.
This song of soul I struggle to outbear
Through portals of the sense, sublime and whole,
And utter all myself into the air:
But if I did it,--as the thunder-roll
Breaks its own cloud, my flesh would perish there,
Before that dread apocalypse of soul.

The poem explained the struggle between expressing one's feelings and the fear of doing just that. Tired of trying to analyze the poem, I put the book back in my bag. The medicine knocked me out and I slept a lot all weekend.

We left Sunday night. I really didn't want to go, but I had no choice. I had to see the doctor and had to get rid of the envelope.

Back home, Mom helped me into my sleep shirt and went to walk Amber with Dad.

I sat at my computer and planned to thank everybody for the get-well wishes and cards, which were so sweet, but I found an email from Daniel. I didn't want to open it, but I couldn't resist.

> **Paige,**
> **I heard from Pierce about your arm.**
> **I'm so sorry.**
> **That wasn't supposed to happen.**
> **I wish I had been there for you, but I was away at the time.**
> **If you'd like to talk, you have my number.**
> **Daniel**

More nonsense! Supposed to happen? *Just leave me alone.* I deleted his email.

I emailed Emma and told her that I wasn't coming. This was so crazy, twice I was going and twice it got canceled. Our regular August trip better happen, or I'll just scream.

I got my journal out of the closet and filled in the latest news. I put in my last song about long distance relationships. There was no point in putting the journal back in the closet until after I got rid of the envelope and could finally close the chapter on Daniel.

***

In the morning, Mom said she was staying home to be with me and would work from home.

She had to leave, so those goons would call. "You don't have to. I'll be fine."

"You might need help."

"I was perfectly fine at Grammy's."

"We were all there to help you."

I tried my hardest to get her out of the apartment. When I asked for croissants, she had the store deliver them. When I asked for a book, she called the bookstore and it was brought over. Normally, I liked these conveniences, but today, I was going insane.

Mom was on the phone with Grammy. I heard the tail end of the conversation as she walked through the living room. "That's exciting though! I wonder who it is!"

She came back when they were done and asked, "Did you notice a car this weekend parked at the entrance of Grammy's street?"

"I did. What about it?" I asked, nonchalantly.

"Grammy had coffee with one of her neighbors and they told her it was a security team for a VIP. Isn't it funny the same thing happened when you were at Martin's babysitting?"

"Oh, yeah, Mom. Did I forget to tell you that I'm the very important person and I have a security team following me around?" I laughed.

"You are important and don't forget that," she said as she kissed my head. If she knew what was really going on, she'd be a basket case right now.

I was going to lose my mind. When I walked out of the apartment, she came along.

"Mom, only my arm is broken. I can still go for a walk alone."

"You might need me." She looked so pathetic that I felt bad telling her to leave me alone. I was her only child and she was going to smother me whether I liked it or not.

***

When I came downstairs, Mom was in the kitchen, talking on her cell and telling somebody that she was working from home. I really needed help, so I ran back to my bedroom. The only phone number I had was Daniel's and since I didn't want to talk to him, talking to the walls would have to do. "Listen, I know you guys can hear me. I have to get my mother out of here. Any ideas?"

My cell rang immediately and it was a private number. "Pierce?"

"Paige, it's Daniel. How are you?"

In my mind, I saw his face, eyes and smile. Being alone in this made me so vulnerable and I really missed him. Why did his number come up private? Did he change his number, so I couldn't reach him?

"Are you there?" he asked.

"I'm here," I said trying to sound indifferent. "I need help. They only call when I'm alone."

"Let me work on it." He sounded very professional and aloof. "Bye."

As I walked downstairs, I had a brainstorm. "Mom, I really want a pretzel from the guy on Central Park South. Could you get me one? I'm just really not up to going," I said yawning.

"Sure, I have to take Amber for a walk anyway. Don't forget to take your medicine."

I nodded and said, "Thanks Mom." I didn't call Daniel back; I knew they had heard.

As expected, the phone rang after Mom left. "Meet us in the lobby in five minutes."

"I'll be right there." Now this all would end. I got the envelope from under my mattress, slipped on sandals, and headed for the elevator.

Daniel was leaning against the wall waiting for me. My heart stopped and my legs felt like rubber. I tried to act calm since there was no other choice. Forget my arm-- that would heal, but my heart I wasn't so sure about. Saying I didn't care was easier when I didn't have to see him.

"Hi," he said. "Ready?"

Afraid that I might break down, I didn't look at him and just nodded.

"Pierce is in the lobby. Just hand the man the envelope then turn around and get back in the elevator. I'll be waiting for you, okay?"

I managed another nod. Please, let it be that easy.

"Don't worry, I'm here. Nothing will happen."

That comment infuriated me and I looked up at him. "I've heard that before," I said as I lifted my broken arm for effect. Daniel had circles under his eyes and looked exhausted. I guess that's what spying on people did to you.

"I'm sorry, Paige. That shouldn't have happened."

"Let's get this over with so that you never have to see me again," I said sarcastically. What was the point of rehashing this nonsense? Nothing he ever said made any sense.

"Paige..." he started, but the elevator doors had opened and someone was in the elevator. He didn't say anything else. What more was there to say?

In the lobby, I saw Pierce sitting in a chair pretending to read a newspaper. Carl glanced at me and motioned to a man sitting on the couch. I had never seen him before. He was a young, black man dressed in jeans and a T-shirt. Not at all what I expected. I walked over, handed him the envelope, turned around, walked back to the elevator and pressed the UP button. Not one word was exchanged between us.

When the doors opened, I got in, turned and saw him talking on his cell. Thank goodness, it was all over. Daniel wasn't in the elevator. I guess that was it. I'd never see him again.

The elevator doors opened and Daniel was standing there.

"Thank you," he said sincerely.

This was excruciating. "I'm going to Long Island. While I'm gone, whatever you have bugged, get rid of it immediately."

"I promise within two weeks, it'll be done. We need to make sure it all worked out."

"What are you talking about? If what worked out? You said that if I handed over the envelope, it was over!" I tried not to yell, but this was ridiculous.

"We just need to be sure," he said calmly.

"Whatever you're talking about, I don't care," I said, frustrated. "Since I did my part, please stop listening to my conversations."

"We will stop as soon as we can, I promise."

Mrs. Braxon came out of her apartment and stared at us as she walked towards the elevator. Noticing that I looked upset, she said, "Paige, is everything okay?"

"Yes, thank you." The elevator door opened and she went inside glaring at Daniel.

As soon as the elevator left, I lashed out by saying, "By the way, I'll be telling Lily everything now. I'm warning you, like you asked, so you can be prepared. I have no idea what that means, but I don't want to be the immature one." I walked away and went into the apartment. Tears streamed down my face, knowing that I'd miss him. They'd better not be able to see me. I'd die if they had cameras anywhere.

When Mom returned, she was baffled at my complete change and asked, "Are you okay? When I left you were fine, did something happen?" She handed me the pretzel.

What could I say? This broken arm did come in handy. "I banged my arm and it really hurts."

Mom put her arm around me and tried comforting me. "I'm so sorry." She kept trying to say the right things, but didn't know that it wasn't my arm that I was crying about.

Later in the day, I called Lily and asked her to come over the following night. I had to tell her about Daniel and hoped that she'd forgive me for not being honest with her.

I sat on my bed thinking that the summer had started off disappointing, turned wonderful and was ending horribly. As soon as all the bugging equipment was removed, I'd be totally free. There was a whole month left before school and though I hoped time would heal this hole in my heart, I knew it wasn't going to be that easy.

The cell rang and I didn't know the number. "Hello?" Please don't be some crazy person.

When I heard a male voice, I got scared. "Hey, its Chad." Thank God! "I heard about the hit and run. How are you?"

"Getting better everyday. What's up with you?" He didn't call to talk about the accident.

"Not much, but I want to ask Lily out and since she lives in Westchester, I wanted to ask you for some advice."

"Lily's coming over tomorrow night. Why don't you guys go out?" I suggested.

"You don't mind?"

"Of course not, I'm leaving for Long Island on Thursday, so I'll see her on the weekends."

"Great. I'll call her now."

Even though I was physically drained, I couldn't stop my brain from racing, so I grabbed the journal and filled in the latest entry. I felt so sad. My cell buzzed and I was grateful for the call.

It was Lily. "Chad just called and said he talked to you. I thought you wanted to talk."

"I do, but we can talk before or after your date. Don't worry, go out with him." My eyes started closing, so I told Lily I'd see her tomorrow.

***

When I opened my eyes, my cell was ringing right near my ear. It was under my pillow. I must have forgotten to put it on my nightstand. Had I fallen asleep talking to Lily?

"Hello," I answered groggily.

"Paige, it's Daniel, I need to see you."

Why was he doing this to me? I know it wasn't painful for him to talk to me, but hearing his voice was agonizing for me.

"Why?"

"We have a problem. There's another envelope. This isn't finished."

"What are you talking about? Please leave me alone," I snapped and hung up the phone. My cell kept buzzing, but I refused to answer and it stopped, so he must have gotten the hint.

There was a note on the kitchen counter from Mom saying she was at the office.

As I was going back upstairs, I heard knocking on the front door. How did they get past the doorman? I quietly reached the door, looked through the peephole and saw Daniel standing there. "Please leave me alone," I said through the door.

"Please let me in."

"I'm in my pajamas." Oh, who cares? What does it matter what I looked like? He didn't like me anyway. Wearing a long sleeved top with long bottoms, nothing was visible anyways, so I flung the door open. "What do you want?" I asked loudly.

"Shh, your neighbors. Can we talk inside?"

"Do I have a choice? I told you I didn't want to talk and you came here anyway." I saw James Haydin walking by with my neighbor, John Costra. Why was he talking to him?

John stopped when he saw me and asked, "Paige, how's your arm?" James Haydin ignored me.

"Getting better. How's Luke?"

"Great. He's been learning to swim."

"Tell him I miss him."

"Will do," he said and walked away with James.

Daniel looked frazzled and I looked away. It was easier that way.

"Why is James talking to my neighbor?"

"Every package that enters the building especially anything that goes to your floor is scanned. Yesterday, John Costra received a delivery and James wanted to talk to him because there's a chance he might be involved in this case."

"What are you talking about? He's my neighbor with a wife and child." All of this was getting crazier and crazier by the minute.

"We're investigating him because there was a bomb in the package," Daniel said it so matter-of-factly that at first I thought I must have heard wrong.

"What? Did you say bomb?"

"Yes, I did."

"But who was it for? Me?" I shrieked.

"We don't know. We need to investigate John Costra though."

"But it makes no sense. If they killed me, they wouldn't have gotten the envelope. Or were they going to kill me after they got it?"

"We're not sure, but they'll be back looking for you and the other envelope."

"But I don't have another envelope. That was the only one," I answered. I found it impossible to break my glance because he still had such a powerful hold on me, but I was reeling from all this bomb talk. "How do you know they'll be back?"

"We just do," he said. "You'll be safe for about seven to ten days if nothing changes."

That was it. The moment he said, 'If nothing changes,' I got irate. "What are you talking about?" I shrieked. "You know what? It doesn't matter. I'm leaving tomorrow, so you need to take care of this by yourself since I don't have another envelope."

"The problem is they think you have it and they won't give up."

"You know, you're crazy because you can't know that," I said.

"The problem is that things are changing so quickly now that you actually might be right. I've already been wrong a few times."

"Finally, I might be right, hallelujah," I looked up to heaven. "I suggest you go investigate the people at my dad's firm since that's how I got that first envelope. How about Maria, the office manager, or Sonia, the secretary? One of them could've put the envelope in that file."

"We are and have been for awhile, but there are over a thousand people in that firm here and many more in London. It'll take too long."

"Well, since I won't be working there, I won't get any more envelopes. They don't want a one-armed photo copy girl."

"The problem is that the catastrophe will happen if we don't find that other envelope."

"I am so sick of all this talk of the future, sci-fi jargon, nonsense. I've kept this crazy secret, but I'm no longer letting you guys call all the shots. Until someone explains to me what's going on, I want you to leave me alone or I will tell my parents."

"I can't tell you anything. It's classified."

"Well, then I don't want to be involved anymore. I want all of you out of my life. Please go deal with bombs, envelopes and goons all by yourself."

"I'll leave. But if the envelope turns up, please call me."

"You'll be the first person I call." After he walked out, I slammed the door.

Lily got in around six and knowing that this drama wasn't over, I was afraid to tell her anything. The bomb part really scared me. Even with the doormen and the NSA security, a bomb got into my building. It could have killed me, John Costra, and who knows how many others.

We went to my room and Lily sat on my bed. "I know something's wrong. Please tell me."

I stared at Lily's face and couldn't hold it together any longer. I was falling apart inside and I started to cry.

I jumped up off the bed and blasted the radio. They couldn't hear me. I wouldn't let them have the satisfaction of knowing how upset I was.

Lily didn't know what was going on and she looked so confused. She hugged me and said, "Please don't cry. Tell me what's going on?"

I took a piece of paper and wrote 'MY ROOM IS BUGGED, LET'S GO OUTSIDE.' Lily stared at me like I was crazy. I nodded that it was true. Not wanting Mom to see my red face, I put on my sunglasses. Lily followed me out to the kitchen and didn't say anything.

"Mom, we're taking Amber for a walk. Call my cell when dinner is ready."

"Okay. Lily, I heard you're seeing a movie with Chad tonight. What time are you going out? I want to make sure you eat."

"He's meeting me here around 7:45. Don't worry. I'll get something at the movies."

"No, that's plenty of time for us to eat together."

When we got outside, Lily asked. "What are you talking about?

Who's bugging you?"

We walked and I talked. Basically I told her everything as best I could since there was so much that I really didn't understand myself.

Lily didn't interrupt, just listened attentively and gasped at times. The car accident flipped her out.

She exploded, "Someone ran you over on purpose! You have to go to the police."

By the end of the story she understood the problem in contacting the police. Even if the police believed me, which was doubtful, the NSA would step in and take over.

We sat on a bench and she just stared at me in a stupor. "You need to tell your parents. I don't know if I trust this agency. It all sounds so crazy."

"I can't. I still believe Daniel. Even if he hurt me, I do trust him."

"What did he mean when he said this will happen in the future?"

"Every time I've asked, he says it's classified. I told him not to talk to me again until he tells me what's going on. That's the reason I'm going to Grammy's. I can't do this anymore." I started getting emotional and Lily comforted me.

"It's probably best that you get out of here."

"You need to know that your house is bugged, too." I watched her face as all of this slowly registered. First surprise, then understanding and then rage showed on her face.

"You've got to be kidding! They took that photo of him from my scrapbook? They were in my house?" she asked, putting two and two together.

"Yes," I began. "Daniel said that someone was watching and

protecting you. Lily, at least you're safe, well unless they try to run you down." I started chuckling because this all sounded so stupid, that it was funny.

Lily looked at me like I had truly cracked up, and maybe I had. "Why are they following and bugging me too? What could I possibly have to do with this?"

"I have no idea, maybe it's because you're always with me. Beats me, this whole thing is going to put me in an insane asylum. I can't figure anything out."

"I can't believe they were going to bomb your building."

"Isn't that insane?"

Lily suddenly said, "I thought we'd never keep secrets from each other."

"I'm sorry, but I didn't want you to get hurt."

"But you did get hurt and I had no idea what really happened. If anything happened to you... I can't even go there," said Lily, visibly distraught.

"Daniel said that I had at least a week before those goons figured out they needed something else. But then he said that he could be wrong, so let's hope that's not the case," I said.

"When you saw him on Long Island, was it him?" Lily asked.

"Yeah, you owe me ten dollars," I said and laughed.

Lily stared at me like I was deranged and she might be right. I felt like I'm losing my mind.

My cell rang and it was Mom telling us to come home.

After dinner, I went with Lily down to the lobby to meet Chad. I made him promise to walk her home afterwards. Chad looked at me oddly and said he had planned to do that all along.

Heading back towards the elevator, I almost walked into Pierce. "Off to work?" He just nodded and walked out of the building.

Mom and Dad watched a movie in the den, while I waited for Lily in the living room and prayed that we'd both stay safe. With nothing good on TV, I picked up my Lord Byron book and read, 'When We Two Parted.'

> When we two parted
> In silence and tears,
> Half broken-hearted
> To sever for years,
> Pale grew thy cheek and cold,
> Colder thy kiss;
> Truly that hour foretold
> Sorrow to this.
>
> The dew of the morning
> Sank chill on my brow-
> It felt like the warning
> Of what I feel now.
> Thy vows are all broken,
> And light is thy fame;
>
> I hear thy name spoken,
> And share in its shame.
>
> They name thee before me,
> A knell to mine ear;
> A shudder comes o'er me-
> Why wert thou so dear?
> They know not I knew thee,
> Who knew thee too well-
> Long, long shall I rue thee
> Too deeply to tell.

In secret we met-
In silence I grieve,
That thy heart could forget,
Thy spirit deceive.
If I should meet thee
After long years,
How should I greet thee!-
With silence and tears.

As I read it, my eyes welled up. By the time I reached the fourth and final stanza, I was a complete mess. The words resonated with me and I could feel the pain caused by the decline of the relationship.

Looking up at the clock, I saw that it was almost twelve and Lily wasn't back. Mom came in and asked me if I heard from her when I told her no, she told me to call. Lily answered and said that they were at Starbucks and she'd lost track of time.

When she got in, we ran upstairs to talk. As Lily got on the bed, she said, "You should date Reed and then we could double date."

"Maybe..." I said loudly, knowing they were listening.

Lily realized what I was doing. "He's so cute and so much cuter than Daniel," she added.

"I know and besides Daniel was such a pompous ass," I said loudly.

I made it unbearable for them to listen to our conversation by putting the music on really loud. Mom ran in and scolded us about the radio's volume and made us turn it off.

I woke up in a state of terror from another nightmare. I remembered being chased and getting killed. The dreams seemed so vivid and felt so real. All this espionage stuff was causing havoc with my sleep and my mind.

***

Waking up and finding Lily there was such a comfort. Somebody finally knew what I'd been going through and could help, or at least give me advice.

As Lily was leaving, she said, "I'll see you Friday night at Grammy's. Oh, I forgot to tell you that Noelle is coming. Should I see if I could change it? We won't be able to talk."

"There's really nothing else to say. We just have to wait and see what happens. Having her out there will be a nice distraction. Besides, she can play tennis and bike with you."

I packed clothes that were easy to slip on, so that I wouldn't have to ask Grammy for help. Mom helped me bring my bags downstairs and left them in the foyer. We would leave right after my doctor's appointment.

At the doctor's building, I saw Pierce in the lobby talking to a guy with black hair. It was creepy that people I didn't know were following me around and listening to my every word.

Dr. Wesley took off the plaster cast and put on a fiberglass one now that the swelling was gone. The new cast was much better, less bulky and more comfortable. He told me that the cast liner could get wet but I still needed to be careful. How do you swim with one arm?

We took a taxi home, had lunch, packed up the car, and were on the road by one o'clock.

11. DREAM

"Learn from yesterday, live for today, hope for tomorrow." Einstein

Sitting in the car for two hours gave me plenty of time to think about Daniel and I knew that I had to get over my anger. Yes, he lied and led me on, but he had never once treated me inappropriately. He had been protecting me and was doing his job. The rejection was painful, but I couldn't force him to have feelings for me that he didn't have.

We got to Grammy's around three and she rushed out the door thrilled to see us. Grammy told me to go lie down by the pool and I left them in the kitchen. I watched the boats in the distance and when I opened my eyes, I knew I had fallen asleep. Except for Amber, I was alone.

I went inside and found them in the living room. "I can't believe I had a three-hour-nap! The painkillers really knock me out. What's for dinner? I'm starving."

"Turkey burgers. We were waiting for you to wake up before we started a ruckus on the grill," Grammy said.

"I made a pasta pesto and Grammy made a tomato and mozzarella salad. Do you want something while we cook the burgers or do you want to wait?" Mom asked.

"I'll wait. I'm going to put on my bathing suit. I'll be right back."

I put my suit on and spotted the NSA boat right in front of the house.

"I understand you guys aren't going to stop tormenting me, but do you have to be on top of me. Move and go someplace else," I ordered.

The cell rang and it was a private number again. Please don't let it be Daniel.

"Hello?"

"It's Daniel. I'm the one out here. Pierce is on his way and when he gets here, I'll move. I don't want you to think we're doing this intentionally."

I didn't know what to say, I was completely silent. I said, "Fine" and hung up. There was nothing else to say.

***

In the morning, the boat was gone. I sat by the pool, read poetry, sketched and wrote depressing, heart-rending songs. Soon, I'd have a whole book of pathetic songs and poems dedicated to my heartbreak. I was miserable. I caught Mom's glances and she understood more than I gave her credit for.

When we went to the store, I noticed that the boat was at the Causeway Beach and it made me feel good that Daniel was nearby.

Noelle showed up before Lily since she had driven out with Aunt Cecile. Lily was taking the bus with Uncle Ian.

After changing, Noelle swam and I sat on a lounge chair. Noelle insisted that I tell her all about my accident. I got hit by a car summed it up, but she wanted more and kept asking questions. Thankfully, I was saved by Lily's call saying that they had caught an earlier bus.

While Noelle read magazines, I went upstairs to check my laptop. I read all the new postings on Facebook, sent some messages, chatted with some friends. When Lily finally arrived, the weekend officially started.

After dinner, we hung out in the pool and gabbed. I had nothing to talk about and realized quickly that without Daniel, my life was quite dull. Lily talked about her job and then about Chad and Zack, the boy that had asked her out from her swim club. Noelle talked about work and then admitted that she had a crush on a boy named Dean who worked with her.

***

Saturday, I spent most of the day by the pool. Lily and Noelle went for a long bike ride.

That evening, we went out for dinner and a movie. As we left, I saw that the NSA car parked at the entrance of Grammy's street was moved to the entrance of Nassau Point.

At Love Lane Kitchen in Mattituck, we got two tables, one for the adults inside and one for us outside. As Lily, Noelle and I sat enjoying the evening, I noticed a car parked across the street. I looked at Lily and with my eyes directed her where to look. She glanced over and shook her head in amazement.

When Noelle went to the ladies room, Lily said, "I'm sorry. This is just insane!"

As we exited the theater, Noelle saw Pierce in the crowd and said, "That guy looks like Daniel's friend, Pierce."

Lily looked at me awkwardly, not knowing what to say.

I blurted out, "Oh, it might be. His family lives out here." Pierce had disappeared at that point, so we dropped the subject.

***

After breakfast, Lily and Noelle went kayaking. I took Amber for a walk and watched them from the beach. As I searched for sea glass, my cell rang. It was a private number.

"Paige," said a male voice I didn't recognize. Did those goons get my number? I would have to leave Cutchogue if I would endanger Grammy. "It's James Haydin."

"Yes? What can I do for you?"

"I need to talk to you. Can you can meet me tomorrow morning?"

"You're here too?" I asked incredulously.

"No, I'm not. I'm arriving tomorrow to see you and then I'm leaving," he said, sounding annoyed by my question. "The team is there and they are protecting you."

His condescending tone irritated me so much, that I snapped, "You have a team guarding me. Doesn't that sound insane to you? Listen, in case you didn't hear, I know nothing and have nothing. So can you please, please, just leave me alone?"

"I wish it was that simple. If you'll see me tomorrow morning,

I'll try to explain."

"You'll tell me what's going on?" I asked surprised.

"Yes, I'll try." He sounded sincere, but since they lie for a living that was debatable.

Curiosity won out and I agreed, "Okay, I'll meet you. Where?"

"Eleven o'clock at the Nassau Point section of the Causeway Beach."

"Okay, bye." What was he going to tell me? All I'd ever heard from either of them was that everything was classified.

After I got back home, I realized how much fun Amber was having running around so I asked my parents if Amber could stay with me. My parents agreed figuring that Amber could keep me company and would be happier here than stuck in a city apartment.

Lily and Noelle got back from kayaking and we sat by the pool talking. Mom came out of the house and asked, "Did anybody see that car at the entrance of Nassau Point?"

Lily glanced at me and Noelle looked confused. "No, what car?" I asked.

"The black one with the dark windows. The security team is back guarding someone."

"Who?" Noelle asked excitedly. "Anybody famous?"

"Nobody knows. All the residents have been trying to figure out what house this person is staying in. Mr. Banes actually knocked on the car window and asked, but they wouldn't answer."

"Wow. It must be somebody really important," said Noelle. Yeah, sure it was.

"Well, this is a good place to guard someone since there's only one way in and out," said Lily.

"Not really," said Noelle. "Since it's a peninsula, if something goes wrong that person is trapped. There's only one road out."

"Well, there's always a boat or a …helicopter," I interjected. There was a helipad on Vanston Road, so it was possible to get out if necessary.

When Noelle went to shower, I told Lily about the call. "Please be careful. I'm not sure if I trust them." Lily plugged Daniel's cell number and his email into her phone just in case.

Everybody started heading home around seven and I didn't want to say goodbye.

Lily hugged me and whispered, "Be careful."

Mom saw my sad face and said, "I'll be back Thursday night and everybody else will be back on Friday. You have fun with Grammy."

After they left, Grammy and I watched a movie. It was nice spending time with her. On my way to bed, I made sure to set the house alarm. Grammy said it wasn't necessary, but I said it was. She looked at me funnily and didn't say anything more about it.

I had breakfast and waited anxiously for my meeting with James. When it was time to leave, I told Grammy that I was taking Amber for a walk and I'd be back around lunchtime.

There was no one on the Nassau Point section of the beach other than the guard at the entrance. His job was to check that the cars had stickers, which allowed the residents access. This area didn't have a lifeguard and was exclusive to the people who lived on Nassau Point. People who lived in Cutchogue used the beach a bit further down at the other end, which did have lifeguards on duty, restrooms and a playground.

I saw the boat in the water up ahead and someone on the deck.

Was James Haydin on the boat? He didn't seem the type to swim ashore. Every time I'd seen him, he was dressed in a suit.

"Morning, Mike," I said to the guard.

He nodded. I knew he didn't remember my name.

"Nobody here, huh?" I asked, looking around the beach.

"Not yet." Most young families stayed near the lifeguard section. As I strolled toward the water, the tide was very low and there was seaweed on all the exposed rocks. Amber sniffed horseshoe crabs on the beach. It moved so I lifted it and threw it back into the water. Just at that moment, a dark car appeared and James Haydin exited. He must have flashed his badge at Mike.

"Hello, Paige, it's nice to see you," he said, trying to be friendly, but it didn't sound genuine. I had felt that he didn't like me from the first time I met him.

"What's this about?" I asked and Amber retreated behind me.

"I realize that I haven't been fair to you and want to tell you what's been going on." His demeanor exuded arrogance and self-importance.

"I thought everything was classified." I looked at him suspiciously.

He nodded. "It still is. I need to tell you something, but it's not about the case."

"I knew it," I retorted and started to leave, so sick of all this cloak and dagger stuff.

"Paige, wait. It's about Daniel." I hesitated at the mention of Daniel's name and turned back to face him. "I need to exculpate Daniel," he stated formally. James looked very uncomfortable.

Did he have to use big words to feel important? Or was it to feel smart? "I have no idea what that means?" I said, looking at him with a disgusted expression.

In a condescending tone like he was talking to an imbecile, he said, "It means I need to clear Daniel."

"What does he need to be cleared of?" I asked. I was so sick of all the vagueness every time either James or Daniel spoke. Why was every conversation with them so tortuous?

"I ordered Daniel to stay away from you."

Well, that was concise and to the point. I stared at him, not knowing how to react. Actually, it didn't matter since Daniel had a girlfriend anyway. It was best that James kept Daniel far away from me. Was that the reason he wasn't around when I got hit by the car?

"So?" I said.

When James didn't get the reaction he wanted, he went for the jugular. "Daniel doesn't have a girlfriend."

My eyes searched his face to see if this was another trick. What was going on?

"I don't understand. Did they break up?" I asked. My heart felt like it was beating out of my chest.

"No, Daniel told you he had a girlfriend because I made him. He was jeopardizing the mission, so I ordered him to end your friendship." Happiness, confusion, annoyance at James Haydin, all these emotions were churning inside.

"Then who's Juliet?" I asked warily.

"That's his ex-girlfriend."

I could tell that this talk was totally beneath James Haydin and he seemed to be cringing discussing Daniel's love life. James looked like he was ready to leave.

I wasn't going to let him without my questions being answered first. James asked for this talk, so he wasn't getting away that easily. "Wait. Why are you telling me this now?" I asked.

James sighed and said dejectedly, "Because Daniel has given up a lot for the agency."

"Why doesn't Daniel tell me himself?"

"When I told him that I was wrong and that he should tell you the truth, Daniel said that it didn't matter now because he overheard that you didn't care for him. No matter what's going on, he's family and I need to remember that."

All those horrible things I said about him were said in anger. In a stupor, I stood there staring at him. "I don't know what to say. I can't believe this," I whispered, afraid to raise my voice. Daniel did like me for real, not just as a job. Probably not anymore, after all the hateful things I'd been saying to upset him. As I was reeling from this news, I heard a familiar voice shouting from behind and I turned to see a wet Daniel hurriedly approaching and he looked irate.

"James, what are you doing?" Daniel bellowed.

James didn't answer and waited until Daniel got closer. "Calm down," James instructed when he was close enough. "You're making a scene." James glanced at the parking lot where a young couple was standing by their car looking worried that an altercation was imminent.

"Why are you talking to her? I just talked to you an hour ago. How did you get here?" he asked angrily, but his voice was quieting.

"By helicopter. I'm on my way to Plum Island. I stopped here to tell Paige that you don't have a girlfriend," James quickly explained.

Daniel's strained facial muscles slowly relaxed as he looked from James to me. Still in a state of shock, I was frozen in place trying to fathom all that was happening. Was this real or was it a dream? If it was a dream, I didn't want to wake up.

"Daniel, I think you and Paige need to talk. Everything else is still classified. I realized that I had no right to interfere in your personal life. I'll talk to you later."

"Thanks James. I appreciate you doing this," Daniel said.

Turning to me, James added, "Thanks for seeing me."

My legs were shaking and afraid I might fall down, I sat on the sand. Daniel sat next to me and spoke quietly, "I'm sorry I lied and I'm sorry that I hurt you."

I was sitting there in silence and I didn't know what to say. I was so happy inside, but I was afraid to say anything and felt if I spoke, he might disappear. I was positive this must be a dream and I didn't want it to end. When he put his hand on my arm to jostle me, it felt so real.

"Can you forgive me?" He let go of my arm and got on his knees in front of me.

"I don't know what to say, I'm still in shock." I really was stunned by the turn of events. In my wildest dreams, I didn't think this was possible. Hoped maybe, but never thought there was even the slightest chance. "But yes! I forgive you."

"I'm sorry, but my uncle ordered me to end things with you."

"Why?"

"The night you showed me that photo, one of our agents was ambushed and ended up in the hospital. They couldn't reach me because I had turned my phone off and James was livid. James told me to put the brakes on our relationship. I told him no way. Even though you had already told me that you wanted nothing to do with me, I was hoping you'd change your mind," he admitted. "The night you had that date with that Billy character, I wasn't supposed to be watching you. But I was really concerned and...jealous so I switched shifts with Frank, another agent and...." Daniel stared at me awkwardly.

Jealous? Daniel really said that? I was completely blown away. "And what?"

"Thankfully, I was there to protect you from Billy... but Frank got killed."

"Oh, my God." Daniel had been dealing with so much. "I'm so sorry."

Looking down, Daniel sighed and said, "Frank was one of the first people I worked with and he always took care of me. I learned everything from him and I blame myself for his death."

"You shouldn't."

"But I do. James blamed me too. That was why he came to your apartment, to tell me about Frank. He was so angry. I underestimated these people and James thinks we have an internal problem."

I didn't know what that meant.

Crestfallen, Daniel looked up and stared at me saying, "So when James said I had to stop seeing you until this case was over, I couldn't disagree with him. Frank died and it was my fault."

"How is it your fault? You didn't kill him!" I said shaking my head. "What happened to Frank?"

"Frank and Tom, another agent, were following Sonia."

"My father's secretary?" I interrupted.

"Yes. We got some information that she was going to be killed. When the agents got there, it was a set up and they were ambushed. Tom made it out, but Frank didn't. If I hadn't switched shifts with him, he'd still be alive."

"I'm so sorry…but you saved me from Billy," I said trying to say something positive.

"The agents would've done the same thing. They'd never let Billy hurt you. I should've been where I was supposed to be," Daniel said.

"I'm so sorry," I repeated, dazed. "But you could have been the one killed."

"Or I could have caught them."

We sat in silence and finally Daniel spoke. "Can we go back and start where we left off? Forget this girlfriend thing ever happened."

"I really need to know something. Please tell me the truth because I can't take much more of this."

"I'll tell you anything that I can."

"How old are you?"

"Nineteen."

"But how can you look exactly the same in those photos?"

"I'm sorry. I can't say. That's classified."

"Let me see your driver's license," I said and put my hand out.

Daniel looked at me and with a 'you got to be kidding' look and said, "I'm in a bathing suit. I don't have my license right now. But I'll show it to you later."

That was all I needed to know, or all I cared to know. I jumped in his arms and hugged him with my one arm. We fell on the sand and Amber ran over to find out what she was missing. She smelled Daniel and went crazy jumping all over him.

"Explain why my dog loves you."

"When we went inside your apartment to put in our equipment, she was really frightened, so I gave her lots of treats and played with her until she was calm," he said, smiling mischievously.

"Okay, now that makes sense," I laughed.

Remembering the shadow I had seen in my window when I had lounged by the pool. "Wait, were you in my room at Grammy's on Fourth of July, while I was outside?"

"Yes. Our equipment wasn't working, so I had to go in and put in a new bug. Amber greeted me at the front door." I hadn't been hallucinating.

We walked up and down the beach and just enjoyed each other's company. Suddenly I realized it was almost one, Grammy must be so worried. Why hadn't she called?

"Grammy, I'm so sorry. I'm on my way home." She had fallen asleep on the couch waiting for me and the call woke her up. I told her I had bumped into a friend and lost track of time. I asked if I could invite him for lunch and she said yes.

I hung up and asked, "Can you come? Even if you're working, you have to eat. Since you're watching me anyway, don't you think the closer the better?"

Daniel was grinning and said, "Lunch sounds great." I stared at his beautiful face hoping he wasn't going to vanish. He pulled me near and wrapped his arms around me. Life was so good!

We walked back holding hands and my body was tingling all over. All the feelings of sadness and despair were gone.

When we got near Grammy's house, I let go of Daniel's hand. I didn't want to make her nervous. I saw through the fence that Grammy was on the patio, so we entered through the side gate. Of course, Daniel charmed her right away and she even told him to call her Gabby.

Grammy was telling Daniel all about Cutchogue. Amber was standing by the empty water bowl, so I went in to fill the bowl.

When I came out, they were talking about nuclear power and Grammy was amazed about how many nuclear plants there were in France.

"There are about 58 plants in France," Daniel divulged.

"I'm surprised about that. We had The Shoreham Nuclear Plant out here, but it got closed after the Chernobyl disaster because of all the public outrage.

"France is concerned, but the French don't want to be dependent on energy from such a volatile region. France has very few natural energy resources so when the oil producing countries started quadrupling the price of oil in the 1970's, the French people backed the nuclear projects."

"After what happened in Japan, they should be scared," I added.

Daniel was knowledgeable about so many things and Grammy looked on approvingly. She smiled at me a few times, letting me know that she liked him.

After we ate, Grammy told us to go swimming. Daniel was in his swim trunks, but I was wearing a long maxi sundress. I ran upstairs to change.

When I peeked out my bedroom window, Daniel was in the pool waiting for me. I couldn't believe that he was here. It was just so surreal. I left a voice message for Lily saying everything was fine and to call me when she got home.

Grammy was doing a crossword puzzle by the pool and when Daniel saw me approach, he gasped looking at my body. "Paige! Oh my God!" he said. Grammy sighed as I walked by and understood Daniel reaction.

I thought my left side was getting better, but from Daniel's reaction, apparently not.

"It's healing," I said, attempting to make light of it. All that mattered now was that my heart wasn't black and blue anymore. I walked to him in the shallow end.

"I promised you that you wouldn't get hurt and look at you," he whispered. "I caused this."

"No you didn't. Frank and I weren't your fault." I wouldn't let him blame himself.

Daniel stopped moping and we had a great time. We got out of the pool when Grammy brought out watermelon.

"Daniel, where are you staying?" she asked, as she put the plate on the table.

"In Peconic. My friend's family has a summer home there."

When Grammy went inside, Daniel said, "Can we go for a walk?"

I threw on a cover-up and we took Amber. We walked to the end of the beach and after we passed the last house, Daniel put both hands on my face and looked into my eyes.

"Paige Devon, I woke up this morning so depressed. Watching you and not being a part of your life has been torture. I never imagined today would end like this."

"I can't believe it either. I almost didn't go see James today," I confessed. "I thought he'd ask me to do something crazy. I can't believe a day could start one way and end so differently." I wanted him to kiss me so badly.

Daniel shook his head and said, "I never thought you'd forgive me."

"If you had told me the reason, I would have."

"Every time I tried to talk to you, you were so angry. You also kept hanging up on me. Then I overhead some of your talks and it sounded like you hated me. I thought it was best that I stayed away."

"I was really angry at you," I admitted. "See, that's why you shouldn't eavesdrop." Memories of some horrific things I had said to Lily popped into my head.

We sat in silence on the sand savoring our time together. I put my head on his shoulder and he kissed it. My ringing cell interrupted our bliss. It was Grammy wondering where I went.

"Sorry, Grammy, we'll be back soon and I have Amber." I didn't want the day to ever end.

When I hung up, Daniel said, "We better get back. I don't want to be hated on my first day."

"I don't think you have to worry. She really liked you."

"We'll see if that continues. Your grandmother was thrilled to have you all to herself and now she'll have to share you with me." He hugged me tightly. "Sharing has always been a problem for me." He reached for his cell. "I'll have someone pick me up."

"Don't leave, stay for dinner," I begged, pouting with my lower lip.

He looked at me like I was the silliest thing he'd seen. "I would love to, but your family will get concerned if I'm over 24/7."

"You're right." I nodded miserably. If Mom knew, she might actually drive right out.

"What should I say when I talk to my parents?" We needed to have the same story.

"Just say what we told Gabby, that I'm visiting with a friend in Peconic, but I'll really be staying on the boat." When he saw my worried frown, he added, "Don't worry. The agency will figure it out before I talk to them, so it'll be believable."

"By the way, when did you bug Grammy's house?" I wondered.

"In June, when she was away."

"How did you know that I'd be out here?"

"We knew," Daniel, answered cryptically.

"But how? Wait. If you've been spying on my dad, you knew we came out here right?"

"I can't say," Daniel repeated. "I don't want to lie to you."

He was back, so I'd just have to accept his job and the limitations to what I'd be privy to. "Why did your uncle go to Plum Island? Isn't it an animal disease center?"

"It is, but the facility is closing," he added and stopped talking.

As we walked back, Daniel was notably quiet. Trying to snap him out of his sudden moodiness, I asked, "Did I upset you by asking about Plum Island?" Did the NSA or EMIT have a base on Plum Island? How many secret government agencies and facilities were there?

"Oh, no. I just started worrying about everything that we're dealing with. As far as Plum Island is concerned, everything is public knowledge. The United States Department of Homeland Security runs that facility."

When we reached the house, we found Grammy in the garden weeding.

"Gabby, thank you for lunch. It was delicious."

"Please come again while you're out here. It was nice to finally see Paige's dimples again." It was true. I couldn't remember smiling and laughing in such a long time.

"She definitely does light up a room when she smiles," Daniel said, agreeing with her.

From the way Daniel looked at me when he said that, Grammy knew that he was much more than just a friend.

We heard a car pull into the driveway and Daniel said he had to go. I walked him out and we hugged goodbye like we'd never see each other again.

"I'll miss you," I said sadly, afraid to let go of him.

"Me too. I just found you again." He kissed my forehead. "I'll call you later."

During dinner, Grammy seemed preoccupied and eventually broached what was bothering her. "Paige, did you know that Daniel was out here?"

"No, Grammy. I had no idea," I fibbed.

"How long have you known him?" she asked.

"Just a short time. We met at the end of June." At least, that part was true.

Later, Grammy and I were watching TV and my eyes began to close, so I told her I was going to bed. She asked if I wanted to go shopping in the morning and I said sure.

When I got upstairs, I realized that Lily never called. She had been so worried about the meeting with James that it seemed odd. I called Lily's cell and her home line, but there was no answer. I hoped she was okay. I started having paranoid thoughts, but if something had happened, Daniel would have told me. I put music on and thought about my day with Daniel. My cell rang and hoping it was Lily, I jumped to get it, but it was Daniel.

"Don't speak. I'll do all the talking on my side, so we have a little privacy."

"How?" I asked.

"I have a jammer on my cell phone. If I want to use it, I can."

"How come they can hear me then, shouldn't your jammer work for me too?"

"There's a device in your house not just in the phone, they hear you anyway," he explained. "I called to say I had a great time today."

"Me too," I said smiling.

"Look out your window."

I got up and there in front of my house was the boat. I was thrilled that he was nearby. "I know you don't like us too close, so I hope you don't mind.

"No, I'm glad now."

"If you need me, just call. Good night."

I was lying on the bed, about to fall asleep when my cell rang and jarred me out of my daze. I answered, "Lily, where've you been?"

"I'm sorry my parents got theater tickets and we just got home. I wasn't able to call you all day because I lost my phone. I called voicemail and got your message. I knew you were okay."

"What happened? Do you think it got stolen?" Thoughts of those goons came to mind.

"I don't think so. I was checking my emails and when the train pulled into Grand Central, I put the phone in my pocket. When I got to work, it was gone. It probably fell out. I'll check lost and found tomorrow. If I don't find it, I'll get another one tomorrow night. So what did James want?"

"I'll tell you everything on Friday, but Daniel didn't and doesn't have a girlfriend."

"What?"

"I know! The best news is that we're seeing each other again."

"Wow! You work fast."

"It all feels like a dream. I really can't believe it," I admitted.

"I had some Chad news, but now it seems pretty dull."

"Stop. What happened?"

"He asked me out for lunch tomorrow," she said happily.

That night, between the medication and Daniel, I slept like a baby.

12. BOAT RIDE

"There are only two ways to live your life. One is as though nothing is a miracle. The other is as though everything is a miracle." Einstein

When I opened my eyes and looked at the time, it was ten o'clock. Oh my God! It took a moment, but then I was awash with emotions that were so confusing. Did that all happen or did I dream it? Please let it have been real. I jumped out of bed.

I had to call Daniel, but first I had to let Amber out. This was extremely late for her; hopefully, Grammy had done it. I threw on my bathing suit and a sundress and ran downstairs.

Grammy was outside talking to Daniel. I was so happy to see him that my heart was pounding out of my chest. She saw me and said, "Good morning, I was about to wake you."

"Hi, Grammy." I was looking behind her, staring at Daniel. I wanted to run to him.

"Good morning, sleepyhead," he said.

"Daniel and his friend stopped by to see if you wanted to go boating," Grammy said. I looked around and a guy was sitting at the table. "I said we're shopping this morning, but perhaps later, if you're up for it."

"Sure, I'd like that."

I sat down across from them and Daniel introduced me to Brad. He was tall, had black curly hair, dark eyes and was quite muscular.

Grammy asked if I'd like some fruit and yogurt, but I said I wasn't hungry. Who could eat with Daniel to stare at? He filled and consumed me.

Daniel came over and as he sat, he placed his hand on my leg. "Come on. You have to eat something. You need to take care of yourself." Feeling his leg pressed against mine and his hand on my thigh caused me to stop breathing.

Grammy seemed pleased that Daniel had intervened and I said, "Fine, yogurt would be great." Daniel could take care of me whenever he wanted.

Brad watched us, but said nothing. The agency wasn't happy with our involvement and I wasn't sure what Brad thought, but I didn't care.

Grammy came back with the food and I obediently ate the yogurt and some strawberries.

"Oh Grammy, did you feed Amber?"

"Yes, a while ago. She started barking at seven."

"I'm so sorry. I didn't hear anything." I felt terrible. The deal with Amber was that she slept in the den. In the morning when she barked, Mom, Dad or I rushed downstairs to take her out, so that she didn't disturb Grammy whose bedroom was downstairs. "I'll let her sleep in my room tonight, so she doesn't wake you." Normally, we didn't allow Amber on the second floor because of Uncle Ian's allergy, but since he wasn't here, it wouldn't matter.

"Absolutely not. You need your sleep right now." As I began to protest, Grammy stopped me and said, "You were in a car accident and you're healing. I don't mind taking care of Amber."

Daniel stood up and said they had to go. As his hand gently brushed my back, my body tingled from the exchange.

At the supermarket, I saw an NSA car with an agent, I'd never seen before. I helped Grammy as best I could, but with one arm, I was basically there for company.

Back home, I called Daniel. "Hi. When do you want to go?"

"Now. I'll be right over. I'm in the channel by Fleets Neck."

I ran downstairs and found Grammy on the phone. When I walked in, she handed it to me and said, "Your mom wants to talk to you." I hoped she hadn't mentioned Daniel.

"Hi, how are you feeling?" She didn't sound angry or annoyed, so that was a good sign.

"I'm getting better."

There was a pause and then she asked, "Grammy said you're going boating with a boy named Daniel. Is that the same Daniel from New York?" Oh no, she knows.

"Yes, it is. I was just about to tell you," I fibbed nervously.

"What is he doing out there?"

"He's visiting a friend in Peconic. I saw him at the Causeway Beach. What are the odds, huh?" I said sounding truly surprised.

"It's uncanny. Chappaqua, Cutchogue not to mention France, it's eerie."

"Do you think he's stalking me?" I asked, feigning astonishment.

"Of course not, but it's still very strange. When you asked to stay with Grammy, you had no idea he'd be there?" she grilled.

"You think I came here because he was?" I asked incredulously.

"Well, the thought has crossed my mind," she admitted.

"I wasn't speaking to him, so how would I know that?"

"You also told me that you didn't like each other. What's going on now?"

"Well, I thought he had a girlfriend, but I was wrong so..." I stopped.

"Okay, and?" Mom asked.

"We worked everything out and we're dating," I said quickly and waited for the hysteria.

There was a long pause and she said, "I like Daniel, but please be careful, okay?" That was it? She wasn't going to overreact. Grammy heard the whole conversation and looked relieved.

Thinking of Daniel, I looked out the window and saw him coming up the beach towards the house. I kissed Grammy on the cheek. "I have to go. I'll be back around six." I turned and asked, "Can I invite Daniel and Brad for dinner?"

"Sure, call and let me know if they're coming."

I ran out and found Daniel sitting by the pool.

"Hi." He got up and wrapped his arms around me. "You're awfully happy."

"I'm happy because I'm with you. My mom knows you're out here."

"How did it go?" he asked.

"Fine, even after I told her we were dating." Suddenly, I realized that we hadn't talked about that. Was I presuming too much? "Was that okay?" I asked, feeling super insecure.

"Of course, that's what I want, too," he said and hugged me. I was so relieved.

The boat was very close to land and Daniel tried to help me up. It was difficult going up the ladder with one arm, so he jumped up on the deck and lifted me in.

Daniel must have just refueled because the boat reeked of gas and Brad was not there.

"Aren't we missing someone?" I asked confused.

"Brad's working," said Daniel.

"Oh, I was going to invite you two to have dinner at Grammy's tonight."

"I would love to come, but Brad will take a rain check. He has plans," he said and winked.

I called Grammy and told her that only Daniel would join us. After I hung up, I started feeling guilty. "Does lying get any easier?"

"It's never easy, but necessary at times. The boat's not bugged, so we can talk freely."

That was good because I was so sick of being spied on. "So tell me about your jammer?"

"It gives me privacy. Remember our first breakfast date on Columbus Avenue?"

I nodded and smiled. "So it was a date?"

"Well, I thought so. When I ask a girl I like out, it's a date." He winked at me. "During breakfast, I turned the jammer on. The team texted and called, but I wouldn't answer so they contacted James. When I got his call, I knew it would be heated, so I went outside."

"That's why you returned in such a foul mood."

"Yeah. I told him that our conversations were off-limits and if there was anything relevant to the case, I'd let them know.

"I thought I had no privacy at all, so I'm happy."

"And that's also why James showed up at your apartment the night Billy attacked you. James went to the NSA apartment to tell everyone about Frank. I wasn't there and since they couldn't hear what was going on, James got angry and stormed upstairs."

"That's right. He didn't know what was going on," I said, recalling that night.

"After we left, he told me about Frank and ordered that I end things with you."

"Does he blame me for Frank's death, too?" James treated me like such a nuisance.

"No. His problem is with me. He says I should've waited until this case was finished before I got involved with you."

"I'm not sure that it's just you. I think he hates me."

"It has nothing to do with not liking you," he said. "He's concerned about the case."

"This is insane. I don't know anything. All this spying is a total waste of your time."

"For now, you are our best lead and we will continue to protect you." Daniel stated.

I shook my head and said, "You really are an oddity."

"You have no idea," he quipped as he stared off into space. The way he said that was strange.

"What does that mean?" I asked.

"I'm just kidding, but why did you call me an oddity?"

"Well, you're a nineteen year-old spy," I said, surprised that he didn't understand.

"I'm an oddball, you're right," he agreed.

"I didn't call you an oddball. I said oddity."

"I know, but I did. Those words have similar meanings. Okay enough, let's go have fun."

Daniel raised the anchor and asked, "So where do you want to go?" I couldn't keep my eyes off him. His bright blue eyes hypnotized me "A beach, or we can go to Sag Harbor, Shelter Island or Greenport. Your wish is my command," he said in a funny accent. He took my hand and I got goose bumps.

I didn't care as long as I was with him. "Wherever you want is fine with me."

"As long as I'm with you, it doesn't matter." He must have read my mind.

"Let's just go for a ride," I suggested.

Daniel started the engine and we set off. We motored towards New Suffolk and I watched the scenery whizz by. Boats zipped around the bay and it was quite busy near Robins Island. Daniel's hair was blowing in the breeze and whenever he looked at me, I just wanted to hug him and never let go. I was staring at Daniel and hadn't noticed a huge boat race by, which caused a large wave to batter us on one side. The boat leaned sideways and since I wasn't holding on to anything, I fell out of my chair. Pain shot through my arm from the fall and I cried out. Daniel stopped the boat and rushed over. He picked me up and placed me on the cushions in the back of the boat. I was totally humiliated and was more embarrassed than hurt. Once Daniel was convinced I was okay, we continued on.

The noise of the engine was so loud that we couldn't talk, so I asked to go to a beach and we headed across the bay to the South Fork.

Daniel helped me off the boat and said, "I'll be right back."

He returned carrying a bag, a blanket and an umbrella. After he put everything down, Daniel presented me with a sandwich.

"You only had yogurt this morning and I had a hunch that you wouldn't eat anything."

"Thank you so much." I took a bite of my sandwich and smiled. "Turkey, lettuce, tomato, onion, honey mustard and mayo."

"I know all of your favorites. I hope that doesn't upset you." It sort of did, but what could I really do about it?

We started talking about his job because it was always the big elephant in the room. "How long have you guys been watching me?"

"We've been watching your dad for a while now. I had to go to Australia for work and vacation. I returned the beginning of June and was watching your Dad. Things went haywire with this case and I was assigned to follow you about two weeks before we spoke."

"So when I saw you at the MET, you were already following me?"

"Yes, I didn't realize you saw me until I heard you tell Lily."

I cringed that he heard everything I said about him. "But you left me and went into the café."

"I had to eat. Someone else took over," Daniel explained.

"Why did you ask me about a movie? What was the point in that?"

"I was in the process of gathering the plants and chestnuts and you noticed me. I decided to talk to you and later, spoke to James about letting me get to know you."

I sat there staring at him. "Why?"

"At first, I really wanted to help you because you were young, but later everything I knew, saw, and heard made me want to know you more. I wanted to see your eyes looking at me and hear your voice talking to me. Eavesdropping on your life wasn't enough."

While I was dreaming about him, he was also thinking of me. "So every time I saw you, it was orchestrated?" I asked.

"Yes and no. I was working those days following you anyway, so if I could, I'd try to talk to you. Like that day you were in the park with that boy. Outside was difficult. Unless I was in the van or in the apartment, I couldn't hear what you were saying because it's so loud out. I talked to you because you seemed upset and I wanted to hear it from you and not the agents."

"Hear me how?" I was starting to get a sick feeling.

"I could hear you through your cell."

Slowly, my mind started working and I reacted, "Wait, are you telling me that I have no privacy outside either? You listen to every one of my conversations?" There was no point in telling Lily things outside.

"I'm sorry." He realized he said too much. "Right now no one can hear us."

"That's just great," I snarled. But if I don't have my cell, how can you hear me?"

"We use listening devices but most of the time we access other cell phones around you."

It dawned on me that in the park, he was so far away from me, but after I chuckled, he looked right at me. "So you did hear me laugh at you that first day in the park?" Daniel nodded. "What a waste of taxpayer money. You really need to find someone in my father's firm because that's where the first envelope came from."

"We've thought of that but that would take more years."

"More years? What are you talking about?"

"I mean we don't have the people to handle that. It's like finding a needle in a haystack. When we found out that you would be the catalyst, we started watching you."

"When you say will or allude to the future, you lose me."

"I've said too much already. Just know I care for you and nothing will happen to you." Looking at me from the side, he said, "Aside from that broken arm, I hope."

"First you say, 'nothing will happen,' then you say, 'I hope'."

"Nothing should've happened to you, but since I spoke to you, I've changed the dynamics and things are off."

"I don't understand." My head hurt and I gave up. "Forget it, I'm tired of all these riddles and I'm not wasting time talking about your job. Let's have some fun. Can we go to Sag Harbor?"

"Your wish is my command," he joked and seemed relieved.

We got to Sag Harbor and Daniel spoke to the dock master to

rent a slip. As Daniel reached for his wallet, I put my hand out and while shaking his head, he handed me his license.

His license verified his age; he was born two years before me. It was nice to finally see proof.

We wandered around and strolled in and out of stores. When we passed a bookstore, I had to go in. Daniel excused himself and said he'd be right back. I didn't know where he went, but he was back in a few minutes.

On the way back to the boat, Daniel bought a blueberry pie and a large sunflower bouquet. Near the Causeway Beach, Daniel called Brad to meet us there. Brad then dropped us off at Grammy's beach and would pick Daniel up around midnight.

Daniel washed up in the outside shower and feeling sandy, I ran to do the same inside.

As we ate dinner outside, Grammy asked Daniel about his uncle. When she heard that he worked for the NSA, she started talking about terrorism.

"I was reading about the various anti-US terrorist groups and couldn't believe how many there are in the world," Grammy said.

"My uncle said there are over forty-five worldwide and those numbers keep growing."

"It makes no sense. If they attack us, then we'll attack them. Everybody loses. I don't know what the point is," I interjected.

"It's a badge of honor to die fighting the infidels, so their own destruction is not a deterrent," Daniel explained. "As far as their religion, the afterlife is much more important than this one."

"I'd always thought that the younger generations would change things," I said.

"Their beliefs are indoctrinated at an early age," said Grammy.

Daniel added, "That's all they know, so hatred and anger are a good recruiting tool."

They started talking about the Taliban. "The destruction of the poppy fields might help Afghanistan get rid of the Taliban regime," Grammy said.

"The problem is that two-thirds of the world's heroin supply comes from Afghanistan and opium production accounts for sixty percent of the country's economy. The Taliban's making well over one hundred million dollars a year. With that much money at stake, they'll fight like crazy not to lose it. Even though the Afghan people don't want the Taliban regime, they know nothing else but poppy farming. The opium traffickers guarantee a minimum price for the crop and the people are desperate, so they cultivate poppy. Hopefully, the agriculture projects being implemented will encourage the people so they can flourish as an agricultural economy like they did in the 1970's. Right now, talks to destroy the poppy crops and therefore their livelihood are making the Afghan people very angry and causing more hatred towards America. Maybe farming pomegranates and vineyards will be a success," Daniel explained.

"Islam forbids alcohol and drug use, so how is selling heroin to the world and creating junkies reconciled with Islam?" Grammy asked. "Do they really think Allah would approve if they only sold to non-Muslims? It seems so hypocritical and non-religious for supposedly such religious people."

"When people are starving, they are just trying to survive," Daniel answered.

"You just said that they can farm other things, so there are other options," I said.

"True, but Afghanistan is often drought stricken and the farmers need advice from water experts. When they learn what can thrive in their region and how profitable it could be, they won't be tempted to grow poppy."

"There's so much wealth in that region from oil, but its still mostly a desert. Why hasn't any money from oil been used to help the poor people and cultivate the land? No wonder there is so much anger in that region," I added.

"That's been the cause for a lot of the uprisings against the governments and royals in the region," said Grammy.

"I can't believe that the Taliban is still there tormenting women though. It has to stop."

"The degradation of those poor women is so appalling," Grammy said.

"If everyone wore those burqas, it'd be one thing, but just women makes it barbaric," I said.

"That's a very contentious issue," said Grammy. "The Koran in some places says women are equal and in other places, it says women are the property of men. Each group makes its own interpretation."

"Since no one can own another human being, I believe it's a moot point," added Daniel.

"I just can't imagine what poor people are going through,"

Grammy added.

At that moment, Amber began whining to go inside.

Noticing that the water bowl on the patio was empty, I stood up to open the door, but Grammy stopped me.

"I'll let Amber in. I'm getting bitten up. If you're staying out here, light the citronella candles and the torches," advised Grammy.

"Okay, we will," I answered.

After she left, Daniel lit all the anti-bug paraphernalia and we went in the pool.

It dawned on me that Daniel had a job and I was still in high school. "What happens when this is over? Where do you go?" I asked anxiously.

"Why don't we worry about that when we have to?" Daniel said and tried to swim away.

Not letting him, I stood in his way and said, "I don't understand." His evasive tactics weren't going to work tonight because I needed to know.

"I plan on staying and living in New York." I was so happy. He added, "I'll have to go away on assignments, though."

"Okay, I can handle that as long as you're not leaving or going to move to London."

"No, I'm not moving to London. I'm not going anywhere," he laughed and hugged me gently. All was well in the world. Daniel was staying.

We went inside and decided to watch a movie. After pestering Grammy, she joined us in the living room. Grammy sat in her chair while Daniel and I sat on the couch at a safe distance. By the end of the movie, we were sitting right next to each other, holding hands.

Once the movie was over, Grammy asked, "What time is Brad picking you up?"

"Around midnight, I hope that's okay?" Daniel asked.

"Of course. Good night, I hope to see you soon."

We sat on the couch and I quickly nestled into his arms. Daniel put both arms around me and we sat in silence.

"I have something for you." He reached into his pocket and pulled out a gift envelope. Inside was a silver bracelet with saltwater pearls and blue sea glass beads.

"It's absolutely beautiful," I said excitedly.

Daniel was pleased. "I saw it today in Sag Harbor and thought of you."

"You shouldn't have, but thank you." I kissed him on the cheek and had done it instinctually, but was still totally flustered afterwards.

Daniel seemed surprised by my kiss and said, "Not as beautiful as you."

I blushed and looked the bracelet. "The sea glass is the same color as your eyes. When did you buy this? I was with you the whole time."

"I saw it in the window and when you were in the bookstore, I called and they delivered it. I'm not allowed to let you out of my sight when I'm the only one watching you."

That's good because it meant he'd be nearby as long as this case wasn't solved. Nothing could compare with the way I felt at that moment. It was like I finally understood what love was.

I couldn't believe that Daniel could mean so much to me and that I could only think of him. All these emotions were so all encompassing that my head spun. I shut my eyes and the next thing I knew I was feeling kisses on my head.

"Paige, I have to leave now. Brad's here." Daniel's voice was so far away and I realized that I had fallen asleep!

"I'm so sorry. I can't believe this," I moaned.

"Don't worry. Your body is recovering. It was nice just being here with you."

I walked him to the door, but I had such a pathetic face that he must have felt pity for me, because he asked, "Can I see you tomorrow?"

"YES! Yes! Yes! Does that answer your question?"

"Yes, your dimples tell all."

I blushed. Of course they do. I adore you, I thought.

"Time for you to go to bed, you look exhausted."

"I will, right after I take Amber out," I promised.

"I'm sorry! I forgot all about Amber. Come on, let's walk her together." Amber ran outside and we held hands as we followed her. Daniel texted Brad to tell him he'd be a bit longer.

I looked up to admire the stars. "I just saw a shooting star!" I shrieked like a little kid.

"It's either the South Delta Aquarids or the Perseid meteor showers," Daniel said. "Both of them are visible this time of year, but I think it's the Perseid because it peaks in August."

"How do you know everything?"

"I've been around a long time," he sighed, and then laughed. "I took an astronomy class."

We sat on the sand and watched the sky. Being here with Daniel was just unbelievable.

"We're like two comets that were pulled together and now we're in the same orbit," he said.

Even though it was scientific, it still sounded romantic. "Is that even possible?" I asked.

"I'm not sure, but new comets are discovered each year, so anything's possible. A while back, two asteroids collided head-on so maybe instead of being in the same orbit, we've just crashed into each other," he joked.

Amber began digging next to us and sand was flying everywhere. "Amber, stop," I yelled.

"Okay that's our clue to head home. I don't want to see Gabby's wrath, because if it's anything like yours, I'll be in big trouble."

I walked him to the front door and he kissed my cheek. "Good night. Call me when you wake up," he said as he exited. When was he going to kiss me on my lips? I set the house alarm and ran up the stairs. I had so much to tell Lily, but it was too late to call her.

13. HARROW

"Gravitation is not responsible for people falling in love." Einstein

The next thing I knew the sun was shining in my face again. I forgot to lower the shade, maybe because I knew Daniel was out there. It was eight o'clock and Amber was barking so I ran downstairs and let her out. And there, sitting on a chaise, reading the paper was Daniel. Amber ran right over to him and almost jumped into his lap.

"It's so nice to wake up to you again!" I exclaimed excitedly.

"I went for a jog and pilfered Gabby's paper. Hoped you'd wake up soon," he added with a twinkle in his eyes. He was in an amazing mood and he glistened from his run. At that moment, Grammy came out in her bathrobe, appraised the situation and looked quite concerned.

"Daniel, have you been here all night?" she asked sternly, looking from Daniel to me.

Shaking my head, I answered, "Oh, no, Grammy, I came out to

let Amber out and found Daniel here reading your paper. He was jogging and stopped by."

She was relieved by that answer and asked, "Would you like some coffee or tea, Daniel?"

"Coffee, but then I have to run. Brad and I are playing tennis this morning." He winked at me.

"Have dinner with us tonight?" I asked as he was leaving.

"I think you should have dinner with Gabby alone tonight. How about we go out to dinner tomorrow night? Your mom will be here. Will she let you out with me?" he asked, jokingly.

"Yes, she will." Thinking of not seeing him till the next day was making me sad, so I suggested, "Come over after dinner. We can go to the movies."

"Sounds like a great idea. What time?"

"Around eight? Why don't you and Brad come over for a swim after tennis?"

"Sounds perfect," said Daniel. Grammy came out at this point and Daniel turned to her and said, "Gabby, thanks for the coffee."

"Would you like to join us for dinner tonight? Of course your friend Brad is welcome also."

"Thank you, but I can't tonight. Paige and I plan to catch a movie after dinner. Would you like to join us?" He constantly amazed me. What boy would invite their date's grandmother to join them at the movies? As I stood there in utter surprise, staring at Daniel in awe, Grammy appeared completely flummoxed.

Grammy said she wasn't intruding on our date. We gave up trying to change her mind. Daniel left, jogging down the beach.

After breakfast, Grammy and I went berry picking at Harbes Farm on the North Road. This was one of Grammy's favorite things to do in the summer. There were so many choices during different times of the year at all the different farms.

One armed berry picking wasn't easy, but I sat in one spot and picked one box.

Unstoppable, Grammy picked five boxes of blueberries. Then, she picked a box of raspberries and a box of blackberries.

Back home, we had lunch on the patio and Grammy left me by the pool to go bake a blueberry pie. I read magazines and listened to my iPod.

Around two o'clock, the boat pulled up and I watched Daniel and Brad jump out. When he reached the patio, he dove in the pool and swam over to me.

"It's been difficult staying away," he said quietly as he exited the pool.

I threw my arm around his neck and gave him a hug. My sundress got damp from his wet body. Looking behind Daniel, I saw Brad observing us with a cold expression. He seemed angry and I wondered if Daniel forced him to come.

Grammy came out and asked if they had eaten and they had. I watched Daniel and Brad swim while I floated on a raft. When they started roughhousing, I got out of the pool.

They left around five saying they had dinner plans. Grammy seemed pleased that it was just the two of us. Our conversation was nothing as intellectual as her talks with Daniel, but we still enjoyed each other's company and it was nice hearing stories about Mom when she was my age.

Daniel called and said he was on his way, so I sat on the white wooden bench near the driveway to wait for him. Amber was with me and when she spotted a rabbit, she took off into the brush. I had to call her repeatedly until she came out and I dragged her inside the house.

Daniel pulled up and I jumped in.

"Hi there. The movie you want to see starts at nine so we have some time."

As we passed the Causeway Beach, I said, "Let's stop here. Want to go for a walk?"

Daniel said sure and we pulled into the parking lot. We ended up sitting in the car talking the whole time.

Almost twenty minutes later, my cell rang and it was Grammy. She sounded really upset, but my phone was breaking up and I couldn't really hear her.

"I can't hear you very well. What's wrong?" Before even knowing what was up, Daniel put the car in gear and headed back. "Grammy, I'll be right there, don't worry. I'm at the Causeway Beach. I'm sure Amber's fine," I said and hung up.

"What happened?"

"Grammy let Amber out on the beach right after we left because she was barking and now she can't find her."

"Should I put out an Amber Alert with the agency?" asked Daniel jovially.

"Very funny, but I don't think that's necessary."

When we arrived, Grammy rushed out, "I'm so sorry, but she

hasn't come back."

"Don't worry. She was chasing a rabbit before. She's around here somewhere."

I ran inside to get Amber's favorite treats and her leash. Daniel and I walked down the beach, while Grammy went to look on the road.

"Amber! Amber!" Daniel and I called as we went up and down in both directions. In the distance, I saw someone walking towards us and recognized Brad. Brad told us that he didn't see Amber on the far side of the beach, but I also knew she wouldn't go to Brad if he called her.

Thirty minutes had passed and I started to panic. Where was she? "Daniel, I don't know what else to do? It's getting dark."

"Amber didn't get off the Point. The guys at the Causeway Beach are on alert. They'll call if she shows up there. There's only one road out of here. We'll find her." We went on the road and as we rounded a curve, we bumped into Grammy and insisted she return home.

We returned to the beach and while yelling Amber's name repeatedly, I heard a lady's voice yelling to us, "Excuse me! Have you lost a dog?" I saw a lady standing on the porch waving to us.

I almost screamed with joy. "Yes, have you seen her?"

"She's here at my house." Daniel and I raced up to the door and there was Amber, playing with a yellow lab. I remembered that she had played with this dog on the beach once. I wanted to cry, scream, strangle her, but all I could do was hug her. Thank you, thank you, I thought.

"We've been worried sick. It's been over an hour. How did she get here?"

"I was walking Cheddar on the beach and she followed us home. I let her in because she was so sweet, but she didn't have a dog tag."

"Sorry, it fell off," I explained.

"Then, I got an overseas call from my husband and got sidetracked. I planned on going for a walk in hopes of finding where she belonged."

"Thank you. I'm Paige Devon, Gabby Tilly's granddaughter and this is Daniel Haydin."

"Nice to meet you both. I know your grandmother; she's a lovely lady. I'm Laura Burke."

I put on Amber's leash and dragged her away. Grammy was so relieved that she almost cried. Since we missed the movie, we stayed home, made tea and got some blueberry pie. We were all emotionally drained, but Amber passed right out on the couch with not a care in the world.

Grammy said, "I'm a little frazzled from all the excitement. I'm going to lie down and relax."

After she left, I looked at Daniel. "Thanks for staying so calm, while I was a crazed idiot."

"No problem, I like crazed idiots," he teased as he stroked my hair, running his hand down my back. It was unbelievable, but whenever he touched me, it was like my body woke up.

We started watching a movie, but I really wasn't paying attention. I was so distracted by his presence. I burrowed myself in his arms and refused to ever leave. We sat like that for a long time in absolute silence enjoying each other and our connection. He kissed my head and I just listened to the beat of his heart. The house phone rang bringing me back to reality.

It was Mom. "Hi. I tried calling your cell, but you didn't answer." I remembered that I put my cell on the outside table when I took off Amber's leash.

"We had a crazy night. Daniel and I were on the way to the movies and Grammy called really upset. She let Amber out and she didn't come back. We came back to find her. It took over an hour, but she was at a neighbor's house playing with her dog."

"Thank goodness. Is Grammy okay? Let me talk to her."

"She was really upset and went in her room. She might be sleeping. Do you want me to knock and see?"

"No don't, she must be exhausted. I'll see her tomorrow. What are you doing?"

"Daniel and I are watching TV. Is it okay if we go to the movies tomorrow night?

"Sure, I'll talk to you tomorrow."

I went outside and got my cell. Shortly after that, Lily called to tell me that Noelle was coming out for the weekend because her parents were going away. It was fine with me since now Lily would have company while I was with Daniel.

I went right back to Daniel who was looking at a book on the coffee table. When I reached him, he exclaimed, "Paige, look at this book!"

Sitting down, I noticed that the title was *Between Sea and Sky: Landscapes of Long Island's North Fork.* "And?" I asked perplexed.

"Remember that book we were looking at in my library?" he asked. "This is the same photographer!"

"Yes, the American Landmarks book. You're kidding!" I said.

After reading the jacket, I learned that the author lived in Southold. We leafed through the photographs and Daniel got a fast course on the beauty of the North Fork or NoFo as Aunt Cecile and the bumper stickers called it.

When Amber barked to go out, I put on her leash just in case she wanted to visit Cheddar again. I thought about all that had happened since the start of the summer. My life had been a whirlwind of excitement, good and bad. Gladly, I'd take the bad if I had Daniel in the end.

Glancing at me, Daniel asked, "Why so quiet?"

"I'm just thinking of everything that has happened in a month. If someone had told me this, I wouldn't have believed it."

"Any regrets?" Daniel asked.

"No. Well, maybe the girlfriend part," I smirked. "And the goons, and the surveillance, and the hit-and-run, and…"

Daniel fell to the ground, pretending to faint. "What a list," he said.

We sat on the beach and I wanted to know more about his ex-girlfriend or girlfriends. "So James told me that Juliet was your ex-girlfriend?"

"Yes, she was."

"Did she call you Romeo like in Romeo and Juliet?" I joked.

Daniel didn't look amused and said, "No, she didn't."

When he didn't say more, I asked, "Is she English?"

"No, she's French and her name is Juliette with a te at the end."

"So tell me about her?"

"There's not much to tell. We dated, we broke up and we're friends."

"You went to France with her?"

"I didn't go with her. She lives in Paris. I called her when I was there."

"She's actually French?"

"Her father is, but her mom is American. Juliette was born in the US."

"What about Australia? You both were vacationing there at the same time?"

"I was working in Canberra and she called me when she came to Australia."

"Where did you two meet?"

"We met in London." Paris, Australia and London? They sure got around.

"At school?"

"No, she didn't go to my school. Can we stop talking about her please? She's not important."

He was right. Why torture myself? He liked me now, but it was so hard not to think about her. "Okay then, tell me about your school?"

"Okay, what do you want to know?" Daniel got visibly animated.

"Everything. My dad said that it's a really old school and has a lot of weird traditions."

"You have no idea! It was really intimidating at first. Even with my dad's help, it was hard to acclimate especially coming from an American school."

"Why?"

"First of all the dress code is nothing like at a normal school. We had two uniforms. During the week we wore a white shirt, black silk tie, grey trousers, black shoes, blue jumper…"

"A jumper?" I asked, rummaging my brain, temporarily forgetting what it was. I knew my grandparents used that word.

"A pullover sweater."

"I knew that. Did…" I was about to ask another question when Daniel jumped in.

"I'm not done yet," Daniel said in a reproachful tone. "We also wore a dark blue woolen uniform jacket, the school blue and white scarf on cold days and, most importantly, a boater style straw hat with a dark blue band."

"You're kidding? Like the gondolier hats in Venice?" I asked incredulously.

"Yes, exactly," he answered proudly.

"That's such a bizarre outfit." I scowled my forehead thinking about it.

"It's tradition and it dates back to Edwardian times. No proper gentleman was seen hatless and Harrow still adheres to all those traditions. We were required to "cap" all teachers when we passed them. It's done by raising the forefinger to the brim, like this." He demonstrated.

"That's crazy and there was a second uniform? That get-up wasn't enough?" I mocked.

Ignoring my ribbing, he answered, "On Sundays, we wore a black tailcoat."

I was incredulous. "You wore a tuxedo?"

Daniel laughed, "Yes, I wore a tuxedo jacket with pinstriped trousers, a black waistcoat, black tie, braces and a white shirt."

"A waistcoat and braces? What is that?"

"A vest and suspenders."

"Everybody wore the exact same thing?" I asked, not understanding this school at all.

"There were some variations if you were a member of certain societies or sports teams."

"What kind?"

"During the week, different sweaters, scarves, neck and bow ties. On Sundays, it would mean grey or red vests, hat with black speckles, or a top hat and cane. It all depended on the group you were in."

"It sounds like another planet. I have to see photos."

"It was definitely weird at first, but I got used to it and everyone became family. After my parents died, I was only able to function because of that school. It pulled me through the darkest period in my life," Daniel answered glumly.

To get Daniel's mind off his parents, I asked him what I had been dying to know. "Did you have any girlfriends at school?" I knew he had one girlfriend and he must have had others. He was gorgeous after all. What girl wouldn't like him?

"It was a boys school, so no, I didn't have a girlfriend there."

"You never saw girls?" I asked disbelievingly. Then how did he meet Juliette?

"Yes, I saw girls. The school had functions with different girls' boarding schools on Saturdays."

Juliette must have gone to one of those schools.

"So why an all boys school?" I asked.

"My parents felt strongly about same sex education."

"Why?"

"Virtually all the top schools are single-sex schools. My dad, being a scientist, explained that research into patterns of brain activity confirmed that boys and girls learn in different ways."

"Is that why you're so smart? Because there were no girls around?"

"If you were at my school, I would've done very little work."

"Very funny! So what sports did you play? I know you like tennis."

"I do like tennis, but I was obsessed with Harrow football at school."

"You mean soccer?"

"Yes, I'm sorry, soccer. Soccer is a kicking and passing game, but Harrow football is essentially a dribbling game. Do you understand soccer?"

"Sort of..." I grimaced and Daniel smiled.

"Okay then...well Harrow football is only played at Harrow, no other school. It's been played for two months every spring season since about the 1800's."

"Why only two months? That doesn't make any sense."

"It's because the grounds are solid clay and during the summer the clay cracks from the heat, but after the winter, it's a slimy, slushy, muddy swamp. In the spring for two months, we get quite muddy playing."

"Sounds great," I said rolling my eyes. "You like poetry and mud?"

"I do, that's part of the fun. Speaking of poems, there is one about Harrow football and explains it all. 'Again we rush across the slush - A pack of breathless faces - And charge and fall, and see the ball. Fly whizzing through the bases.'"

"I'll pass," I joked.

"It really was fun. I'm crushed that you're so skeptical." He acted hurt by my reaction.

"Sure you are. Wait, did you say bases? That sounds like baseball."

"We had to score a 'base' by kicking the ball between two vertical posts."

Puzzled, I asked, "Do you like any sport that I'll actually understand?"

"Well in school, I also played polo."

"You ride?" I shrieked.

"Yes, and I know you do as well," he grinned.

"I can't believe it. I know so few boys that ride. Most boys I know think it's a girl's sport."

"Not in Europe. Polo is very popular."

"I can't believe that you ride," I said, shaking my head in amazement. We talked about polo for a while and somehow we got back on soccer. I told him that I thought it was rather boring.

"It's different in England. When we're in London, I'll take you to a game and you'll see."

I just stared at him wondering if I heard him right.

"Did you just say, 'when we're in London'?"

"Do you think you're going across the pond without all of your chaperones going?"

Reality set in. "No! I thought I'd have peace there. You're all coming. Are you kidding?"

"Yes, we're all coming; please don't argue, it won't work," he said adamantly.

"I'm thrilled you're coming, just not that your posse is," I said. "I want my privacy back, but I'll pass on that for now, if I can keep you."

"You definitely can keep me," he said.

"When were you going to tell me?"

"Soon, but we started talking about soccer and I slipped."

"Such a bad spy!" I laughed, "Are you staying at your house? Is it near my grandparents?"

"Yes. Surprisingly, my house is only a little over a mile away," he said.

"You're kidding?"

"No, I'm not. I can't wait for you to see it."

"What are we going to say to my parents? Please don't tell them that you have a home there."

"I figured as much. Every time you were with me, they'd think you were at my house."

"Should I pretend you're not there?" I asked.

"No. If anything happens, I'll need to be with you. Or if they see me, I don't want them to hate me." We decided that a job interview sounded the best.

"I was so upset that Nana broke her leg and my visit was canceled, but if I went, I never would've met you."

"That's right! You weren't supposed to be here this summer!" he exclaimed.

Daniel was deep in thought and I had no idea why. "I was supposed to be in London. Why does it matter? Nana's accident had nothing to do with what's happening here."

"Probably not. I have to get going. I'll keep away tomorrow until it's time for the movie."

"Please come in the afternoon. Mom won't be here till early evening." I smiled and batted my eyes for effect.

He laughed and said, "Paige Devon, you're incorrigible." I nodded happily. "It's time I left. It's past midnight."

"Time goes too fast when I'm with you."

"That's funny because for me time stops." We hugged and said goodbye. Would he ever kiss me? I couldn't take this much longer!

***

I woke up in the same clothes from the day before. "Ugh." I remembered lying down thinking about Daniel, planning to put on my jammies, but that never happened. Knowing today was going to be different worried me. Mom's presence would absolutely change things. Amber was barking so I ran downstairs. I found Grammy walking to the kitchen to let her out.

"Morning, Grammy, I'll take care of Amber."

As I walked outside, my cell rang and I heard Daniel's glorious voice. "Good morning. Did you sleep well?" I realized that he was on the boat watching me, so I waved.

"Good morning. I crashed and woke up fully clothed."

"So, you were that tired?" he asked, sounding amused.

"I guess. One moment, I'm lying down and the next it's morning."

He laughed, "It's called exhaustion. Wait, I'll meet you at the bend on the beach and I'll walk Amber with you." I couldn't wait. Just seeing him would put a smile on my heart.

He jumped in and swam over. As he hugged me, I got damp, but it didn't matter. Everything was perfect except for my one and only problem. Why hadn't he kissed me yet? We'd only been a couple since Monday, but that's all I could think about.

As we walked, Daniel had his arm around me. "I have to go to DC for the weekend. I'm catching a flight out of Mattituck tomorrow morning." In a matter of seconds, my happiness was shattered.

"Mattituck?" I questioned. "There's no airport there."

Daniel smiled. "There is. I'll be back on Sunday." Seeing my sad face, he added, "You know that I'll miss you too, but I have to go for work." I didn't want to act like I couldn't live without my boyfriend for a couple of days, but since our relationship was filled with spying and goons, there really was no normal way to act.

"Don't look so sad. You'll have Lily and Noelle this weekend," Daniel said.

"Where are you staying?" I wondered.

"I have an apartment in McLean, Virginia."

How many more surprises were there? "What? Where else do you have homes?"

"That's it. I promise. After school ended, I lived with James in DC. Once I started working, I got my own place. The EMIT offices are in the CIA building in Mclean, so I moved nearby."

"How far is James from you?"

"He's in Georgetown, only eight miles away."

"That's really close."

He looked down the beach. "Paige, I better get out of here before Grammy sees me."

"I'll call you later," I said.

Daniel jumped in the water and swam to the boat.

When I got back, Grammy said that Mom was on her way. Why was she coming this early? She was supposed to be coming after work. Seething, I called her cell to get to the bottom of the change in plans. She said her meeting was canceled and she left earlier. I really hoped that was the truth.

When Mom walked in, Amber went ballistic. She really missed her and so did I.

We ran out to do some food shopping and Mom did not bring up Daniel at all. I was grateful for that because in the past we'd just argue about him.

On the drive back home, she finally brought up Daniel.

"He's good, but he's going to visit family in DC tomorrow morning," I answered stoically. I hated making up stories and being dishonest.

"Oh, that's too bad. Dad and I wanted to invite him and his

friend over Saturday for a barbecue." At first I got annoyed, but I did tell her we were dating. What did I expect them to do, ignore him?

"That would have been nice, but he can't," I answered and it came out sounding so pathetic that Mom glanced over at me.

"Why don't you call him and invite him and his friend for dinner tonight before the movies?"

"I'll ask him," I said and reached for my cell. I told him I was with Mom, invited him to come over for a swim and relayed Mom's dinner invitation. He said he'd check with Brad and tell us when he came over.

"He'll let us know later," I told Mom.

After lunch, Grammy and Mom gardened and I read my poetry book. I read the biography of Elizabeth Barrett Browning. She began writing when she was young and received critical praise. When she was older, Robert Browning, an unknown poet, started writing to her. After five months, they met and fell in love. Against her father's wishes, she married him and was disinherited. She left England and moved to Italy where she lived a happy life. She died at the age of fifty-five from a life-long illness that doctors were never able to diagnose. In her husband's arms, she died and her last word to him was "beautiful." How tragic! I began reading her poem called "Change Upon Change."

> Five months ago the stream did flow,
> The lilies bloomed within the sedge,
> And we were lingering to and fro,
> Where none will track thee in this snow,
> Along the stream, beside the hedge.
> Ah, Sweet, be free to love and go!

For if I do not hear thy foot,
The frozen river is as mute,
The flowers have dried down to the root:
And why, since these be changed since May,
Shouldst thou change less than they.

And slow, slow as the winter snow
The tears have drifted to mine eyes;
And my poor cheeks, five months ago
Set blushing at thy praises so,
Put paleness on for a disguise.
Ah, Sweet, be free to praise and go!
For if my face is turned too pale,
It was thine oath that first did fail, --
It was thy love proved false and frail, --
And why, since these be changed now,
Should I change less than thou.

How I related to those words! It described a carefree love, but things changed. Winter symbolized the end of their love and the poem alluded that it was false. It was similar to what had happened with Daniel and I, but our relationship has been given a second chance.

The next poem SONNET #43, FROM THE PORTUGUESE surprised me. I had heard the famous first sentence before but never knew it was a Browning poem. I always thought the line 'How do I love thee? Let me count the ways' was from Shakespeare.

How do I love thee? Let me count the ways.
I love thee to the depth and breadth and height
My soul can reach, when feeling out of sight
For the ends of Being and ideal Grace.
I love thee to the level of everyday's
Most quiet need, by sun and candle-light.

I love thee freely, as men strive for Right;
I love thee purely, as they turn from Praise.
I love thee with the passion put to use
In my old griefs, and with my childhood's faith.
I love thee with a love I seemed to lose
With my lost saints!---I love thee with the breath,
Smiles, tears, of all my life!---and, if God choose,
I shall but love thee better after death.

The words made me think of Daniel and I understood the depth of the emotions the poet was trying to convey. How can you measure love and be able to express the magnitude of the feelings involved? It's impossible to define the emotion of love, longing and desire. Sure, poets and writers have tried, but they can only write about their own view of love. Every person has his or her own idea of what constitutes love, what it is or what it feels like.

Closing my eyes, I thought about how these fourteen lines were able to deliver so much passion and meaning. "Sonnet 43" expressed such absolute love.

I felt my hair being stroked and I opened my eyes to see Daniel in all his beautiful glory. Deeply immersed in my thoughts, I was oblivious to his arrival.

"Hey, no boat. How did you get here?"

"I borrowed Brad's car. What are you reading?" Glancing at the book, his eyes widened, "Elizabeth Barrett Browning, a little more light reading?" he joked. "Very British of you."

"Well, I am half-English, besides the class is called English Poets."

Daniel sat down next to me and leaned in to see what poem I was reading. Embarrassed because this poem really affected me, I blushed.

"How do I love thee? Let me count the ways," he read and then he smiled at me. "I like that poem and all it implies."

Staring into his eyes, I thought he was alluding to the fact that he loved me, but since he'd never even tried to kiss me, maybe I was wrong.

Luckily, Mom came out of the house just when my insecurities were getting the better of me. Carrying three water bottles, she approached Daniel, smiling warmly. "Daniel, it's so nice to see you." She kissed him on the cheek. I was happy that she was being nice. "My mom told me you were a godsend when Amber was missing. Thank you so much."

"You're welcome."

"Can you have dinner with us tonight?"

"Yes, I can, but Brad has other plans."

"Well, I'm glad that at least you can." She handed each of us a water bottle and left to bring one to Grammy in the garden.

Suddenly, Daniel seemed a million miles away.

"Is everything okay?" I asked, as he stared at me. I sensed he was about to say something, but then nothing came out and he looked anxious. I got nervous and presumed that it had to be work related. "Did something happen? Are those men on Nassau Point?"

Daniel shook his head. "No. Everything's fine. Can we go for a drive?"

"Sure, let me tell Mom." I went to find her and she said to be back at six for dinner, so we had three hours to do whatever we wanted.

When I returned, Daniel was staring off into space, oblivious that I was back.

"We have to be back at six. Are you okay?"

"I'm fine, but we need to talk. Let's get out of here." What was wrong with him? He was so distant.

14. SECRET

"Everything that can be counted does not necessarily count;
everything that counts cannot necessarily be counted." Einstein

Daniel drove out to the Point Beach at the end of Nassau Point Road. I hadn't been there yet this summer. There were a few cars parked on the dead end road. When I got out of the car, Daniel reached for my hand and I relaxed feeling his touch. Hand-in-hand, we walked down the stairs to the beach and the silence was killing me.

I blurted out, "Did something happen? You're beginning to freak me out."

"I keep going over and over this discussion in my head, but there's really no way to buffer what I need to tell you. Please, believe that I never meant to hurt you," he said imploringly.

I was so confused and didn't want to presume anything, but his tone was so ominous. *Oh... no...he's breaking up with me again.*

"Can we sit down, over there?" he said, pointing to the left of the stairs. There were people near the steps, but it was deserted further down. I stared at the shells and stones underfoot, trying to fathom what was going on. After we sat down, all I could do was gaze at the water, unable to look at him because I knew I'd cry.

"Can you look at me? I need to see your eyes," Daniel pleaded.

I refused to look at him. Why make this about him and his needs?

"I don't think it's necessary. Just go on and break up with me already. Why do you keep torturing me? I don't understand," I said, trying to mentally shield myself from the oncoming heartache.

Daniel swung me around searching my face with his eyes. "I'm not breaking up with you! I need to tell you something and afterwards, you might want to break up with me."

"I don't understand. What are you talking about?" I asked, baffled beyond belief. Me break up with him? That wasn't a possibility.

"Last night, I realized that I couldn't continue our relationship unless I told you everything," he said tensely. I was scared to hear what he had to say. "I called James this morning and told him that I was telling you the truth. As my superior, he advised against it, but as a relative and on a personal level he understood. Since I have to go to DC anyway, I decided to tell you, see what your response is and then fix things if necessary."

"Fix what and how?" I asked irritated by his mumbo jumbo.

"I have to tell you something and if you can't handle it, I'll understand. Just know that I've never told this to anyone and you must promise me that what you hear, you'll never repeat." All I could do was nod my head. "Let me start from the beginning." Daniel took a deep breath. I tried encouraging him by rubbing his arm.

"Go ahead, tell me. We'll figure it out. Don't worry." I braced myself. *How bad could this be?* Crazy things were running through my mind. Is he married? Does he have a baby?

Daniel sighed and continued, "My father and mother met when they were both at Oxford. Dad was a year older and after he graduated, he started working for a research laboratory. My mom joined him after she graduated."

Both his parents were scientists. I knew that.

"Britain was the first country to seriously study the feasibility of nuclear weapons. As a result of those studies, a group of scientists invented something and broke off from the weapons studies. My parents worked for that division and were involved with a new invention. A group of scientists including my parents moved to Washington DC to bring the invention to the US." Daniel was watching my face as if something about the story should sound odd to me. It didn't so he continued. "I was born in DC, my brother, James, was born in England."

Brother? He never mentioned a brother. Maybe that's the guy in the photo from Florence. "You never told me you had a brother."

"Paige, James isn't my uncle. He's my older brother." He watched my face with trepidation.

Uncomprehending, I sat there trying to understand what he was talking about, but confusion was winning out on any logical explanation as to what he was saying.

———

"Were you or James adopted?"

"No, he's my full brother," Daniel said.

I started to realize that this was impossible. Did his mother freeze fertilized eggs? I wondered. "What are you talking about?" I asked totally confused. I couldn't take it anymore.

Daniel succinctly said, "I was born on November 11, 1949..." He stared at me.

I realized that he'd said 1949. *1949?* "What are you saying? Is this a joke?"

"No its not. I was born in 1949." Daniel watched as the confusion swirled in my eyes.

How old was he? I felt like hyperventilating. This wasn't happening. He was older than my father! Stunned and incredulous, I gaped at him not grasping how this could be true.

"How is that possible? Your license said that you were nineteen," I stammered and tears welled up in my eyes.

"I am. Let me explain."

How could he look so young? Plastic surgery? I was inching away from him on the sand, sliding backwards, trying to get away. How could I have been this wrong about him? *Please wake up, Paige.* Why did my fairy tale have to turn into a nightmare?

"Please, let me finish," Daniel sounded frantic.

"What else is there?" I screeched. Why was I starting to cry? Getting angry with myself, I brushed the tears aside and stood up. I didn't want to know anything more. My world was shattered and I felt pure and unadulterated fear. Was he a pedophile? He hadn't even kissed me, so none of this made any sense.

Daniel reached for me, but lowered his hands when I said threateningly, "Don't touch me!"

"Please, let me tell you the rest," he pleaded.

"Are you crazy?" I hissed through clenched teeth.

Every emotion went through me: disbelief, confusion, sorrow and rage. "Why have you done this to me?" I screamed.

People on the beach were looking at us, noticing our raised voices, but I didn't care. At least there were witnesses because I was terrified of this man. Nothing, absolutely nothing, was making any sense. My first instinct was to run, but my feet weren't moving. In a recent nightmare, there was a man pursuing me but even though I was running as fast as I could, I was stuck in place. This had to be a dream! All of this was impossible! Everything began spinning, and momentarily my mind blacked out. I stood there gawking at this stranger, trying to will myself to wake up. Opening and closing my eyes repeatedly wasn't working.

"Please, calm down. I can explain everything."

I had trusted him. How could he explain any of this? Daniel waited for me to compose myself and appeared taken aback by my anger. Reasoning was slowly coming back to me and I looked at him warily. Taking deep breaths to calm myself, I settled back onto the sand to the apparent relief of Daniel. I needed to know what he had to say. Whether it was morbid curiosity or plain hope that maybe he had a feasible story to explain this, I prepared myself to hear what he had to say.

"Okay, go ahead," I said trying desperately to control my emotions. Holding my hand up, I instructed him to stay away from me. Daniel moved away and left enough space between us in the sand, so that I felt comfortable.

Daniel began, "I was born in 1949, but physically, I'm nineteen and will continue to be that age because of my job."

"What are you talking about? You were born in 1949?"

"That's the classified part that I need to tell you about."

I stared at him trying to figure out how he could be so old. Nothing in his appearance fit the age that he was saying he was. I tried guessing. "Is this some science experiment?" His uncle worked for the government, it was plausible. "Or did you guys discover the fountain of youth?"

"None of those things. You're jumping to crazy conclusions and I have so much to tell you."

"Okay, go on." I sat there staring at his face and realized that somehow deep down I knew there was something extraordinary and unique about him. From the time I saw the photo of him in Florence, I had consciously avoided asking questions because I didn't want to know the answers if it meant losing him. Crazy photos of him and fear for my life hadn't deterred my wanting to know him. Neither had the disclosure of the surveillance equipment. I chose to close my eyes whenever Daniel said the word 'classified.' I could've walked away a long time ago and only did before because Daniel had pushed me away. Daniel was right. I needed to know what was going on. He was telling me, whether I was ready or not.

"I'm here from the past," he said, in such a low tone that at first I thought I heard wrong.

"Did you say the past?"

"Yes."

"You're actually serious?"

"Yes. The invention was a time machine."

He watched me as my eyes widened. "While working on nuclear power and Einstein's theories of relativities, the secret of time travel was unearthed." Daniel talked while I sat there spellbound. Scientific terms were being bandied about and I had no idea what he was saying. Time travel was foremost on my mind and thoughts of that took precedence over the theories involved in creating it. Who cared about the specifics? A time machine! Suddenly, all those crazy comments alluding to the future that Daniel and James had made in the past made sense.

"You can go to the past and the future?" I asked incredulously.

"No, I can only go back to my time, which is in October 1969," Daniel explained.

"I don't understand."

"I can't go back before my own time, only into the future of my time. Travel to the past was abandoned because there were casualties and aging problems when the agents returned."

"But how come you don't age?"

"It's called time dilation. The time machine is propelled at such great speed that aging doesn't occur. This was discovered in the early 1940's and it's been improved so many times since then. When I joined the agency, it was 1967 and most of the kinks had been worked out. Now years later, the machines are even better. The scientists from the past and the future are constantly updating them and discovering new things about them."

"How much time passes in your time while you're here in the future?"

"Eight months in the future is about one day in the past. Paige, I didn't graduate high school last December. I graduated in June of 1967 and began working at the EMIT offices in July. They wouldn't let me into the actual program until I turned eighteen, which was in November."

"This is so unbelievable. Can you stay in this year forever?"

"I can only stay for eight months in any year that's not my own."

"What do you do the other four months?"

"We work for two months at the EMIT offices and then we have a two month vacation. During those four months, we're not allowed to time travel or there can be serious health issues. Time travel is very draining on the body and since there's very little down time when we work, we need to fully rest before we can travel again. When we're active, we can work six days a week and need to time travel if we have to. There've been times where I've conflated the past and present from pure exhaustion."

"What does that mean?"

"I've mixed the years up and thought I was in the past when in actuality I was in the future or I've combined data from multiple years. That's the job. I can't complain since I knew what it entailed before I signed up and knew that I had to fully immerse in each case."

As he talked and explained everything, I got totally absorbed in the story and forgot all my previous emotions. We sat on the sand chatting like this was a regular conversation.

"You're so young. Why did you sign up for this?" This was such a bizarre existence.

He smiled weakly and said, "To make a difference and save lives, but it took a lot of persuading on my part to get hired at my age. My knowledge of the program gave me an advantage, as did my parents and brother. They eventually allowed it, only after certain requirements were met."

"What do you mean knowledge? Isn't this all classified?" I said sarcastically.

Daniel grinned and added, "It was difficult for my parents not to bring their work home. James and I put two and two together after some eavesdropping. Whenever our parents had co-workers over for dinner, we were always sent out of the room as soon as the meal was done. Most of the time we were thrilled to be excused, but one time James overheard something about the time machine and told me. When James started working with Dad during school breaks in high school, it was impossible to keep it from us. James wasn't in the top-secret area, but he wanted to work in that area. I had every intention of being a scientist also, but my plans changed after my parents' crash," he said.

"But why?" I asked. There seemed to be something he wasn't saying.

Daniel confided, "To try to save my parents. I hoped for a long time that they'd figure out how to travel back in time safely." Daniel started throwing rocks into the water.

We sat there for a while in silence and I kept looking at his profile not believing his real age. "I don't understand. How come you haven't aged if you go back for four months every year?"

"I haven't been going back to my time. I've been travelling to other years for my four-month rest and in doing that I don't age. All the other agents that go back to their time do age for those four months."

"Are there other travelers that are your age?"

"No, just me. They decided that it was a great cover and have allowed me not to age, but the choice has been totally mine. The hiring age at EMIT is twenty-five."

"When agents stop traveling, do they age normally?" I envisioned a horrible sight.

"Yes, we age exactly like everyone else does."

"Why can't you stay longer than eight months?" I wondered.

"Because when we return to our own time, we're ten years older."

"Why?"

Daniel shrugged, "We don't know. It's one of the side effects of time travel. Most of us don't stay past eight months because the change is permanent."

"What do you mean most of you?"

"Some agents do stay longer and go back ten years older." Before I could ask why, Daniel added, "Their spouses age so it starts getting really obvious. Others though refuse to age and just do cosmetic changes."

"Like making their hair gray?" I asked and Daniel nodded. "Eight months? Some months have thirty days, others thirty-one, and what about February?"

"It's exactly two hundred forty days but we just say eight months. There's a department at EMIT that's responsible for tracking the agents times and notifies us one week before so we can get ready to leave and wrap things up. We overlap agents so everyone knows what's going on."

My head was throbbing trying to wrap my brain around all of this. Daniel sat there with both hands rubbing his eyes, looking drained.

"What is it that you're trying to stop?"

Daniel looked at me awkwardly and said, "I've told you before, we're trying to stop an attack on the United States."

"I know, I know," I smirked. "You've told me that repeatedly. I want to know what kind of attack."

"A nuclear disaster aimed at multiple nuclear plants simultaneously."

I remembered the nuclear conversation with Grammy. "Who's trying to do this?" I asked. I had an idea and waited for him to confirm my suspicions.

"Groups of radical Muslims."

"I thought so. Why is it so hard to stop this? My goodness, you have a time machine!" I said. It sounded so surreal.

"We can only work and stop what is going on where we have time machines. One big problem is that Hezbollah has been working with the Mexican drug cartels and they have been smuggling the extremists into the US. They even have tunnels on the border that have been difficult to locate."

I just stared at him.

"Every time we think we've averted something, it still happens because there are people involved that we don't know exist. We can't have agents patrolling the entire border, there isn't enough manpower in EMIT. We have to allow regular law enforcement and the military to assist us. The agency supplies them with data, but it only helps if they follow through on the information."

"But why wouldn't the law listen to you?"

"They do, but there have been times that things weren't dealt with in a timely manner. We can't tell them that we know a terrorist will be somewhere at a specific time. If he's going to a meeting, we can say we heard through a phone interception. But there are some cases where there is no way we could explain the things we know and we find out later on that they didn't take care of it or went before or after the terrorist showed up. Since EMIT can't divulge the time machine, some things slip through the cracks. We can't be everywhere."

"There are so many people watching me. That's such a waste of manpower," I said, while pulling my hair back into a ponytail in frustration. "Why am I still involved in this?"

"I don't know. None of this makes sense. At the moment, you're the best lead, so we're not letting you out of our sight." Stunned by everything, I scooped sand in my hand than let it run through my fingers. This little concrete act was allowing me to stay sane.

My sand diversion was interrupted, when Daniel said, "There's something else."

"Okay?" I answered hesitantly. What more could there be?

"For years we've watched your father because we narrowed

down the lead to the company your dad was representing. It's been difficult to ascertain who's involved because we first were focusing on the French firm. Then the leads moved to London and then to New York. So many people work at all three firms that it's been difficult. But when the information moved to NY and your dad's office, he was the only connection. Your dad started working with the French company when you were five so we traveled to that time and traveled forward trying to find out who these people were, but we found nothing. That's how you have a picture of me in Florence and the Eiffel Tower."

"You've been watching me since I was five?" I interrupted him. Is that why he's looked familiar? He's always been around in the background of my life. Or was it that I'd seen his photo on my wall for years? I'm sure I didn't put that David photo on my wall though, so Mom probably did to torment me.

"Different agents, including myself, have been investigating your father. We never thought of you, and never checked your father's personal life, even though I've watched you grow over the years. Things abruptly changed in June of this year, so we went back to see what happened." Daniel stopped.

"And?" I insisted. "Go on."

"We still don't understand how or why things changed though," Daniel said.

"What do you mean? What changed?"

"Things in your father's life that had never happened before and that's when we started watching and guarding you and your mom," Daniel confided. "It started with your father being mugged. That never happened before."

"What are you talking about my dad was never mugged."

"We went in and changed the outcome."

"When did it happen?"

"Beginning of June. Then everything took a crazy turn, but we were watching you." Daniel looked out over the water momentarily and then his gaze reverted to me. His look scared me.

"What?" I asked shuddering, as I suddenly felt cold all over.

Daniel leaned in closer and said, "You were killed."

"How is that possible?" I asked. "What are you talking about? I'm not dead."

"We fixed it." Seeing my confusion, Daniel added, "Let me explain." He ran his hands through his hair as if trying to find the words to do that.

"You had never died before, so there was a change somewhere," Daniel said. "When you got killed, we changed the outcome and knew that you had to be involved somehow.

This was all too much. "When did I die?" I demanded, panic setting in.

"The day in Central Park when I got you away from those men."

"Do you mean if you didn't come from the past to me here in the present, I'd be dead?" So I shouldn't be here. Death was my destiny and science was the only reason I was alive.

"Yes," Daniel answered concisely. "But, it shouldn't have happened."

Shocked, I got up and started walking towards the Point. How was any of this possible? Daniel was giving me space to comprehend everything, but my death trumped the time machine now.

As I approached the osprey nest, the birds began to make such a racket squawking that I sat on the sand far away from them. Daniel had been following me and sat down next to me. I played with the shells not believing that all this turmoil was happening in such a beautiful setting. Looking up, I saw diaphanous clouds float by and boats sailing in the bay.

"What happened to me?" I finally was able to blurt out.

"You were shot."

"But why?" All those dreams of being shot popped into my mind.

"We weren't sure."

"Why didn't you follow them?"

"We've tried that twice with different outcomes. We never let you get killed again, but they were in different places as if they were warned where we'd be. It makes no sense and that's why James thinks it's an inside job. He's talking conspiracy theories, but I can't believe that. Either way, with killing you or not killing you, we haven't been able to stop this catastrophe from happening; somehow other people know the info. It's been so confusing and we have no idea what's going on."

"I can't believe this."

"I wanted to get to know you, so I talked James into letting me be friends with you. I thought that way we could watch you more closely, protect you and see what we were missing."

"You wanted to get to know me, even though you knew I really should be dead?"

"You weren't supposed to die. All the times we watched your dad before, nothing happened to you. I told James that we needed to find out why your whole family's destiny suddenly changed. That's why you're being watched so carefully. We bugged your homes, cells and started surveillance on you. Now, things have changed again, your broken arm and a second envelope. We have to find the people involved and figure out what's going on."

"When I gave them the envelope, didn't you catch them?"

"No, the man was just a messenger. He was paid to take a photo of the paper on his cell and send it to them. He knew nothing else."

"That makes no sense. How do they keep getting away from you?"

"We really don't know, every time we go in they're one step ahead of us. Whenever something happens, we travel back to before the incident, but the same things happen at a different time or place. We don't know how they're doing it. James is adamant that someone in EMIT is helping them."

"Like what things?"

"You first got hit on Central Park South but the next time it happened on Central Park West and on a different day. James fixed it once, but when it happened again, he said it was best to focus on the catastrophe and stop changing things unless it was a fatality."

"Why?" I wondered.

"He felt we were wasting time and travel trips."

"Of course he did," I said sarcastically. "If they can change things, they must have a time machine, too."

"It's possible, but highly unlikely. All the time machines are in secure locations under heavy guard and only authorized personnel have access to it. Only the scientists and the top stratum know where the plans are stored. Someone can't just steal the designs. It's impossible."

"It's possible other scientists discovered time travel, too. There are a lot of brilliant people in the world. Couldn't someone have told somebody else of its existence? And maybe they've been trying for years and finally succeeded."

"I don't think so because we track all our travels and nothing changes anywhere in the world. The only changes have been with you."

"That's crazy. How far in the future have you gone?" I asked wondering.

"Only to the end of this year. We have a different team that's responsible for future travels to discover what catastrophes will happen in future years. That group consists of agents and scientists who travel back and forth sharing the latest technology available from the future. Then the older time machines are updated. I'm in the group that actually works on stopping the issues that the scouting teams uncover."

"But why only to the end of this year? Why haven't you gone into the future?"

No one can travel more than fifty years from his or her own base year. Since my base year is 1969, I can only go as far as the year 2019, but we only deal with one year at a time. Once the issues are solved, we move onto the next year."

"Why?"

"The same reason as why we can't travel to the past. Medical issues."

"If you stay here permanently, this would be your new base year and you could go much further into the future?" I asked thinking out loud.

"Yes and no. First, I'd need to get authorization to change my base year and second, I'd only be able to time travel to the end of this year until EMIT moved on to the next year. Paige, no one in the agency has ever changed their base year."

"That's surprising. Why not?" I asked bewildered.

"Why do you say that? Think about how hard it would be for you to leave your family."

"I didn't think of it like that. I was just thinking about the adventure part of it," I answered, understanding what Daniel was alluding to.

"Future travel is much more involved and complicated than just going into a different year. EMIT only enters one year at a time, takes care of what it needs to do in that year and then we move on to the next year. The travelers that go into the future to fact-find never leave the lab facilities. They find out everything they need from news on the computers and we use that info to handle whatever case we're working on."

"But why don't they leave the labs in the future?"

"If we exit into a year and engage there before we know what needs to be stopped, we can seal events and we might not be able to stop or correct them. We have to deal with one year at a time. The changes we make in this year will affect what happens next year. If I check next year's issues today, it wouldn't be as accurate. What we do in this year will alter things in the future."

"How do you know about what changes?"

"Our cells record everything that happens, including our locations. All day our cells sync the information to the EMIT offices including video recordings. The staff updates all that information constantly on the computers. Whenever a traveler goes to the future to check things out, he loads all that data on a flash drive and another agent returns immediately with the new information."

"Why not the same traveler?"

"We have to wait twenty-four hours before traveling again because it's bad for our bones."

Someone else had to have a machine. Daniel had to be wrong. "Is there a country that has any inkling or suspects the existence of time machines?" I insisted.

"The only country that we're concerned about is France," Daniel finally revealed. "We haven't been able to detect if they have one yet."

"So what is the plan?"

"Well, I have to tell you that James said if we can't stop this soon, we might have to start from scratch."

"What does that mean exactly?" I asked nervously.

"We'll have to start researching again from the beginning of this year to give us more time to figure this all out. The bad thing is that you wouldn't know me."

"Are you telling me that I could forget you?" Somehow, I found that difficult to fathom, but if I could forget getting killed, I could forget Daniel. "No! I don't want that." Is that why James told me that Daniel didn't have a girlfriend because he knew that I might soon forget him?

"James will allow our relationship for now because he knows how much I care for you. I'm trying to get him to not to alter things on the day we met and then everything will be fine."

"I don't want to forget you." After his reassurance that he'd work everything out, I tried to compose myself and prayed that he really could.

"Honestly, I think all the changes that are happening might be my fault."

"How could that be?"

"Not the things that happened before I talked to you, but afterwards. If I didn't talk to you, your daily routines would've been different and that's why now there is utter chaos."

Well, he had me there since he was so right. After we met, I couldn't stop thinking about him and constantly searched for him. I'd never acted like that before.

"What did James say about your theory that you've caused the changes?"

"I didn't tell him. I'm afraid he might make me stop seeing you."

"Then don't."

"I'm not, but he's pretty positive the changes are being done internally."

Daniel's tone suddenly changed and he became very serious. "When I learned you were hit by the car, I went into the future to see what was going on and it was bad. By intercepting phone calls, we learned that they knew the NSA was close to catching them and they...."

"What? I got killed again?" I asked impatiently.

"Yes. You were abducted by gunpoint and shot."

"Just great! But if the catastrophe happens even after they kill me then somebody else has what you're looking for."

"Their informant was adamant that you had the envelope. One of the callers said you should have been tortured and not killed because their plan needed to be postponed by six months while they got what they needed from another source," Daniel said through clenched teeth.

"Who was the informant?"

"We don't know. It was data picked up through satellite monitoring, but I think you have whatever it is they need."

"I don't understand this because I don't have anything."

"When we get back to the city, we have to figure out where it could be and prevent your death and the nuclear attack."

"Where could it be?" I asked worried that I had to go back.

"I have no idea. Let's start with your apartment. Maybe in your dad's office?" he suggested.

"I brought files home before so maybe it's in one of them," I answered feeling encouraged.

"We'll start there."

"I can't believe this." I felt dazed and foggy. "Daniel, I'm really scared."

"I'm not letting you out of my sight. The reality will set in once we get back to Manhattan and you had to know everything."

"Do you have to go to DC in the morning?" Panic started setting in and Daniel watched my face, as I grew more and more terrified.

"I'm sorry, but I have to go for a meeting. You'll be safe while I'm gone, I promise. Nothing happens until you get back to New York and I'll be there waiting for you."

"Are you sure?"

"Yes, I wouldn't leave if you weren't. I also want to see what's going on in the future. Reports from agents aren't specific enough because they're only reporting the specifics of the case. I'm interested in your outcome, even though that's constantly changing, so I need to access all the data about you," he tried explaining.

"If things keep changing, how can you be so sure I'll be safe?"

"Because they never come to Long Island, they always stay in the city."

"But I never got hit by a car before either, so they could come here."

"James assures me you'll be safe and even if anything does happen, he'll take care of it."

After calming down, I suddenly realized that James wasn't on Long Island. "James isn't here, how can he promise you or me anything?" I started getting really scared.

"And if there's a bad agent what if he comes here? Or what if he's here already? Wait, how can you fix anything if it happens when you're traveling to the future?"

"Calm down. James is coming back here while I'm away."

"Where is he? Plum Island?"

"No, he's in New York."

"But why? You said that he's normally in DC."

"Yes, he's in New York to oversee this operation because he's second in command. James comes in towards the end of the operations, reviews what's been done and decides what the next steps should be."

"Who's in charge in New York?"

There was a long pause and then he said, "I can't say."

"But why not? I know who your uncle is and he's more senior than the guy in New York."

"The less you know about this and the personnel involved the better. I'm only allowing you to meet people who you need to know," Daniel said.

"What do you mean?" I asked.

"If anything happened and you saw Pierce, Brad or James, you would know that you were safe, so you would go to them. I need to give you their cell numbers. Can I have your cell?" I handed him my phone and he put in their contact information.

"Speaking of Pierce. Is he really from Chappaqua?"

"No, he isn't."

"If I wasn't here this summer, my Dad would've been dealing with this?" I said out loud.

It seemed like he wasn't listening but then he stopped. "Wait, that's right, you weren't supposed to be here this summer. Maybe I should travel to save your grandmother from falling in London. Then you won't be involved in this and you'll be safe in London. At the same time, we won't meet," he said resignedly. "I can bump into you again after this mess is solved and hope you'll like me again."

"Forget it. I'm glad we met, even with everything that's happened."

"I wonder if your grandmother fell before or if this was new."

"You think everything could have changed because of Nana's fall?" I asked.

"I'm not sure. We've never watched you before."

"But weren't you bugging our house? Wouldn't you have known if Nana had fallen before?"

"No, we never bugged your house before and never paid attention to personal data, just your dad's business dealings. We put our surveillance equipment in your apartment three weeks before we met in the park. So as far as your grandmother's fall is concerned, I'm not sure if that was supposed to happen or not. I'm going to ask James to check the other times if he could."

What he was implying was crazy, but so was everything else he'd told me. "How can you check though?"

"If James thinks it's important, he'll review your dad's phone calls from all our time travels. They could also view the satellite images and send someone to see exactly how the fall happened," Daniel explained. "I'd go if asked, but right now I need to check the future. I can't do both and be back on Sunday."

After what seemed like hours, I began to get comfortable with the story and asked about the invention. Daniel looked at his cell and slid the top off. I saw how different it was.

"Can I see it?" I asked when he was done. "Now I understand why you think my cell is old. This is scary looking." There were weird symbols and buttons. It looked so foreign.

"Only EMIT has these. Everything I do is recorded and videotaped."

"Everything?"

"That involves the case. They know where I am at all times. Our personal interactions, I have on a private file just in case. All data has to be saved so we know what happens on every visit to be able to document changes. All the information is sent to the EMIT office. There, the staff uploads all that transpired that day into the main computer and then it's in the system. Our cells help them track our movements so everything is monitored. If something needs to be changed, the agency knows exactly where in time to go back to. All the info the agency has, we can access from our phones."

"But Daniel, the computers from the past are so different."

"Computers and all electronic equipment are the same in the EMIT offices for all the years. Whenever we need anything or there are new inventions, its sent using the time machine. Technology is the panacea for the EMIT program."

"All the time travelers can't go back before 1969 or just you?"

"There are a few that can go back as far as 1967, but the original time travelers from the 1940's and 1950's are now retired," Daniel explained.

"How do they find time travelers?" I asked. Maybe they were all spies from the CIA.

"The first group of travelers were recruited from the CIA, but they found it difficult and a lot of them resigned after completing the required ten years. So when NASA started recruiting for their astronaut program in the late 1950's, EMIT started getting the time travelers from there."

"Why?"

"The astronaut selection process consisted of a series of intense physical and psychological screenings. EMIT picked from the people NASA rejected."

"If they weren't good enough to be astronauts, why would they make good travelers?"

"EMIT didn't pick anybody who failed the psychological screenings. The maximum height requirement to be an astronaut was no more than five feet eleven inches because of the limited cabin space. The EMIT group would find travelers from the taller candidates that NASA couldn't use and from other applicants that NASA didn't want."

"That's why all the agents I've seen are tall." Honestly, I thought it was to be intimidating. "That's how they were picked? If they were tall?" I joked.

"No." Daniel shook his head at me. "They looked for candidates that had little or no family to hold them back. After that, they were told about the EMIT program."

"But if somebody refused to be a time traveler and rejected the job, wouldn't they go blab to everybody that there was a time machine?" I asked.

"Yes, some refused and when they did, one of our agents went back in time."

I didn't get what he was saying and then I understood. "Oh and didn't ask him."

"Correct. Keeping the time machine secret has been the most

important part of the new recruiting process. From that point on, EMIT changed the length of service to forty years for continuity and to ensure that the program remained clandestine."

"I don't understand. There have been so many disasters. Why didn't EMIT fix them?"

"So many events are happening simultaneously that it's impossible to fix them all. We zero in on the worst catastrophes and stop those. There aren't that many time travelers."

"But why? It sounds very exciting."

"You have to commit for a long time and watch your family and friends grow old and die. It wreaks havoc on your personal life."

"It must be so hard," I said understanding what the issues were.

"It is. The first five years we're assigned a partner to learn all that time travel entails and how to do the job competently."

"How many travelers in total are there?"

"I can't say, but a new traveler is hired only when another traveler retires to keep the program as secretive as possible."

"But you told me," I said.

I was the first person that Daniel had trusted with his secret. Suddenly, it clicked and I gasped, "Oh, if I freaked out, you'd have someone travel right before you told me and not tell me."

"Yes. James gave me the authorization."

"How come James isn't a traveler?" I struggled with the implication of this. If Daniel stayed here in my time, he would watch his brother die. If he went back to his time, he would age with his brother and I would lose him.

"He was engaged and had no interest. As a matter of fact, he was angry that I signed on, but he wasn't able to change my mind."

"If a traveler marries, he tells his wife, right?"

"Yes, the spouse is told, but a lot of marriages end because of the aging issues and time spent away from home. It's a lonely existence for both spouses."

"What happens when they divorce? How do you keep the ex from telling all about it?"

"With a combination of hypnosis and a type of nepenthe from the future."

"What's a nepenthe?"

"A drug that erases specific memories. The hypnosis targets the memory and the drug completes the erasure of it. The job memory is changed to whatever the couple had told family and friends."

"Like traveling salesman?" I chuckled and Daniel nodded.

Tired of sitting, we continued down the beach towards the Point. Seeing the sand bar, I walked out into the bay. Daniel followed. We got so far out that when I looked back all I saw was water because the tide was coming in.

Daniel warned, "I suggest we go back unless you're planning on swimming with one arm."

After giving him a snide look, I turned around. Daniel headed for shore first and I copied his steps gingerly, fearful of falling in. Safe on the beach, we resumed our discussion. Our walk was a nice distraction. We passed the noisy osprey nest and sat on the sand.

Daniel looked at me and asked. "I need to know. Can you deal with this or not?"

"I'm sorry that I got so upset before, but when you told me the year, I lost it."

"I understand. It's a lot to process."

"As long as you're staying this age, I can handle the rest."

A sigh of relief passed through his lips. "A big weight has lifted. I couldn't stand deceiving you. It never mattered before, but it does now." That comment made me smile.

"I'm drained. Can we talk more later?"

"Sure, I'm spent too."

This really had been quite an emotional afternoon and could've been a total disaster. I couldn't imagine Daniel not a part of my life. Realizing everything he knew and had done, I was intimidated by him. No wonder he was so smart, he had lived and learned so much.

Daniel put his arm around me as we walked towards the car. "I won't let anything happen to you." I knew Daniel would keep me safe or wouldn't rest until I was.

He kissed my head and whispered, "Everything's going to be okay. We'll be okay."

15. GREENPORT

"It is a scale of proportions which makes the bad difficult and the good easy." Einstein

Mom was relentless in talking to Daniel about going to college. Grammy looked at me and when I rolled my eyes at her, she asked him a question. I was glad that she changed the subject.

They started talking about the Middle East and terrorism again. I didn't want to hear anymore, so I surreptitiously mouthed to Daniel, "Let's go." We got up to leave for the movies.

"Gabby, thanks for everything. It was a pleasure to spend time with you this week," Daniel said as we made our exit.

"I really don't want to see a movie. Can we just go for a ride?"

"Sure, how about Greenport?"

It sounded great to me. As I stared out the window, I saw the trees swaying in the wind and asked, "So please tell me why were you collecting those nuts and plants in Central Park?"

"Oh, some scientists in my time asked for them."

"I knew that it was weird! Why?"

"In my time, there was a chestnut blight, a fungus, which almost wiped out the chestnut trees on the East Coast. They're working on developing resistant chestnut trees to the blight and getting present day specimens will help."

I looked at him incredulously. "You're saving the world and you're also worried about chestnut trees?"

Laughing, he said, "You said I was an oddity."

I shook my head. "Amazing."

"The basis of all science and technology that is present today was started in the past. All future years are working on things that have already been discovered and updating and creating new technology from old. Everything is co-dependent on each other."

"Tell me more about your parents."

"After Oxford, my dad joined the Tube Alloys program." He looked at me as if I should know something about that, but I shook my head no. "The Tube Alloy was the code name for the nuclear weapons program and where the principles for time travel were discovered. A separate team was put together to study that and my dad joined the new group. They eventually succeeded and the time machine was built."

As he drove, he rattled on about scientific stuff. At one point he looked over and said, "Do you want to hear this?"

"Yes, go on," I insisted.

"New areas of physics were being explored such as nuclear power, electricity, magnetism, and shock waves. The goal was to achieve military advantage during WWII. There was information that Hitler was also researching nuclear power."

"If that ever happened." I winced at the thought.

"Weapons like rockets, the atom bomb, and radar technology were impossible to keep hidden, but the time machine has been a very well guarded secret."

"Yeah because you guys go around and eradicate people's memories," I said jokingly.

Daniel glanced at me and his expression troubled me.

"I have to tell you something. When I go to DC tomorrow, I'll check the repercussions you knowing. If the outcome is bad, I have to come back to right before. That's my deal with James."

My face went white. "No. Why? I won't tell anybody, I promise."

"I trust you, but I have no idea what the consequences might be. I'm telling you everything in the hopes that everything will be okay."

"But how can you check that?"

"If the future events stay the same and nothing horrific is added, we'll know."

As he drove through the center of Greenport, I was freaking out. Daniel kept trying to reassure me, but it sounded hollow. He couldn't guarantee that everything would be fine, definitively fine. I didn't want to forget everything he had told me. Daniel parked in the lot across from the gelato shop and saw how upset I was. He promised that whatever happened, we'd still be together and I felt a tiny bit better.

Knowing that there was nothing I could do about it, I asked him to finish the story.

"You sure?"

"Yeah, maybe it'll keep my mind off the fact that you might erase my memory."

"I hope that won't happen."

"I know. Go on tell me the rest, please." I needed to focus on something else or I'd cry.

"Okay. They initially created two machines and experimented by first sending objects, and later animals, back and forth. After many trials, they felt ready to try human travel. In the beginning, they were sent to the past and future with mixed results. After some casualties, the machines were adjusted and eventually perfected. Wherever the time machine was, was where the agent exited. Because England, the US, and Canada were united through the war, England informed them of the nuclear findings and time travel machine. Known as the 'British Mission,' a team of scientists went to work at Los Alamos on the nuclear bomb and to set up a time machine. In Canada, a joint British-Canadian laboratory was set up and a time machine was constructed there. Once that was in place, time travel between the three countries was possible. Dad remained in England and was in charge of the time machine there."

"How many time machines are there in total?"

"I can't answer that, but there are machines in Australia, Canada, New Zealand, the United Kingdom and the US."

"How did Australia and New Zealand get involved?"

"The UK–USA Security Agreement established an alliance of five English-speaking countries for the purpose of sharing intelligence. The alliance comprises of Australia, Canada, New Zealand, the United Kingdom and the United States. The countries involved are known as AUSCANZUKUS. AUS stands for Australia, CA is Canada, NZ for New Zealand, UK is United Kingdom and of course you know what US stands for."

"With all those countries involved, how can you be sure that it hasn't leaked?"

"The program is top secret, only the top personnel of each country know of its existence. Only the actual time travelers know of each other. All that the other NSA agents know is that we are agents from another department. EMIT is an elite group in the NSA, but not everyone in EMIT are travelers."

"Are Pierce and Brad?"

"I can't say."

"Why?"

"It's one thing telling you about me, but I can't talk about other agents."

"Fine. You can only travel between those five countries?" I asked.

"For now. They've been working on a traveling time machine for quite some time and soon we'll be able to travel anywhere."

"That's amazing."

"It is, but it's dangerous depending on what country we end up in."

"Is a traveling time machine safe? Have there been deaths?" I asked, worried about Daniel.

"A few, but the issues have been corrected. The main problem is making sure the machines go where they are programmed to go."

"Have they been seen?" I asked.

Daniel said, "Yeah, a few times, but there were two major sightings where a lot of people saw."

"Recently?"

"No, the worst one happened on July 7, 1947 and was one of the reasons my father had to come to DC to take over the Time Travel program at the CIA. Do you know anything about the Roswell incident?"

"The UFO story with aliens?" I had read something about that.

"Yes, but it wasn't a UFO. It was the first attempt to launch a traveling time machine. At the Los Alamos Laboratory in New Mexico, they sent a test machine to the Lawrence Berkeley National Laboratory in Berkeley, California. It was to appear at the 7000-acre remote experimental test site, called Site 300. Something went wrong and the time machine appeared 226 miles away in Roswell, New Mexico. The agent was found dead inside, shriveled and aged beyond recognition and that started the UFO stories. James showed me the pictures after it was recovered and it did look like an alien."

"Why was your dad called to DC?"

"A lot of the scientists in DC were sent to Los Alamos after the Roswell fiasco, so Dad was moved to DC to be in charge of the Time Travel program there," he explained. "Last year, they finally thought all the kinks were worked out, but just in case they decided to do the test in Europe not wanting another Roswell problem. A traveling Time Machine was sent to the Piedmont area in Italy from London. Again, something went wrong and it appeared in the South of France. They got it out of there, but France went crazy with UFO sightings."

"Wow, people actually saw it?"

"Yeah, there were some witnesses that reported an object touched down, left scorch marks and zoomed off."

"Did it?"

"No, the truth was that it appeared and disappeared, but that wasn't reported."

"Why wouldn't it be?"

"I guess that would've sounded too crazy, so no one admitted to seeing it disappear."

"I still can't believe that this hasn't leaked out."

"Only high-ranking personnel who pass security clearance procedures are permitted near the machines. There are retina screenings, finger print checks. No one can get in without proper identification. Besides, even if there was a breach, we could go back in time and correct it."

"Hopefully, you won't have to correct telling me."

"Me too, but I wanted you to know everything before I left."

I didn't know what to say. I had no idea what would happen when Daniel went into the future. I hoped that nothing would change, but that was out of my control.

Trying to change the now somber mood, I asked, "1947, huh? It's taking a really long time?"

"Yeah, it is. With stationary time machines, the locations are locked, but with a moving machine there are many variables to deal with. It should be a fait accompli by next summer since the traveling time machines in the future are working."

"Can't they send one from the future?" I asked.

Daniel appeared impressed with my suggestion.

"No, the traveling machine is too big, but some scientists are recommending we built one huge time machine for just such issues." Before I could ask another question, he said, "Come on, enough of this. Let's go have some fun."

"Please, just a little more," I begged.

Daniel sighed and nodded his head for me to continue.

"But if it's traveling around, aren't people going to see it?"

"Hopefully not. That's the reason it's taken this long to perfect it. An agent will exit the machine and press a button and it will disappear to the lab. When the agent needs the machine to return, it will reappear."

"Where would that button be? A cell? What happens if you get caught?"

"You're right and that's why the device will be implanted into the earlobe."

"Won't that hurt?"

"It's very small. Let's get some gelato."

"What does EMIT stand for?" I asked not moving.

"This is the last question," he insisted and I agreed. "Our team initially was part of a group called Echelon. For security issues and to hide our existence, our division was named E.M.I.T-Echelon-Matrix of Intelligence Travelers. EMIT spelled backwards is time."

"Wow! I didn't realize that!"

"That's it. Let's get out of the car," Daniel ordered.

I could've sat there and listened to him all night. This story was just so incredible.

While we crossed the street, we held hands and his touch made me tingle. He was the most amazing person and the thought of him leaving was making me more anxious by the minute.

"Do you have to go?" I asked. Daniel stopped a few feet from the entrance and twirled me to face him. His eyes stared into my soul and he kissed me right on the lips. It was a fast kiss but I almost fainted. This was the first time his lips came anywhere near mine.

"I'll miss you too. I'm so accustomed to seeing you every day, even when you hated me." He noticed that I was breathless. "Are you okay?"

"Your kiss just knocked me out, that's all."

He gave me a quick kiss and I couldn't stop smiling. "Well, at least you're not gloomy anymore," he grinned.

"After that kiss, why would I be?" I said blushing.

He laughed. "Let's go inside."

The store was crowded as it usually was during the summer months. I got a chocolate and stracciatella while Daniel got coffee and caramel. We walked down to the pier and saw a long line of people waiting to get into Claudio's. Winding around the back, we sat on a bench near the carousel and watched the kids scream trying to grab the brass rings.

After I told Daniel about all the times Lily and I made our parents bring us, he pulled me up and tried to lead me inside.

"What are you doing?" I squirmed, trying to plant my feet firmly, so I wouldn't move.

"Come on, let's have some fun."

"Okay," I laughed. "Why not?"

We picked horses side by side and Daniel helped me on.

Busy enjoying each other's company, we didn't grab at the rings not wanting to make any kids angry. The carousel was inside a glass structure and with the dark night sky outside and the lights shining inside, it was magical.

After four rides, I had enough and I walked out feeling a little dizzy. "That was fun. Thanks."

"You're welcome, and you were right, I did feel like a kid." Daniel scooped me up in his arms and carried me until I begged him to put me down.

We stopped at a coffee shop. Daniel got coffee and a sparkling water for me. We sat out front and I started to think about him being here from the past.

"Can I ask you something?"

"Of course, you can ask me anything."

"Where do you prefer being?"

"What do you mean?

"Your time or here?"

"Well, that should be perfectly clear to you, I prefer being here with you." My heart jumped and I couldn't help smiling. "My life is here now with you. Never forget that."

I looked at his beautiful face. "I'm so happy you said that."

"I'm glad." He looked at his watch and said, "We have an hour, what do you want to do?"

"Can we go to the Causeway Beach until I have to go home?"

"Aye, aye, Captain," he joked.

Walking to the car, we both were extremely quiet and I started worrying again. "Daniel, I'll understand if you have to change things."

"Let's hope for the best. Now, let's have fun on our last night on Long Island together."

Our ride back was quiet. Thank goodness for the radio. Arriving at the beach, we saw a couple walking a dog, heading away from us. It looked like Laura Burke and Cheddar. The man must be her husband.

Daniel retrieved a towel from the trunk and we walked down to the water and sat down. It was dark, but the stars twinkled overhead.

I looked at Daniel and he started to kiss me. It was the most amazing, tender and loving kiss. I didn't want it to stop. My heart was pounding and my blood was racing. I couldn't breathe; the kiss was so intense that I felt dizzy. I almost fell back on the towel and he grabbed me.

"You okay?" he smiled.

"No."

"I wanted to kiss you for so long, but couldn't because I wasn't honest with you."

He cradled my face in his hands and kissed me again. We clung to each other as we shut the world and all the drama out. We were in our own bubble and no one could hurt us or keep us apart.

I clung to the possibilities and forgot the worries. We laid on the towel and watched the stars above. We began kissing again and I felt such a rush of emotions and sensations course through my body.

Kissing him was more than I could've ever imagined. Things got a little heated. Daniel abruptly stopped and sat up. Why did he stop?

"Let's start heading back. Okay?"

He tried to look at me, but I was covering my face. "Are you okay? Did I hurt your arm?"

All the emotions I'd been feeling since I'd met him, all the drama, the secrets, they had all just exploded and tears were streaming down my face. He didn't say anything. He just hugged me and let me cry.

When we got to the driveway, he pulled me close and gave me another kiss. My breathing intensified and I hoped he wouldn't leave.

"I want you to promise me something," I said.

"What?"

"If you need to change things, you'll still stay and be a part of my life even though I won't know your secrets."

"I told you before, I'm not going anywhere."

"I'm holding you to that."

Daniel walked me to the door and said, "Please be careful."

"I will. I'll miss you. Maybe with you gone, I'll get my poetry reading done."

Daniel played with my hair and said, "Poetry, huh? One of my favorite quotes is 'Love is the poetry of the senses." That was apropos because everything about him was poetry to my senses.

"That's beautiful. Who wrote it?" I asked. "You?"

"No, a French novelist named Honoré de Balzac did," he said. "It's time for you to go in."

We kissed and I went inside in a state of bliss. I couldn't believe that I had almost run away from him today.

Mom was watching TV and asked about the movie. I told her that we just went to Greenport and said goodnight. My cell rang. It was Daniel, so I ran upstairs.

"Hi. I'm happy that today turned out the way it did. I was really worried. Sleep well. We'll talk in the morning." What a beautiful voice!

I couldn't sleep so I started scribbling a song and called it 'A Little Different.'

Gasoline rainbows and laughter on the saddest of days,
They're beautiful to me in all of the strangest ways.
They're perfect like the gentle way you push the hair out of my eyes
Before you lean in and kiss me for a bittersweet goodbye.

Well maybe it's clear to you like it is to me.
I happen to see things slightly differently.
And your friends, all of them, they say I've changed you,
But why does that matter cuz I know for a fact that you've changed me too.
I'm not the same as when I met you.
And guess what? I think I like it.

Who cares if we're a little different?
Who cares if we're not what they say is okay?
We don't need to listen.
We might be messed up in their worlds,
But we're just perfect in my world.

Then of course there are those who have a few more decades than us
And they say it can take a lifetime to build love and trust.
They dismiss teenage relationships as crushes that won't ever

last.

But what if this crush is one that just won't pass?

They say that romance ain't what it used to be
And that the love letter was killed by technology.
But I couldn't live without the thousands of texts that we send
Or the hours of time on the phone that we spend.
The hours of time that we spend.
The hours of time that we...

Who cares if we're a little different?
Who cares if we're not what they say is okay?
We don't need to listen.
We might be messed up in their worlds,
But we're just perfect in my world.

Who cares if we're a little different?
Who cares if we're not what they say is okay?
We don't need to listen.
We might be messed up in their worlds,
But we're just perfect in my world.

***

The next thing I knew, the sun was blinding me and kisses filled my thoughts. I knew I was madly in love with Daniel and that's all that mattered. It was nine and I needed to hear his voice.

"Good morning. Where are you?"

"Good morning, sleepy head. I'm near the airport."

"I wanted to see you before you left."

"I thought of that too, but I knew I'd miss the plane if I did. Don't do anything crazy while I'm gone."

"Oh yeah, with my one arm?"

He laughed and said, "I'll call you as soon as I get back."

This weekend would drag until I saw him again. Hearing lots of barking, I threw on a bathing suit and rushed downstairs to see what was going on.

At the front door stood Mrs. Clark talking to Mom and Grammy while her dog, Ranger and Amber chased each other around the house.

"Good morning. Sounds like they're having fun," I remarked as two fur balls raced by.

"Morning, would you mind letting them out through the patio and just keep an eye on them?" Mom asked pleadingly.

I grabbed some magazines and scooted the dogs outside. They tore off on the sand and jumped right into the bay. I sat by the water and watched them. Mrs. Clark eventually came out and took Ranger home. Amber collapsed on her dog bed from sheer exhaustion.

After some breakfast, I grabbed my poetry book and read the biography section on Percy Bysshe Shelley. Perhaps to be a good poet, you needed to have a life full of turmoil and angst. Shelley had a tumultuous life and his scandalous relationships with women had overshadowed his writing. He died at the age of thirty from drowning.

One poem was called Mutability. After looking up the definition, mutability means changeable.

We are as clouds that veil the midnight moon;
How restlessly they speed, and gleam, and quiver,
Streaking the darkness radiantly!—yet soon
Night closes round, and they are lost forever:

Or like forgotten lyres, whose dissonant strings
Give various response to each varying blast,
To whose frail frame no second motion brings
One mood or modulation like the last.

We rest – A dream has power to poison sleep;
We rise –One wandering thought pollutes the day;
We feel, conceive or reason, laugh or weep;
Embrace fond woe, or cast our cares away:

It is the same! –For, be it joy or sorrow,
The path of its departure still is free:
Man's yesterday may ne'er be like his morrow;
Naught may endure but Mutability.

'Man's yesterday may ne'er be like his morrow.' That line really struck me with its poignancy especially because of Daniel. Changes, that were wanted or not, occurred in everyone's life. That was how I spent the day, reading, fantasizing about Daniel and worrying.

When Lily and Noelle arrived, they wanted to hear what happened with Daniel. Noelle didn't understand why the music was on so loud in the bedroom.

"I don't want my mom to hear," I fibbed and told them everything except for the time travel stuff.

Noelle went to the bathroom and Lily asked, "Aren't you worried about all this spying and those men that are after you?"

"Yeah, but I'm hoping that it'll all end soon." Noelle came out and we stopped talking.

We had dinner outside and it began drizzling. The awnings kept us dry but the winds were strong, so we moved inside to finish.

***

Saturday morning, the sky was dark and it was still raining. After talking to both moms, we decided to go out for breakfast and drive out to Orient Point.

Grammy had already eaten so she declined our invitation, as did the dads. They were golfing at the North Fork Country Club as soon as the rain let up.

After eating yummy blueberry pancakes and omelettes in Southold, we went outside to see the sky brightening and saw peeks of the sun through the clouds. We were about to take the North Road and head to Orient Point. when Lily saw signs for Horton's Point Light House. She asked if we could show Noelle the beach with the humongous rocks.

Then, we stopped at the Lavender farm in East Marion. The aroma was amazing. After picking our own lavender and taking pictures, we set out to the beach at Orient Point, the tip of the North Fork. While collecting beach glass, we saw the ferries going to and from Connecticut.

On the way home, Mom and Aunt Cecile stopped at their favorite winery in Southold, Croteaux Vineyards to get rose wine. Sitting in the car waiting for them to return, Lily said that the picturesque scenery reminded her of the South of France.

Back home, we spent the rest of the day in the pool and had a barbeque that night. Mom offered to take us to the movies but after calling, there was nothing we wanted to see.

***

On Sunday, Noelle and Lily went bike riding while I tried to finish my poetry homework. I didn't want to take any of it with me to London.

As I sat by the pool, I looked at my cell. It was almost three o'clock and I still remembered everything. My phone rang and when

I saw it was Daniel, I jumped for joy.

"I see you're still alive," he joked.

"So what happened?" I asked eagerly.

"Well, nothing horrific, so believe it or not, it'll be fine with you knowing my secret."

"YEAH!" I screamed. "I was so worried."

"I'm leaving DC shortly. Call me when you're home. I need to see you," Daniel said.

Even though I couldn't wait to get back to the city to see Daniel, I'd miss being at Grammy's so much. Besides being a special place because of my family, Nassau Point would now also be the place where Daniel and I became a couple.

Saying goodbye to Grammy was quite difficult.

"Grammy, thanks for letting me stay with you."

"Don't be silly. I loved it. Next week, you're off to London and you'll forget all about me."

"No, I won't," I protested.

"I'm kidding. Please say hi to Nana for me."

Tears and hugs ensued and finally, we were on our way. Afraid of what awaited me in New York, I was miserable the entire ride home. Only thoughts of seeing Daniel kept me rational.

16. RETURN

"Only a life lived for others is a life worthwhile." Einstein

Our arrival at the apartment was uneventful. Amber was a little disoriented at first, but after finding her favorite squeaky toy, she settled right back on the couch with it. I went to my room and felt as if so much time had passed.

I dialed Daniel's cell and the need to see him was overwhelming. "Hi, I'm home."

"Great. Can I come over?"

"Yes. I can't wait to see you."

"Paige, I don't want you going out today or tomorrow, not even to walk Amber unless you're with me, so feign sickness with your parents. I'll explain later."

"Okay," I said nervously.

I found my parents in the kitchen looking through the mail. "Daniel's coming over. Okay?"

"Sure, no problem," Mom said.

The doorman announced Daniel, so I waited for him in the hallway. Exiting the elevator, he engulfed me in his arms and I melted as our lips met. What I felt for him was unbelievable!

Daniel's eyes twinkled as he said, "Has it only been a few days? It feels far too long."

"I missed you so much." Daniel put both hands on my face and kissed me again.

The elevator door opened and we released our grasp as Mrs. Braxon exited giving us a surly look. Exchanging pleasantries didn't change her furrowed expression one bit. As soon as she turned her back, I kissed him, but Mrs. Braxon turned and gave me a reproachful glare. I quickly dragged him through my front door.

My parents heard us in the living room and came out to say hello. Dad and Daniel immediately got into a debate about English soccer and the Liverpool team.

Amber was sitting on the couch and was licking her leg like crazy. Mom went over to see what was going on and presumed it was a tick since there were a lot on Long Island, but found a large lump instead. The skin all around it was raw and enflamed and Mom said she'd call the vet in the morning.

We went to watch TV in the den. Daniel said, "I'll be over as soon as you call tomorrow and we'll search your dad's office."

"Okay, but why can't I go out?"

"You're supposed to get abducted. Again, things constantly change, but nothing can happen if I am always with you."

"What are you talking about? They can kill both of us," I answered nervously.

"That won't happen, we have security."

"Wait, if they kill us, time travelers can go and change it, right?" Something was nagging in the back of my mind.

"Yes."

"How come you didn't save Frank, the agent that died?" I watched as Daniel's shoulders hunched over from hearing Frank's name.

"I figured you'd ask why we saved you but not Frank, one day. That's one of the reasons why James thinks we have someone inside the agency working against us. There's always a traveler on duty at each machine in case something needs to change. The window to correct a death is thirty minutes, after that, the event occurs."

"I don't understand."

"All the times you died, we had thirty minutes to undo it."

"Are you serious? Why didn't you tell me this before?"

"I almost did, but since I had to leave you for the weekend, I didn't want to worry you. So much was thrown at you, I wasn't sure if you could deal with much more."

"What happened with Frank?" I asked.

"The agent stationed at the closest time machine was sent away into the future, but there was no information as to who sent him. So when James called to instruct the traveler to go back in time before the murder, he wasn't there. Then he called the other machines on the East Coast and mysteriously all those guys were on travels also. There was no time to get someone else there in 30 minutes. There's an internal investigation going on right now. In all these years, that was the only time we lost an agent like that. Because of Frank's death, backup procedures have been implemented, so this never happens again."

Daniel looked so upset. I looked into his beautiful eyes and said, "I'm sorry about Frank, but all we can do now is try and stop this." Daniel closed his eyes and looked exhausted.

I stared at him and thought of something. "Why weren't some of the past political assassinations corrected?"

"Because the thirty minute window wasn't discovered until 1981. That window is absolute only for changing someone's death, not other things and was discovered by accident. An agent was at a location where someone died. Since he needed to alter something else, he phoned it in. Another agent went back in because the time machine's location was nearby and discovered that someone that had been killed was alive. That was the first time that someone's death was reversed. EMIT hadn't known that was possible before, so there is someone at each time machine in case of emergencies."

"But if I die in the future?" I babbled, getting lost with my train of thought. "I should be dead?" This was so hard to understand.

"It hasn't happened yet."

"But...."

"Don't worry about the future; I'll take care of it," Daniel said, not as confidently as I would've liked. "Do you know what Einstein said about the future?"

I shook my head no.

"I never think of the future- it comes soon enough," Daniel answered. "Can we just relax and watch a movie? Time travel knocks me out."

I grabbed a pillow and put it on my lap. "Here, lie down."

Daniel did and I scratched his head while we watched the movie. He was so quiet that I think he fell asleep.

I heard Mom coming downstairs to take Amber for her last walk and saw that it was almost midnight. I paused the movie and Daniel sat up.

"Do you want me to take her?" I called out.

"No, your dad and I feel like taking a walk. He's finishing something up and will be down in a few minutes," Mom answered and went in the kitchen.

"I better go. I'll be downstairs in the apartment."

"Where is it?" I wondered.

"Fifth floor, apartment four. If you're ever in trouble, go there." I walked him to the elevator.

When I got into my bedroom, I got my journal out of the closet and wrote for about an hour. Since my last posting, a lot had happened. I wrote about everything in Long Island except the classified things. I took his photo from the Eiffel Tower out and put it back in my bag. Why hadn't we taken any pictures while we were in Long Island? I felt like screaming! I had left my camera home thinking that taking pictures with one arm would be difficult. I should have taken some with my cell.

It was impossible to sleep. I had this sense of foreboding or was it just my imagination. Being told you're supposed to die could do that to a person.

I had nightmares all night again and woke up constantly. At Grammy's the dreams were minimal, but here, the terror-filled dreams had returned.

***

In the morning, I found a note from Mom to call her at work.

I called and asked, "Hi, Mom, what time will you be home tonight?"

"Around five thirty, you'll be all right won't you?"

"Yes, don't worry, I'll walk Amber. Can you call me when you're coming home?"

"Why?" she asked suspiciously. Great, she thought I was up to something with Daniel. I was, but not what she was imagining.

When the doorbell rang, I ran down and opened the door. Daniel entered, picked me up and proceeded to kiss me passionately.

"Wow, now that's a good morning!"

"I could do better," he grinned mischievously and kissed me again.

"How can you so easily melt me?" I asked.

"Because I love you," he smiled, still holding me in his arms. "As much as I'd prefer to kiss you all day, we have to find that other envelope."

Daniel said he loved me! He actually loved me! I stood there in shock watching him as he walked in to the living room.

Turning to find me still in the foyer, he asked, "What are you doing?"

"You said you loved me," I grinned.

Daniel came back, put his arms around me and lifted me up so my face looked right into his and said, "Yes, Paige Devon, I love you but I thought you already knew that."

"No, but I hoped. I love you too," I whispered because I had a lump in my throat.

"I'm glad because you're stuck with me," he joked.

"I'm fine with that."

Putting me down softly, Daniel kissed me.

He snapped me out of my euphoria by saying, "Paige, let's get to work because the sooner we find the envelope, the sooner this'll be over."

"Fine, but I'd rather kiss you," I whined.

Daniel shook his head grinning and dragged me upstairs to dad's office. We searched for hours and nothing.

When my stomach began grumbling, I realized it was almost one o'clock. In the kitchen, we made sandwiches and decided that we'd check my parents' bedroom next.

Their bedroom was so soothing and tranquil. The furniture was white and the bedding and curtains were all blue toile. I felt really bad snooping around their personal things.

We found nothing and Daniel said, "Maybe because of my involvement and with things constantly changing, you haven't been given the second envelope yet and it's still at the firm."

"It's hard to search there," I said.

"I'll send people there tonight. Don't worry. We'll get in."

Amber was barking by the door and I realized that I'd forgotten to walk her. Going outside and getting some fresh air got us both out of the doldrums. We walked up Central Park West and turned around when we got to the Museum of Natural History.

I wondered if Mom was home, so Daniel called someone and

said she wasn't. It was so weird that strangers knew all about my life.

John Costra walked out of the building as we approached and I realized that Daniel never told me what EMIT had found out about him. He stopped to talk, so I introduced Daniel.

"Lucia and Luke are coming home early. Lucia has an audition for a Broadway play."

"When will they be back? I really miss them."

"Not sure yet. Lucia is waiting to hear what day her audition is."

After he left, I asked Daniel, "I'm presuming he's been cleared or you would've told me."

"You're correct and if we didn't find that bomb, he'd be dead right now."

"I can't believe it. What was the point?"

"The bomb was to scare you, not to kill you."

"I'd be responsible for John's death and Luke wouldn't have a dad.

"It didn't happen, so get it out of your mind."

"What if Luke and Lucia were home?"

"They weren't," Daniel said trying to calm me down. "Everything that comes into this building is being scanned by an EMIT agent. We have video surveillance on all the floors, all the elevators and all the stairways. No one can get to you without us knowing about it."

So they had seen me cry in the elevator and the hallways. "You don't have cameras in my apartment do you?" I asked anxiously.

"No, only on the outside."

"Good. What did James say to John when he talked to him?"

"James met him in the lobby and was keeping him busy, while an agent put surveillance equipment in his apartment. James said that he was thinking of buying an apartment and asked questions about the building."

"Did James say he knew me?" If John asked me I had to know.

"Yes. He said that I was a friend of yours and he was coming with me to look at your apartment. John asked if your family was moving, but James said no he just wanted to look at the layout."

Back upstairs, Mom called to say that Martin, Marina and Anna were coming for dinner. Dad wanted to see Martin before we left for London and Daniel was welcome to join us.

"My mom wants to know if you'd like to have dinner with us tonight. My brother and his family are coming."

"Is your brother going to interrogate me, too?" Daniel asked.

"Martin won't. Don't worry."

"We'll see," he said grinning. "What time is dinner?"

"I think six."

"I'll leave and come back. I don't want your mom to think the worst."

"You're right, I told her to call before she came home," I said feeling guilty. I hoped we put everything back in the right places.

"See you soon," Daniel said trying to hide his frustration, which was written all over his face.

Exhausted, I sat in the living room waiting for Mom and watched a silly movie. Hearing the door open, Mom entered the apartment laden with groceries and Carl was behind her carrying more. I jumped up to help as best I could, wondering what Carl and the other doormen thought of Daniel constantly coming and going out of the building. I'd have to ask Daniel what they told the doormen because Carl looked at me strangely as he left.

"Why didn't you use a cart?"

"There were none. People take them into their apartments and forget to bring them back."

Entering the kitchen, a bag that was precariously placed in my right arm was about to fall so I yelped. Mom turned, dropped her bags on the floor and rescued the groceries from me.

"Mom, when I see the doctor on Wednesday, do you think this cast will come off? I can't take it anymore!" I said, getting upset.

"Sweetie, the doctor said six weeks and since it's only been three weeks, the answer is no. It'll be off soon enough. It hasn't stopped you from having a great summer. Am I right?"

"You're right. Why am I complaining?" I said, beaming.

"Speaking of Daniel, is he joining us?"

"Yes, he is. I told him to come at six."

"Okay. Marina will be here around then, too. Dad and Martin more like six-thirty."

Mom cooked and we had a great time talking until she brought up Daniel. Mom called him 'poor boy' so many times because of his dead parents that I left to change my clothes.

In my room, I checked my computer and found that all was fine in the world of my friends. I texted Lily and asked her to come over on Tuesday so that we saw each other before I left. I suggested we do something with Daniel and Chad.

Daniel arrived and we sat in the kitchen chatting with Mom while she cooked. I couldn't wait for Martin and Marina to meet him.

When Carl informed us that Marina and Anna were on their way, Daniel and I walked to the elevator to help Marina with the baby.

While waiting, I got some kisses and as our lips locked, the elevator door opened and Marina stood there staring at us.

"Well, hello. This is quite a surprise," Marina said, as she looked at both of us one at a time.

"Oh, hi, Marina. This is my boyfriend, Daniel." I said smiling when I realized it was the first time I had introduced him like that.

Before I could say more, Marina introduced herself. "Hi, boyfriend Daniel. I'm Marina and this is Anna."

"I've heard a lot about you. It's nice to meet you."

"Unfortunately, Daniel, I've heard nothing about you." Marina looked at me with a 'why haven't you called me?' face and looked hurt.

"Marina, I'm sorry since my accident, I haven't been calling anybody," I said.

Instead of making things better, Marina appeared more annoyed and said, "I'm not just anybody. I'm family. I called you twice last week and you've never returned my calls."

Oh my God. I did get one call and I forgot to call her back! I apologized profusely. But there weren't two calls, just one! Daniel had to do something about my cell.

I was playing with Anna when Amber started getting finicky by the door. Mom made a move to take her out, but Daniel offered to do it and walked to the foyer.

"That's very kind of you, Daniel, but Amber won't go with you. If anyone tries to walk her, she runs away." Just as she finished her sentence, Amber sidled up to Daniel to allow him to clip the leash to her collar.

Mom was stunned. "Great Amber, make me look like a liar." Mom shook her head in amazement. "I've never seen her voluntarily go to anyone like this before. Maybe it was all the time you spent with her on the Island."

"Probably," I said. "I'll come with you."

"Play with Anna, I'll be right back."

As Amber limped out, I asked "Mom, are you taking Amber to the vet?"

"Yes, I have an appointment tomorrow. I have to know what that lump is before we leave. I don't want Grammy to worry."

Mom went to check on the food and as soon as we were alone, Marina pounced on me. "Okay, spill it. Who is he and where did you meet?"

"I met him in Central Park at the end of June. I thought he had a girlfriend. We bumped into each other on the Causeway Beach and I found out I was wrong. That's basically the whole story." God, please forgive me for all these half-truths.

"Well, he's gorgeous and seems very nice, but that's all I have for the short amount of time, I've talked to him," Marina admitted.

Knowing that people were listening to the conversation, I had no intention of gushing about Daniel. As I crawled around the floor chasing Anna, the door opened and Dad, Martin and Daniel entered the apartment together.

"Hi, everybody," Dad said. "As we walked up the street, I said to Martin, 'someone has a dog that looks just like Amber. When we got closer, I saw that it was Daniel and was amazed that Amber went outside with him."

Mom laughed. "I was floored too. She must have spent a lot of time with him."

"What can I say dogs love me," Daniel joked.

All evening, Martin seemed cold and distant. During dinner, Martin mentioned that people should take things slow in relationships and Daniel tapped my foot under the table. I looked at him and saw Mom glancing at me. I realized that besides this being a get-together because we were leaving for London, my parents were using Martin to tell me to slow things down with Daniel. Was this some sort of intervention? It didn't matter what they thought. It only mattered what Daniel and I thought, and there was no way we were slowing anything down. Daniel was my destiny. I knew it and so did he.

Martin, Marina and Anna were at the door leaving and Dad got a phone call. He put the call on hold. "I have to take this. Good night, I'll see you when we get back." He left looking upset and I presumed it was about some case.

It was still very early, but Daniel left with them. I wondered why he didn't stay. In my room, I waited for his call. "You miss me already?"

"Always, you know that."

"Me too. I'm sorry about Martin."

"I expected it so don't worry."

"It's so annoying though. My parents must have asked Martin to say something. What's totally absurd is that Martin and Marina started dating in high school."

"It's understandable. Your parents see this raffish bloke appear and try to steal their daughter. Don't get mad at them. What I would give to have my parents around. You're very lucky. I'm leaving now for your dad's office. Call me when you wake up."

"That's why you left so early. I forgot you were going. Please be careful."

Right after we hung up, Lily called. "Hi, Lily. Are you coming tomorrow?"

"Yeah, I told Chad about it."

"I forgot to tell Daniel, but it'll be fine."

Again that night, I had terrifying dreams and woke up a lot. I wondered if my sub-conscious was trying to tell me something or were they premonitions of what was to come. Was it possible that they were memories of what had happened to me? EMIT went in and saved me, but was it possible that those events remained in my subconscious?

***

The morning was dark grey and wet. Needing my Daniel fix, I called him.

"Why are you up so early? It's only seven!" he asked.

"What are you talking about? You were the one working. How'd it go?"

"We found nothing. It's really frustrating. Do you think you could go and look around?"

"I doubt I'll do any better, but I'll see if Dad can have lunch. I'll call you when Mom leaves."

When I walked into the kitchen, Mom was finishing the clean up from last night.

"Did you ask Martin to say something about relationships or was that all Martin?" I asked.

"We like Daniel, but you're rushing into a serious relationship."

"I'll be eighteen in December. You can't tell me who to like or to date. Martin and Marina met in high school, so Martin saying anything is so ridiculous. It's like the pot calling the kettle black. Don't you think?" I asked angrily.

Mom looked frustrated, but didn't say anything to rebut my comment.

"Where's Dad?" I asked.

"He went in early. There was an emergency. Sonia called in sick on Friday. Yesterday, she didn't come in and when she didn't call, the office got concerned. Maria called Sonia's parents in Massachusetts and they hadn't heard from her either. Maria went to her apartment in Brooklyn last night and got the super to open the door. Sonia wasn't there, but her pocketbook with her wallet, cell phone and keys were. It's like she just disappeared. They notified the police and now it's a missing person's case." My heart stopped beating.

"Hopefully, everything will be okay," she said.

Walking backwards, I said, "I'm going to go to Dad's office, maybe I can help somehow."

"I'm sure he'd like it, but call him first, he might be going crazy."

I knew if I called, he'd tell me not to come and I was going. As I reached for my cell, it rang. "I didn't want to tell you about Sonia. I didn't want to scare you," said Daniel.

"When did you find out?"

"Last night, when your dad heard it from Maria."

"I thought you were watching her, what happened?"

"The agents had no idea she ever left her apartment."

"Wasn't she being bugged?"

"We didn't bug her apartment. There was a tracker on her cell, but since it was left behind that didn't help," said Daniel.

"Did Sonia disappear before?" I asked wondering.

"No. Things are changing so rapidly that it's impossible to go by past events.

Quickly dressing, I went back downstairs. Mom was taking Amber to the vet and then going to work. The minute she left I texted Daniel, and shortly after, there was a knock on my door.

I opened the door and found Luke standing there. Lucia was behind him smiling.

"Hey neighbor! Luke's been begging since six to come say hello. I couldn't hold him back anymore."

"I missed you," I said and picked him up with my good arm. Good thing he's light. As I hugged him, I began twirling him. Lucia came forward dodging his flying feet. I put him down and he beamed his tanned face at me.

"You got so dark!"

"I've been swimming without my swimmies," he proudly informed me.

"Wow, that's great!" Turning to Lucia, I asked, "How are you?"

"Good, I had to come back for an audition. How's your arm? I can't believe what happened."

"I know. It's getting better. I just want this cast off."

The elevator door opened and Daniel came walking down the hallway. He was his usual breathtaking self. Lucia watched him as he approached and raised her eyebrows at me.

"Hey, Paige," Daniel said and kissed me on the cheek.

"Lucia, Luke this is my boyfriend, Daniel. Daniel, these are my neighbors, Lucia and Luke."

"Well, well," Lucia said, "It's very nice to meet you." Luke was behind Lucia peering up at Daniel cautiously.

"You too," Daniel said and got down on his knees to chat with Luke. As he showed Luke a magic trick with a coin, Lucia gave me the thumbs up sign. I nodded. After we said we'd get together soon, Daniel and I went into my apartment.

"Come here, beautiful," he said as I walked into his arms. The scent of him was so familiar that I would know it was him with my eyes closed. After showering he always smelled of citrus shampoo and verbena soap but otherwise he smelled of tea and sandalwood.

I was so worried about Sonia. "Do you think she's okay?"

"We'll try and find her, but I don't think it'll be a good outcome, so be prepared."

I hoped that Sonia was okay. When terrifying scenarios began swimming in my head, I realized that I wasn't helping anybody and needed to get empowered somehow.

It finally came to me. "Do you have a gun?"

"Yes," he answered and showed it strapped to his leg.

"Where was it on Long Island? You were in shorts."

"The boat or the car and when we were out, I always wore long pants."

"Can I have a gun?"

"No." Seeing the fear in my face he added, "I'll be with you. Don't worry."

I closed my eyes. All the sleepless nights filled with nightmares were getting to me.

Daniel asked, "Are you okay?"

"I'm so tired. Almost every night, I have crazy dreams about getting hurt or killed. Do you think it's possible that I'm reliving real memories?

"I'm not sure," Daniel answered. "I guess it's possible. Those things did happen to you, but since you're the only person I've ever spoken to about this, I can't be positive. I'll ask the scientists about it."

"Thanks. I keep dreaming of this man that was recently found in the park with amnesia."

"You are?" Daniel asked sounding amused.

"Yeah, why's that funny?"

"That guy did try to kill you. We gave him a drug to forget things and he had a bad reaction."

"And you just left him in the park?" I gasped.

"He's not a good guy, but don't worry about him. His family

finds him at the hospital."

"Will he get his memory back?"

"No, but he'll stop being a criminal."

Daniel got a text that a car was waiting for us downstairs. It was time to leave.

"You'll be safe inside. You met Jared, right?"

"Yes..."

"He's one of our men. I'll take you up in the elevator. I'll let Jared know that you'll be there and I'll be in the lobby. Everyone else will be outside."

"But he's been there three years!" I realized the day Jared walked me to the library had been staged. He was protecting me.

"Three summers, actually. Call me when you're leaving."

It was almost one o'clock and Dad wasn't there. Maria said he was in court. I told her I wanted to leave him a note and hurried in to his office. Five minutes into my snooping, I heard knocking and I cautiously opened the door, but it was Jared and not some crazed terrorist.

"Daniel told me what you're doing and I'll be right outside if you need me."

"Thanks Jared. No one is helping him today?" I asked, looking at Sonia's empty desk.

"One of the other secretaries is helping from her desk and a temp is coming tomorrow."

An entire team of professionals had been here and found nothing, so my visit was absurd.

I glanced at the old photos of me on his bookshelf and cringed.

They had to be changed as soon as possible.

I looked around and I was right. I found nothing. As I exited, Jared looked up expectantly. I shook my head. "Did they look through Sonia's stuff?"

"Yes, they searched her apartment, too." Of course they did. I called Lily and told her to meet me at Dad's office. Frustrated, I sat at Sonia's desk and talked to Jared. I noticed Jared's left hand and he had the same three tattooed dots that Daniel did. That's what the bandage was covering. Was that the symbol for all the EMIT people? James Haydin didn't have it, but he didn't seem like a tattoo kind of guy. Maybe it was the symbol just for the time travelers. I'd have to keep an eye out for everybody's hands.

Jared got called away. It was weird that he worked at the firm and also at EMIT.

I remembered that Mom had gone to the vet, so I called to see how Amber was. She said the vet found some strange electronic gadget embedded under her skin. They put a tracker in Amber! I was going to kill Daniel.

"Dr. O'Reilly had no idea what it was. He gave me the disc and said that it happened within the last week. Maybe while she was roughhousing on the sand, it somehow got lodged in. Thank goodness she has such sensitive skin and we saw it."

After the call, I called Daniel. "Did you implant something in Amber?"

"No one from EMIT did that. I just checked. It might not be anything at all, but I want to see that disc. Can you get it from your mom?"

"OK. Amber was with us the whole time except for that one hour we lost her."

"The neighbor was Laura Burke. I'll have her checked out."

I was getting paranoid without knowing what the gadget was, but if it was a tracking device and EMIT didn't do it, that meant the bad guys were on the island.

It was almost five o'clock when Dad showed up.

"Buttercup, what are you doing here?" he asked and gave me a big hug, while I winced. There was no rhyme or reason to when Dad used my nickname, but here it was humiliating.

"Dad, please don't call me that at work."

"Sorry, I forgot where we were for a minute. Been a bit pre-occupied." He began looking at the mail on his desk.

"Its okay, Dad," I added, changing my tone. "I heard about Sonia and I came to help."

"That was nice of you. Sonia's disappearance is so bizarre. I don't know what to make of it. Her parents are frantic." He reached for his briefcase and started putting files inside. "Let's go home."

"I'm waiting for Lily, but you can go."

"No, I'll wait with you. I need to return some phone calls anyway," he said.

I went to the bathroom and called Daniel.

"Do you think you'll walk home?" he asked.

"Probably." It had stopped raining and Dad loved to walk.

"We'll be right behind you."

My cell rang. Lily was in the lobby and I went to tell Dad.

17. CONCUSSION

"The fear of death is the most unjustified of all fears, for there's no risk of accident for someone who's dead." Einstein

The sky was still overcast and it looked like it was about to rain. Dad was undeterred and we proceeded up Sixth Avenue. Looking around, I didn't see Daniel. As always, traffic was at a standstill because of rush hour. On Central Park South, I saw a black van pull up alongside and presumed it was the agency tailing us home. When we reached Columbus Circle, Daniel appeared and I was so relieved.

Daniel and Lily walked behind Dad and I. It was too difficult to walk together. When Dad asked Daniel a question, Lily joined me in front to let them talk. I looked around nervously and noticed that Lily was watching me. "Are you okay?"

"I'm fine, just really tired. I haven't been sleeping well. So tell me about Chad," I said, wanting Lily to distract me.

As we got closer to home, the tension was slowly receding. The light changed, but Dad and Daniel missed it and didn't cross, so Lily and I stopped to wait for them. The van that I mistook for the agency pulled up and two men jumped out. One grabbed Lily and the other one leaped on me. They covered our mouths and began pulling us towards the van. All I saw was sheer terror in Lily's eyes pleading for help. I turned and saw Dad's horrified expression from across the street. Daniel started yelling and the one holding me got startled and released me. They raced across the street maneuvering around people and cars. Daniel tackled the guy, but the van with Lily sped off. *Oh my God!*

Daniel looked up and the guy pulled out a gun. Dad lunged at him. Suddenly, Dad crashed to the sidewalk with such force that I didn't know what happened. Had he been shot?

"DAD!" I shouted and rushed over to him. After a few blinks, his eyes stilled and then closed. Looking up, Brad was handcuffing the man and Daniel was on the phone.

"Daniel, help me, please," I screamed. Dad was unconscious and unresponsive.

Daniel kneeled near my father.

"Is he dead?" I was too scared to look.

"No, he's breathing."

"Thank God!" This was my fault. I should've told him about the danger I was in, that we were all in. I'd endangered my whole family. *LILY! WHERE WAS SHE?* My head was about to explode. Please let her be okay, I prayed. Don't let them hurt her. Please, let Dad be okay.

Pierce and James came running from across the street. Instantly, there was a throng of people everywhere and I saw James brandishing a badge. At least ten agents swarmed the scene; men I'd never seen before.

"We need an ambulance!" I was frantic. "Where's Lily? Please find her!" I pleaded with James Haydin. They must have a tracker in Lily's phone. I didn't know what to do. Terror overcame me as I grasped that Dad and/or Lily might die.

"A car is following the van and an ambulance is coming for your dad," James informed me and walked away to talk to some men.

"What happened? Did he get shot?" I was hysterical.

Daniel put his arms around me as I sat on the sidewalk next to dad, freaking out.

"No, the gun never went off. When he lunged at the guy, he tripped."

"I have to call my mom." I reached for my cell and Daniel stopped me.

"Before you call, we have to have the same story."

I looked at him like he was a stranger. My father was lying on the ground unconscious and Lily had been abducted and he thought I cared if we had the same story. "Are you crazy?" I shrieked. "I don't care. My father's hurt and Lily's gone." My call got postponed anyway because the ambulance arrived and I rushed over.

As the medics prepped Dad, James came over. "Lily's fine. She'll be here shortly." I was so relieved. *Thank God!* If anything had happened to Lily, I would've died. I should have warned everybody. I knew how dangerous this all was.

"Paige, call your mom and tell her your dad fell and we're on the way to the hospital," James instructed.

A black car pulled up. I watched as Lily jumped out and ran to me. On cue, we both started crying and I held on to her so tightly. Seeing Dad on the stretcher, she asked, "What happened?"

"He fell and smashed his head on the ground or a pole. Are you okay?"

"I'm okay, they didn't hurt me. They wanted me to warn you that you better give them the info or the same thing will happen to you that happened to Sonia. What are they talking about? I thought you gave them the envelope."

"They're after another one."

Lily's mouth dropped. "I can't believe this." Lily leaned on a parked car and looked white as a ghost. "We're all still in danger?" she asked.

Daniel put both hands on Lily's shoulder to steady her because she looked like she was about to keel over and tried to reassure her by saying, "You have security, don't worry."

"I have security! Big deal! I was just abducted. Where was my security? What about my parents?" Lily said shaking.

"No, they're not involved in this, and they're perfectly safe," added Daniel.

"How do you know that?" Lily demanded. Lily was giving him a hard time, not wanting vague answers, but grew more and more frustrated as that's all she kept hearing. Lily was right. Since everything was constantly changing, Daniel saying our parents were safe was ludicrous. My dad wasn't supposed to get hurt. How could Daniel guarantee anything anymore? Tired of their verbal debate and knowing Lily wouldn't win, I went over to the ambulance.

While Dad was being put in the ambulance, Daniel and Lily came over. Someone I didn't know approached Daniel and I heard Sonia's name.

"What happened?" I asked, but I knew the answer before he told me.

"She was found dead," he whispered in my ear, so Lily didn't hear. My body was shaking and fear was becoming a common emotion. How much more of this could I endure?

I mustered the courage and called. "Mom, Dad fell on the sidewalk and he's unconscious. We're on the way to the hospital." Mom became frantic and said she was on her way.

I got in the ambulance and Daniel kissed me on my head. "We'll be right behind you. Lily will ride to the hospital with me."

I closed my eyes and prayed that Dad would be all right. When the ambulance stopped, I opened my eyes and Dad looked small on the stretcher and so pallid.

As they wheeled him into the hospital, I stared at his unmoving form and my eyes filled with tears. After all, this was my fault. When I was asked to keep this secret, I never imagined anything like this was even possible. Everything I was involved in was dangerous, yet somehow I felt safe and believed that my family would be unharmed.

My parents always said if someone told me to keep a secret from them not to listen. So what did I do? I ignored their advice. All the red flags and all the warnings screaming in my head didn't dissuade me either.

Because of that decision, I was standing in a hospital staring at my dad who was in a catatonic state. Why didn't I tell my parents! Warn them about what I was involved in! I told myself that I was protecting them, but was I just being selfish?

Entrenched in this bizarre world where everything seemed so impossible, but was actually real, I succumbed to the adventure. All my perceived notions about what I would and wouldn't do in certain situations went right out the window.

Suddenly, I noticed movement and saw Dad thrashing around. I rushed over to him. Looking around confused, Dad stared at me and appeared to be waiting for an explanation. "Dad, are you okay?"

He mumbled, "I think so. What happened?"

"You hit your head. We're at the hospital." Mom rushed in and was thrilled that he was awake.

"Oliver, how are you feeling?"

"My head hurts." A door opened and a doctor headed towards us.

"Hello, I'm Dr. Carr. The nurse said you arrived unconscious. It's a good sign you're up and about. We need a CT scan, stat." An orderly wheeled Dad away.

"What happened? The ambulance report says he fell and hit his head?" the doctor asked Mom and she looked at me for the answer.

"I'm not sure. I think he tripped and hit a pole or smashed his head on the sidewalk." This hadn't been a good summer for my family, first Nana, then me, and now Dad, not to mention Lily's abduction.

"As soon as I have some news, I'll find you," the doctor said and left.

After all the insurance information was given, Mom went to

make the necessary phone calls to the health insurance company. James, Daniel and Lily were sitting in the waiting room and poor Lily looked ashen. I hugged her and all I could say was, "I'm so sorry. I wish they had taken me."

"If they took you, I don't think they would've let you go."

"Probably not, but I wouldn't feel so guilty. If anything happened to you…" my voice trailed off and tears welled up in my eyes.

"Calm down. I'm trying to forget it or I might break down again. Let's worry about your dad right now." She was right.

James and Daniel were whispering and I wasn't sure what they were planning. James asked if we could all go outside. Daniel took my hand as we exited the hospital. When I glanced over, Mom was still on the phone.

Outside, James said, "Please tell your parents exactly what happened on the street today."

Confused, I asked, "We can say that some men tried to kidnap us?"

"Yes," James responded dismissively.

"My parents are going to freak out!" I said, flustered by the absurdity.

"Trust me. I'll take care of everything," he answered and seemed annoyed by my questions.

"Even that Lily was taken?" I asked, looking at Lily, who shrugged, not understanding what was going on either.

"Yes. Just tell her it was a mistake. A prank gone wrong," drilled James. "Just leave out the gun part, please."

"Okayyyyyy," I said in a sing-songy voice. Mom was going to have a fit and this wasn't going to work. When we got back inside,   . Mom was looking for me.

"What's going on? Are you okay?" she asked looking concerned.

Before I had a chance to answer, James stepped forward and introduced himself, "I'm James Haydin, Daniel's uncle."

Mom shook his hand. "Lena Devon. What happened to my husband?"

"It was the craziest thing. Dad, Lily, and I were walking home and we bumped into Daniel at Columbus Circle. As we walked up Central Park West, Lily and I got ahead of them because they got caught at a light. We were across the street and a van pulled up. Two men jumped out, grabbed us and started dragging us inside."

"What?" she exclaimed. Staring at me in horror, she cupped her hand over her mouth.

"Somebody yelled and the guy who was holding me let go, but the other guy dragged Lily inside the van and drove off."

Mom looked at Lily. "What? How did you get away?"

"It was a mistake and they let me out," Lily said.

"What mistake? What happened to Oliver?" Mom asked puzzled.

"Dad and Daniel ran across the street and the next thing I knew Dad was on the ground unconscious. He tripped and hit and smashed his head."

Mom glanced over at James and Daniel and asked, "Were you there, James?"

"Not when they were accosted. Daniel called me after he called the ambulance. I was in a cab on Eighth Avenue on my way home. I arrived shortly after. The police were already there and basically it was a prank gone awry." What was he saying? There were no police, just NSA.

"A prank?" she shrieked. "What are you talking about?"

James continued, "Apparently, some guy was trying to frighten his ex-girlfriend. He asked his cousin to scare her, but he mistakenly grabbed Lily."

"Are they crazy? I can't believe this! My husband's lying in a hospital."

Mom believed this crazy story, which absolutely surprised me. At the same time, James does work for the NSA. Why wouldn't a person believe him? Why would he lie?

Looking at Lily and me, she added, "I'm so glad you two are okay."

"Thank you for being there to help," she said addressing James. "Of course and you too, Daniel. I'm so glad you were there."

"No problem. Glad to help any way I can. I'm really sorry." Mom didn't catch it, but Daniel was looking at me when he apologized.

He wasn't responsible for this mess, but I was angry with everybody, even myself.

"What if Oliver had been alone with the girls? What would've happened?" she said. "Were they arrested?"

"I'm not sure. We followed the ambulance here," answered James.

It felt like hours when the doctor finally came out. He said that there was no blood on the brain, but Dad had a bad concussion and needed to stay overnight.

With a loud sigh, Mom rushed to his room and we all lingered outside. Peeking in, I saw her stroking his hair and talking to him. Step by step, I slowly entered and stood staring at my father. What had I done? Guilt consumed me and I couldn't look him in the eyes.

Lily came in after she called Aunt Cecile. "Aunt Lena, I spoke to Mom and she's waiting for Dad at the train station and then they're driving straight to the hospital."

"Let me go call her. There's nothing they can do. Lily, you told her what happened to you?"

"Yes, she's really upset, I told her I was okay, but maybe she'll believe you."

"I'll do my best," Mom said, as she walked out of the room.

I said, "Dad, I'm so sorry. Are you okay?"

"Don't worry. I'll be fine. My head's hard as a rock."

I know he was trying to make me laugh, but that was impossible. "Not funny Dad."

"What actually happened? Everything's a bit fuzzy. I remember walking home with you and Lily then I woke up here."

Dad listened as I told him, but he didn't remember anything.

"You're kidding?" Dad said at the end.

"No, she's not," said Mom, as she came in. "What an asinine prank. Oliver, you should sue them for medical bills, pain and suffering. Paige and Lily should sue, too. They've been traumatized and they could've been hurt. Those guys have to be punished."

"Lena, let's talk about this later. There's been enough excitement for one day."

"Fine, but I could scream! Lily, your mom isn't coming. She said to call her later."

"I will."

"Girls, let's go home. I'll feel better making sure you two are safe inside. Will you be okay if I stay here with Dad tonight?"

Lily nodded at me, so I said, "Mom, we're good. We'll just watch a movie and try to relax."

"Lena, no. I'll be fine. Stay home and sleep there."

"No, I'll walk the girls home and I'll be back," Mom said. "Girls go find Daniel. I want to talk to Oliver for a minute."

I hugged Dad and told him to get better. He smiled weakly and squeezed my arm.

I put my arm around Lily and helped her up. She looked like she would fall over. We found Daniel in the hallway talking to Pierce. James was gone.

"Mom is walking us home and coming back to stay with my dad tonight."

Pierce got on his cell and that's when I noticed it. On his left palm, there were three black dots. It had to be a traveler thing.

While we waited, Lily called Chad and told him what had happened.

"Lily, tell him to come over. We can all hang out at my house tonight."

I glanced at Daniel and he nodded. "Everything will be okay," he whispered in my ear.

When we got to the apartment, Daniel offered to walk Amber.

That was good, because I was never leaving the apartment until this nightmare ended.

Mom went upstairs and came back down with a small bag.

"Please feed Amber. She gets antibiotics twice a day after meals for the infection."

"She'll just eat the pill?" I asked.

"No, after she finishes eating, wrap the pill in American cheese or cream cheese."

"Okay. Is there food home or should I order a pizza?"

"Whatever you want, but there's a lot of chicken left from last night and there's fresh corn. Don't remove the husks. Put the corn in the microwave for four minutes."

"Okay, I will." I looked over at Lily and she wasn't looking very good.

"Bye girls. I'll see you tomorrow morning." Mom kissed both of us goodbye.

Lily collapsed on the couch and stared at me in disbelief, finally saying, "This is really scary. I have to tell my parents. I can't keep this from them."

"Everything will be okay." I tried to calm her down, but it wasn't working.

"What if Daniel is wrong and they're in danger? If anything happens to them I'll never forgive myself."

"You can't tell them. It's complicated."

"I'll talk to Daniel when he gets back and I'll decide then," Lily stated firmly. I'd never seen Lily that upset, but then she'd never been abducted before either.

When Daniel returned, I took Amber into the kitchen to feed her and left them in the living room to talk. Honestly, I'd heard enough and just wanted to escape from it all. After Amber ate, I give her the medicine and I set the table for four. In case Chad was eating with us, we'd be ready. I put the chicken in the oven to warm up and started the corn. Preparing the meal made me feel like it was a normal night, but I knew it wasn't. No matter, I would enjoy this moment of fake bliss and have dinner with my boyfriend. As I turned to get the glasses, Lily and Daniel entered the kitchen.

"I told Daniel that I will give them time to find these men, but if anything happens to my parents the deal is off."

Daniel went to the beeping microwave oven and removed the corn.

"What happened to the guy who grabbed me? Where is he?" I asked Daniel.

He didn't look up from buttering the corn. "He's being interrogated."

Obviously, he'd had enough of this topic too or he didn't want to talk in front of Lily. I saw him reach for something in the fruit bowl on the counter.

I asked Lily if Chad was eating with us. She texted him and when we didn't get an answer, we started eating without him. Chad showed up when we were eating ice cream.

As Lily told Chad what happened, he was shocked. "Did they get arrested?" he asked.

"We don't know," answered Daniel. "We left for the hospital."

Lily's phone rang and she went to pick it up. "It's my dad," she mouthed, as she walked into the other room. I walked to the dishwasher and started loading the plates.

Lily rushed back in saying, "We have a problem. My dad is calling the police station."

"Why is that a problem?" asked Chad curiously. Lily looked at me for help.

"Lily was afraid that her dad would sue the guys who pulled the prank," I answered.

"Why's that a problem? Those guys terrorized you," Chad asked, looking at Lily.

"I don't know." She shrugged her shoulders, not knowing what to say.

"Those guys should get punished or fined. You could have gotten hurt," Chad insisted.

"I'd rather forget it ever happened. I don't want to relive it over and over again." With a frown, Lily walked towards the living room, saying, "Let's watch a movie."

Before I could follow her, Mom called to see if we were okay and to tell me that Dad was doing fine. I told her that Daniel and Chad were over. Remembering about my appointment, I said, "I'm seeing the orthopedist tomorrow at one. Should I go alone?"

"No, I'm coming with you. We'll talk in the morning. Don't worry, we'll figure it out."

"Are we still going to London?" I asked feeling terrible that I was thinking about our vacation, while Dad was in the hospital.

"We'll know tomorrow. Take care of Amber. Love you."

Daniel had heard my end of the call and put his arms around me in a bear hug. We joined Lily and Chad in the living room. I threw my shoes off to get comfortable and sat on the floor against the couch.

"What does everybody want to watch?" Lily asked.

"I don't care, but nothing scary. I've been having nightmares all week."

"How about a comedy? We need to laugh," suggested Lily. While she surfed On Demand, Daniel went into the kitchen to take a phone call.

I went to get some water and as I got near to the kitchen, I could hear that Daniel's voice sounded upset. When I walked in, he hung up.

"What's the matter?" I asked.

He shut the kitchen doors and picked up a disc from the bowl to show me. "This tracker that was in Amber is from the future and it's not being made here yet."

"So EMIT did put it in her," I said angrily.

"No, that's the problem. Everyone in EMIT is adamant that we had nothing to do with it. James is investigating and we have to find out who did this."

I just couldn't talk about this anymore. "I'm sorry, but I need to lie down. Please come upstairs with me."

Daniel said sure and followed me out, but he was preoccupied texting.

"Lily, we're going upstairs. You guys watch whatever you want."

"Okay…" she said, but she looked concerned.

Daniel had been in my bedroom before, but not with me. While I sat on the bed, Daniel looked at the photos on my wall.

"Come sit with me?" I asked.

"I don't think it's such a good idea," he said.

"Why?" I smiled.

"Because you might misbehave," he teased.

"I don't have the strength and I'm physically and mentally drained," I joked. "Did you forget I almost got abducted, Lily did get abducted and my dad's in the hospital?"

"I was just kidding. I know you had a horrible day. I wish I could make it all go away, but James won't let me," Daniel said, as he got on the bed and put his arm around me.

"Yay, I won," I said laughing and then realized what he said. "Wait, you asked James if you could change today?"

"Yeah, but he said no. I feel really responsible, but he said we can't waste trips."

"You did everything you could."

"No, I should've walked right next to you and not let you get so far in front."

"Let's forget about it. I don't want to think about today."

We started to kiss. Everything disappeared but us. I was lost in Daniel.

He caressed my back and asked, "Penny for your thoughts?"

That question brought me back and I asked, "Will everything be okay?"

Daniel stroked my cheek and kissed my lips. "Yes."

After another kiss, he added, "I hope so." I shut my eyes and nuzzled into him. I tried to get those images of today to disappear.

Something was shaking me and when I opened my eyes, I found Lily sitting on the bed.

"Paige! Wake up. Amber needs to be walked. Chad's gone and I'm afraid to do it alone."

Daniel opened his eyes and was temporarily confused. "I'll take care of Amber. I'll be right back."

"Lily, how did you stay awake after the day you had?" I asked sitting up.

"I wanted to spend time with Chad and the movie was funny."

"I'm glad you had a good end to this horrible day."

"Do you want me to sleep in the guest room?" she asked with a smirk.

"Lily, nothing happened, we just fell asleep. Well, we kissed. Stop making those faces, it's annoying."

Returning just as I said that, Daniel asked, "What's annoying?"

"Lily," I explained.

Daniel said, "Okay. I won't ask."

"It wasn't anything important, I assure you," Lily said. "What's going to happen when my dad calls the police station?"

Daniel thought a minute then said, "They'll probably tell him that there's no report of the incident and they don't know what he's talking about."

"Then what?" I asked.

"He'll probably want to talk to James."

"I don't understand. Why did we say it was a prank?"

"We had to explain it as a one-time problem not as a continuous one or your parents would panic. If they knew of the NSA involvement and the ongoing threat to you, they'd be terrified." That was true. Daniel yawned. "Paige, I better get going."

"No, please stay," I begged and looked over at Lily for help.

"Please stay. After what happened today, I'd feel so much better," Lily said.

Looking at each of us, it was obvious that Daniel was torn. "Okay," he said, watching my pleased expression. "I'll stay in the guest room."

"No stay with me, it'll be fine."

Daniel was about to say no but changed his mind. "Fine, do you have an extra toothbrush?"

I nodded and told him where to look in the bathroom. I closed my eyes and fell asleep while he was still in the bathroom.

***

As the morning light streamed in, I looked over at beautiful Daniel sleeping in my bed.

When I heard a noise in the hallway, I presumed it was Lily. My bedroom door opened and Mom was standing there at first smiling and then she saw Daniel.

"Come into my room, now," she said through clenched teeth and walked out. She slammed the door so hard that Daniel woke up.

He sat up and looked concerned. "Damn, I forgot to set my alarm. Was that your mom?"

I sighed and nodded yes. "I think I'm dead."

Daniel laughed while he put his shoes on. "I better go. I knew not to stay, but I couldn't say no after what you went through yesterday." He kissed and hugged me. "I hope your parents won't hate me. It makes dating difficult."

I said, "She'll calm down eventually. Why didn't the agents warn you?"

"I have no idea, most likely to teach me a lesson for always turning off my equipment."

Daniel went downstairs and I went across the hall. She was sitting on her bed fuming. "Mom, nothing happened. As you saw, we were fully clothed."

"Why did he stay over?" she asked seething.

"I begged him to stay because we were scared to be alone."

Lily came in and said, "Aunt Lena, I asked him to stay, too."

Seeing Lily pacified her and she said calmly, "You should've asked me. I'm not sure I would've said yes, maybe if he slept in the guestroom. I thought you knew better. Since you two were traumatized yesterday, I'll let it slide, but know that Daniel is never allowed up here again. Do I make myself clear?"

"Yes, but nothing happened. Pretend he was a girl sleeping over."

"He's not a girl, so stop with the wise comments."

"Blame me, don't blame him. I begged him to stay." I stormed out in a huff.

Lily followed me out and said, "Calm down. She's just worried about you ...and your dad."

"It's just dumb. We just slept."

"I have to take a shower," Lily said and left. I knew she thought I was overreacting since she always said that whenever I got upset.

"Fine, I'll be in the kitchen."

I made tea and waited for her and wondered if I should walk her to work.

When she came in to the kitchen, I said, "Don't go to work today."

Lily looked nervous. "I have to go. Pierce will meet me in the lobby and take me by car."

"Good. I don't think I can handle a repeat of yesterday," I said, exhaling with relief.

"Me either. My mom is freaking out. She wanted me to take the day off and come home, but I'm working on a project that has to be finished today. It'll keep my mind busy."

I walked Lily to the door and hugged her tightly. "Call me when you're in your building." I was worried. Yesterday, we had security and those goons got to us, so they could do it again.

Mom appeared after Lily left and seemed more peaceful, or was pretending to be.

"I'm running to the hospital. I'll leave you the address for the doctor's in case you have to meet me there. Although, I hope to be back with your dad and we'll go together," she said, as she wrote the address on a piece of paper. Mom looked exhausted.

"Why didn't Dad come home with you?" I wondered. I was so wrapped up in being angry that I forgot to ask where Dad was.

"Before the hospital releases him, he must be examined by the doctor. The doctor hasn't made his rounds yet this morning. I came home to shower and change. I'll call and let you know what's going on as soon as I know."

The minute she left, I called Daniel and he came right over. I swung the door open and his smile warmed me all over. He must have just gotten out of the shower because as he kissed me, his wet hair touched my forehead.

"It was nice having you with me all night," I said happily.

"I was thinking about you all morning," he said, as he kissed me quickly. "What happened with your mom? I took a quick shower so I didn't eavesdrop."

"She was angry, but she calmed down after Lily told her we asked you to stay."

"I'm glad. I really don't want to upset your parents."

"Neither do I," I admitted, even when they annoyed me.

We sat on the couch and Daniel said, "I have to tell you something."

"Is it bad?" I asked.

"Well, I'm not sure, but we have a problem. The Laura Burke we met the night Amber went missing wasn't the real Laura Burke. The real Burkes have been in California all month visiting their daughter who just had a baby."

"What? Who was she?"

"We have no idea. She must have put that tracker in Amber."

"I can't believe this!"

"James is checking all the surveillance footage. Maybe we can get her license plate and track her that way."

"How about that man that grabbed me yesterday?" I asked. "Did you find anything out?"

"Yes, his name is Gilles Barnes. We'll ask him about that woman today and see if he'll tell us who she really is. We have to find her and find out how she got that tracker from the future."

"What else did he tell you?"

"Basically, it's what the agency suspected. This involves a terrorist group called Chakir. Since they need to fund this attack, this is all about money and access to it. The terrorists are looking for the banking information for close to ten billion dollars. Only three people were given the information to access the account. One of the three men, Omar, a chemical engineer, works in the technology division at a French firm and your dad is their attorney on a lawsuit. Omar put the banking information in some files involving the lawsuit and for some bizarre reason he put the data in three separate envelopes. Omar's new secretary sent the files to your dad's New York office by mistake." Probably the same one that called us early that morning, I thought.

"When Omar asked for the file, she told him that she sent it to New York. When Emir, the leader of the group, called for the information to transfer the funds, Omar had to tell him what happened. Since Omar was no longer useful, Emir had him killed after first torturing him to make sure he wasn't lying and trying to steal the funds for himself."

Even though I was still shocked by all the brutality, a part of me was getting numb. "Why didn't Emir just go to the other two men, get the information and access the account?"

"When they heard that Omar was killed, Gilbert and Farid thought they were next and went into hiding. Emir got two teams together to handle the problem. One group is searching for Gilbert and Farid, while Gilles and his group tracked down the envelopes in

New York. Gilles paid someone at the law firm to get the files out."

"Who?"

"A file clerk named Todd Madison."

"I can't believe it. He's so nice," I said shocked. I would have never suspected him. He seemed so nerdy, but maybe they threatened him. "How did he do it?"

"Todd labeled all the files that your dad worked on by number and sent them one by one to your apartment by messenger whether your dad asked for them or not. Gilles would be told and he'd meet the messenger to search through the package. If your dad hadn't requested the file, the messenger brought the file back to Todd. When Todd told Gilles that there were no more files, they knew something was wrong since they only found one envelope. Todd overheard Sonia ask you to take files home. He realized that there were files in your dad's office that he didn't have access to and he alerted Gilles. That was the day in the park that I stopped them. Eventually, you gave them that envelope. There's still one piece missing of the password in the third envelope to access the bank account."

"How did the information get into more than one file?"

"I don't know. Maybe somebody in New York was working or looking through files and didn't know where the envelopes belonged and just stuck them wherever. Even if they had looked inside the envelopes, it wouldn't have made any sense.

"Did catching Gilles change anything?"

"One of the agents went into the future and the attack still happens. Even if they don't find the envelope, they eventually find one of those two men, get the money and proceed with the attack. If they find that last envelope, it happens sooner. Without the envelope, the attack is put off by six months. At least, we know what we have to do, but we need the information to access that ten billion dollars."

"Where did all the money come from?"

"Gilbert worked for a French bank and stole the money in a trading ponzi scheme. He put the funds in a Swiss account, but Emir wanted the money moved to Singapore and called Gilbert, who was on a flight to China and was unreachable. That's when Emir called Omar to transfer the funds and… the rest of the story you know."

"Don't most people put their money in Swiss banks? Why did they move it?"

"With new laws to counter money laundering, they got worried. Switzerland has been participating in joint task forces that target the financing of Al-Qaeda terrorist cells. Switzerland has helped find and freeze these assets. That's why the group decided to move the funds to Andorra. It's getting harder to hide ill-gotten money because a lot of countries are working together now."

"Singapore doesn't care?"

"It's business for them. Singapore is the most enticing for crooks now and offers depositors privacy and protection. In order to promote itself, Singapore now imposes steep fines and long jail sentences for personnel who leak information to international authorities."

"But why wouldn't Emir know the banking information? It doesn't make any sense," I said.

"I have no idea. Perhaps it was a good faith gesture to show the men he trusted them or he didn't put his name on the account, so that the stolen money wouldn't trace back to him."

"What happens now?" I asked.

"James sent agents to look for those two men."

"It was Gilbert and who was the other man?"

"Farid. He's a nuclear physicist and works for a French nuclear company. Gilles said that Emir is desperate to find him not only for the banking data, but for his expertise to help in the nuclear attack."

My cell rang and it was Mom. "Sweetie, I don't have time to come back to get you. I'll meet you at the doctor's office."

"Okay, I'll leave now." I went in the kitchen and got the address.

"I'll have a car take us over," Daniel said as I came back and texted on his cell.

"How about you just drop me off at the building? I'm not sure how Mom will be."

"I'll deal with it. I'm not leaving you alone until this is solved."

"Okay, it's your funeral," I said jokingly, but was glad he was coming.

Sure enough, as we entered the office, Mom looked livid when she saw Daniel. Rising from her chair, she beckoned me to follow her into the hallway.

"I really don't understand what's going on. Why are you two always together?" she whispered to me. I didn't answer her because a group of people got off the elevator and were standing staring at a directory. I walked back into the waiting room and sat down next to Daniel.

Mom walked over and said, "Daniel, I don't want to find you in

Paige's bed again. Do you understand me?" Thank goodness no one was sitting nearby to hear her.

"Yes, I do. I'm sorry. I should've had Paige call you." Why was he being nice to her?

"Mom, please stop being so rude," I snapped.

"Watch your tone, Paige," she said threateningly.

"You're not being fair. I already told you it wasn't Daniel's fault and the reason we're together is that he's my boyfriend."

Daniel looked embarrassed and tried to hush me. "Paige, stop."

Mom looked furious, but instead of yelling at me, she walked away and sat far way from us.

"I suggest you stop fighting with her unless you want to get grounded," Daniel advised.

"I know, but I was so angry that I couldn't help myself."

We waited almost thirty minutes before my name was called.

Daniel squeezed my hand and said, "I'll be right here when you come out." Hopefully, no one on the doctor's staff wanted to kill me except for my mother.

As Mom and I entered, she said under her breath, "We'll talk about your behavior later."

I knew I should apologize. "I'm sorry about before Mom." She didn't say anything.

After examining my arm, Dr. Weston said he wanted to see me in three weeks.

"We're leaving for Europe this Saturday. I'll see you when I get back," I said.

After we walked out, Mom said, "We can't go. Dad can't fly

because of his concussion."

"Poor Dad, but I just can't believe this. My trip to London has now been canceled three times. Nana's leg, my arm and now Dad's concussion."

"I know. It's been a crazy summer," Mom agreed.

Daniel was reading a newspaper and when he saw my sad face, asked, "Are you okay?

"I'm fine, but we're not going to London. Dad can't fly because of his concussion."

"We'll go another time. There's no other option," Mom answered. "I have to get back to the hospital to get your father. Please walk Amber when you get home."

After we walked Amber, we sat in the living room to wait for Dad. Almost an hour later when they hadn't shown up, I called Mom, but her cell was off. Mom finally called and said that Dad was exhibiting memory loss and they were keeping him another day.

I hung up and turned to Daniel. He heard what was going on. "What if he has brain damage?"

"He's probably okay. They just want to be safe." Daniel held me while we sat on the couch.

"Can you check Dad's condition in the future? If he's going to be okay?"

"I'll see if I can, but James might not allow it."

As if on cue, my house phone started ringing. "I can't take it anymore."

"Just answer it."

"No…okay." I relented. I had no choice, but it felt good to

refuse, if only for a moment.

"Hello?" I answered nervously.

"We need that envelope," a gruff man's voice barked.

"I'm looking for it, but I can't find it."

"You have till Friday. After that there will be problems for you and your family." Tears streamed down my face as I dropped the phone.

"How do they know I'm home alone? If they're outside, don't you see them?"

"We have no idea where they are? We think they might be in one of the apartments across the street?"

"I can't handle this anymore," I said and started to cry.

"It'll be okay, calm down."

"You don't know that, things keep changing and no one's safe." Keys were jingling in the lock and Mom entered to find me hysterical.

"What's going on?" she asked and looked at Daniel accusingly.

"I'm worried about Dad," I said honestly.

"The doctor said it'll take time, but he'll be fine," she said and started to head upstairs.

"Thank goodness. Are you going back to the hospital?" I asked.

"In a little while. Martin is with him now. Do you want to come back with me?"

"We'll walk over later." I realized quickly that was the wrong answer.

Mom stopped on the stairs and glowered down at me. "You can go see your father alone."

"Yes Paige, it's not necessary that I go," added Daniel.

"Please come and wait for me outside," I said. Little did she know, he'd be there whether he was asked or not.

"Can I speak to you upstairs, please?" she asked curtly.

Daniel stood up and said, "I need to go. Call me later."

I walked him to the door and kissed him goodbye. I turned to find Mom watching me with a worried expression. Now that Daniel was gone, she came back downstairs.

"This is getting ridiculous. That boy is always around. Don't get me wrong, I like him, but this is all too much. You two are attached at the hip. Why are you rushing into such a committed relationship? You're too young."

"No, I'm not." What was the point of fighting? "I'm not talking about this anymore."

"Dad and I think you should go to London on Saturday. You need a break from Daniel."

I was taken aback. "Are you kidding me? You want to separate us?"

"Of course not, but maybe you'll get some perspective on this relationship."

"You're not being fair."

"Your priorities have changed and I'm worried about your last year in high school."

"Why? It's the summertime. School hasn't even started. My GPA was a 3.9 last year."

"Let's hope you keep it that way. Your education comes first."

"Ay ay Mom," I said and saluted her. This was ridiculous.

"One other thing, Paige. If you ever talk to me the way you did at the doctor's office, you'll be grounded. Understand?"

"Yes," I said and stormed off.

Upstairs, I lay on my bed. She came up and asked if I wanted anything to eat and I said no.

"I'm going back to the hospital. See you later."

Five minutes passed and Daniel was at my door.

"I'm sure you heard."

"I did, and if you were a mom, you'd feel exactly the same way."

Not interested in talking about my temper tantrums and overreactions that Daniel was alluding to, I kissed him instead.

Daniel took my hand and led me upstairs. "Let's focus and try searching your Dad's office, the den and the master bedroom again. It has to be here," he said.

Almost two hours passed and we found nothing. I had to get out of here.

"I want to go see my dad," I said, resigned to the fact that my life would be in turmoil until this was resolved one way or another.

In the agency car, I stared at Daniel.

Daniel noticed and asked, "What's the matter?"

"Nothing, I was just thinking about my life with you and my life without you." I pressed against him and he embraced me tightly. When we reached the hospital, Daniel walked me to the room and I peeked through the window to see Mom sitting on the bed. Dad was in a semi-private room and an older man was in the other bed.

"I'll wait out here," Daniel said and kissed me.

Entering the room, Dad smiled when he noticed me. "Buttercup,

I'm glad you're here."

"How are you feeling?" I asked and kissed him on the cheek. There was a weird smell permeating the air.

"Fine. I wish they'd let me go home," he moaned.

"What kind of memory loss did you have?" I asked.

"Your father couldn't remember what he ate for breakfast today. As a precaution, they want to keep him one more night. The doctor said that sometimes happens, but usually goes away in a few days," Mom explained and tried to sound upbeat.

"I'll be back to normal in no time. Don't worry. Our family is having quite a summer, huh?" Dad said, pointing at my arm and his head. "And there's Nana. Maybe it's the universe telling us all to slow down and stop rushing around."

"Maybe," I agreed, knowing full well that wasn't it at all. Nana's fall was an accident, but not Dad's or mine.

"Since I'm not cleared to travel, you should go and stay with your Aunt Lucy and visit your grandparents."

"Mom already told me. It's only two weeks. Can I please stay at Nana's?" I begged.

Mom shrugged her shoulders and he relented. "Okay, she'll be thrilled to have you. Lucy says she's doing great and she'll love your company. Let me ask her first."

"Aren't you going to miss Daniel?" Mom asked suspiciously.

"You know, Mom, we can be apart for two weeks," I answered. She was right, not seeing him for fourteen days would have been unbearable.

Dad looked at me disapprovingly and said sharply, "Don't talk to your mother in that tone."

I apologized when I saw how upset he was. This wasn't the time to fight about Daniel. Lying in the hospital bed, Dad, a tall man, looked so small and pale.

"Are you staying here tonight or coming home?" I asked Mom.

"I'm not sure, but Daniel is not to sleep in your bed tonight, understand?" she snapped, forgetting about Dad and looked at his reaction.

Dad stared at me with such shock and annoyance. "Please, explain."

"Nothing happened. We were afraid to be alone, so we asked Daniel to stay over."

"What were you afraid of? The incident was a prank and we have doormen," he said.

"Two men grabbed us and then tried dragging us into a van. Lily got kidnapped than returned," I said succinctly. "We were scared."

Not the best time to make an entrance, Daniel walked in and the room fell silent.

"Good evening, Mr. Devon. How are you feeling?" Daniel asked politely.

Dad glared at him. "Getting better," he answered coldly. "I need to speak to your uncle. Can you give me his number or ask him to call me?"

"Sure, I'll call him now." Reaching for his cell, he asked, "Is everything okay?"

"My brother-in-law called the police station and was told that there was no report made."

"That's strange! When we left, the police were there. Right, Paige?"

I tried not to lie. "I don't know. I was flipping out about Dad and Lily."

"Let me call him." James didn't answer, so Dad gave Daniel his cell number to leave on the message. Daniel got a call and went out in the hall to answer it.

I left Dad's room and found him waiting for me. "How'd it go? They seemed okay."

"No, they were pretending. They're sending me to London to get me away from you."

"Great, we can fly over together now."

"Great?" I asked bewildered.

"They'll come around when they realize we're meant to be together. Don't worry," he said as he kissed my scowling face. "Is your mom coming home tonight?"

"She said she wasn't sure, but you're not allowed to sleep in my bed." Then, an idea popped into my head. "She didn't say anything about the couch in the living room."

Daniel shook his head. "Absolutely not. Let's get food. I'm starving."

We walked over to a little Italian place on Columbus Avenue. We ordered a pizza and shared a salad. Daniel wanted to search for the envelope in the morning and wanted to relax tonight.

In the apartment, we made ourselves comfortable by putting all the couch pillows on the floor. Leaning on a pillow, looking gorgeous, Daniel kissed me. It really wasn't a great idea being alone with him because I could barely control myself.

"Okay, time out." Daniel stood up. "Paige, we need to slow down."

"Why?" I wasn't ready to do anything more, but was curious to what he meant.

"It really isn't the right time."

"What time then?"

"A time when you're not worried about being killed, you don't have a broken arm, a time when it's all about us and not a catastrophe."

"I just wanted to know how you felt. Some of my friends have told me they've been pressured by their boyfriends and…"

"And you wanted to know where I stood." I nodded. "There's no rush. I have very traditional views."

"I haven't been with anyone," I said, feeling very uncomfortable.

"Yes, I know."

We sat quietly and held each other staring at the TV. I envisioned girls surrounding Daniel and wondered how many he was with. The movie droned on in the background. Every once in a while, he stroked my arm, kissed my head and asked, "Are you okay?" Sick to my stomach, I nodded and hid my face in his chest. There was nothing I could do about Daniel's past, but I could be a part of his present and his future.

My cell rang and it was Lily. I put her on speaker.

"Hi, Lily. I'm with Daniel. You're on speaker."

"How's your dad?"

"He's still at the hospital."

"Why?" she asked.

"He couldn't remember what he had for breakfast, so they want to keep an eye on him."

"I'm sorry. I want to come over tomorrow, but I'm scared to walk."

"Lily, I'll have you picked up. Don't worry," said Daniel.

"Thanks. Can I invite Chad over?"

"Sure, I'll see you tomorrow."

After we hung up, my phone rang again almost immediately. "Hi, Mom. Is Dad okay?"

"He's fine. I wanted to let you know that I'll be home soon and sleeping there tonight."

"Okay. Bye." I looked at Daniel and rolled my eyes.

"What did she say?" asked Daniel.

"She's coming home to chaperone us."

"That's wise of her," he joked and started kissing me. I couldn't think straight.

When we heard the door open and Mom walked in, looking ragged.

"Hi you two. What are you..." She stopped speaking as she surveyed the messy living room and shook her head.

"Sorry Mom, I'll clean it up."

"Daniel, your uncle called and said he called the police station and was told the same thing. There was no report filed about the incident." She was actually being pleasant to Daniel and it was probably because I was leaving for London.

"Now what?" I asked.

"James said he'd look into it through NSA channels, but he thinks that the boys might have powerful connections and it was buried. I will be so disgusted, if that's true." Mom left the room.

Daniel stared at the wall, deep in thought, and finally said, "Paige, EMIT has one week left before James orders us to start back at the beginning of the year to give us more time."

"But if you can keep going back in time, how can this attack happen? Don't you keep trying until it's stopped?" I asked.

"No we can't keep going back. The scientists can't figure it out, but at a certain point time travel to certain years gets blocked. We can still enter those years but none of the changes we make stick. We try not to go back until we have no other options. The scientists thought that the definitive number of entries per year for changes was one hundred, but one year we got blocked at sixty entries and we don't want a reoccurrence of what happened that year."

"What year?"

"The year of 9/11." All the chaos of that day began bombarding my brain. Dad was in London on business and Mom had picked me up early at school. We went and stayed at Aunt Cecile's house when we were able to leave the city.

"How many times has EMIT entered this year?"

"Almost fifty."

"That's why you kept saying that James didn't want to waste a time travel trip for my arm and dad's concussion. James doesn't want this year to get blocked. What happens if you can't stop this or the year gets blocked?" I asked, understanding that the event would happen.

Daniel looked uncomfortable. "We'll worry about that when we have to."

When we heard Mom coming downstairs, Daniel kissed me and said, "I better get going."

After he left, Mom said, "I'm taking Amber for a walk. Want to come?"

"I'm really tired. I'm going to bed. I'll clean this room in the morning, okay?"

She said fine and gave me a kiss goodnight.

Seeing my journal on the nightstand, I quickly jotted down the crazy events.

Daniel called my cell. "You okay?"

"Yeah, but I wish you were here."

"Me too. Now go to sleep and please have pleasant dreams tonight."

18. ENVELOPE

"The only reason for time is so that everything doesn't happen at once." Einstein

The next morning, Daniel called my cell and woke me. "Morning, beautiful. Your mom just left to go to the hospital and I need to see your face."

Laughing, I said, "Give me fifteen minutes, I need a shower."

"Okay, I'll run and get breakfast. What would you like?"

"I would love a blueberry muffin and you, of course."

"Okay, you'll have both shortly."

Jumping into the shower, I daydreamed about him. Remembering our last talk, I started thinking about this attack, the what-ifs, Daniel leaving and me not remembering him. I descended into a panic attack. By the time he arrived, I was in quite a state.

"It'll be okay. No matter what, we'll figure it out." Daniel's confidence calmed me.

"Anything new on those two guys you're looking for?" I asked.

"Gilbert and Farid, right?"

"Yes. Unfortunately, we're down to one. Gilbert, the banker, committed suicide." That meant only Farid was left and that made me shudder.

"Why didn't your agents change that outcome?" I asked, perplexed since they were watching him.

"We found out where he was and the agents saw him enter a building. They decided to wait before entering and arresting him."

"But why?"

"For safety reasons, they wanted to first find out what was in the building such as terrorists, explosives. When they were confident it was safe, they went in and found him dead. They never considered suicide. It was past thirty minutes, therefore, it was too late to change anything. Our agents are going into the past to search for Farid because we have not been able to find him in the present."

"I can't believe this."

"Let's eat breakfast then start our hunt again," Daniel said, trying to distract me.

As we ate, something occurred to me. "Daniel, don't you know if I find the envelope or not? When you go into the future?" I asked.

"No, we don't know. That's the frustrating part. Everything keeps changing."

"But if I've never found it, maybe I don't have it?"

"I don't know, but I won't let anything happen to you."

When we finished breakfast, I left Daniel in the kitchen and I went to clean up the living room. I didn't want Mom to come home and have a fit. The throw pillows were placed back on the couch and the magazines that were scattered on the floor were neatly stacked back on the cocktail table. Peeking from under one chair was one of my sandals. I wore them last on the day Lily got abducted. Where was the other one? On my knees, I looked under the couch. Holding the fringe to one side, I saw my sandal, and there was something else! Next to the shoe, there was an envelope. Reaching blindly under the fringe, it was hard to reach with one arm and I fell over. Lying on my back, I grabbed for the envelope.

I was afraid that my eyes were playing tricks on me and hoped that it was the envelope we'd been looking for. How did it get under the couch? Vaguely, I recalled coming in one day with a package for Dad and throwing it on the couch. All the contents had spilled out. The envelope must have fallen out of the redweld folder and fallen under the couch.

"Daniel, I think I found it!" I screamed, as he came in from the kitchen with a cup of coffee.

"Found what?" It took him a second to realize what I meant. "Are you kidding?" He put his cup down.

"No, it's been under the couch this whole time!" I screamed.

"Are you sure?" he asked and took the envelope from my shaky hand. He ripped it open and the paper had words on it that I didn't understand, Sabah Al Khair along with strange symbols. Daniel smiled. "I knew you had it."

"What does it mean?"

"It means good morning, how appropriate, since it sure is."

"What about the symbols?"

"I'm not sure. Let me call James. He'll have someone look at it

---

and figure it out."

He grabbed his cell. "James, Paige found it. Do you want to come up and look at it?"

"I can't believe it! I'm so happy," I shrieked with joy.

The front door opened and my parents were standing there. "Hi, you two. What are you happy about?" Mom asked me.

Daniel and I looked at each other in unison and nothing was coming to me.

I ran over to Dad and hugged him. Maybe that would give me time to think. "I'm so glad you're home."

"What were you so excited about?" asked Mom, not letting me off the hook.

"Daniel got a job in London. He's leaving this weekend, too. Isn't that great?" I hadn't planned on telling them, but there was nothing else I could think of.

"How exciting is that!" said Dad, but it sounded very sarcastic.

I looked at Daniel and he seemed unfazed by the disapproving glares from my parents. They would have been thrilled if he got a job in London, just not while I was there for two weeks without them. At the same time, maybe they'd figure he'd be busy and I'd be alone, at least during the day. Possibly, the added bonus that Daniel would stay in London while I returned to New York would please them.

"Where are you working?" Dad asked.

"I'll be interning at an engineering firm." Daniel didn't skip a beat.

There was a knock on the door. Mom turned around in the foyer and answered. James Haydin was standing there and she invited him in. We introduced Dad to James. Mom raised her eyebrows at me as if she was asking me a silent question.

"Oh, James called and told Daniel about the job. He was nearby, so I invited him over and told Carl to let him up when he got here." It was getting so easy to lie. James had to know my parents were home, but he had to get that envelope.

"We'll get going. Come on Daniel, I'll tell you all about the job."

Thank goodness, James went along with the story since I'm sure Daniel was using his jammer and he had no idea what we were talking about. I just prayed Mom and Dad didn't ask James any questions.

"Sure. Paige, want to come?" Daniel asked. I looked pleadingly at Mom, then Dad.

"Go ahead. I'll be very boring," Dad said.

"Daniel, I need to grab my bag from upstairs. I'll meet you in the lobby."

When I came back down, they were sitting in the living room waiting for me. "Did you know Daniel was job hunting in London?" Mom asked accusingly.

"No, I didn't."

"Where is he living?" she asked.

"I don't know. He just found out about the job fifteen minutes ago," I sighed.

"Please let us know when you find out," she demanded.

Dad just listened and watched from the couch, not sure what to make of the news.

"Okay, I'll, see you later. Bye." I wanted to get out of there as quickly as possible.

Daniel was alone in the lobby texting. "Hey, I thought we weren't going to tell them."

"I'm sorry. I was so excited that I couldn't help it."

Daniel tried reasoning with me. "Now that they know I'll be in London, they can change their mind about letting you go."

"I don't think they will. They already told my grandmother I was coming," I said, praying I was right.

"We'll find out soon enough. At least, they'll warn your grandparents about me as opposed to me just appearing one day. Since I'm supposed to be working, you'll have to come to me every day," he said, raising his eyebrows jokingly.

"See, there was a method to my madness even if I didn't think of it until now. You're right about my grandparents knowing. If I had to lie to my grandparents or my parents every time I talked to them, it would kill the fun for me," I confessed. "By the way does James own the house in London with you?" I couldn't imagine Daniel inherited all the real estate.

"James inherited my grandparents' house in London and my parents house in DC," Daniel said as we exited the building and jumped into the waiting car.

Could I dare to believe my life was going to be normal again? No more bugging or spying? I couldn't wait to have my life be private again. When we entered the apartment, I heard voices in the kitchen and I saw from Daniel's face that he wasn't pleased. At the kitchen table, James was sitting and talking with a girl. She had shoulder length, brown wavy hair, dark eyes, light skin and was very pretty. As Daniel walked to the table, she glanced up and excitedly jumped up from her chair.

"Daniel, bonjour." She kissed him on both cheeks and Daniel looked stunned. "It's so good to see you," she said.

"You too," answered Daniel and awkwardly reached for my hand.

"Who is this pretty young girl?" she asked. I didn't like the way she said young.

Daniel looked at me and said, "Paige, this is my friend Juliette. Juliette, this is my girlfriend, Paige."

"Hi," I said in a state of shock, smiling like an idiot, knowing exactly who she was.

"Oh, girlfriend! It's nice to meet you. Quelles belles fossettes!" What cute dimples! Her mentioning my dimples annoyed me and I didn't respond, pretending I didn't understand. Daniel squeezed my hand as I grinned awkwardly at this woman.

James stood up. "Daniel, I called Juliette to help with questioning Gilles Barnes. I forgot to tell you with everything that's been going on."

"Juliette works for the NSA?" I asked, not directing the question to anyone. *Was she a traveler too?*

"Yes, I do," she answered. The way she said that annoyed me.

Ignoring her, Daniel said, "Yes, she does."

James interjected, "Juliette, we have to go. Daniel, I'll be back in half an hour. Please wait. I need to talk to you."

"Goodbye Daniel, it was so nice to see you," she said and kissed him on both cheeks again. As she raised her left hand to his shoulder, I saw the three-dot tattoo on her hand. Turning to me, she said, "Au revoir, Paige. It was nice to meet you."

"Bye," was all I could manage to say.

When they walked out of the room, Daniel said, "I'm sorry. I didn't know she was here."

"Is she a traveler?" I asked, but I already knew the answer and wondered if he'd tell me.

Daniel looked torn, but finally said, "Yes. That's how we met."

There was no point in telling him that I knew. We'd talk about that another time. Right now, all I wanted to know about was Juliette. It was one thing hearing of an ex-girlfriend, but it was totally different now that I met her.

"When did you two break up?"

"Two years ago."

"Who broke up with who?"

"I broke up with her," he said.

"How long did you two date?"

Daniel looked uneasy. "I believe we stayed together as long as we did for companionship."

As long as they did, what did that mean? "How long did you date?" I asked again.

"On and off for about five years."

"Five years!" I felt numb.

"You know my job. It was more off than on, but yes." Flabbergasted, I stared at him in disbelief. I heard footsteps and James entered the room.

"Daniel, let's talk about the next step in the library. Paige, make yourself comfortable."

Daniel didn't move. "We need to talk about Juliette." James stopped in the middle of the living room and looked at Daniel with a confused look on his face. How come men are so obtuse? "I wish you had told me she was here."

James sighed and answered, "I've been a little busy. Your love life is the least of my concern. We're trying to stop a disaster here. Please focus on that and know that she is here to do her job. I'm confident she's over you."

That's what I wanted to hear, but I wasn't sure that James was accurate. When she had looked at Daniel, I had sensed something.

He turned to me. "Thank you for your help. We couldn't have done it without you." James looked at his cell and said, "Daniel, I'm sorry, but I have to go take care of something. I'll be right back. It shouldn't take long."

After James left, Daniel asked, "Are you okay?"

"Yeah. It was just weird finding your ex here."

"I know. I planned on telling you about her since I knew there was a possibility that you two might meet, but I thought I had time. I had no idea she was in New York since she's been investigating the staff at the nuclear plants."

Daniel got a call and went into the library.

When he came out, he said, "That was James. One of the agents just got back from the future and the attack was stopped."

"Oh, I'm so happy that means I'm getting my life back."

"Yeah…but I'm still not letting you out of my sight," he said weirdly and that troubled me.

"I don't understand. Why?"

"Because things just aren't adding up," Daniel said as he played with my hair.

"Now you sound paranoid," I teased, hoping Daniel was wrong.

Daniel looked at me and shook his head, saying, "I know."

"Let's be happy that this is over. Has Farid been found?"

Smiling, he said, "I'll tell you later." And he began kissing me. Daniel and I were the only two people alive.

When we heard a door slam, we glanced up to find James walking towards us smiling.

"Daniel, I'm going to DC tonight. Can I see you in the other room?"

I realized that Daniel and I would now be a normal couple. Well, as normal as we could be with a time traveler as a boyfriend. Daniel returned and was in such a good mood.

"I'm off duty and you and I are going on vacation." I jumped in his arms. He was mine completely and entirely now. "But while in London, we'll have some surveillance," he added.

"Why?" I asked annoyed.

"I'm still not so sure about your safety. James agrees, so we're just going to see what happens next. Someone from the agency might be involved."

"But why? There are no more envelopes, the attack has stopped and you have the bad guys."

"I don't want to scare you, but Gilles Barnes has no knowledge of that fake Laura Burke woman or anything about that tracker. We have no idea who implanted Amber. Since that tracker is from the future, I'm concerned." He started kissing me and said, "So, no arguing."

Who could argue with him kissing me? At least we'd be together and I'd pretend that the surveillance team didn't exist.

My cell rang and it was Mom telling me to come home that Lily was there. After everything that happened, I had forgotten about Lily. I wondered why she hadn't texted me herself.

As we walked home, Daniel told me the rest of the saga. Right after I'd found the envelope, EMIT arrested Farid in the South of France. He wasn't cooperating, so they planned on giving him the truth serum. He said that international law forbids the use of the serum, but the one that EMIT uses was from the future and was totally safe and untraceable. The NSA was accessing the bank accounts and freezing the assets. Another team was working with the European authorities to locate everyone responsible for the plot.

When we walked into the kitchen, Lily and Mom were talking.

"Hi. Why didn't you call me you were on your way?" I asked Lily.

"I was talking to Chad the whole way here and I figured you were home."

"So what are your plans for tonight?" Mom asked us.

"I don't know yet. How's Dad? Is he sleeping?" I asked.

"I'm not sure. Would you go up and make sure he's not working?"

"No problem." I looked over at Daniel and Lily and said, "Why don't you guys think of something to do tonight?"

I peeked in and Dad looked like he was sleeping. I turned to leave and he called out, "Paige, don't go. I just had my eyes shut."

"How are you?" I sat in the chair next to the bed.

"Same as before, fine. I'll humor your mom and the doctors, but Monday I'm going back to work."

Mom was going to have quite a battle keeping him home.

"I'm sorry about London."

"It's only for a little while. Maybe we'll go for a long weekend in the fall. We'll check your school schedule and see what days you're off and work around it. We'll go for Thanksgiving."

Looking at him confused, I said, "Ah, Dad, Grammy would get really upset." Thanksgiving was always at Grammy's house on Long Island. It was tradition. How could Dad forget that? Was his concussion messing with his memory? I had to tell Mom.

He furrowed his brow and looked bewildered, but then there was a flicker in his eyes. "You're right. What was I thinking?" he laughed, shaking his head. "I meant for Christmas." Nothing else that he said troubled me, yet I was still scared.

Downstairs, Lily was texting and Daniel was reading the newspaper. I couldn't believe all the things that had taken place recently. As I stood there watching Daniel, he glanced up and smiled. Everything I had been through was worth him.

I found Mom in the kitchen and told her about Thanksgiving. She said she'd watch him.

Back in the living room, I told Lily that we found the other envelope and she was so relieved. When I told her that Daniel and I were going to London, she said she was jealous.

Daniel suggested an Italian restaurant and Chad met us there. Afterwards, we went to a movie. Out and about like a normal couple and not having to worry that goons were going to attack or kill me was very liberating.

"Lily, stay over tomorrow night, too. Your parents were supposed to pick up Amber on Saturday, now they don't have to. They could swing by and get you instead on the way to Grammy's."

"They did want to see Uncle Oliver. I'll ask my mom," Lily said.

19. LONDON

"Truth is what stands the test of experience." Einstein

Lily woke me when she got up. I rolled over to see that it was seven o'clock. Lying in bed staring at the ceiling, I decided to get my packing started, so that Daniel and I'd have more time together. Thoughts of his beautiful face kept me very focused. When Lily came out and saw me packing, she was surprised and kidded, "I know you want to see Daniel, but I'd still be sleeping."

"If you could see Chad, you'd be up early too," I said, knowingly.

Lily left and I called Daniel.

"You got up early this morning. For me I hope?" Daniel asked.

"Always for you."

"I'm very glad. Let's pick up breakfast and go to my place. How about in thirty minutes?"

"Okay."

I walked by my parents' room and the door was shut so I went downstairs. Mom was in the kitchen reading the paper.

"I was afraid to go in your room. Is Dad still sleeping?" I asked. Mom nodded. "I'll see him later. I'm meeting Daniel for breakfast."

"Okay, have fun." I was waiting to hear a lecture, but there wasn't one.

The elevator door opened and there he was standing against the wall in the lobby waiting for me.

"Hey," he grinned and I walked into his arms.

People were entering the lobby, so we separated, but held on to each other tightly. On the way up Columbus Avenue, we stopped at a bakery and picked up some pastries, muffins, fruit and coffee.

After breakfast, I wandered around the apartment and snooped, knowing that Daniel was the real owner of the apartment.

In the library, I found photo albums on a bookshelf. I handed one to Daniel and asked him to tell me about the photos.

"You'll be so bored. They're just pictures of me when I was young."

"I want to see them. You saw pictures of me. Wait, you were there when I was young," I huffed. Daniel grabbed the album with one hand and my hand with the other. Pulling me into the living room, he motioned for me to sit on the couch.

Page by page, Daniel lovingly told me about each photo and explained what was happening in each. Whenever, the photos were of his parents, his voice sounded wistful. At the end of the album, I decided one was enough because there was plenty of time to see the rest.

Daniel got up and got his guitar. "Don't I owe you?" he joked, facing me.

"Yes, you do."

"I wrote this song for you," he said.

"Really!" I was so surprised. No one had ever written anything for me.

"It's called Mental Crossroads. I hope you like it, but if you don't just lie," he kidded.

"He's standing at a mental crossroad,
Drowning in his frantic thoughts.
Should he tell her the very secret
That might rip them apart?

He spent his whole life trying to look past it,
But now it stares him in the face.
It could lead to his life being shattered
Just as it was falling back into place.

Who knows where decisions will lead us.
I think life is just a tapestry
Of little coincidences, hard decisions.
Who knows where fate will blow us,
So let's just cross our fingers and open our minds.
Maybe that's how we'll find our way.

She spends all day thinking,
Lying on her bed with a distant stare.
She always thought that she loved him,
But for this secret she was unprepared.

Part of her wants to run away from the relationship,
But part of her wants to run straight into his arms
To hear him tell her it'll be okay now,
To reassure her they can keep moving on.

Who knows where decisions will lead us.

———

I think life is just a tapestry
Of little coincidences, hard decisions.
Who knows where fate will blow us,
So let's just cross our fingers and open our minds.
Maybe that's how we'll find our way.

And by the way if you're wondering about them.
Well they turned out okay.
I guess the world has a way of working everything out
The way it was meant to be.

Who knows where decisions will lead us.
I think life is just a tapestry
Of little coincidences, hard decisions.
Who knows where fate will blow us,
So let's just cross our fingers and open our minds.
Maybe that's how we'll find our way."

His singing voice was much lower than when he spoke. When he finished, I started clapping and said, "I loved it. What a great song!"

"You inspired me."

"Really? That's the same reason, I wrote some too."

"You did? When do I get to hear yours?"

"Probably never. Mine are sappy. I'm so glad I never sang them."

"I've heard you sing and you have a great voice."

"It's so weird the stuff you know about me," I said shaking my head and I looked down the long hallway at all the closed bedroom doors. "Can I see your bedroom?"

"Sure, come on," he said and helped me up.

After I walked in, I almost fell over. On one wall there was a huge framed corkboard and there were at least fifty pictures of me from different years. I swung around and looked at him as he watched, smiling.

"So I have a picture wall, too. Do you like it?" Daniel asked.

"How did you get these?"

"Over the years, we needed to take pictures of your family to show the new agents. Whenever you aged they took new ones and James put the discarded ones in your file. After we met, I found them and made a collage for my wall. It's my homage to you," he joked as he walked over and started kissing me. No wonder James didn't like me, it all made sense now.

Regaining my composure, I looked around his room and saw there were also pictures of his family and grandparents. His room was quite sparse and it was apparent that he didn't spend too much time there. The focal point in the room was a beautiful wooden four-poster bed.

"Now that's a very royal bed," I joked.

"It was my parents, so I kept it."

"It's beautiful," I said. As I walked further inside, I noticed an open door leading to another room. Peeking in, I saw that it was an office. On one wall was a framed poster that read, "Keep Calm and Carry on" with a crown overhead. "What's this?"

"It was a poster that my dad had in his office. In 1939, the British government put these posters up to calm Londoners anxious about the war with Germany."

Everywhere I looked, it was spotless and it was diametrically opposite to what I envisioned. At the same time, Daniel wasn't a typical nineteen year-old guy. "This apartment is so clean!"

"I have a housekeeper who comes in weekly."

"But if you're not here for months or even years, why use a housekeeper?

"It still gets dusty and I want it to be clean when I do come."

"How do you pay for it?"

"EMIT has a department where a staff takes care of all the travelers monthly bills."

"They think of everything."

"They have to."

"What about laundry?"

"I have a washer and dryer down the hall and there are laundromats and drycleaners that pick up and deliver."

"But if you're not here?" I asked.

"The doorman holds it and when the housekeeper comes she puts it in the apartment."

When I sat on his bed, I really felt uneasy.

Daniel asked, "You okay?"

"Yeah, suddenly I got very nervous," I admitted.

"Paige, you wanted to see my bedroom, I didn't suggest it." He was right.

He leaned over to kiss me and we fell backwards on the bed. Delicate kisses brushed my face, my neck, and my shoulders, ending at my collarbone. He was driving me insane. Things were escalating when Daniel stopped, looked at me and stroked my face.

I noticed his tattoo and had to ask, "What is this for?"

Daniel was reticent to answer me, but finally said, "It's the markings of where my hand goes on the machine."

"I don't understand."

"Under each dot, there is a tiny chip. The three chips and my fingerprints authorize the use of the time machines."

"Wow." Every day I learned something new.

"Let's get out of here. It's almost one and I'm starving."

When we exited the Dakota, I almost collided right into Eden. Paul and Billy were with her.

"Paige, how are you? How's your arm?" asked Eden in a happy mood. Eden had called after my accident, but I never called her back.

Billy said nothing and when he glanced at Daniel, he looked scared.

"It's fine. This is my boyfriend, Daniel. Daniel this is Eden, Billy's sister, and Paul, Eden's boyfriend. And you know Billy," I said in such a sarcastic tone that Eden was surprised.

"Hello Eden, Paul," Daniel said, ignoring Billy. Eden glanced from Billy to Daniel to me confused by the apparent animosity.

"Is there something going on here?" she asked.

"I was going to call you, but I got hit by a car and honestly, I forgot, but I need to tell you something about Billy."

Billy was getting agitated and flustered. "Nothing happened. I don't know why you're bringing it up," he snapped.

As I talked, my voice cracked with hatred, "How dare you? You almost raped me."

Eden gasped, "What are you talking about?"

"I went to the movies with Billy one night and he attacked me. Daniel saved me."

"Oh my God," said Eden, staring at Billy in disbelief.

"She's lying," Billy countered. "She's making this all up."

Paul stood silent not knowing what to do.

"No she's not, you jerk," Daniel said. "I wanted her to call the police, but she refused."

"Eden, the only reason I didn't call was because we're friends. You really should tell your parents. He needs help. I can't be the first girl he's tried taking advantage of and one of these days he's going to hurt someone, if he hasn't already."

Eden stared at me and didn't know what to say.

Billy looked disgusted and said, "Don't believe her. She's crazy. She came on to me and I turned her down, so now she's out for revenge."

I laughed and wanted to get away from him. "Eden, have fun in California. Email me when you can." As we walked away, I called out, "Get help, Billy, you need it."

Eden and Paul stood there in shock. My legs were shaking from the heated exchange.

"You really should've pressed charges," said Daniel.

"It would've been his word against mine."

"You forget. We have it recorded."

"And what would I've said to the police as to why I recorded my date? What would I have said to my parents about the surveillance in our apartment?"

"We would have figured out something," Daniel answered.

"It's over. I never want to think of Billy again. How come he looked so scared of you?"

"I paid him a visit and had a little chat with him," Daniel

snickered. Whatever he had said or done, Billy deserved it.

"So where are we going?" I asked, as we entered the park.

"To the Boathouse."

"I love that place. Can we go for a boat ride? You'll have to do all the work though."

"No problem, I rowed in school."

"Of course you did, but that was a hundred years ago," I chided.

"You're going overboard," he retorted and hugged me.

Musicians and performers were everywhere. Hand in hand, we talked and teased each other all the way to the restaurant.

Daniel requested a table on the deck and we sat in the wicker chairs overlooking the water. The table next to us was celebrating something. They were clinking champagne glasses.

"You can't legally drink!"

"I do have an ID that says I'm twenty one if I need it for work, but I'm not much of a drinker. One wine or one beer is really my limit."

Looking at the lake and the boats, I saw the gondolier and remembered that at Daniel's school everybody wore a boater hat. "Instead of a row boat, how about a gondola ride? You'll feel right at home with that hat," I joked.

Daniel smirked. "You are so funny."

"I'm kidding. If we do a gondola ride, you can relax too." Daniel agreed and left to make arrangements.

After we ate, we walked around until it was time for our ride. Daniel said he booked an hour.

Gliding effortlessly through the water, cradled in Daniel's arm, I had no worries.

"So do you miss the boater hats?" I teased.

"Sometimes," he answered.

"Do you think Harrow still has the same traditions? You were there so long ago."

"Little has changed. They pride themselves on tradition."

I told him all about my grandparents, my Aunt Lucy and Uncle Blake, my two crazy cousins, David and Liam and all about Emma and her brothers, Lane and Damian. Daniel might like them since they were theoretically the same age. I'd been emailing Emma all about Daniel and she couldn't wait to meet him.

Walking back home, I had a text from Lily inviting us to join her and Chad at some party. There was also a voicemail from Mom to call home.

"Hi what's up?" She wanted me to come home and have dinner with her and Dad.

Having heard my side of the conversation, Daniel knew. "Dinner with your parents, huh?"

"Yeah, but I'll see you right after. I got a text from Lily about a party. What do you think?"

"Whatever you want to do is fine with me."

At my building, Daniel said he had some packing to do and would wait for my call.

Mom was in the kitchen cooking, so I ran up to see Dad. Newspapers were flung all over the bed and he was talking on the phone. He smiled and patted the bed for me to sit and wait.

When his call was done, he asked, "What have you been doing

all day?"

"Daniel took me for lunch at the Boathouse and then we took a gondola ride."

"That sounds like fun," Dad answered. "Is he joining us for dinner?"

"Mom never told me to invite him."

"We wanted to talk to both of you about London," Dad added, confused.

"I'll go downstairs and ask her."

The salad spinner was whizzing and Mom was so deep in thought that she jumped when I entered the room. "Are you okay?" I asked.

"Yes, I'm thinking about a new project at work."

"Dad asked if Daniel was coming for dinner, but you never mentioned it."

"I didn't?" I shook my head. "Yes, please invite him. I thought I had. Between Dad, you leaving for London and my job, I'm all over the place."

I called Daniel and he jokingly said he was nervous to come over.

When I went back to see Dad, I found that he was sleeping. Tiptoeing out, I went into my room to finish packing. I picked a week's worth of things since I could do laundry at Nana's. I needed to leave room in my luggage to go shopping in London. My favorite store there was Topshop. The New York store didn't have a lot of the things that the London store had.

As I grabbed some shampoo from the bathroom, I saw Lily

coming up the stairs.

"Hey, how was your day?" she asked.

I told her what happened with Billy.

"I'm so glad Eden knows. What did Daniel say to him that he was so scared of him?"

"I don't know and I really don't care. I never want to think about Billy again," I answered.

The doorbell rang and I ran downstairs to find Daniel in the foyer with Mom.

"Daniel, I'm sorry about forgetting to invite you before. I've been a little overwhelmed with things," I overheard her saying.

Dad came down looking comfy in sweatpants and a T-shirt. Dad was in a silly mood and was telling us jokes that I thought were quite dumb. My parents finally got to the real reason for this dinner.

"Paige, since you're staying with Nana, you can't stay out really late every night. Nana will be worried sick and wait up until you get home. She has to rest, so please be considerate," Mom rambled on. Glancing at Daniel, I shook my head. We planned on spending our days together so it'll be fine to cut our nights short since I also wanted to spend time with my grandparents.

"How are you getting to the airport tomorrow?"

"I have a car service getting me. Can I pick Paige up since we're on the same flight?"

"That would be great. You'll be able to help with her luggage. It'll be hard with one arm. By the way Daniel, where are you staying?" asked Dad.

"With some friends from school." Lily glanced over, but knew not to say anything. After all the rules were explained and Daniel put on full notice, we were excused. We escaped to the den.

"That was intense," breathed Lily.

"Yes, even while I'm in London, they'll be ruling with an iron fist. Are you okay Daniel?"

"I'm fine. They are just being good parents."

"I know, but it's really stifling sometimes."

We all watched TV and waited to hear from Chad. I left my cell in my bedroom, so I ran upstairs to get it and checked Facebook. It was amazing how unimportant it was now.

Daphne and Grace had sent a few messages and from the wording, they were annoyed. They texted that a group of seniors going off to college were throwing a 'Hello to College Bash' at a local YMCA and asked if I wanted to go with them. This must be the party that Lily was talking about. I called Daphne and she was happy to hear from me.

"I thought you ditched me," she confessed.

"I'm sorry, it's been such a crazy summer. My grandmother, my arm and now my dad, I'm sorry. I'll make it up to you. I promise."

"You left out one other thing… Daniel."

"Yes, and Daniel."

We talked for almost twenty minutes. "Come and bring Daniel and Lily. You'll know a lot of people there. I saw Billy last night and he said that he and Carla were going. Did I tell you that they were dating?" Billy and Carla what a great pair! Since I had no interest in seeing Billy, I wouldn't be going.

I filled Daphne in on all the details of what happened with Billy.

"That's crazy." Daphne was appalled.

"Please be careful around him."

Promising to call as soon as I was back from London, I ran downstairs.

"Did you get lost?" asked Lily.

Daniel looked up from a magazine.

"No. I had to call Daphne and after talking to her, I don't want to go to that party. She said Billy was going and that he's dating Carla. Do you believe it?"

"Wow. A match made in heaven." Lily shook her head.

"Did you ever tell Chad what Billy did to me?"

"No. I wasn't sure if you wanted me to," Lily answered.

"Please tell him. I don't like Carla, but nobody deserves that. Maybe he's different with her."

"She probably didn't say no, so there wasn't a problem," Lily guessed.

"Let's stop talking about Billy. I'm so sick of him."

When the doorman called, we went down to the lobby to meet Chad. It was funny how Reed's name was never brought up.

"Lily text me and tell me what's going on."

"Okay. If we get tired of the party, maybe we'll meet up with you," said Lily.

"Sounds good. Have fun," answered Daniel as Lily and Chad took off.

"Can we take a walk and then go to your place?" I asked.

Daniel's eyebrows rose and he said jokingly, "I might not let you leave."

"Oh yeah! Maybe I don't want to leave."

We wandered around talking and ended up at Lincoln Center.

I saw some military people walk by. "I can't believe you're in this crazy program, but eighteen year-olds enlist and go to war, so what's the difference."

"It wasn't that easy to convince them. I first had to meet some stipulations."

"Like what?"

"I had to go to college first."

"Are you kidding? You've already been to college?" Daniel nodded. "Where?"

"I went to Yale. I'm sorry, but I really forgot to tell you."

"But how were you able to do that?"

"Let's get some dessert and talk in my apartment. It's not a good idea to talk out here." Daniel dragged me into an ice cream parlor.

The whole way back to the Dakota, I just stared at him and wondered how much more was there that I didn't know.

As Daniel scooped the ice cream into bowls, he told me all about it. "The agency had me go to the year 1970 to start school. When I finished, it was 1974.

"How was that possible?"

"It was actually very easy. I went in for every four-month semester, left between each semester to go to a different year. I did that for four years and got my degree. After that, I was assigned a partner to learn everything about time travel."

Just as I was going to ask a question my cell rang and it was Lily. The background noise was so loud that I could barely hear her. What

I could make out was that the party was out of control and they wanted to meet us.

"Lily we're at the Dakota. Do you want to come over and watch a movie with us?"

"Now you'll be forced to behave," Daniel said when I hung up.

"Really, what about you?"

"I always behave."

"Sure you do," I teased and we started kissing.

They must have been really close because it seemed the bell rang a few minutes later.

When they walked in, they were absolutely shocked by the apartment.

In the kitchen, Lily asked, "Did you hear me when I said the party was raided?"

"No, what happened?"

"It was a good thing you didn't come. Billy came to the party drunk."

"I can't believe it."

"It gets worse. He got into a fight with somebody over a girl."

"It was Nick Logan. I spoke to Nick afterwards and he said that Billy approached Josie, his girlfriend, started flirting with her and when she told him she wasn't interested, he grabbed her breasts," said Chad. So Nick and Josie are dating! Too bad, I was hoping Reed would date her.

"Did Lily tell you what happened to me?" I asked Chad.

"Yeah, I couldn't believe it," said Chad. "I heard that Carla broke up with him right before the party, so that might have set him off tonight."

I turned and looked at Daniel. "I wonder if our talk had anything to do with this or that I told Daphne."

Daphne or Paul might have told someone and it could've spread like wildfire this afternoon on Facebook and Twitter. Carla wouldn't care that he tried to force me, she'd only be angry that he was with me.

"Let's be grateful we weren't there because I would've decked him and I would've been arrested," said Daniel. I wonder what happened when an NSA agent got arrested. Probably nothing.

Chad continued, "Somebody called the cops. When they showed up, the fight was over. We snuck out a back door."

Each couple took a couch and we put on a movie. This time, Lily fell asleep on Chad and when the movie was over, I had to wake her up to go home.

***

In the morning, I found a note in the kitchen. "Dad and I went to get food for lunch," I read out loud. "I'm so glad he's feeling better."

"Me too," agreed Lily. Lily started searching for breakfast and suddenly stopped. "Oh...I forgot to tell you. Chad said Reed is dating some girl in Canada."

"That's so great," I shrieked. "But wait, she lives in Canada, that's not good."

"No she doesn't. She's lives in Connecticut and she's a figure skater."

"I thought it'd be a girl hockey player. I'm happy for him, but Carla won't be."

While Lily had cereal, I called Daniel. "Good morning, what are you doing?"

"Morning, I'm at the Dakota finishing some last minute arrangements."

As we were eating strawberries, Mom and Dad returned. Dad sat on the couch and read the papers, while Mom arranged the flowers she purchased in a couple of vases.

"Dad, you look good."

"Thanks, Honey, I'm fine. I spoke to Nana this morning and I told her what time you'd be in and that Daniel was dropping you off."

"Thanks. Lily, come upstairs and keep me company while I finish packing," I said.

An hour later, I heard the doorbell ring. We went downstairs fifteen minutes later and found Aunt Cecile and Uncle Ian munching on grapes in the kitchen.

We sat down for lunch and when we were on dessert, Martin, Marina and Anna arrived. All Anna wanted to do was crawl around after Amber.

I carried Anna to my room and we danced around with her. When she started getting cranky, I found my bubble blower. That amused her for a little while, but as soon as she started crying, we took her back to Marina.

Marina was in the kitchen getting coffee. "Anna wants you." Marina reached for her crying child. "Can we talk?" I asked.

"Sure, what's up?" she asked while she rocked Anna.

"Can you tell me what Martin's problem is with Daniel? I keep meaning to call you, but things have been so crazy."

"Yes, I know. I'm hurt that you've been so unreachable this summer. I called you a bunch of times this week and you've never returned any of my calls."

"Marina, I swear I didn't get them. I would've called you back." Daniel had to get my cell phone debugged. This was crazy! Everyone is going to hate me!

"I thought so before, but now I see you're just too pre-occupied with Daniel."

"You're not being fair. I didn't get your messages. My cell phone is wacky."

Marina looked at me skeptically, like she didn't believe me and said, "Then get a new phone. You keep saying there's a problem with your cell, so why aren't you getting a new one?"

She had me there.

"Martin and I like Daniel, but we miss you and you need to remember you have a family."

"I do. It's just been a crazy summer," I tried explaining.

"That's not an excuse. Everybody has things going on. We thought we'd see you more since you were home, but it didn't happen and the lack of communication was upsetting. You used to call to chat and see how Anna was."

"I'm sorry." Marina was right. I got so sucked into this vortex of Daniel that nothing else mattered. I now understood how Eden felt being with Paul.

"Is that why Martin seems mad at me?"

"Martin's not used to his little sister having a boyfriend, so you'll have to be patient."

I went into the living room, got a pastry, sat down next to Martin and talked about nonsense.

Soon enough, it was time to leave. Martin brought my luggage down and the entire family insisted on seeing me off by coming to the lobby. It really was quite comical.

When Daniel arrived, he was greeted with quite a crowd. Amused, he couldn't help chuckling and when I passed him, he quietly said, "What a send off!"

"Be quiet," I snickered, embarrassed by the entourage.

"Paige, it's very nice. I'm joking," he whispered.

"Daniel, please take care of Paige for us," Mom said approaching the car.

"You don't have to worry, Mrs. Devon. I won't let anything happen to her."

I could see that Mom had tears in her eyes and I gave her a big hug. We jumped in the car. I was absolutely free until I got to London. As soon as the car was out of sight, I felt Daniel's arm around me, pulling me close to him.

"Alone at last," I whispered and leaned in for a kiss. "I missed you today."

"Hopefully, you won't be sick of me by the time we get to London."

"That's not possible," I said.

Newark Airport materialized into view. The driver pulled up to departures at British Airways and we exited the car.

Boarding passes in hand and luggage checked, Daniel took me to the lounge and we called my parents to tell them that we were at the airport. Then, Daniel called James and asked if there were any new developments.

When he got off the phone, he seemed puzzled.

"What's the matter?"

"It's crazy, but James said there was never going to be a nuclear attack. We had stopped it a long time ago. He had to go to a meeting and he'd tell me more when I got to London."

"What?" I asked confused.

"When they started investigating Frank's death internally, they found a lot of discrepancies with Seth's data. He's one of the scientists. They gave him the truth serum and found out that he kept the nuclear attack going to keep EMIT busy. He's been feeding us bogus information. When they pulled him off the case a few days ago, that's when they found out that there was something wrong. We thought it was the envelope that fixed everything, but today they found out that the event was stopped months ago. He kept altering the data so that the event kept showing up."

"Why?"

"He was trying to steal and sell the time machine."

"I don't understand. What about the terrorists and all that money?

"That part of this was real, but even if they got the money it wouldn't have worked."

"I'm so confused."

"EMIT stopped everything you were personally involved in and saved your life, but whether the terrorists got the envelopes or not, the event had already been stopped. Seth was helping them dodge us daily by giving them information of our whereabouts. That's also why things kept constantly changing."

"But why didn't you know about this if you went in the future?"

"Seth put in a code that covered his tracks. We weren't able to override it until he gave us the password and that only happened after the truth serum."

"Who was he going to sell the machine to?"

"The highest bidder, but it was between China and France." Daniel shook his head. "James was right. It was an inside job. They are still interviewing Seth. James said they'd ask who the fake Laura Burke was and why they put the tracker in Amber. We'll know more when we get to London."

"So other countries do know about the machine. How do you handle that?

"We'll erase Seth's memory of the machine and he'll have nothing to sell. The important thing is that we got him and he will no longer work at EMIT. Even with some of the bad things that happened in this case, I met you, so for that I'm thankful."

While I read magazines, Daniel spent the rest of the time on the phone gathering information and talking to other agents about Seth.

When we got onboard, I turned right, but Daniel grabbed my arm and pulled me left.

"Paige, I upgraded your seat. It's one of my perks when I fly," he said winking. "Besides, I still have to watch you, so it's still business."

First class was great, but we were sitting in the middle aisle so there was a partition between us from the seat down. I pushed a button and a wall panel rose and Daniel disappeared from view.

"Hey, you're sick of me already?" he called out.

"I was just playing," I said as it came down. "I'm so glad that this mess is almost finished."

"It sure has been a whirlwind."

"You know since the first time I saw you in the park, I couldn't stop thinking about you."

"Well, I was thinking about you before that day," he said, trying to one up me.

"But that's not fair, I didn't know you existed," I said making a gloomy face.

Laughing, he leaned over and kissed me. "You'll have plenty of time to make it up to me." He bent down and reached inside his bag and pulled out a red box with a white bow. He held it in front of me and said, "Something for you to remember our trip."

"But we haven't even been to London yet."

"Okay, it's a pre-trip present," he conceded. "Please open your present."

As he held the box, I pulled the ribbon off with my right hand and lifted the lid off. I reached in to find a necklace. On a long silver chain, there were three charms. One was an hourglass and as I turned it over, the sand fell from the top to the bottom.

"As I've said before, time stops when I'm with you," Daniel explained.

The next charm was a crystal obelisk. "I love obelisks. Ooh, but you know that!"

Daniel smiled. On closer inspection, in the center there was a thin piece of blue metal wire running from the point to the base of the obelisk. It looked like the same type of crystal I had seen at Daniel's library but in a different shape. The third charm was a silver **P**.

"It's beautiful, thank you." As I held the **P** in my hand, Daniel took it flipped it upside down and twirled it to show a lowercase **d**. How remarkable! My letter **P** whether uppercase or lowercase could also be the lower case letter **d** for Daniel. "That's unbelievable!"

"I know, I thought the same thing so I got one, too." Daniel pulled out the identical chain with a lowercase **d** charm on it that he was wearing under his shirt. He flipped it to show it become a **P**. "It's a **d** for Devon and a **p** for Paige," he said smiling.

"No, it's a **d** for Daniel," I corrected him. "This is amazing! I'm never taking it off."

"That's good, because neither am I," Daniel stated. "I saw them and thought of you. Do you know there was a study done in London and it said that it takes a man 8.2 seconds to fall in love? That first day when I spoke to you in the park and looked into your eyes, I knew I was in trouble." Daniel leaned over, kissed me and everything was absolutely perfect....

Hearing a commotion behind me, I looked around my partition and saw Juliette entering the first class cabin.

Because of my audible gasp, Daniel stood up to see what had happened. When I looked over at him, he looked visibly angry.

"I'll be right back." Daniel walked straight back, through the galley between First Class and Business Class and reached Juliette on my side of the plane. She was getting situated with her belongings and smiled when she saw him. Daniel whispered as he spoke, but from his facial features I saw that his jaw was clenched during their exchange. Daniel left and Juliette sat down in her window seat. When she noticed me looking at her, she gave me a Cheshire cat smile that made my skin crawl and waved.

Sighing as he sat down, Daniel turned to me and said, "Juliette's working on a new case and has to go to London."

Not wanting to sound paranoid, nevertheless, I had to ask, "Do you believe her?"

Daniel looked at me apprehensively and seemed to be debating his response. Guardedly, he asked, "Why would you ask that?"

Suddenly, I felt pathetic. "I don't know, it's a feeling I get," I admitted sheepishly.

"I had the same gut reaction. When we land, I'll call James and find out for sure."

"Was this the only flight she could take?"

Daniel shook his head and made a smirk, "I have no idea. Maybe she didn't know we were on this one."

"Sure," I said cynically.

Knowing she was on the plane, really bothered me, but there was nothing I could do about it.

Suddenly Juliette was standing right next to me and greeted me warmly, "Paige, nice to see you again."

Before I could answer, she looked over my head and said, "Daniel, I was told to tell you to contact the London office when we land."

Daniel nodded and she walked away. There was no more contact between the three of us for the rest of the flight. Every time I passed Juliette on the way to the rest room, she appeared to be sleeping.

By pretending that she didn't exist, Daniel and I had a great time on the plane to London.

The End

The story continues in the next book.

REMIT

ACKNOWLEDGEMENTS

I want to thank the following people for their help and support:

Most importantly Betsy Voreacos, the book is better because of you.

Andrea DaSilva at AD NetworkNY for all her help.

Joe Srednicki, my brother, for liking the book even with all the "girly parts."

James McKee for all his support.

Renee Sokolowski Smith, my cousin, for all her help.

Magaly, Adam, Marleyana and Vincenzo Cross for their love.

Michelle Maffeo, my beautiful goddaughter, for always making me smile.

Debbie, Vince, and Stephanie Maffeo for being the kindest people I know.

Miria Pace for reading my book, long before all the edits and reedits. I wonder if she'll recognize it or miss things that she might have liked in the original version.

Regina Rohn for always pushing me forward, being a great friend and her wonderful spirit.

Jan Boyle for her kindness and advice.

EMIT

coming soon

REMIT

The EMIT Series by Barbara Cross

www.facebook.com/EmittheBook

Barbara Cross lives in New Jersey. Amber the field spaniel is real and is still a wonderful couch potato. The character of Paige is modeled after her daughter Alix and Lily, after her niece, Jane. Barbara loves the young adult genre and this is her first book.

www.barbaracross.com
Cross.Barbara@aol.com

www.ingramcontent.com/pod-product-compliance
Lightning Source LLC
Chambersburg PA
CBHW031413240626
47154CB00001B/11